The Empire of the Black Suns
Volume III: Dark White

Acknowledgements

Due to the speed at which I wrote this book compared to the previous two volumes in the series, I have very little to say about its production, other than that my parents feel insulted to have been left out of the acknowledgements until now. So, Ivan and Sandy, here's your mention.

I suppose I'd like to thank everybody for putting up with me for the last ten years of my life. There's a deep satisfaction in having finished this portion of the series, having solidified the stories and lives of these characters that I've spent a decade dreaming up.

It's refreshing to know that I can move on to *the rest of my life*, now, knowing that I've written down the one story which I knew I always wanted to write. I'm still not done though with this prematurely flat writing career. To the five readers who it may interest, there's still *The Empire of the Black Suns: Volume IV* to come, as well as a new detective-noir thriller series.

Once again, the biggest thanks go to Imogen Holdsworth, Particia Miller, Oliver Thomas (and kids, Fred, Dash, and Jaz), and Andrew Walley, whose interest and readership have shaped this series greatly, and whose enthusiasm have forced me to believe that it is worth publishing.

Enjoy reading.

Episode 1

Archaeology Without a Degree

Chapter 1
Certain Death

I tumbled through the cosmic tunnel, red lightning thrashing and burning on its perimeter, erupting in dazzling fits of brightness. Light crashed into my eyes, through my body, through my soul. The world encapsulated the tunnel, racing over at dangerous speeds. A three-dimensional cross section of the earth which tore open before my eyes and stitched itself over my toes. Mad colours dashed.

My hand was being held, pulling me through the cosmic rip. I couldn't see it, nor the rest of my body, but I still had the distinct *feeling* that I existed. That put me at ease.

The end of the tunnel came near – the crash and rumble of the world rushing to my ears. It came quickly, a halo of white light blaring towards me.

I flew from its mouth, ejected across a grassy field. I landed hard on my left shoulder and tumbled over my bag, groaning as shots of pain cascaded through my body. I grasped at my upper arm, coming to a stop as I slumped over *Anastasiya*, the Legendary of Teleportation.

"*Gah!*" I shrieked, gripping at my shoulder. It had only been a few weeks since tearing a muscle, and all of the quatra healing in the world couldn't make it feel like I was improving. The visions, however, still haunted me.

Anastasiya dragged herself out from under my limp body, and I slumped to the grass in her wake, wallowing in my own pity.

"Are you okay?" she asked, her voice softer and nimbler than the gentle breeze flowing overhead – the words so delicately placed that they almost didn't make it to my ears. I cocked my head up, towards her.

"Does the landing ever get any easier?" I asked.

"It's hard, isn't it?" She squatted down to my side. , Anastasiya hoisted me up, grabbing at my good arm. My left arm hung, the pain of impact slowly dissipating, but always biting at me. I grumbled once on my feet.

"I think riding though a *tear in space* is about as difficult as it sounds, actually," I noted, and dusted the grass and its crusty frost off my body. Taking a deep breath, I held my hands by my side to re-establish my connection to that around me. With my left hand being uncooperative, my connections were weak, but I still managed.

We stood on a meadow – a gentle breeze singing softly by, rustling Anastasiya's long, blonde hair. Hints of a far-off spring wafted across the frosted field, the scents of pollen and sunlight drifting to my nose. Near me, a patch of pink flowers bloomed hesitantly.

In the distance, cresting the gentle rise of the meadow, was a set of stone houses and a low, stone wall. Behind them, bearing over the village, were the peaks of mountains. We sat in a wide valley between the rugged hills, where the air was crisp, and fresh. I could feel it in my palms.

"Are you sure this is the place?" Anastasiya asked finally, patting herself down of frost. She looked over to the village. "I wouldn't want to have gotten it wrong."

"I'm sure of it," I said, marvelling at the sights. I'd seen the images of this village before, in the photo albums in Dad's chest. The spire of the church rose high over the buildings I could see, and I immediately recognised it for its stark-white column, red roof tiling, and blue cross.

"Are you going back for Simone?" I asked the Suneva of teleportation. Her cheeks flushed red, and she looked to her feet.

"Not yet," she said softly. "It takes a lot of quatra to make a jump that big. I'll need to rest for an hour or two."

"An hour or two?" I gulped.

"Teleporting isn't like moving air. You blasting wind is like me teleporting to my arms reach. Coming from Melbourne to a northern Greek village –"

"– *Macedonian* village –" I corrected her.

"– is like you blasting a whole room full of air from your house to here. It takes a lot of energy, and a lot of practise in storing it."

"I can imagine, then," I said, marvelling at the concept.

I trekked on, leading Anastasiya up the muddy hill. Taking careful steps in the sloppy ground, I attempted not to slip. In my eloquence, I only fell twice onto my ass to reach the stone wall. I vaulted it, and blasted air down to land. The blast was lopsided – almost no air coming from my left arm as my shoulder screamed in the pain of moving it, and I stumbled onto my knees. I grunted, annoyed at my boundaries. I was no longer as free as I imagined myself being.

"You've got to be careful," Anastasiya said quietly. "You might hurt yourself."

"I know," I said, standing. "It's hard to remember – but it shouldn't be. I couldn't even get my arm above my head a few days ago, and look at me now." I lifted my arm up before me, past horizontal to the ground. My hand climbed to eye level, and then my muscles yelled and barked. I dropped my arm, wincing. Anastasiya gasped.

"Don't hurt yourself!" she gawked, her eyes bulging and her hands reaching for the weak arm. I shrugged away, turning back up the hill.

"It's alright," I said. "But if we've got two hours to kill, we might as well grab a coffee."

"You don't want to see your Baba and Dedo?" she asked.

"Not without Simone – at least, not on purpose before she gets here," I said. "Come on, let's find the main strip."

The field past the stone wall housed goats and sheep happily grazing. We tip-toed our way past them, and sleuthed around the decrepit cottage which guarded the pasture.

We stalked in the side-alley between the dwelling and its fence, before bursting out onto the main street of the town. As in all mountain villages, the houses' fronts came right up to the asphalt of the road – which itself was only the width of a single car. The road dawdled across the hill in front of us, then turned sharply up it. I walked us towards the bend.

"Why have you come to see your dedo, anyway?" Anastasiya asked as we walked. I couldn't help but notice the condition of the buildings on this single-street village. The houses appeared ancient – square piles of hand-made bricks held together by cobwebs and sweat. Many of the dwellings appeared abandoned, missing entire parts of walls or roofs. Some grassy fields to the sides of the road had animals grazing around a pile of stones – what must have at one point been buildings which were left to rot.

"He was a *Kiin*, like me and my dad," I said. "We're close enough to the supposed area that the *Vochduh* lived in, that he could know about their city, and their scriptures."

"What would that help you do?" she asked, genuinely curious. We reached the bend in the road, and clambered up the steep, uphill drive.

"Well, my main objective right now is to get my friends back," I puffed. "Celeste is out there, fighting with fists. I'm not interested in that. I need to get Natalie back to her family, and to do that, I need to find out how to bypass destiny."

Anastasiya stopped in her tracks. I thought she might have been tired from the climb, but she was shocked instead. She held a hand to her chest with her mouth agape.

"You want to bypass destiny?" she asked.

6

"Yes, because –"

"But destiny is the duty of a Suneva. It's our *right* to purpose in the universe," she interrupted my answer, stopping dead on the road. "Why would you want to give away your life's meaning?"

"Well," I started, moving past her to continue up the hill, "the Vochduh seemed to think that it was a curse – the trade-off for having power."

"A curse?" she asked, catching up. "That's almost blasphemous."

"Would you consider the White Witch a blasphemer?" I asked. "Because both Natalie and the past *Ocras Quatrona* believe that quatra and destiny are too dangerous."

"I…" the girl choked on her thoughts, then coughed. "No."

"And how can you know that the thoughts about destiny are even yours, and not planted?" I asked. If my recent healing visions had taught me anything, it was that Omercronius had vast power to show me ideas, and influence my decisions. The more I reflected on it, the more I found myself agreeing with Natalie. She and Tess were right.

"I can't be sure," Anastasiya said. "It's the first time I've ever considered that."

"See, it's worthy of thought." I said, and pulled our path left, around a corner house. We could see the main strip of shops in the village now – only two or three, with chairs flooding into the already narrow street. A few villagers sat, but it was mainly empty.

"But I still trust destiny," Anastasiya said. "My callings have helped me through enough."

"And that's fair."

"But what do you think the *Vochduh* will be able to tell you about denying the control of Gods?" she craned her eyes reverently to the sky as she talked.

"I don't know if they knew anything," I said plainly, "but they did study and revere the Sunesca for their *freedom* from Gods. The Vochduh had to have discovered *something*."

Anastasiya grunted at the mention of Sunesca. Although her grunt, through her frail voice, resembled more of a chirp, I understood it's connotations. Anastasiya didn't trust Sunesca. It was a sentiment Celeste eluded to when Simone revealed her abilities, and not anything I thought I'd have to worry about.

"I wouldn't think it like you to hold a grudge against anybody, or anything," I said to her as we neared the tables and chairs in the street. I took a seat under the awning of the closest café. The clouds departed as I did, letting the

7

yellow glow of midday break through the bleak grey sky. The hillside seemed to glow in the green of thick trees beyond the dusty village. I smiled.

"Oh, I don't *really*," Anastasiya said, shying from the confrontation. She took a seat opposite me. "But, I grew up with the old stories. My family were very traditional."

Now I grunted, grinning. Anastasiya was the first truly traditional Suneva I had worked with. Natalie wasn't traditional – Tess seemed to protect her from the old ways of the *Liktan* empires. Celeste, despite her familial Suneva upbringing, was far from a model *Liktan* Suneva.

"Where is your family, anyway?" I asked, peering aside into the restaurant. It was in better condition than the surrounding buildings, but that didn't afford it much merit. Fashion was of the least concern in a place as isolated as this. The chairs we sat in were straw, maybe handwoven. Each table was different, and all must have been built at least fifty years ago. Ours rocked as I leaned around to catch the attention of the server – an older man, with greying hair and wrinkled skin. He shot me an odd glance, clearly not recognising the new faces in his café, and slunk over cautiously.

"They're at home. I came from a village a little like this one, near Ukraine," Anastasiya answered. "I left home a while ago when I went to study."

"And you never finished?" I asked, but she didn't have time to reply before the server was upon us.

"*Iassu*," he greeted us. I smiled.

"*Iassu*," I greeted back. "*Silo di Liktan?*" I asked if he spoke the Suneva language. He squinted and tilted his head, responding in Greek which I couldn't understand.

"*Makedonski?*" Anastasiya asked. The man smiled and nodded, grabbing out his pen and pad. They continued talking in the tongue for longer than it took to order two drinks. I let my mind wander, feeling the gentle air currents which passed by. The wind here was relaxed. It swayed easily between the stunted trees of the roadside, slipping lazily between shuffling feet on the road. It swirled up, into the sky, into the beam of sunlight which blessed the quiet town. It did not gust, and it did not stammer. It moved like the tranquillity of pure peace. I released a sighed breath.

"James?...*James?*" Anastasiya called. I was pulled from my blissful daydreaming. The waiter was looking at me expectantly – perhaps a little too enthusiastically to be waiting on a simple coffee order.

"Greek coffee, if they do it, please," I smiled to Anastasiya.

"No, James, he wants to know if you know somebody."

"Who?" I asked, shifting in my chair to sit upright.

"John Ivanov," she said. "He says you look just like him."

John Ivanov. I looked to the man, his eyes smiled with a hint of concern. His hands fumbled in each other, waiting on my response.

"How does he know John?" I asked Anastasiya, and she asked him.

"They were friends growing up, before he moved away," she reported.

"He's my dad," I said to her. His father, my *Dedo*, changed the family name when he came to Australia, to prevent his son getting ostracised for his ethnicity. Dad never went by his Macedonian last name, but I'd seen it written around the house.

"He asks how he's doing," Anastasiya reported to me. "He's wondering if John came to visit with you."

My heart sank. I sucked in a deep breath.

"He's coming, maybe next year," I lied. "His health is good – better than ever."

Anastasiya translated the words and the man's eyes glowed brightly with joy. A heart-breaking smile crawled across his sun-crinkled face. Guilt pitted at the bottom of my stomach.

"Can you ask him where my dad's parents live?" I asked.

"He says he'll draw you a map," Anastasiya reported. The man bowed at me as he retreated to the kitchen. The coffee machine whirred and spluttered, echoing against the bricks of the interior.

"Why didn't your dad just come with us?" Anastasiya asked. "I would have taken him here."

"He's dead," I said, flatly. "He's been dead for over two years now."

"Oh…" the Russian girl said, falling further into her shell. Her long, blonde hair covered her whole face.

"Oh, I'm sorry, I didn't mean it like that," I said, leaning over the table. She peered from between her curtains. "It's just a fact, the man is dead."

My words didn't seem to console her, and Anastasiya remained quiet as we drank our respective coffees and watched an hour pass by. Not long after we were done with our silent drinks, the waiter returned with instructions drawn on a serviette. By his survey of the town, there were only five roads. We were to continue along this main one in the direction we were previously travelling, then head right, up the hill. Dedo's house would be at the end of the trail, near the crest of the knoll before the plateau-meadow which footed the mountain. I thanked the server, paying the bill and swiftly leaving before any more questions about my father arose. I lead Anastasiya along the main road again.

"So, you don't want to wait for your sister now?" she asked as we turned the corner.

"I'll wait," I said. "But I want to find the house before the sun sets. It will make it easier when you get back."

She smiled and nodded, falling back in behind me.

Houses trickled out of sight as the path of the road pushed into the scrub. We trekked through an archway in the forming forest, scraping past tall conifers and overhanging vines. Flowers sprang close to the ground, smattering the roadside in white and yellow dots. The natural alleyway was dark, and steep. The road had long ago stopped being paved, and the dirt track had treacherous footing.

Not noted on the café owner's drawings were the switchbacks – three in total – which climbed gently up the increasingly steep hill. It became almost like a cliff, with trees no longer bothering to hold onto the sharp embankment. Sun was lost to us as the forest engulfed the sky. We continued climbing, sweating in the late-winter cold. I had to stop to catch my breath and hold my arm, which groaned in the pain of being swung. I didn't believe I'd ever get used to its constant inconvenience. I summoned quatra to dull the ache.

Finally, we crested the hill. The forest was still thick, but the steep slope fell away for flatter ground. The path here appeared even less worn than it did down below, with limbs of trees hanging below head height. I stumbled my way through the barrage of leaves and sticks, finally pushing past the last branch to break out of the forest's edge.

My black cloak rustled as the branch cleared, revealing a cottage sitting on a meadow of tall, dry grass. Flowers, just as tall as the house, and purple in colour, dotted the field all the way to the base of the mountain.

The cottage was elegant, made with newer, sturdier bricks. It was squat, with a wide face, and a shallow, tiled roof. The smell of a bubbling, strong stew wafted from the hearth-smoke which poured from the chimney. A goat toddled around by the front door. He bleated at me, and I smiled.

The shadows of the day were long – the blackness of the cottage being cast over me as the hot, summer sun set behind the peaks of mountains.

Confident, I strode towards the front door, which was inset under a small veranda. The goat moved away as I approached, calling nervously. Before I could reach the door, the shadow of a tall man appeared behind it, and it opened outwards to meet me.

The man was wearing a long, blue and green robe. His feet did not touch the ground.

"*James!*" Anastasiya gave a hushed yell into my ear. My arm was tugged back, and the illusion before me slid from my vision like paint washed off a canvas. I was only at the foot of the forest, staring at a dying cottage.

The chimney had half collapsed, with only a trickle of aromaless black smoke crawling from its face. One entire wing of the cottage was reduced to a pile of rubble – a few remaining feet of walls where sheep were now housed. A window on the face of the building was boarded over, but the front door was nicer than the one I had seen moments ago – the only thing which appeared to have *improved*.

"Olomb has been here," I said as the Russian teleporter pulled me back. We squatted behind the shrubbery of the forest, eyeing the building from between leaves.

"What?" she asked. "How do you know that?"

"I see his memories," I said. "I don't control what I see, but they're always important."

"What?" she asked again, bewildered.

"He gave his thread to me. As scary as it is, parts of his mind are merging with mine."

Anastasiya didn't have a response to that, past gawking. I slung my bag around my shoulder and dove my hand into it. I pulled out the little red book I'd taken here with me – Olomb's diaries.

"Have you read Olomb's diaries?" I asked her.

"Like any good *Liktan* citizen, yes," she replied.

"Great," I smiled. "Then you'll know that he never states *how* to get to the *Vochduh* city, leading most to believe that it didn't exist. But he *does* describe the sights and places along the way."

"I don't remember a cottage being in the sights," she said. "A *village*, sure – but there are so many villages."

I frowned, looking over the small house again. Kuvalik had been here, and he had been greeted by a levitating *Vochduh* monk.

"Well," I said, turning to the girl. "You're just going to have to trust me that he's been here, and that it's on the way to the *Vochduh* city. I'm sure of it."

"Okay," she nodded, turning back to the cottage. "I'll trust you on it. But I'm not sure how much I like snooping like this. It doesn't feel right."

"You call *this* snooping?" I asked. Her face was nervous, her lip almost quivering. I stepped back, and pulled Anastasiya into the thick of the scrubs.

"We'll come back here later, then," I said, and she immediately calmed. "Let's walk back to the town. Maybe we'll find hints of it in the diaries."

"That sounds good to me," she smiled, brushing aside her long curtains of hair. Her smile was cute, her cheeks rosy red against her white face.

I led her back to the path, down the switchbacks and into the town. As we walked, she produced a black stone from her pocket – so reflective in the sprays of light that I thought it was wet. She handed it to me, and when between my fingers, I could feel that it buzzed with energy. In its marbled reflections hung a slight pink sheen, like a sparkling mist.

"What's this?" I asked her.

"An infused onyx," she said.

"Infused onyx? –" I trailed off, observing its wavering shimmer. "What does it do?... *How* does it do anything?"

"This is what witchcraft used to be – infusing stones with quatra," she said, smiling at me. "The White Witch is really a *soulcrafter*. This magic with *crystals* is what ancient Suneva were known for where I'm from."

"Huh," I smiled, eyeing the stone. "So how does it do stuff?"

"I don't know," she said, "nobody does. But you can track your own quatra scent in a stone of onyx from anywhere in the world. It helps me find places when I'm jumping back and forth."

I didn't air a response. The stone was energetic – I was an unskilled witch, but its energy was clear to me.

"Hold this and it means I can find you without trying," she broke the pause. "I already left one in your house."

"You did?"

"Yes," she smiled. "It will make it easy to find Simone and come back."

"That's good planning," I commended her, finally pocketing the stone.

"I always like to plan well," she smiled sweetly, and swung her bag back around her shoulder. Up ahead, the town came into sight.

***

Simone complained on the whole journey up the switchbacks to the cottage. Hours had passed since Simone had been teleported to the village – and landing wonky on her foot when falling out of the tear in space had set her on an awful mood.

"Dad wasn't exaggerating about the walk to school, then," Simone grumbled, halfway up the rugged slope. "I don't even want to imagine this in the snow, like he complained about."

"It did take a lot to make him complain," I said. "If anything, this is *harder* than his stories claimed it was."

"I'll never doubt him again," Simone said, then trailed off. She would never *have* to doubt the man again, of course, for he was dead.

The sun was starting to set in the sky overhead, with the shadows of the mountains stretching long over the village. I was eager to reach the top of the steep incline, so that we wouldn't be caught in the forest during the night.

Finally, we reached the plateaued meadow – the sun still hanging on the obscured horizon – and walked across the untamed, stony grass to the cottage door.

Gravel crunched underfoot. A group of ravens burst from the crumpled western wing of the cottage, taking flight from between the sheep. Anastasiya jumped, teleporting to the other side of the yard without a moment's pause. Simone caught me as I stumbled, and I found my breath in her arms. She just rolled her eyes, and continued towards the door.

Simone went to grab the door's knocker – a rusted, brassy ring – but hesitated. She craned her head around to me.

"How long has it been since we've seen Baba and Dedo?" she asked.

"I was seven last time, wasn't I?" I asked.

"Yeah, because I was nine," she said, her eyes trailing off.

"What are you thinking?" I asked, and reached around her to grab the knocker. "Too afraid to knock?"

"No," she said, forcing my hand aside. "I just hope they recognise us."

"They will, now come on…"

"They could have dementia, you know," she said, suddenly very anxious. Her voice was shaking.

"I doubt it," I said. "Now you're just sounding like me. I mean, if anything, *we* are bound to have changed more than them. Think about how traumatic this is for their old people brains."

Her face dropped, aghast. Possibilities raced through her mind, streaming behind her eyes.

"Now that's only another stupid thing I'd say. They'll be so happy to see us," I smiled.

"Something bad will happen here. I feel it," she said, turning from the door.

I stepped back, my heel finding the edge of the porch. Simone's face was entirely serious, and I looked at her quizzically.

You made an oath to always believe her. I reminded myself. I took a breath.

"What, and why? How do you feel it?" I asked.

"I don't know," she said. "It's the same feeling I got the night Dad died."

"Oh…" I hushed into silence.

Her eyes begged me for confirmation, but I had none to give her. I danced around my nervous smile, keen to hide my thoughts.

"I don't doubt you," I said, skipping around conclusions. "If we get into trouble, we can be *anywhere* instantly. I think we'll be fine."

Anastasiya smiled at my comment, and was keen to add a few terms and conditions to my statement, but was interrupted.

The door creaked open.

Simone spun quickly, trying to make her best smiling face. The door was pulled in slowly, by a solid hand which latched around its side. Anastasiya hid away, behind me, but I bustled up next to Simone.

The woman who appeared behind the door was not old, certainly not our Baba. She would have been about Dad's age – in fact, she shared a remarkable number of his features. She bore his inset eyes, and strong nose.

"Teta Dejana?" Simone gasped. Of my dad's two sisters, Dejana was the eldest, and had chosen to come back to the village with Baba and Dedo back in 'eighty-eight – a decision not highly regarded by our Father.

"Simone?" she scrunched her brow. "James?"

"Yes! It's us." Simone smiled brightly.

"And this is my friend Anastasiya," I said, moving out of the way. Anastasiya peeked around me like a silent mouse, making a meagre smile. She said hello, in the same dialect she'd used in the café. My auntie raised an eyebrow, but greeted her back. I couldn't read the woman's face - she was surprised to see us, but certainly not emotional.

"Is your dad here?" she asked, peering around us. "You wouldn't have left him behind, would you?"

Simone and I immediately gave each other a curious glance, squinting.

"You…you *don't* know?" I asked.

***

14

Baba sat down at their dining room table – incidentally, also the main kitchen bench, due to the size of the interior. The inside of the house was old, and claustrophobic instead of cosy. The furniture which lined the floor was newer than the cottage, if only by one hundred years, which didn't say much. There was a state of the art television from the fifties sitting in the north corner of the room. It buzzed with its cancerous cathode rays, basking us in dangerous light. Without its glow, the room would have been entirely dark, as the electric lighting could barely persuade the shadows to depart.

Baba laid photos across the table in front of her, and Simone gathered over her shoulder. Auntie Dejana and I sat at the table, the mood sombre. Finally, Baba laid a certificate on the table, for the death of Simon Ivanov, my Dedo, dated at the fifth of November, nineteen-ninety-six.

"I can't believe it," I said, holding the certificate. "I swear Mum told you..."

"And I sent a letter," Baba said. "Why do these things not work? Who knows." She lowered her head, shaking it. I grimaced.

"Can I have a look?" Simone asked, and I handed the page to her. Across the table was an album of loose family photos, many picturing Dad and Dedo. I found a particularly nice one of them in front of their Melbourne family house. Dad must have been just my age, and his father the age that Dad should have been now. Dad had a football in hand, Dedo had a great grin across his aging face.

"He wasn't sick, was he?" Baba asked us.

"No," I replied, "it came from nowhere. An unpredictable heart attack in the middle of the night. We tried to save him, but...well..."

"He died of heart attack?" Baba asked, her expression growing concerned. Her hand dashed across the table, landing on mine and encompassing it. I dropped the photo I was holding as her tight grip threatened to crush my bones.

"James, you be careful," she said. "It is in family!" Her eyes were dead serious. I met her expression.

"What do you mean?" I asked.

"Your Dedo died from a heart attack, too." Auntie Dejana said. "You might want to keep an eye out for it when you're older."

I gulped, meeting the serious faces around the room.

"James..." Simone interrupted my train of fatalism. "What date did Dad die?"

15

I didn't have to think to get the answer – the memory was engrained in my mind, preserved perfectly.

"The fifth of November, nineteen ninety-six." I said robotically. Simone turned Dedo's death certificate to me.

"And what date does this say?" She pointed to the date printed.

"The fifth of November, nineteen-ninety-six." I repeated the words. My eyes widened. "They died the same way, on the same day?" I gawked. Simone nodded.

"That's destiny," Anastasiya contributed, her quiet voice barely breaking over Baba's laboured breath. Simone glared at the Russian girl dangerously, slapping the certificate onto the table.

"It's a tragedy, is what it is," Simone grumbled.

"You're saying that they died on the same day, from the same thing?" Auntie Dejana caught up. Simone and I nodded, but Baba groaned and shook her head. She turned to look out the window, at the pink light of sunset.

"This is the weird thing that surrounds your dedo," she said. "All of this weird things which happen like this. *Zondeca*, eh?" She coughed.

Baba wretched herself out of her seat, and shuffled towards the curtains. She grabbed them in her strong, old hands, and tugged them apart – revealing the blinding yellow of the setting sun.

"Why it has to happen to men I love, I don't know," she turned suddenly from the glorious light of the evening, her shadow casting over us. "You are *Zondeca* too, yes?" she asked, directed at Simone and myself. *Zondeca* was the *Vochduh* word for Suneva, I remembered from Dad's texts.

"I am a *Vochduh*." I said, then pointed to Simone. "Simone is a *Zalach*. Anastasiya is…" The girl shot me a nervous glance. "…A different *Zondeca*," I said, she smiled.

"Eh," Baba nodded. "You came here for Dedo, didn't you?" And she stepped back towards the table – a silhouette against the blinding yellow light. Simone rushed to the old woman's side once more.

"No, Baba. We came to see both of you."

"I was hoping Dedo would be here, though," I said, and Baba nodded, knowingly. She didn't take offence – lord knows that she hadn't visited us, either.

"You wanted him to tell you about the *Vochduh*," she read me like a pamphlet. I nodded guiltily, and swung my bag around, off my back. I reached in, and pulled out her cookbook.

"My recipes!" she rasped in delight. I set the tome atop the counter, and opened it to the back pages, where Dad had written in Vochduh. I slid it over to Baba, but she frowned.

"Eh, I can't read *Vochduh*," she said. "I know the letters, but this words, they are special. I don't know them."

"If I couldn't read them," Anastasiya spoke up from behind me, "then we should have known that your Baba couldn't."

That wasn't necessarily true – my Baba did live with a man who spoke *Vochduh* and talked it with his son. I had tried to get Anastasiya to read the pages before, but she had the same comment as my Baba– the words were specialised. Words like *quatra* have no English equivalent, just as they wouldn't have an easy Slavic equivalent. As I sighed, standing, Baba happily flipped through the cookbook.

"Thank you from bringing this back to me," she smiled.

"That's okay, Baba," I said, walking towards the window, towards the blinding gaze of the sun. I shielded my eyes with my hand, just catching a glance at the shadow of the mountains as they cast over me.

And here I was once more – having made the journey for the third time now, staring out of the familiar cottage window again. Tomorrow I would make further negotiations with the *Vochduh* king, and maybe he would accept the treaty. I knew that he wouldn't, but I had hope left. Nerios wouldn't lead me on this path if it was one of futility. I trusted the ghost Kuvalik on that, just as I had trusted his thread for many years.

This was the last leg – the kingdom would be just beyond here. I got out my diary and noted down the scene as I saw it.

"*The Valley of the Setting Sun*," I penned it.

Chapter 2
Through Frenchmen and Brimstone

Esteemed Argol members stood, gathered by the round table illuminated by tendrils of pink flame. The pale glow danced around the small dungeon – more like an alcove of a cave, supported by ancient masonry.

Celeste bore over the table, palms flat upon it. In the centre, spread around for all to see, were floor plans and blueprints, with her delicate handwriting scrawled across many of the sheets. Suneva, all in their human forms, nodded as Celeste talked – including her mother, Juliette Leroux, who stood opposite her in the dank, catacomb complex. Celeste noticed, as she recited her plans, that one corner of the eccentric room was particularly dim in their appraisal of her lecture. They did not nod, they did not agree, and they did not speak. They stood with arms crossed, leaning away from the diagrams. This nagged at Celeste.

"The plans we got from *Anderson* indicate that the castle's sleeping quarters are here, past the gardens, in this quadrangle," she said in mottled mix of French and Liktan, pointing to the map. "There are then five entrances we could take – the rooftop above the eastern wing, the rear, the first story end of the western hall, and the central lobby, which is the most dangerous. However, with the recent death of Boekidin, there is a greatly diminished chance of detection. Without an intelligence head, the castle is relatively undefended. We need to use this gap in their defences before it gets fixed."

"And what do we do when we find the White Witch?" a balding man said, who had been nodding along to her plans earlier.

"This is a rescue, I believe that she'll come willingly," Celeste said. She stood tall as she talked, making sure to pump her chest, arch her back, and lower her voice. She was by far the shortest person in the room, shorter than her mother, and the most slender of form. Celeste had to generate a serious presence to command this lot of hulking men.

"If I'm right, Hesslik is using the same mind control technology he used on *Vectra*, the Legendary of Gravity. There will be a small device attached to her neck, altering her thoughts somehow. If we remove it, she'll snap out of the illusion. I know Zamelle – she's not as brash as to leave our cause on a dime. Hesslik must have sabotaged her."

There were nods and hushed murmurs of agreeance, except from the quiet corner. Juliette quietly praised her daughter's speaking, but the crowd's attention was drawn as one of the dissatisfied men stepped forward to bear himself over the table. His name was Michael Richard, or *Canivaer* – a prominent Argol figure in Flanders. Juliette tried to hide a sneer as the man took a stand. Celeste made her face blank, arching herself to be taller.

"If you don't mind me asking, Miss Leroux," Michael began, "why, if we have the plans to invade Hesslik's castle, wouldn't we go in for a single mission to take out Hesslik, instead of retrieving the White Witch?"

The table hummed, as if they hadn't even considered the option. Michael and his friends smiled smugly, but Celeste had prepared for such questioning. She smiled, and spoke confidently in the dim, pink light.

"The White Witch is incredibly powerful," Celeste started, "in fact, I'd say she's got more social and physical power than a Legendary. If we tried to attack Hesslik with her as our enemy, we wouldn't make it past the forest's edge. She will be able to sense and predict our every move. She needs to be on our side if we're to win."

The man stifled a chuckle, and scrunched his face in amusement. Celeste eyed his dissent, unable to keep her face straight. This brought more joy to his expression.

"So, you've recognised their power, and you want to march us right into it?" he scoffed. "We could work *around* her to get to Hesslik, if she's as powerful as a *Legendary*. Speaking of which…" he paused to eye the room. "Where is *ours?*" he asked. "Wasn't *Vectra* on our side?"

A silence was drawn in the cavern, and eyes settled to the young Iva Argol. Her expression fell – she wasn't prepared to tell them that her sister had run off again, but lying wouldn't do, not when she was asking Suneva to put themselves on the line.

"She left," Celeste said. She said it with such purpose, that she had almost convinced herself that she sent her sister away.

"She *left?*" another man asked, not from the argumentative corner. "What do you mean *she left?*"

"She walked out," Celeste said, as if the answer should have been obvious. "You can't stop the Legendary of Gravity from doing anything. Not even twenty of us could."

"And yet you expect us to stop the White Witch?" Michael cut in, perfectly. Celeste groaned. Manipulation, she hated to admit, she was practiced in. Politics, however – and leadership – these were out of her retinue. She was cornering herself – starting to sink in a sea of arguments, the holes which she pierced into her own hull.

"Why don't you just admit," Michael cast another blade, "that this is a selfish rescue mission for your friend?"

"*What?*" Celeste jerked, clawing at the table. Pink flames danced on her tongue. If her eyes could kill, there'd be a dead man in the room.

"Of course it is," Michael grinned. "And after we're done with this one, there'll be a mission for both Maiki and Ferrad."

"Why would I do that?" Celeste growled. "Maiki doesn't want to join us, and Ferrad won't help anybody. They're not necessary."

"Why should we listen to this girl, anyway?" Michael asked the crowd now. "Her father might have handed his title to her, but she's the one who ran away from him *because* of his ideals, whilst we supported him every second of the way. Whilst we kept those *pig* cops at bay."

"How dare you!" Celeste spat, unable to control her emotions. Furious, dazzling flames licked from her mouth, forming her words. The table smoked under her fingertips. Across from her, Juliette Leroux flicked her wrist and drew her staff – a sleek, silver rod with a crystal ball end. It slopped with violet plumes, and her eyes glowed the same colour. Celeste was reminded again that she hadn't been able to teach even her mother the secret of the pink flames. They alluded all *Ivaer* except herself.

"I am the bearer of the pink flames!" she asserted. "I am the most powerful *Ivaer* in existence – my coming was foretold by the first flame bearers. I am the rightfully handed heir to this position."

There were some nods of reverence behind the now scared and confused faces bordering the table. Michael kept his face straight, and his response straighter.

"Your father wouldn't have said such a thing," he replied. "His passion was that we were all equal, and all deserved to be ourselves. *Sur san Suneva*, after all."

"Don't talk about him like he's dead!" Celeste groaned. "He's literally in the next room. He approved of this plan! He..."

Celeste gauged the expressions around her, all awkward, all looking away, including her mother. Celeste no longer had support, and she didn't know how to claw it back. She looked down to see her sword formed in her hand, and she jumped – she must have summoned it in her anger, and lit it with roaring pink flames. The crowd was trying to ignore the feat, but they had shuffled away, and Celeste was left petrified and panicked. This meeting was beyond saving.

"The meeting is over," she said quietly. "Everybody please leave. Except for you, Michael."

Alexis LeGrand, the Capo of Melbourne, shot her a concerned glance. He would back her up, if she wanted it. Still, Celeste waved him away, and he left – grabbing Juliette and taking her with him to stop her from staying too. Soon, with the shuffling of feet across the dusty floor, the room was emptied, bar the two debaters.

"Couldn't stand me spreading the truth?" Michael asked, his voice entirely condescending. Celeste tried to ignore the jab, sighing to recompose herself. There was a strategy to be played here – something her father would have excelled at – but she hadn't mastered.

"You're being selfish, you realise?" Michael continued to cover her silence. "The Argols aren't your personal army, even if your father handed you the reigns. We were loyal to him because he proved that his interests lay with the community. You are yet to gain loyalty – he would never have dragged us into personal missions."

"No, he took care of his dirty work himself, in his house, where nobody but I could see," Celeste said, and surprised herself with the potency of her comment. "At least I'm open – and this isn't a personal mission," she asserted. "Hesslik is a danger to the community. He's meddling with powers which he shouldn't have access to – which none of us should. He's already gotten rid of threads."

"So," Michael slapped his palms together, "we take out Hesslik directly, by avoiding the White Witch."

"*No*," Celeste insisted. "She's our key to gaining trust from general Suneva – and our key to saving the Suneva."

"And you expect that we can take her on?"

"We can only try to disarm her," Celeste said. "But if we don't try it, we'll never know. Our only chance to win is by trying."

The man hummed. He nodded, finally.

"It's risky," he said, "and you have simply *assumed* that the same technology to trap *Vectra* is being used here, yes?"

"Yes," Celeste admitted. Michael frowned. "At least I'm more honest than my father." She tried to save herself. Michael fell into thought.

"You need to build some loyalty before you can pull stunts like this, miss," he said. "I don't trust your judgement, but I trust your name – don't ruin a name that took so long to build. You've got a lot to learn from your father; humility included."

A lot to learn from my father? Celeste fumed to herself, able to hide her suddenly building rage. She'd learned enough from her father – the blood of two people stained her armour still. That was far too many.

Still, Michael was right, Celeste did need to learn something from her father – leadership. She wasn't the leader this group needed – although she desperately wanted to lead them anyway. Why had her father stepped down? He could still talk, and plan, and be himself. He'd only lost his flames.

"Leadership and humility, sure," she replied after an angry pause. "Thank you for your *honest* feedback. I'll have to take your words into consideration."

The man straightened up, and almost flinched back.

"I didn't expect you to agree with me…" he said, bewildered.

"Well, maybe I'm more self-critical than you give me credit for. I did follow the Code to find two Legendaries, after all," she said. "You will help me in this mission, won't you?"

Michael bore over the sheets on the table. He ruffled around the blueprints, and took in her delicate handwriting.

"I'll stay loyal. I won't give up on this community because I disagree with you, especially not without giving you a chance."

"Good," Celeste said with her nose high. Although, realising how pompous she appeared, she dropped her posture. "Thank you," she said demurely, and quickly left the room.

Michael glanced again at the scattered papers. He shook his head.

***

Chad sat in the meadow clearing of the forest. Streams of spring light broke the crisp air, settling in rays upon his face. His legs were crossed, his hands rested in his lap with poise. He meditated on his connection to the earth.

The earth rumbled around him – silently, slowly. The cycle of nature was a part of Chad, and he was a limb to its will. The roots of plants housed the souls of the forest, and connected the ground to the sky. Through roots he could feel the sway of flowers in the wind, and the strength of trees. Animals pattered across soil, their footprints bouncing like drops of water in a small lake. The ripples of their movements could be felt in the roots of grass, and the footprints of leaves who fell from trees when birds rustled away.

There was peace here in the soft soil, with nature. This, he felt, was where he was meant to be, where his powers were meant to take him. One with the world and its cycles. Animals were born and died in this very dirt, and so his soul would perish here.

Chad was truly at peace – or he would have been, if it weren't for that screaming voice bouncing in his skull, the one telling him that he was wasting his time doing nothing, saving nobody.

But the voice was wrong, Chad smiled gladly. The world was beautiful, and its beauty would be wasted if he didn't observe it. Was art any less beautiful if nobody could see it? He was an observer trapped in a burning gallery – the forces destroying it were beyond his ability to hinder. If he spent time fighting the fire instead of admiring the work, then its beauty would be wasted. Better to be the observer than the foolish fighter.

Still, the stream of the void moved overhead – the waters of destiny running their course. They ground on his soul like a boulder in the tide, pushing to make him move. Chad couldn't tell if his peace here was a fabricated effort to ignore the divine will, or his own decision. He no longer trusted the path laid for him – and destiny tried its hardest to wear him down.

"The earth cannot be moved," Chad said aloud, in his strong, deep voice. The flowers bent to his commands, their roots straining in the soil. "Like the earth, I am the ultimate force. Nothing moves rock except for rock itself, and so no force of destiny will move me except for my will itself. As the earth moves, others move for it. It does not bow to currents. It does not bow to a master."

The urge to act still screamed at him, but he felt better for resisting it now. It could not move him., for he was of the earth. Chad took a deep breath, and let his connection to the rock and the world grow. Here, there was serenity. Only birds chirping and trees swaying to be heard.

"You know that you're wrong, right?" A female voice broke the natural noise. Chad perked up, and dug his fingers into the soil. He could feel every disturbance of the ground – every branch of every root, every berry which had landed from the bush, every footfall past and present. There were no footsteps of people near him. He flicked his head around, trying to spot the intruder to his clearing.

"A Kidin?" he asked aloud, although he'd only intended to think it.

"No," the voice replied. It was clearly in the real world – it didn't have the echo quality of a kidin intrusion. Chad also had no wet-thickness in his skull.

"Then who?" he asked.

23

They did not answer his question.

"You say that the earth does not move, except when it wants to move – but you're wrong," the woman said. Her voice was deep and soulful. Chad couldn't decipher their accent, but one was present. "The earth spins about a star, and that star about a galaxy, and that galaxy about a supercluster. The Earth is just as much a part of the flow of destiny as everything else – it just moves on a grander scale. There are much larger forces at play than rocks shifting."

Chad stood, summoning his axe-staff and examining his surroundings. He stalked slowly in a circle.

"Rocks do not *deform* except by their own will," Chad countered the woman. "Rocks are solid. They stand on their own – invincible."

"Except when gravity pulls them down," the woman continued, "just like it pulls the whole planet around. What about when water erodes rock? Or when magma shifts the crust to make mountains?"

"Ah," Chad raised a finger, "but it takes rock against rock to form mountains; and it takes the earth to break a falling rock."

"And the rock does not *fall* due to rock, nor does the crust move because of rock. Great forces act, and they can break the unbreakable, and move the immobile."

"Yes, but–" Chad attempted a defence, but he was cut off. It was lucky too, because he wasn't going to say anything particularly intelligent.

"The rock is still just a pawn to higher powers," the girl continued. "It is strong, but in its resilience and immobility, it is useless against them. It is more of a pawn to the forces that surround it than the air. At least air can move out of the way when danger comes. The rock just sits there, like you right now."

Chad squinted, still stalking and searching for his debating partner. He stepped out of the flowery clearing, into the tall spruces. Their voice became no more distinct, and their presence still did not appear.

"You see, that's where you're wrong," Chad rebutted. "Rock might have to yield to the tides and forces of this world, but I do not. I am sentient – rock is not. I can see how I'm being manipulated, and I can make decisions to fight the powers which pull me. I have found peace by fighting them."

"Peace, through fighting?" the girl asked. She chuckled.

"Yes," Chad said solemnly.

"Oh Chad," they said, "there are still forces in this world which can move you."

Chad's feet left the ground. He was thrown into the air.

24

Chapter 3
The Valley of the Setting Sun

I had awoken from my short vision, whispering the name of the valley which cut the mountains before us, the same valley that Kuvalik and Olomb had visited before me. *The Valley of the Setting Sun.*

I panicked when I realised where I was, and where I had just been. I should have felt blessed to be steered into the right path, but the frequency of these delusions was beginning to frighten me. I used to summon them – like I did to stop Chad choking at the hands of Sheriff Johnson – but now they came to me uninvited to show me some truth. Olomb told me that he could no longer distinguish between the thoughts of Kuvalik and himself. How long would it take for my mind to meet the same fate?

Anastasiya jumped at my mention of the valley. She tore into my bag, pulling out Olomb's little, red book, and flung it to the relevant page. She read its passage.

I walked through the Valley of the Setting Sun, far in the north of the country. I continued north through it, following the passage of the Vochduh people. Between the mountains, I found the spire in the meadow, upon which lay the foundation of Vochduh society.

***

Simone, Anastasiya and I stayed the night at Baba's house, on one mattress upon the cold floor, then set out the next day. We walked across the meadow, and scaled down the rocky mountain face, into the forest, to the stream which separated the gigantic peaks.

We had set off with our rucksacks full of food and water, but it became quickly apparent that the trail would take longer to traverse than we had assumed. Down near the stream, the forest was thick with trees and scrub. Making a path here was difficult, but not as treacherous as walking higher up the mountain face, where crumbling rock lay at one's feet. We chose to rough the bush, sticking close to the stream forming the valley.

By the time we reached the first fork in the path, the winter's sun was a quarter of the way through the sky. It hung on the cloudless, crisp day, teasing us as if it could *actually* create warmth.

25

The forest fell away around the fork, giving us full view of the hulking mountains which loomed to our every side, watching over us. Two streams combined here - our branch and the left branch becoming one, flowing together to the right. I reached the intersection first, and stopped, admiring the peak of the mountain before us.

"Which way should we go?" Anastasiya asked me.

"Not sure," I said, turning back to her and Simone. There was distance between them – Anastasiya still uncomfortable around the Sunesca. "The diary said to head north, following *the passage of the people* – whatever that means."

Simone swung her rucksack around and pulled out a compass. She fiddled with it as she caught up, spinning whilst walking.

"We had to have been walking west when we started, if we walked into the sunset," she said, "but we followed the mountain around, and we're facing north-west now."

"So, which path for north?" I asked. Simone gave me a judgemental glance.

"Right, James. We go right," she pointed. "Don't you know your cardinal directions?"

"Hey, no need to get snooty over it." I surrendered, one hand in the air, the other hanging painfully. I picked up a large branch from the ground to use as a hiking pole, and descended right, into the thick scrub and along the flow of the creek.

I needed the pole. The slope was muddy, and numerous times I caught myself shooting my left hand up to grab a branch, only to be met with the pain like it was tearing off the bone. Simone was concerned at first, but as I continued she just shook her head, and trudged onwards.

The wind followed us with the stream. It curled between the branches along the faces of the valley. Leaves twisted and fell in the gentle eddies it left behind. With my arm having made a *slight* recovery, I could now just sense the breeze in my palms. Focussing on this – and my careful steps – took my attention off the pain of my shoulder, which became constant as we trekked on.

"Is any of this familiar to you, James?" Simone asked as we settled for lunch. She held her compass to me – the needle shaking dramatically before setting. It was pointing almost due east. "This valley has taken us all around the base of a mountain. We're now nowhere near travelling north. Hopefully we don't get lost."

"No, actually," I said, taking in the scene. We sat down on a network of roots, sitting above the mud. I pulled out a sandwich from my bag – lovingly made by Baba. "I haven't had any memories come to me today."

I was glad, too, because every memory I didn't experience helped to keep the line between Olomb's mind and mine defined. I sighed, looking down to the packet of fresh pita in my hand, wrapped in vines and leaves. I tore the inedibles away, under the starry night sky. Not an ideal place to sleep, but it was better than nothing.

The wind whistled by, rustling my black robe, a warm summer breeze. It put me at ease.

Black Robe? I slapped myself in the face. I couldn't see my arm move, but I did feel it strike my face. I also felt the horrible, crippling pain of moving my left arm to slap my own head, and gagged as fire consumed me. My eyes blared open – despite the fact that they had never closed – as I was once again in the midday forest.

"James, why the hell did you do that? You could hurt yourself," Simone said, dropping to her butt with lunch in hand. Anastasiya wordlessly rushed to my side. She grabbed my sore arm and held it still as I griped with pain.

"I just *had* a vision," I whined. "So, yes, we're on the right path."

Simone hummed, sceptical. "Aren't these visions good?" she asked. "They're like, free guidance, right? You just know the right path because you've already done it before."

I squinted my disapproval at her remark. "*I* haven't done anything before, *Kuvalik* has," I protested, "and that's the problem. These memories are coming to me so smoothly that even *I* think they're mine. But they're *not*."

"What's the issue?" Simone asked. "Why does it bother you so much?"

"Because I'm not him, and I didn't ask for this!" I blurted. Her face dropped at my outburst, but I continued with the rant. "It's only been a month and a bit, and I already can't distinguish between his memories and reality. How long until I start responding to his name, or forgetting my own past?"

Simone didn't have an answer. She hushed, and quietly munched on her sandwich. Anastasiya sat beside me, on the tree's thick root.

"You already feel like you're losing yourself?" Simone asked. Her tone was serious now.

"No, it's hyperbole," I explained, "but it's still scary. At least when I summoned the memories, I knew that I wasn't *actually* him, or living them. Now

27

that *they* come to *me*, I can't be sure. Even if it changes suddenly from night to day, I can never tell."

"That's horrifying," Anastasiya agreed.

"Do I look any different when they happen?" I asked the girls.

"Yes," Anastasiya said. "You keep doing what you were doing, but your eyes go blank."

"Slap me," I demanded to them both. "When it next happens, that is."

"Are you sure?" Simone asked. "There's got to be a better method than hurting yourself."

"I don't know it," I said. "I need to be bought back. I don't want to get stuck in there."

Simone and Anastasiya nodded grimly, and turned their attention to their food. I flooded my arm with quatra whilst we ate – just enough to keep me from slipping into visions of the churning sea. I'd somewhat mastered this in the last week – although the healing was apparently much slower.

With the added energy, I could feel the breeze fully in my palms. My arm went numb, and hot. The wind rushed through the valley, phased by no object. It shook the trees as it went, determined in its mission.

***

The scrub pulled back as we left the edge of the mountain's face. Now all that we trekked through was long grass, with the occasional bush of some strange mountain fruit. As the sun fell through late afternoon, we reached a junction unlike any other. Five mountains came together – six valleys – all at different elevations, conjoined at a central lake where the streams met.

"That's it for following the stream," Simone said as we approached the tide of the natural spring, "if we were even doing that anymore. Where do we go from here?"

"Do we head north?" Anastasiya asked. Simone spun with the compass, and frowned.

"Two of the valleys are just as north as each other," she said, and pondered. "James?"

I had not seen this lake. When I looked at it, day did not turn to night, my personality didn't change, I didn't wear a black robe. I stroked my chin with my right hand.

"Kuvalik and Olomb have nothing," I said.

28

"So, we're lost?" Simone asked.

"Maybe," I said, "but there's still more to Olomb's directions. We went north, then…"

Follow the passage of the Vochduh people. His voice echoed in my head. I grunted.

"Then we follow the passage of the Vochduh people," I repeated the words. "Maybe they left markings, like *Ivaer* leave candles all over the place…"

"Or footprints," Anastasiya suggested.

"I'd be surprised if either of those things can last five hundred years," Simone pondered.

"Can't know if you don't check it out," I suggested with as much cheer as I could muster. I turned to step along the water's gravelly shore. I held my hands by my side, trying as hard as I could to sense the world around me.

Footprints could leave anomalies in carbon – although picking the patterns in shifting, constantly wet gravel and dirt was a long shot. Still, I tried.

Carbon glowed in my minds eye like burning on a heat map. I could visualise its heavy clusters of bright red against a blue backdrop. Images of grass, animals, shrubs and bugs began to coalesce in my fingertips. The image was faint, and disturbed by static. My left arm didn't hurt being held straight down, but there was something wrong with its connection.

"Stupid wind," Simone cussed from behind me. Her voice pulled me out of my concentration, and when I tried to focus again, I found only static.

"What's wrong with it?" I asked.

"Half of it won't stop," she said. "It's not even too fast to steal energy from, it just won't let me take its flow. *Come on*," she tensed, hands clenched by her sides. Anastasiya winced at the scene - energy stealing made her almost as uncomfortable as the mention of the Sunesca.

"Well," I said, stepping back towards the scene, "think about the sheer *volume* of air here." I attempted to connect to it. I felt it in my palms now, my unstable connection stretching halfway across the lake. The centre of the valley wasn't an eddy as I expected, but rather, a channel for a remarkably directional wind. It travelled to my right – all of it that I could feel. "I mean, from down here to the tops of the mountains, all flowing. That's got to be mega-tonnes of it. I'm not surprised you can barely steal speed from it."

Simone grunted. "It's not that," she said. "I should be able to take from pockets of it – but I can't."

29

"Well then, take from the stream," I suggested, and turned my head to the floor for signs of fossilised footprints. "The air here is strange, anyway."

"I agree," she said. "There's other energies mixed in with it. Maybe that's why I can't use it as a source." Her hands were extended by her side, and the stream's energy flowed into them. Anastasiya looked away, coming towards me.

I connected to the winds of the valley again, to confirm my feelings. Yes, they did move so *uniformally*. The gusts weren't like others I'd seen. These movements were carefully calculated, almost *controlled*.

"The winds here *are* behaving unusually, though," I said. "Feel for it. It's unnatural."

"I'm not sure what I could tell you," Simone said, grabbing into her soul connections "You've got more experience than me with this…"

"It's from Suneva," Anastasiya said. "If you can't *steal* from the winds, then that means they're powered by quatra. They *are* unnatural. Sunesca can't steal from the divine."

I didn't want to grimace once more at Anastasiya's distaste for my sister's abilities, but she did have a point to prove in her bigotry. Simone and Salak Kuul had mentioned that Sunesca couldn't take energies which had quatra sources – only demons had that power. As I studied the air, I realised that this must have been the unnatural flavour to its movements. This was the quality that *I* gave the air – although I hoped I was more in tune with the skies than to move it so obviously unnaturally.

"This feels a bit like your air, James," Simone agreed. "You're right, it's clearly unnatural."

"*The passage of the people*," I thought aloud, "it must refer to the winds – the winds of the Vochduh people. We've been following them this whole time."

"Yes, my thoughts too," Anastasiya agreed. "Why wouldn't Kuvalik be direct with his instruction, I wonder?"

"I don't think he ever wanted anybody finding this place," Simone said. "*Kuul* seems to think that he wanted to protect the *Vochduh*, for whatever reason."

Anastasiya grunted, the answer was good enough. Re-establishing my connection to the strange winds, I left my hiking stick in the mud, and led the three of us down the stream. I followed the path of the people, through the rightmost valley.

A dirt trail, formed through hundreds of years of use, still surviving the reclaiming hands of nature, lay beaten onto the rocky mountainside. The path was ancient, the passage of the Vochduh people, following the winds of the valley. It wound up the mountain, bringing us higher up the hill and around its face, before descending dangerously. The trail was uneven, broken, slippery. Grainy gravel shifted underfoot over smooth, hidden rock. The path undulated, over rotting logs and roots, over precarious rock faces. Eventually, as sun began its set behind us, the shadow of another great mountain bathing us in its darkness, we reached the foot of the mountain's far side.

We reached a meadow, rich in tall grass and vibrant flowers, surrounded by a forming perimeter forest of high trees. In its centre, in the last light of day, stood tall a column of wind-beaten rock – grassy at its top like icing to its form. The spire, upon which lay the foundation of Vochduh civilisation.

The old Vochduh King's directions had been true then – even if a little cryptic. I noted it in my diary, my black robe fluttering in the wind. Without the flow of my cape, I might never have been able to follow the path.

Black Robe.

I growled, clawing back to reality. It *was* sunset, I was in shadows, there was a spire with grass and vines like icing standing before me. I now had no idea at which point I'd entered the vision, because both scenes looked almost identical, as if the two had mixed – two memories stitched together. I slapped myself in the face with my good arm, and stumbled forward, across the meadow, catching up to Simone and Anastasiya.

"*The foundation of Vochduh society,*" Simone said, frowning. "Well, it looks like the society died way before we got here. There's nothing around."

The flowers in the field held a shared distinctive petal. They each grew to the same shape – long and tall, closed, elegant – but in a multitude of different colours. I'd seen these plants before – and not as Kuvalik, either. Where had *I* come across this flower?

"There's a Suneva on the top of the spire," Anastasiya said, her hands by her side, gripping into the quatra field.

"I didn't see anybody up there before," Simone noted, squinting at the spire's peak. From our view near its base, amongst the flowers, one couldn't see *anything* about the pillar's top. I certainly didn't remember seeing a figure atop the structure – but then, I couldn't trust what I had seen.

"It's worth looking at," I said. Aware that any attempt to climb the rock formation would leave my arm in severe pain, I summoned my *alis*, the form of Maiki. The Suneva representation of my soul crawled from my thread, over my skin and clothes, and locked into place. The pain in my arm was gone – although,

31

it could not heal this way – and I immediately felt at ease under the quatra armour of green, silver, and black.

I leaped off the ground, pushing off a jet of air, and dug my long, silver claws into the rock wall. I leaped again, grappling my way up the structure's tall, narrow face.

Below me, Anastasiya reached through space and pulled herself through it, onto the spire's top, where she looked down upon me smugly. Simone opened her bag and pulled out a pair of gloves she'd prepared earlier – a set of silicon claws designed to mimic my Suneva hands. Stealing from the current of the nearby stream, she propelled herself upwards much like myself.

I grappled myself over the edge of the rockface, and slumped onto its grassy top. Anastasiya stood perplexed before me, staring at the only thing atop the spire. I hauled myself to my feet and stood beside her.

It was a colony of bright purple, shimmering flowers, with the same petals as those below. They grew directly from stalks, sprouting from a single cluster though a crack in the rock, much like garden clovers. I now recognised the flower.

"An Argol woman in Athens trusted us to deliver one of these…" I said, bending down and feeling the petals. Through my quatra-metal fingers, I could sense their delicacy, and their mystique. "The Vochduh King used to make his tea with the petals, apparently."

"No Suneva up here, then?" Simone asked as she flipped through the air, landing upon the grassy top. She bustled up to Anastasiya.

"This plant is the Suneva," Anastasiya said. "It has a thread, and it's using it."

"Huh…" I nodded. "So, this is probably the *Kiin of the Valley*, then?" I chuckled – although both Simone and Anastasiya took my joke seriously. "I wonder what drinking its tea would do."

"Well, why don't you try it?" Simone suggested. "I mean, apparently this plant is the foundation of the Vochduh society – unless anybody sees any other foundations of society around here."

"There should at least be a temple somewhere near…" I said, trying hard not to look into the setting sun. "Dad wrote about it as being right up in a cliff. I saw it in a vision, too, a few weeks ago. It's so high up, it should be hard to miss."

I leaned into the plant, metallic claw out, and grabbed at one of the stalks. The flower stem was strong, it wouldn't have broken if my fingers weren't sharp enough to pierce stones.

"You mean that Dad wrote about this place, but didn't write how to get here?" Simone asked. "Why would he do that."

"I don't know," I said, standing. "Maybe it's a respect thing. He didn't write much except for a few lines, anyway."

As I lifted my head to inspect the flower, a blinding beam of light hit my eye. I grunted, and turned around, only to face directly into the sunset. "Damnit!" I hissed, my eyes burning. I looked toward the sprouting plant on the ground, where I knew it was safe to look, and comprehended my confusion. How was I hit by sunlight in two opposing directions?

A spot of intense brightness lay on the grass by the flower's stems. It's beam, which cut through the hanging pollen in the air, came from up high. I followed the beam, shielding my eyes as I looked to its source. High in the east-most mountain, jutting from the sheer, jarring cliff face, was the overhang of a temple built into stone, its brilliant rocks reflecting the sunset.

"There!" I pointed high onto the cliff face. "There it is." *The Vochduh Temple.*

Chapter 4
The Ledge

Standing on the stones at the base of the temple, by the valley's dried stream, the structure's lip stretched much higher than it seemed before. The cliff face was totally sheer, the rock almost entirely smooth. I'd fought myself away from a vision, seeing myself as Olomb about to embark on the vertical journey. Coming from the memory, I was faced with the preserved marks of his climbing knives – where they had sheared into the rock. I felt the mark with my metal fingers.

Dad's personal accounts said that he had scaled the whole wall to reach the temple. Apparently, according to one text in the library, it is the honour of a *Kiin* to fly up the face – which suggested that some form of flight was common amongst them. I also saw this in a vision of Olomb's – the same vision that taught me how to command air with my breath.

Annikida came up behind me, admiring the scope of the cliff face. She had let her Suneva form take over her, her bright pink eyes lighting the rock through the shadow of dusk. Her antlers hung tall against her meek, white helmet.

"Do you want me to get us up there?" she asked in her small voice. "It is getting dark. We should camp out in the temple."

I turned to her, then back to the ledge of the temple. It was so high up – higher than many skyscrapers. I remembered from Olomb's memory that there used to be monks who would sit upon the ledge and create updrafts. Without them, this would be a very difficult climb – more difficult than Olomb had experienced it. I turned to Simone, whose mouth hung agape at the structure.

"You can take Simone," I said. "But it's an honour of a *Kiin* to make their own way up this face."

I wasn't certain if it was an honour, but I felt less stupid than admitting that I wanted to do it to prove myself as a *Kiin*. I felt that ascending this temple was some right of passage – surely it had to be. Dad wrote about it, didn't he?

Simone immediately turned to me, her face offended.

"You think that I can't make it up?" she asked.

"What, no, it's just dangerous, is all…"

"I pissed off a whole magical society by being their number one enemy. I think I can handle danger," she smirked.

"That's different," I insisted. "What if you fall climbing this thing? It's a stupid idea, no?"

"What if *you* fall?" she persisted.

"Then I pull up. I've got free energy. You don't, and you don't have armour."

"Olomb managed," she shrugged. "Like you said, there's honour in the climb."

I grunted, but she was right.

"You're usually smarter than this," I grumbled. "I'm the one to make stupid decisions."

"Now you know how stupid *you* sounded insisting to climb this thing out of honour yourself," Simone chuffed. "The things you Suneva do for destiny and tradition…"

Annikida squinted, her offence obvious in her balled fists.

"Although I'm serious, I want to try the climb," Simone steeled herself. "I reckon I can make it. I have the power of air."

"That you do…" I hummed, and felt my guilt spike as she stole energy from somewhere, throwing herself high onto the sheer cliff before us. Her silicon claws gripped in tight, and she thrust the next hand and foot up, starting her climb.

I turned to Annikida, and shrugged.

"I guess you're the only one teleporting up, then," I said, and leaped onto the wall.

***

Simone dug in with her claws, feeling the energy which danced all around her. The earth moved, rocks rumbling; heat rose from somewhere, down, under the stream-bed; animals chirped, their songs displacing the air, turning it into a symphony of vibrations. Energy appeared like waving ribbons in her vision, streaming from their source, each type a different colour. The world was full of energy – it would help her in the climb.

She channelled this ambient kinetic energy – that of the tumultuous air, whose red ribbons danced in the breeze – into her pushes as she leaped from one hand-hold to another. As long as she didn't power her connection to silicon, her latticed nails would tear into the cliff face, and she would hold on.

I had passed Simone by this point – she could see my black, quatra-metal ass up above, as I bounded and pushed with the fluidity of the wind. To her, I danced through the skies – I controlled the air as if it was an extension of my arm. I moved it with grace.

Simone found it difficult to move with such poise – *Salak Kuul* had only been teaching her to use air as an exhaust, not as a skill. Still, she could push, and that was enough.

Simone paused to catch her breath, making the mistake to look down and admire her progress. The ground was so far away now, composed of hard rocks with jagged faces. She gulped.

And that Russian girl was down there too, watching Simone with her innocent, pink, Suneva eyes. Like glass, there was no emotion behind a Suneva helmet. That said, the girl didn't show any emotion regularly. Simone knew that Anastasiya didn't like her, some sort of traditional bigotry towards Sunesca. *What petty crap.* Simone grumbled to herself, pulling her silicon claw and slamming it into the rock above.

How petty, She repeated, *I expected more from a Legendary. We're in the same social struggle, what right does she have to hate me? Why would she choose to hate, anyway?* Although Simone promptly remembered the years she spent hating the Suneva because of her own identity confusion, and was quick to divert her train of thought.

Anyway… she climbed further, panting despite the rest. She was over half way now – still a while to go. *I'll show her. She's afraid of what I can do, but I haven't given her anything to fear yet. She'll see…*

Yes, it was true that Sunesca abilities were quite frightening – silencing words in the throat, taking the light from one's eyes, muting sounds by the ear, stopping a moving car – but Simone wasn't at this level yet. It would take a lot of work, and she was keen to be a good *Kiin* too. If Simone could help me save the Suneva, she'd have plenty of time to learn it all. If not, she'd have to learn without my demonstration.

Simone roared up the face, furiously grappling with fists and pushing with feet. She was panting hard – without quatra to motivate the tiring muscles, this was a hard effort. Still, she scrambled on, up the cliff, bashing at the stone.

Simone drew energy more heavily now. She thought she could feel it in her blood, becoming her own. *Kuul* had said that Sunesca were only a vessel of energy – transforming it into exhaust and abilities. Maybe that wasn't true, after all. Simone tried to keep the energy sitting warm inside her, un-transformed, but it couldn't, and it burst from her skin, blowing air away from her, forcing it into new patterns around her body.

Somehow, it seemed to be helping. The currents swirling made her lighter – they pushed her upwards. With Simone's own pushes – sucking in energy around her to it's last drop - she surged up the rock. She now made ground on me, although I was taking the climb slowly. Why would I need to be cautious when I had armour and *kiin* abilities?

Simone bounded onwards, energy flowing, moving itself out of her body upon being drawn in. She trusted it to move where it helped her.

She shouldn't have.

An ounce of excess energy ran through her fists, powering Simone's connection to silicon. She slammed her claws into the wall, where they squished like putty.

And suddenly without any handhold, Simone fell.

Annikida looked on, emotionless through her antlered helmet. She reached out to Simone, and teleported. Simone expected to find herself held, but the girl had disappeared.

Simone twisted in the air, trying to grasp at scraps of energy around her. The dancing ribbons extended to her palms, but as quickly as she'd drawn them towards her, they were already flying out of her range. Panic took hold. The ground came fast.

Simone screamed. I turned to lock eyes as she fell towards the earth. Her body twisted, her hands flailed and grasped around her.

I leaped from the rock face. I was so far up, so tired now, but I could do it again. I'd have to — for some sense of honour. It felt wrong to enter the temple without having earned it. I felt this deeply.

I twisted, blasting air behind me. My head-fin kept me stable, my blade-like chin directing wind, letting me steer. I kept blasting jets from my feet, desperate to catch my sister. She fell almost inhumanly fast, but I could fall faster.

Rock zipped by my stomach. The sheer face like a road underneath me — the ground ahead a wall in the middle of it. It was coming quick — almost too quickly for me to reach her.

Metres from the ground, right where I wanted to pull up, I finally caught Simone's hand. I grappled her in close, taking her in a bear hug. My back to the ground, I tried to pull up. "Grab me!" I yelled, letting go of Simone to direct the air currents. I slammed the flow atop us to a halt, driving pressure under my back desperately.

My body was yanked from it's trajectory, pulled in an arc with sickening force, but it wasn't enough. Zipping away from the cliff, my back crashed into the rocks of the dry creek, and we bounced. I held Simone tight through the tumble, protecting her as we scraped and rolled across the hard ground, finally skidding to a stop. We both collapsed on the creekbed, our bodies buzzing with adrenaline.

Then Annikida appeared next to us, dropping her armour to hoist my body to sit. Simone righted herself, her hyped and dizzied form slumping over mine.

"Thank you," she whispered to me, grappling my body in a painful hug.

Anastasiya pulled something from her pocket — a shimmering clear stone — which she handed to Simone. I instantly connected to the dense carbon in the pink-shimmering rock. It was a diamond.

"What's this?" Simone whispered, her voice still straining for breath. She regarded the item with a raised eyebrow, only letting it touch the very tips of her fingers.

"It's a healing stone," Analstasiya said, pushing the rock fully into Simone's palm and closing her fingers over it. "You have no quatra to heal, this rock gives you some of mine. You have the pathways to use it."

Simone hummed, accepting the gift, and put it into her pocket.

"Let's camp here tonight," I said, groggily. "Rest and regain some energy to climb tomorrow."

"You still want to climb?" Anastasiya quizzed.

"Yes," I said, although my mind flashed to my mother, who had taken serious issue to my judgement calls. She thought we were in Macedonia for the sole purose of seeing Dedo, to deliver to him these texts that Dad had found and translating them, nothing more. I winced at the thought of the woman's face. "The scripts said to enter honourably, and I don't feel like defying tradition. It's climbable."

Anastasiya hummed, her face growing nervous, and she peered through the valley to the moon above. "I don't know that we have enough time for climbing."

"Why not?" I asked.

"It's just...they'd have to have sensed it," she said, still staring at the moon. "The amount of quatra I used to get fully across the globe, the White Witch would have to have felt it. She'd have to be coming for us."

I sweated at the implication. We stood no chance against Natalie – even though she was the reason we were here, facing her now was not ideal. I needed answers first.

"We'll be here tomorrow regardless," I pointed out. "I don't think I'll find the *destiny-loophole* in one day. If she's coming, we'll just have to hope that we sense her and can escape in time."

Anistasiya's eyes furrowed – she was displeased, but she did not put up a fuss.

"I'll set up a fire pit, then," she said, and pulled herself through space, disappearing into a physical anomaly.

***

In the morning sunrise we grappled the face of the rocks. Simone leaped ahead of me, at my insistence, so that I could catch her if she fell. It took hours to reach the ledge of the temple. It had loomed over us the entire morning, a long overhang jutting out from the rock face just enough that it threatened to be unclimbable.

As I reached it, I looked below. At least two hundred metres in the air, dangling on a cliffside by my sharp, metal claws, I could feel myself sweat through my armour. The fall was impossibly long. Simone, hanging next to me, arms dead, refused to follow my gaze. We craned our heads backwards, across the valley, to gauge the lip of the temple's protrusion.

I reached for the edge, but not even my elongated, armoured arms could grasp it. I sighed, and looked to my sister.

"I'd really hate to think that we came all this way and can't get around the edge," I said. "I've got one idea, but if it doesn't work, I honestly think I'll just teleport up."

Simone tutted playfully. "Dad made it up without a legendary. You even said that he couldn't fly."

"Oh…yeah," I hummed. I had, of course, remembered Kuvalik climbing into this temple as Salak Nolver, but Dad? I thought I'd stopped living under the long shadow of John Grey, but I still had a toe in the darkness if I couldn't round this lip as a more powerful *Kiin*.

"And Olomb did it without air…" I added. How had he done it, though? The memory wouldn't come to me – in fact, every time I'd let Maiki embrace me, the memories seemed to be locked out. I liked this, although it appeared now that I needed the hint.

"I'm going to attempt something," I said. "Although, I'm not sure you should try it."

"Why not?" Simone asked. I began to scale back down the rock.

"You'll see," I warned.

Two hand holds down the wall I paused, peering again at the ledge's edge. I'd given myself an angle to the face of it, hopefully enough. The lip had to have been two metres in length, and past its edge, if I miscalculated any leap, was nothing but distant mountain peaks and blue skies. *My God this is high up.*

I could see the arc I wanted to take before me painted on the thin, high air. Unsure of myself, but brave, I tensed.

And I pounced.

Air blasted from my feet, and I soared upwards and away from the sheer cliff. I vaulted under the protrusion's face, twisting around mid-air to face it. I fell away from it, though, faster than I predicted. There was nothing to catch on this fall, nothing but a long, *long* drop to gravel and rocks. I clenched up, throwing another gust of air down at the cliff.

The blast extended my arc, throwing me towards the ledge, only just. I hit my peak height just as I rounded its lip, and I threw my hands at the vertical stone of the landing.

My claws crashed into the front face of the lip, barely reaching. I clenched to set them into the stone, but my weight was still flying outwards, and my claws slipped, scraping at the rock as my body continued flying away. My blood boiled to horror, my eyes bulging. I could recover, right? Swoop towards the wall, land back on it without crushing my body and falling to my death...

Hands grappled at mine, and my claws finally stuck just at the last millimetre of ledge face. Annikida was reaching over the cliff, holding me in place. With a sturdy handhold, I hoisted myself over the lip's edge, coming to flop on the platform to lie with a smile.

"What do I do?" Simone shrieked. How did I forget about her? I made my way to my hands and knees, crawling over the face of the ledge. The drop caused my head to spin – I could have vomited into my helmet. I turned back to Annikida.

"Grab my legs," I instructed, and once pinned, dangled my chest and arms over the ravine. I had enough of my stomach on the stone that the armour would grip.

"Jump for my hands," I instructed.

There was a pause, before Simone said "Fuck...okay." And I waited, my hands dangling, my fingers outstretched.

Simone then landed in them, her hands clawing at mine after what must have been a spectacular leap. Her body soared outwards still, just like mine had done, and I heard a scraping.

Annikida was slipping. *I* was slipping.

And Simone was still pulling us out to the ravine.

My first instinct was to grab – grapple at something – *anything*. I took my left arm away from Simone and lurched my chest upwards. As I slid, my legs came around, bringing Annikida with them. I dug my claw into the ledge as Annikida came over the side of it, clawing into my thigh for dear life. Both girls gripped to my limbs with the same vigour.

The load hit as my legs swung down. My arm strained, and the rock cracked. I could feel it before I could see it – the structure was weakening. My eyes bulged.

"Climb!" I yelled, my body swinging on the rockface – with no free limbs to throw air and stop the movement.

"Climb!" I screeched again. The rock was failing under my grasp, cracking again, the shudder of it sending a shockwave through my body.

My swing came abruptly to a halt. Simone, stealing my energy, pounced off my body. She leapt past the ledge, going so far as to do a front-flip, before landing steadily on its face.

With my other arm free, I raced to slam it onto the stone. I strained to pull myself up, but Simone held my head fin and yanked it tight. Together we hoisted myself and Annikida onto the temple's landing.

I screamed triumphantly, and fell onto my back. Deep gushes of breath poured into my helmet. My chest rose and fell – despite the logic which concluded that Suneva chests should do no such thing.

"*Omercronius*," I huffed. "That...that was something. Simone, you saved the day there."

"I didn't save anything!" she gushed humbly. "You held us all together."

"Team effort, then," I smiled beneath the helmet. "*Sweet cheese* – I didn't think it would be that intense."

I slowly wretched myself off the ground. At first, I could only crawl, and so I crawled from the overhang into the temple proper, where I sat upon my knees. Simone did the same, writhing up next to me. I reached back to pull Annikida away from the lip, and into the safety of the building. The girl was shaken into silence.

"Wow..." Simone uttered to the sight. I, pulling Annikida to safety, had the view of the entire mountain range in my vision. Peaks, capped in dusty rock and frost, extended infinitely under the pale-yellow morning light. Birds moved like specs of life against the painting of the still earth.

"I know," I uttered to Simone, sitting Annikida up in the shade of the temple. She abandoned her armour to become Anastasiya.

"No," Simone insisted, grabbing my shoulder and turning me. "Not the view. *Look.*"

The temple extended beyond my eyes. Columns of faded jade and sky-blue marched through the lobby, like the legs of giants, supporting the cavernous roof. The tiles on the floor, cracked and broken, lay as a suggestion to a long-lost, beautiful and intricate pattern of reds, yellows, and stone greys. The space was wide and tall, but not dark. Light fell from the roof in pools of pure white – raining down from massive skylights.

The lobby was flat, but rose on a small stair set by its rear, leading to a central grand doorway on the far wall – an entrance to an elaborate chamber. On the back right, elevated and tucked into a dark corner, was an equally impressive portal. On the left and right walls of the vast space, past the central column rows, were three sets of doors, each leading to unknown rooms.

41

I let the armour of Maiki slide off my body – choosing instead to let my arm heal. Instantly, I was imbued with familiarity of my surroundings. There were many memories of this place floating in my mind. None of them were mine, of course.

"It's beautiful," Anastasiya said. She was on her feet, standing next to me.

"It used to be even prettier," I said. "In Olomb's memories, the tiles glistened in the skylights."

I stepped cautiously into the grand hall between the thick columns. My steps rang throughout the cavernous entranceway, echoing off all surfaces. Up ahead, I could see an odd feature of the floor which I wasn't familiar with – it looked as if the floor had fallen away. I snuck forward to investigate.

Despite our loneliness in the temple, I felt as if I was trespassing. I knew there were eyes staring at me. There were faces judging me – hidden, somewhere. I glanced nervously as I tip-toed my way towards the anomaly. Simone joined in, stepping just as cautiously into the grand cavern. Anastasiya seemed reluctant to enter the temple at all.

I reached the crack in the floor, and crouched to inspect it. Tiles had fallen away here into an aqueduct running beneath the floor. This temple had plumbing. Along with the skylights obviously built by *Raduk*, it was clear that the *Vochduh* Kingdom attracted all kinds of Suneva into their temples and cities. I dipped my hand into the water, crystal clear and still flowing. It must have been coming from the mountain top.

"Look at this," Simone said, over by a portal on the rightmost wall. She stood under a hook, next to an ornamental column. A black robe hung before her. It wasn't my robe.

It wasn't Olomb's *robe*. I mentally slapped myself.

"That's a Sunesca robe," I stood and walked towards her.

"Interesting," Simone nodded, feeling the material. She outstretched it on the hook, investigating its form. "I wonder why it was left here."

"I don't know," I mused, "could have been someone's spare."

"I wouldn't leave this behind. It feels expensive," Simone noted, and outstretched it to me to feel.

In my hands, the material was lightweight, but incredibly dark. One would expect to be able to see their fingers through a fabric so thin, but it seemed to absorb every drop of light. The surface of the cloak was so dusty, and cobweb covered, that it must have been left here for hundreds of years. This was definitely not my cloak. I don't know where I'd left my cloak.

Olomb's Cloak, God damnit.

Simone removed it from the hook and swung it around her body. It had large, loose sleeves, and a long hood which shaded the face to the nose and mouth. There were no buttons to hold it shut, although I could see a ribbon on its inside which could hold the waist tight. It was perfectly her size, trailing down to her ankles, and not interfering with the floor.

"Do you know why they would make the robes black?" I asked her, although I'd heard the answer somewhere before. Nolver would have known it. "I mean, if I was going to make a robe, I wouldn't make myself look so...scary."

"*Kuul* told me this, actually," she smiled. "He said that a Sunesca can transform heat before they can light. The black robe catches all light that lands near it and turns it to heat. It means you've always got energy to use.

"They really thought of everything," I nodded, admiring the form of the cloak.

Anastasiya stepped up to us hurriedly. Her footsteps cracked through the cavernous temple. I spun to her, but Simone seemed unfazed.

"You're just going to *take* that?" she asked Simone, aghast. Simone seemed to expect such interrogation.

"If I'm going to be a proper Sunesca, I'll need to adhere to the traditions," she said. "You're quite traditional, aren't you?"

"Yes, but..." the girl nervously squeaked, before being cut off.

"I don't think I could accurately recreate this, so I'll have to take it. Stealing is in our nature, isn't it?" Simone said smugly, gesturing to the material. "You don't see anybody as old and dusty as this robe around, do you?"

"No," Anastasiya stifled, "but can't you *feel* the energy here? We're being watched."

"I don't think it's surprising that ghosts attach themselves to a temple," I noted. "I expected it, really."

"I don't mean *ghosts*," Anastasiya squeaked.

Behind her, in the peripheries of my vision, a shadow darted. I snapped my head to it, to see no sign of it. I could feel the air grow colder and crisper. I could see the light dimming slowly.

"Demons..." I said. A resonating caw echoed from the shadows.

The darkness in the temple was liquid. It had eyes, and ears, and could steal your life-force. There were several beings here, lurking behind columns, around corners. Pebbles on the floor rustled, and ancient wind chimes rattled in the temple's many doorways. Our observers kept themselves at a distance, waiting for us to move.

"You can't defeat a demon," Anastasiya's voice wavered with genuine fear. "What do we do?"

"Defeat?" Simone huffed, she locked eyes with the girl. "Not everything is a threat. Why should we have to defeat them?"

"You just stole their robe!"

"And they haven't attacked, *look*." And Simone gestured to the temple lobby. The space was practically electric with anticipation. "They're just people living their...deaths..."

"If they attacked us, they could kill us," Anastasiya stood her ground. "They're unstoppable. By being in here, we're at their leisure."

"You're assuming a lot. You know nothing about these dead," Simone stifled a yell. "They're *people*, not thieves nor murderers. Or, they *were* people. People can be evil, Suneva can be evil, Sunesca can be evil. But they're *not* evil by design. How about you let them act before you judge?" she snapped. Anastasiya had more to say, but Simone would not let her say it. She turned to me.

"Where's the library?" Simone asked me. "We're finding the secrets to Suneva freedom."

"Back right door," I said, pointing to the corner with an elaborate doorway, which had grown darker in the last moment. At least, that was where I remember Kuvalik going in the vision of the *Vatje na Vochduh* writings.

Simone stepped towards it, closer to the gathering shadows. They swum across the room, congealing like sets of ribbons, dancing in front of the impressive stone arch.

Anastasiya squeaked, frozen. I grabbed her hand and pulled her along behind me, up to Simone. My sister's stride was natural, unhindered by fear. Her face was straight – not brave, vindictive, stubborn, scared, or any other conceivable emotion. As she confidently mounted the stairs to the archway, the ribbons of blackness swirled with increasing intensity.

Then there seemed to be a *command*, something felt instead of heard, to *stop* before the arch. The blackness had formed fully now in the door, a cloud of soot, stone, and ribbons that blocked all light. It was this being which told us to halt, I knew now. Had this thing invaded our minds? I wasn't sure how I knew what it wanted.

Then it commanded of us to tell our purpose. It delivered this intrustion through a *compulsion* to speak. It was bizzare.

"We're here to find what the Vochduh learned about destiny," Simone said. "We wish to create freedom from destiny for the Suneva."

The demon's body hummed. Around the cavern, grunts, howls, and groans echoed and spat. The space billowed with the shrieks of the dead and damned. I shuddered.

The demon wanted to know who we were.

"I am *Salak Nera*," Simone spoke. "This is my brother, Maiki Leukess. We are both of Vochduh heritage. This is Annikida…" She gestured to the Russian girl. "She is the Legendary Suneva of Teleportation."

The wails of the rocky temple hushed. The demons stopped their growling, their swirling shadows slowing. The ribbons of the demon before us fluttered, as if about to fall, but he held himself together.

I am Salak Becha, head guardian of this Library. His voice resonated in my soul. *We have guarded this space from acts of destiny since its first creation, and will do so for centuries to come. Long research went into the answers you seek, which lie beyond this doorway.*

You have our blessing to find them, although I warn – only one Suneva ever did comprehend the path to freedom, and many before and after him have tried.

"Thank you," I said, although by the time I did, the shadow of his body was already disappearing – scattering, back into the nooks of the temple's darkness. Revealed beyond *Salak Becha's* shadow, was a great light. It cascaded out of the stone archway onto our faces, blinding us momentarily until we stepped into the room.

Daylight streamed in with impossible intensity from a small skylight at the pinnacle of the room's domed roof. The library was a spherical cutting into the mountain, two storeys tall, whose entire circumference was lined with shelves. The archway from the temple led onto the second story catwalk, which encircled the space halfway up the circular wall. Before me was a tablet held on a lecturn – the *Vatje na Vochduh*. Observing the shelves around the room, it seemed that many of them were empty. Entire rows had vanished, either destroyed by rot or explorers,

45

or having never been filled to begin with. On the floor of the cylindrical room sat rubble of smashed stones, amongst a set of stone stools for reading.

"*Cheese*, this place is huge," I noted. "Where the hell do we start finding answers?"

"I don't know," Simone gaped, taking in the room herself. "We'll have to just start with book titles, I guess."

"But, just *look*," I continued my gawking. "I mean, look how many *tablets* there are even amongst this stuff. Some of this is truly ancient. I doubt we'll be able to read *half* of it."

Simone frowned, her excitement dashed in one single comment. She turned to me, her eyes sceptical.

"How much of it will we be able to read?" she asked. "Weren't we hoping to have Dedo here with us to help with the language barrier?"

My stomach fell, and I suddenly felt very stupid. I hadn't learned Vochduh, I couldn't, so we had hoped on Dedo joining us to teach us. But he was dead. "Well, like all good libraries, there'll be more than one language in here." I laughed nervously. "Maybe some liktan, probably a lot of Vochduh. Maybe some Macedonian that Anastasiya could help with…" and I peered over my shoulder to the girl, who was shuddering in the entranceway.

"The demons could probably read Vochduh, if we asked them nicely," Simone stroked her chin, peering back to the lobby. "I'll try and find the books we *can* read first, though."

"I can't believe we're doing this," Anastasiya blurted, words spilling as if she'd forgotten how to talk. Her tone was desperate. "Trying to get rid of destiny – kind-of-fine, but taking the honour and blessings of demons to do it? Doesn't that just seem wrong to either of you?"

Simone grumbled, swatting a hand of dismissal and turning towards the books. Anastasiya waited for an answer, whilst Simone analysed the closest spine.

"Well?" Anastasiya turned to me. I had no problem with propositioning demons for help. I might have been traumatised by *Kuul*, but I had learned to not hate him. I had to give these demons a chance, as they held the answers I needed. They were probably the Sunesca test subjects of Vochduh philosophers.

"I think this is a good idea," I said, a guilty smile on my face. "If the demons trust us in here, then I trust them."

"How?" she snorted.

"Like you said – they could kill us at any time. If they didn't want us reading the books, they wouldn't have let us any further."

"And you don't think this room is a trap?" she squeaked. "'*Only one Suneva ever did comprehend the path to freedom*', what do you think happened to the others?"

Simone growled, grasping at the book she held in her hands. She tossed it to me, and I caught it. The thing was thicker than any book I'd ever read. The weight of this research finally dawned on me as it heaved on my arms.

"It's in Liktan. *Read,*" Simone groaned to me, before switching her attention. She stomped on the stone catwalk, past me, toward Anastasiya. The *Kida* held her grip, as if to reach out and jump through space at any moment.

"How about you air your problems with me *right now*," Simone growled at the girl. Beyond the two, I could see a hint of darkness congealing in the stone archway. "Because frankly, I'm sick of your shit. You've got a big problem with not only me, but everything to do with the Sunesca. I've tried to be nice to you, but I've had it. So, spit it up, *princess*. What's your issue?"

Anastasiya's eyes narrowed. She puffed her chest.

"Whoa, hey!" I let the tome down and ran between the two girls. The air separating them sat rotten like curdled milk. "Come on, let's just calm down and…"

"Princess?" Anastasiya remarked. "Says the fake activist. You hated Suneva and Sunesca alike since the day you were born. What made *you* change, *Fairysmog?*"

"Oh no," my eye twitched. I ducked away.

"Fancy you telling me off for being afraid of demons. You're the biggest hypocrite to grace the Suneva sphere," Anastasiya harked. "When I came for your brother, I thought I was going to join Iva Argol, the White Witch, and Hesslik's fiercest defector. I just got an action blogger."

I slunk away, palming my way around the wall until I found the exit. "I think I'll make us all some calming tea – fit for a king!" I interjected, and slipped through the stone archway. A demon's shadow hung above me, a single ribbon of its corporeal being buzzing.

"I tell you why I changed," Simone's voice echoed. The main chamber, as I stepped into it, was frighteningly cold, and the air abnormally still. Obscuring the light, standing over the exposed stream in the lobby's centre, were four shadow figures made of swirling, charcoal ribbons. I almost fell over at the sight, but composed myself to walk towards them.

"I feared Suneva because they were powerful, and I would never have that power," Simone's voice rang, "then I found that I was like them. I could see their energy, but I couldn't use it. It was a cycle of self-loathing. Hell, I got so deluded,

47

that I thought I was a saviour sent to protect people – the one person who could see and deliver us from the enemy. Do you know how degrading and toxic that kind of isolation is?"

"So, you projected hate?" Anastasiya stabbed. "I barely think you can tell me off for…"

"I spread concern," Simone interrupted. "The community generated hate, and I stupidly gave them what they wanted. I became the embodiment of it."

I stepped carefully towards the stream. My footfalls did not sound as I did so. The demons seemed to take delight in the ruckus caused, their ribbons dancing vibrantly.

"So, you find out that you're the thing you hate, and you do a total switch of opinion. How graceful," Anastasiya spat. "Tell me, what of *the community* now? You've just left them to breed more hate. You've done nothing to stop it."

"I…"

"You didn't address the issues!"

I knelt by the stream, in front of the four demons there. They stared at me, with their eye-less, featureless whirlwind bodies. I tore carbon from the tiles nearby, and shaped it into a crude, diamond teapot.

"I don't suppose this happens with every guest, does it?" I asked them, but they had no reply for me. I sighed, and filled the pot with water from the stream.

"If I told them I was a Sunesca, they'd think I was manipulating them this whole time," Simone argued. "That would have generated *way* worse outcomes. Did you ever read the personal messages of some of the blog users? They went nuts for a conspiracy. They'd believe *anything* they made up as long as somebody would agree with them."

I pulled cardboard from my backpack, setting it down in a ring of broken tiles. I tore the carbon from the bottom piece, setting it alight in a dazzling flame. The fire built, and I added some sticks from my bag – which I'd collected in case we needed to cook up here. I set the diamond teapot amongst the smouldering pittance.

"You're going to have to fix your mess," Anastasiya said. "You can't run from it forever."

"You can't fix extremists, and if you can, I'll do it later," Simone said. "For now, I'm out here trying to preserve the Suneva. Is that good enough for you?"

It would take a while for the water to boil. In the meantime, I removed the flower from my pocket. It was slightly crushed, but still glowing with its enchantment. The demons regarded me with keen expressions.

"The flower of the kings," one said to me, aloud.

"Yes, I heard that he used to drink its tea," I said, competing to be heard over the nuclear argument echoing from behind.

"The last king who came drank from it," the demon said. He stood on the left end of the crowd, with the most excited ribbons of darkness. "It helped them to think."

"How did he make the tea?" I asked. I wasn't quite sure what to do with the flower in my hand.

"It is shown on the tablet in his chambers," the demon said. "I will help you read it."

They wafted past me – their dusty, looming figure sweeping right through my head. I summersaulted backwards, out of the way, and jumped up to follow.

"Tell me then…." I heard Simone's voice, "I get why you hate *me*, but why do you hate Sunesca and demons? What shit did your entitled-ass parents spout at you?"

There was finally a lull – a deafening silence as Anastasiya found her words. I followed the demon up the steps to the central doorway, to the *Vochduhvlad*'s chambers. I paused outside the stone archway, waiting for her answer.

"A demon possessed me as a child, and held my identity at ransom. I couldn't tell anybody or he'd out me as a legendary to the world. My parents were very accepting of all Suneva and Sunesca – as Olomb's codes always taught. My hatred has always been my hidden guilt."

"Holy shit…" I exclaimed aloud, and looked to the demon, who was ushering me into the large, stone throne room. I hurriedly clambered after him, my legs shaking.

The room was tall, taller than the library's dome. It was long and thin, with both walls ornamented with tapestries of carved rock. At its end, in the centre, was an impressive throne of pure diamond. The tapestry of basalt on the left of the chamber had split, with half of it strewn across the base of the camber in pieces. The righthand side, where the demon stood, was preserved. I limped over, my mind too preoccupied with shock to walk properly.

The demon pointed to a pictogram. It had four panels, which showed a hand picking a leaf from the stem of the flower, then sprinkling both into a pot.

49

"The writing says to crush a segment of stem and a full petal in the hand. You must crush enough for the juices to flow, and only that much. The flower should not be pulverised, or cut."

I nodded, observing the Cyrillic writing. I let my eyes wander over the wall of text, away from the pictogram, and towards the chamber's entrance. I scanned for words which I knew – Zondeca and Zalach coming to me immediately. Then, I hit a word I did not expect to find, written in a list of words which seemed to have been carved by different hands.

Muhrakiin.

"Muhrakiin." I pointed to the word. The demon wafted over, observing the carving with me. "That's my dad. Who wrote this?"

"I know that he's your father, Maiki Leukess," the demon said. "Above it is Nekridah, his father. Each man wrote it by his own hand. Your father even left space for you…" The demon formed a finger from one of his ribbons. It pointed to the blank area of basalt below my dad's name.

"What is this list, then? A guestbook? Hopeful Vochduh looking to solve destiny?" I asked. The demon chuckled, and pointed to the lists' title at the very top of the stone. Both craning my head and reading in foreign letters made my comprehension slow, but I got it eventually.

"*Vochduhvlade.*" I read.

"Yes." The demon said. "It is the list of the Vochduh Kings. Your arrival has been awaited since your father's death, *Vochduhvlad.*"

Chapter 6
Written in Stone

I handed a diamond mug to Simone and Anastasiya each. I held my own, still hot from being poured. We stood around the central sitting area in the library, on the bottom floor. The two girls sat silently, despondently. Emotions had boiled over, but each girl was too stubborn to admit their apologies for the argument. Still, the curdled tension had entirely dissipated. There was an air of understanding within the library's cylindrical wall.

The demon who had shown me how to make the tea, *Salak Kallid*, hung by the bookshelf. I asked him, with the permission and comfort of Anastasiya, to help us translate the texts we would choose to read. He complied, trying to be as invisible as possible.

Simone sniffed the tea, then winced, and handed it back to me.

"I don't know," she said, "there's something weird about this tea to me. I think I'll stick to water."

"Sure you don't want the drink of kings?" I asked.

"Not really," she said. "I'll wait to see what it does to you first."

"Fair enough," I said, scooping away the mug and leaving it on the floor by the pot. I took a small sip of the tea, as did Anastasiya.

Its taste, clearly, was floral. The flavour was heavy, and intense, though. It was like drinking perfume out of a bottle. My face scrunched, but the aftertaste was so lovely, that I had to take another sip.

"Nerios, that's *odd*," Anastasiya remarked. "I don't think that does a lot for me."

Odd, I thought. I immediately felt lighter, happier. My arm even throbbed less. I took another sip.

"Okay," I addressed the group, "let's each pick a book in a language we can read and get going?"

Each nodded, and set in radially opposite directions out to the shelf. Simone went to Salak Kallid, and started to chit chat as she searched spines. I pondered books on my side of the cylindrical shelves.

"Hmm..." I hummed aloud, fingering the spines of books and tablets. Many of them were in Liktan, and many appeared to be useful, but not many were on the topic of destiny cancellation. *Air pressure and hand gestures*, *Whirlwind physics*, *Gliding Essentials*, *The Omercronian Agenda*.

My arm, set on its own compulsions, moved itself towards a volume before I had even comprehended the title. When I caught my hand, I saw the title on the spine – *Destiny and Control*. Around it, near the bottom of the bookcase, were several similar titles which my hand did not automatically migrate to. *Price of Divinity*, *Salak Freedom*, *Compulsions and Denial of the Cosmos* – amongst many Macedonian and Vochduh works which I couldn't translate. I sipped my tea. Damn, it tasted good.

Omercronius wants me to read this book, I decided. Omercronius wouldn't want to relinquish his control, would he? Surely, he wouldn't guide me towards severing my link to destiny. I pushed the book back, stepping away from the shelf. My decisions were being guided.

"Simone," I fought the compulsion to stick with the choice my hand had made, "I don't trust myself to choose a book. Come here and tell me which one you'd choose."

"What, why?" she asked.

"Because Omercronius wants me to read a certain one," I said, and took another sip of the delicious tea. It's tangy, fruity flavours danced down my throat. "That either means it's important, or the exact opposite of what we need. I don't think Anastasiya or I can be trusted to choose on this matter."

"Okay..." Simone said, and walked her way over. She quickly perused the relevant titles whilst I sipped my tea. I could see why the old kings used to drink this to concentrate – my brain felt so activated. The air around me was so much crisper to the touch. My spatial awareness was incredible.

"This one," Simone said finally, handing me the book I'd picked before.

"Interesting," I noted, grabbing the book. I walked it back to the central podium and opened it up. "This is the one that Omercronius chose. Maybe it's useful."

I had another sip of the tea as I leafed over the first page. Except, it wasn't a sip, it was a gulp, and by the end of it, I was out of tea. I'd been drinking it much more enthusiastically than I'd thought.

"Right..." I hummed, looking at the first page.

Destiny, seen as a divine pathway to life's purpose, has often been the subject of much scrutiny by Vochduh scholars. In this study, we analyse the effects of control and speculate the ideologies of...

"James, what's happened to your thread?" Anastasiya asked, her eyes wide. I looked up to her.

"What do you mean?" I asked, pawing at my neck. "What's happened to my..."

My vision dislodged, soaring behind my eyes, through them, past my brain and into my systems. I rushed through my hands, into my palms, and my fingers. My fingers were the air. They were the room. I was the room. Suddenly, I was one and connected to all of the air in the temple. The vast space of the lobby cavern, the lush and tall throne chamber, and each of the side rooms behind the vaulting columns of the grand entrance. I could see it all at once in my mind. My vision and awareness were everywhere, omnipresent. I could sense every eddy and vortex which pushed and waned, as if my fingers were right there to sense it. Every nook and cranny in the intricate diamond throne caressed my touch. I could feel the pressure of the library's dome at the same time as I could feel the swirling of convection in the monk' quarters. I was *vast*.

"*James?*" Simone asked. In one breath, my mind fell back into my body. The universe of my collective connections collapsing into the singularity of my brain. I jolted into my regular senses. My sight was saturated to distortion, as if my eyes were wired to my brain through guitar pedals, all pressing overdrive. Her voice bounced in my head, glowing in my consciousness as if it were light rather than sound.

"James?" she pestered again. Her voice rang, and vibrated, and scraped the corners of my being. I had to shut my eyes to comprehend the sensation. It *wahed* like a synthesiser with a heavy modulator, whose control was being cranked by a madman.

"Silence!" I yelled. My own voice had the same effect, wracking my brain. I was going to be sick, I could feel it. I could sense the shock in all of those around me. I was connected to them. Silence came as I commanded it.

I sighed in relief. My breath, rather than being separate to me and pushed by my lungs, was a part of my body. It originated from me. I and it were one in the same, just as it was one and the same with the ambient atmosphere around us. The line between my fingers and the air was obscured – blurred. They melded into one at the event horizon of my body. My body was not separate from it. I was the air, but the air was not me. I could control it. I twitched my finger, and the room spun into a wind.

This level of connection was *other*. I was not literally the air, and I did not simply control it. This connection was somewhere between unity and control, yet simultaneously *beyond* both catagories, beyond my human comprehension. I became aware that I was floating in the air – levitating in it. One with it, yet its master. Floating in an unescapable state of existence.

The collections of the library tugged on my soul. They called to me. I had a connection to them, as well as everything else in this space. One called to me more intensely than the others. I pointed in its general direction.

"Simone," I said, breaking the silence, the sound reverberating around my skull, "pick a book from over there."

My eyes were still closed. I didn't have to open them to see Simone, or know where her footfalls landed. She disturbed the air, as she was not one with it in the way that I now was. Her hand glided over the section of library I had pointed to, and she picked a book. She picked the one which called to me.

"Good," I praised. "Please, bring it here."

She gently stepped over, trying not to make noise. She put the book down in front of me.

"It's in Vochduh, James," she said, opening it. "I don't know that you'll be able to…"

I opened my eyes. There were words on the page, but the words didn't matter. This book held *ideas*. I analysed the first page, and I could sense the man who penned it. I could see him, working papyrus paper with an ink fountain pen. I knew his thoughts, I knew his research. I had a connection to him, and the words he wrote. As I read them, they shifted, and swam. They came alive in colour and meaning, and they made sense to me. I could know this whole book just by touching it.

"This book talks about the waters of life that control us," I recited aloud. "The author is concerned about the visions he's had of the sea and the beach. He calls the space *The Void*. He says that the waters are those of destiny. They represent the flow of the universe. He thinks the sea is inescapable."

"How did you…"

"Don't ask, just pick another," I instructed Simone. She obliged, coming to carry away the two books I'd just read to make space, but they were heavier than she expected, and she stumbled. Simone tripped right into my injured shoulder – her elbow shoving directly into the tear.

My vision flushed white hot. My ears boomed like a broken amplifier. I could feel every cell in my arm, every broken link, every healing molecule. I could feel the blood blushing around the wound. The calm before the storm. I could feel the rip in my body moaning. I could *hear* it.

Then it screamed.

It whirred in my ears. Deafening, blinding. It wailed like a cosmic guitar under every distortion imaginable, all cranked to the max, with a demon stomping the strings. It roared and cried in the rhythm of the universe. I could feel it, hear it, see it, live it – the beat of life itself. It was syncopated, rocking, rebellious. When I opened my eyes, I was flying through a tunnel of red and white stripes. For every red the guitar wailed, for every white the pedals cranked and it faded. It matched my throbbing, which now I hardly felt. I heard it. I saw it.

I was elevated. I flew through space separate from the physical world. No longer could I feel the temple in my fingers. There was no air to be one with, to control. Simone's cries to me were distant, choked in the base of the tunnel of light.

Bright white ahead approached fast. I braced, unprepared for what I might experience next. I hoped to land back in the real world, without this heightened connection. This new experience was beyond alien, it was inhuman – an incomprehensible, indescribable experience of the world which I would never be able to replicate without the king's flower. I came to the end of the tunnel, and I wished myself into it.

Light faded. Wet, cold, I was flailing near the shore of a drab ocean. Tiny waves lapped away from the nearby shore. My hand crashed into a bank of sand. All around, there was turmoil, but here, there was calm. I clambered further up the beach, and rose to stand on it. The water was thick and green, too opaque to see to the bottom, even where I stood at a few inches deep. To my left, distant along the strand of the beach, was a pyramid temple.

This was the place of the outwards-flowing waves, the realm of my quatra-visions. Only now I was out of the water, a cheap ending to my usual struggle with the sea, to simply wake up on the beach. Seeing the temple, I ran across towards it. The water slowly rose to meet my ankles, tide rising to touch me.

Then it tripped me, my foot yanked by a grapple of the tide, it fell from under me and I was pulled into the shallow water. Quickly, the ocean grasped at my body, forming a rip to drag me off the sand.

Panicking, I plunged my feet to the fast disappearing floor, and anchored them there. The current fought with me, but I was a worthy opponent, and step-by-step I hauled myself from its insane grip, coming finally again to dry land. I stumbled further up the beach now, resting at the foot of the dunes, away from the water.

The air was warm, but no wind blew here. The temple was reachable now – finally, and I could see the monk residing in it. He was a distant shadow, poking his head around a square column of the pyramid's pinnacle room. I ran towards the structure.

From the land, as I ran, I could see the vastness of the ocean and its beach. It ran along the coast further than I could see, with waves extending out into the distant waters from the sandy shore. The pyramid came closer, and as it did, the extent of its size was revealed.

Its greenish, stone steps rose into the sky's oblivion. The sky, much like the landscape, was a dull, endless expanse of overcast grey. The angle of the pyramid's incline was such that I couldn't see the room at its peak.

If I could scale a cliff I could scale some stairs, I decided. I connected to the air around my palms, and pushed down, to leap high onto the pyramid.

Except I didn't. There was no air here, or *anywhere* around me. What was I breathing? The rise of my chest told me that I was, in fact, taking breaths, but of what? I tried to use my senses, but there were no connections to be had in these surroundings. There was no carbon to the dirt or stone, or air to the atmosphere. This place was alien - unconnectable. I had jarringly been thrown from what must have been the highest state of connection achievable, into a state of nothing. I sighed a breath of this places' not-air, and took my first step.

And after my first step, I decided to run. I had not dreamt a vision which lasted so long as this one. I wanted to reach this pinnacle and see its purpose before I was pulled from this nightmare. As I ran, I did not become tired or fatigued. My chest did not rise or fall faster. Even without the shell of Maiki, my shoulder did not hurt.

The temple kept expanding before me, as if the stairway were a cruel, laughing treadmill. The extravagant top room awaited me, coming no closer, impossibly out of reach. I continued running, sprinting towards the vision's end, knowing I wouldn't make it.

Then I did, jogging atop the temple's landing, peering into its greenish, stone room. I looked back down the staircase, to see that it was, in fact, miniscule. The time which it took to reach this step seemed to collapse in my memory, as if insignificant - both as infinite as it felt, and shorter than a light-metre at the same time. I narrowed my eyes.

From this vantage, I could see that what had appeared to be an infinite expanse of beach, was actually part of a long cove. Either side of the long, sand strand was bordered by an outcropping of sea-sharpened rocks. The raging waters themselves had no boulders in their wake, no interferences to their surging waves. There were, however, figures bobbing in the sea. Others were trapped out there, like I was.

"Hello," a voice, wise and old, called from behind me. I turned into the temple. It was ancient, and undecorate, but sturdy. The man before me appeared to be its opposite – young in appearance, with the decorative jade and blue robes of a Vochduh monk, and sleek of frame. His skin was dark, and his eyes were closed. He looked peaceful.

"Hi," I said, stepping up to the man. "Finally, I'm here. Tell me what this vision means. Quickly, before it ends."

The man eyed me curiously, and stepped closer, striding the temple's stones. "This is no vision," he said, "and I am not some apparition of yours. This is the realm of quatra – The Void, and I am its guardian."

56

"What?" I stammered. "No, this isn't some other *place*. I've seen this vision before." I scanned the temple and the beach. "I've seen this place just by meditating."

"I know," the Guardian said. "I've seen your little head bobbing up and down just out there." He pointed to a patch of the sea beyond the shore. "Most Suneva will never see this place, but you have always been floating close to the surface."

"But I'm not actually *here*, am I?" I asked. "I mean, I'm in the Vochduh temple. I didn't just teleport away…right?"

The Guardian hummed, and stepped his high-held nose past me, to the rooms edge, where he watched over the cove.

"This place is the origin of all threads, and all connections," the Guardian said. "What you're seeing is not real in the way that you would call things real – in fact, you're not *seeing* anything at all, as there is no light here. What you experience is your soul trying to comprehend a realm made entirely of quatra – in the same way that your experience of life is just your brain computing arbitrary signals to generate a perception of reality. This is a different kind of reality, which your soul is building."

"Why am I here?" I asked. "How did I get here?"

"Many Suneva who sit close to the surface of their sea will experience visions," he said. "The sky here lights with the future, and connections to others. It is painted by the Gods who hold each sea. You have seen beyond the veil – it's not uncommon. What *is* uncommon is leaving the sea. You have pulled yourself out of the flow of life. You have become destinyless."

"Wait…that was it?" I asked, stepping next to the man. He was tall, unnaturally so. "All I had to do was get high and hurt myself?"

"I suppose," he replied, "although I do not think you'd have made it out of the sea if Omercronius had not willed it. They control the tides of this cove."

"So, there are other coves controlled by the other black holes?" I asked.

"Yes," they said, starting to walk. They embarked the steps. "Come," the Guardian instructed. "Your father left a message for you."

"He did?!" I asked, skipping alongside him, down the steps. Walking next to the Guardian, the stairs did not play tricks. The ground was coming towards me at the speed I expected it to.

"Yes, he came to the land briefly after death," the Guardian said. "He went back into the sea to find *peace*."

"I see," I said, remembering his last moments – his soul consumed by dying light.

I peered out to the sea as we descended on the stairs. I found the bobbing bodies more disturbing now – this wasn't merely a vision, this was reality. If I touched the water, I'd become stuck in it, but surely the only way to help those under the control of destiny was to drag them out. Did it even work like that? As I stared, I witnessed a whirlpool start to form. Waves encircled its event centre, growing quickly outwards, revealing a lying man in the vacuous spiral.

"What's that?" I asked the Guardian, pointing. He regarded the display dismissively, barely stopping to look.

"That happens sometimes," he said. "I do not know what it means."

From the temple's base, the Guardian led me away from the shore, over a large dune. At its crest was dull-green vegetation, and standing at its top amidst the plants, I had a vantage to inspect the landscape. It was wild, yet dull, constructed of stunted vegetation painted in dull greens, clinging to the crests of dunes. Not far beyond the sea, the grass and shrubs gave way to lifeless sands, and a desert which extended on past my vision. There was a single sandy trail in the valley of the hills, leading deep into the scrub, towards the desert.

"If this place is so different, then why does everything look so earth-like?" I asked. "I mean, why bushes and grass? This place could look like anything."

The Guardian grunted. "It appears however your soul wants it to appear. It doesn't look any set way at all."

I hummed, and knelt to touch a plant. In my hand, it felt to be in the shape that I saw it. How could it exist any differently to others?

The Guardian led me down the dune. He did not walk towards the path that traversed the hills, instead, we battled through the thickening brush, directly away from the Omercronian sea, towards north. The Guardian would hold branches aside for me – a hint that he had to be having the same experience as I was.

He led me to a stone tablet which jutted from the dune, eroded at its edges by wind-blown sand. I swept away the dust in its precisely carved message, revealing the text written in *liktan*. I lifted it off the ground to read it.

Simone, you are not the first Suneva to come here. Investigate the other temples. There is something strange about the seas.

"Simone..." I frowned.

"It's a strange spelling of Simon," the Guardian said. "I pictured a man carving a tablet to be careful."

"It's my sister's name," I said. "I have her thread, after all."

"Yes," the Guardian said, scanning me contemplatively. "Your soul is strange. I haven't heard of this happening before."

"Thanks," I said, returning the stone table to the ground. "Did he say anything else to you?" I asked the Guardian, but he had already risen and started walking back towards the temple.

"Yes, we talked sometimes," he said. "Nothing of significance. He asked me how to return to reality, but I do not know that answer. Then he asked me how to make a message…"

"So, how did he make it?" I asked, looking back to the tablet. Now, it appeared much further than the distance I had walked from it. The dunes around had grown larger.

"It is quatra. If you are a witch able to repair armour, you can make objects here."

"Oh, well…I didn't want to plant a message anyway," I chuckled half-heartedly, jogging along to walk beside the Guardian.

There was a scream. A scream of death. It tugged at my soul.

It cut through everything, coming from every direction at once. From the sky, in which hung a dull, shining moon, to the soft sand which wasn't sand at all. It reverberated in my soul, ringing me like a harmonious bell, shaking me still. I felt my soul tear, and from my body rose a powerful pink aura.

The sky flashed bright white, and I craned my neck up to the forming storm. The flash was not lightning, however – it came with a distinct feeling, of raw, intense power. It was white quatra.

Oh no.

As the sky flashed, I caught a glimpse from within its clouds of a spire, jutting from a meadow. On it, a flower burning, wilting, *dead.*

"Oh shit!" I yelled aloud, "Guardian, Guardian!" I looked for him, but he had walked off, already at the base of the temple. I yelled all the way down the dune, sprinting. Muffled crashes and wails blasted from every direction. White light tore through the sky like the storm of gods. I reached the tall, ancient young man, and spun him by the shoulder.

"How do I get out of here?" I asked frantically. "Something is really *wrong.* I think my friends are under attack!"

"I do not have that answer, just like I did not have it for your father," the Guardian said, removing my hand and turning to ascend the staircase. "To leave, you must return to the sea."

Return to the sea? I looked out to the beach, its waves lapping. Bodies were out there, stuck in the passage of time, pawns to the powers of the world. But I was free, finally. If I returned, how would I get back to freedom? The flower was dead, it could not help me.

"There's got to be another way," I said. The Guardian did not turn to answer me.

The sky roared once more, burning my vision in blinding white. The lightning flash had come from the eastern area of the sky, fading slowly from it as its thunder crack rolled overhead. In the waning light, I caught a glimpse of my sister's face – stoic, strong, eyes blazing with energy. I saw a fire behind her eyes, or, rather, behind her head. A book was burning.

"Oh *Cheese*, they're burning the library!" I yelled. I could see it in the sky, painted across the clouds obscurely. The vision was halfway between a projected idea and an image of the scene. The sky roared with a mighty crack, strong enough to shake my footing, and a tablet was smashed across the library floor, by hands which I didn't recognise.

"No, no, no!" I cried out. The secrets of the ancient *Kiin*, the secrets of their connection and understanding of air, of their ethics, their history, of the people of whom I was apparently now the king. *The secrets of Kiin flight.*

There's a way out of here. I thought desperately. *Falling out of these visions is like going to sleep – like blacking out.*

But I had always blacked out in the water. There was something about the water which could do this – drown you into sleep. I couldn't go back into the sea, but surely I could convince myself to fall asleep otherwise.

I lay down at the foot of the temple, and rested my head on the sand. My eyes were wide open, the sounds of chaos rippling through the flashing sky. Waves lapped away from the soft shore near my feet, the water wading close by.

It could get me. I panicked, realising that I wasn't sure how tides here worked. I scrambled to my feet, throwing aside any time for hesitation, and ran from the water. I sprinted through the trail cutting the nearest dunes, forcing myself into the thick vegetation.

I ran to the stone plaque created by my dad, which sat now in the cradle of a bush. I landed my ass next to it, and collapsed into the coarse sand, forcing myself to lie there. I rolled over, closing my eyes tightly, wishing the blaring rumble and flashes of the storm away.

Sleep. I ordered myself. *Fall to sleep.*

Chapter 7
The White Witch Marches

Celeste sat in her office, in the chair which was once her father's, deep in the Parisian catacombs. She swivelled on her throne, behind the desk on the stage of the white marble room. The main light was off, the room bathing in the intense glow of her pink flames, which burned the length and height of the room through the rear glass wall.

Her father's green flames had once taken that glass fireplace, and it was by Adam's order that Celeste had replaced them. The green wall of fire used to tell a story, one of hardship, of sorrows, of respect, of glory, of community. They glowed intensely with their colourful story. The tendrils of Celeste's pink flame danced, but they did not glow nearly as brightly.

From her childhood memories, she knew that her father's wall of flames could ward off the shadows better than hers did now. They demanded something more than hers, they embodied a greater authority which drew respect. By contrast, Celeste's flames danced a mark of arrogance as they burned hot against the white room. In their higher energy they were weaker to the soul. They had more, but did less, like spoiled children born into luxury. Celeste swivelled away from her shame, towards the desk.

Why did her father have to be struck down? The footsteps he left in this Suneva world were monumental. He was the *Green Dragon* after all. What would Celeste be? The *Pink Dragon*? That sounded like a fluffy teddy-bear, not the boss of a Suneva community. She couldn't even rule an office space right, let alone a mob of followers. Hesslik's plans to subdue the Argol influence were working, and it was all due to the late Boekidin's ex-agent, Fisira.

That filthy *Fisira*. Celeste wished that the girl hadn't lost her thread so that Naxaer Argol's wasn't extinguished in vain – so that *Celeste* could be the one to take her down. The daemonic witch apparently had no control of her actions – she had been wholly possessed. That somehow made the whole ordeal worse to Celeste, it made her father's death an order from a higher power. The Argols were betrayed by an act of destiny, one from the black hole Amasos.

By Veritas I will make this all work. Celeste stewed over her social debts, watching the door to the office. She was excited about the next guest who would be coming. He had even rung in advance to make an appointment – although he was always welcome. She hoped that her sour mood would not ruin the meeting.

Just as she had the thought, the door swung open. Celeste perked up in her seat – the flames behind her growing in ferocity as her eyes dilated. A smile came to her face, her mood automatically cheery.

As soon as her body was flushed with excitement, it was replaced by disappointment. The man to walk through the portal was none other than Michael Richard, the man who often opposed her decisions. Celeste deflated into the chair, her flames spittling with the same intensity behind.

"Tona Argol," he greeted overly-formally, nodding politely as he stepped towards the stage. Celeste sighed, and rolled her chair towards him, lazing over the desk.

"Yes, Michael?" she asked.

"My scouts spotted the White Witch leaving the castle in a white van, heading north. She had in the van a Liktas agent, two Sunesca, and other unidentified equipment."

Michael had Celeste's attention. She sat tall, engaged.

"Two Sunesca?" she asked. "I didn't think Hesslik hired Sunesca as agents."

"He usually doesn't," Michael said, "this might be the White Witch's doing."

"Oui," Celeste agreed, "but what is she trying to accomplish with two Sunesca?"

"A Sunesca is a common defence against another Sunesca," Michael suggested.

"I know that," Celeste narrowed her eyes. Michael didn't speak to undermine her, but she couldn't help but receive it that way. "I just wouldn't expect her or Hesslik to have any business with any Sunesca, let alone *multiple*."

Michael hummed, nodding in approval. "It's strange, but the men want to know if your orders have changed now."

Celeste furrowed her brow. She clicked on the computer, sending the screensaver away and revealing the blue desktop. The calendar revealed the date to her – three days out from her intended strike, just the day she suspected it was.

"No, plans don't change unless she comes back after the strike date," Celeste said. "We only have an advantage in the castle, where we know her quarters and the layout. To chase her north, into whatever battle she has planned, is way too dangerous. We stick to our strike plan."

Michael smiled and nodded through her evaluation.

"Pleased, are you?" she asked.

"Yes," he smirked, "it's a good evaluation. Your father gave the same one."

"My father? ..." she asked. *He consulted your father before he consulted you.*

If the pink wall of fire didn't look imposing before, it certainly did now, as its licks of flame burned to the fireplace roof. Celeste didn't speak, although neither did Michael. His smug smile told more than words could, anyway.

"Yes, well, I'm sure that my father has the same opinion," Celeste replied, surprisingly calmly, "and I'm sure that my father would have told you that I'm more than capable of making the correct decision."

"He did," Michael said.

"But you don't believe it, do you?" Celeste said.

"No," he said. Celeste sighed, and there was a brief silence.

"Do you even enjoy living in his shadow?" Michael asked. The question was honest, and asked without devious intent. "Do you think you're ready to lead these people?"

The answer in Celeste's head was a resounding *'no'*. She didn't believe that she was fit. She was living in the valley of the Green Dragon's footstep.

"He could appoint a new leader to take the stress off your shoulders," Michael suggested. "Somebody who could follow his vision. You'd even be free to help Maiki, and rescue the White Witch."

He could. Celeste considered the idea, but was immediately repulsed. Imagining this community of Suneva under anybody else's control? It might have been selfish of her, but she *wanted* this prestige. She was hungry to fulfil her name. *This* was her destiny. *This* was her ambition. She wasn't meant for the role now, but she could grow. People weren't static.

"He *could*," Celeste said, "but I think you're forgetting one thing."

"And what is that?" Michael asked.

"It doesn't matter if my father appoints a new leader."

"Why do you say that?"

"Because *I* am Tona Argol," Celeste smiled, leaning back in the chair. "He has given that power to me, and his word no longer goes."

***

Simone and Anastasiya watched my body hang in the library, my limbs lolling limply. I stayed in the air, stuck, as if lame on a string. My eyes were shut, but rolled under their lids. My mouth ran, mumbling.

"He's never done this before…" Simone said. She came up to me and tugged my arm, but she couldn't pull me back to the ground. My body resisted it.

"His thread is massive," Anastasiya noted. "I've never witnessed anything like it. There's so much power."

Simone hummed. She figured that I had to wake up and come down at some point – I wasn't dead yet, it seemed. She went to collect our sleeping bags, to lie under me for when I fell.

When she returned, Anastasiya had taken a seat on the far side of the library. She had produced from her bag a small sack, and was sorting through its contents. Simone decided to pick a book from the shelf and attempt to read it.

Using her own instincts – free from the pull of destiny – she pulled a tome from the cylindrical bookcase. It had no title on the spine, but the cover was written in Liktan. Simone summoned Salak Kallid to help her read it.

The text failed to capture her interest. It talked ad nauseum about the conversion of quatra into will, and the discussion of free will compared to the free will of air currents. The author, who was a pompous philosopher, drew comparisons between the force of the ocean and magma, and the will of the black holes controlling the free will of air and Suneva respectively.

Simone yawned, and instead focussed intently on Anastasiya. She appeared to be pulling colourful rocks from her sack, and rolling them in her hands.

"Bored?" Salak Kallid asked. "Perhaps a different book?"

"No, no. I don't think I'll learn much from these books," Simone said, and looked to my limp, hanging body. "These will help James, not me. I want to learn something useful to me."

"I could teach you," the Salak demon said. His voice was young, and surprisingly smooth.

"You'd do that?" she asked. "Is that against the rules? I'm already an apprentice of Salak Kuul."

"There are no rules," the demon replied. His body was invisible, his presence signalled only by his incorporeal voice. "The Salak Order strive to educate all Sunesca in the arts of their powers. It is an honour to learn from many sources. Variety sows the seeds of wisdom."

Simone nodded, still watching the Suneva of teleportation. This was a very honourable, selfless viewpoint for demons to hold. It's not something even the least judgemental would come to expect from such a class of creature.

A rock left Anastasiya's hand with a glowing shimmer. Simone's eyes narrowed.

"What are you doing to those rocks?" she asked from across the room, cutting off Kallid and his conversation. Anastasiya looked up with a smile.

"I'm infusing it," she said. "Opal acts as quatra storage. I need to have stores of quatra to travel far distances. What's in my thread is never enough."

"And you're expecting to make a big leap soon?" Simone asked, noting the sheer number of rainbow-striped rocks which must have been in the now glowing bag. Anastasiya looked to the sack, and her face paled.

"Possibly," she said. "I've been feeling an urgency – an impending fear. I need all of these, if something goes wrong, to get you and James to safety."

Simone nodded. She could not feel this impending fear – she wasn't a part of the emotional manipulation that was being a pawn to a higher power. This was to her advantage here in the library, but a hurdle elsewhere. To Simone, Suneva seemed to be connected to a web of consciousness. Like spiders, they could sense disturbances through it, and they knew what was coming.

Simone pulled out the similar rock Anastasiya had given her a day ago at the base of the temple. It was white-clear, and brilliant in the light of day. Simone twiddled it between her fingers. It seemed entirely innocent, in fact, she wanted to keep holding it. It was pretty. It was special. It was hypnotising.

It was manipulating her thoughts.

Destiny.

Simone walked across the library, over to Anastasiya.

"Thank you for the healing rock," she said to the girl. "I feel fine now, though. You can keep it. Have another battery."

"Oh, okay," Anastasiya said, palming the clear crystal. "If you're sure. You might need it again."

"That's okay, really," Simone said. "You keep it."

"Alright," the Russian girl smiled. Simone turned, and walked back towards the demon.

I remained in the air, peacefully. Simone decided to leave the library until I had come to, and learn from the demons of the temple.

***

A wet thump rang through the lobby, between the many pillars.

Simone perked up, abandoning her lesson. She ran to its source, barging through the library's arch to enter on the first level catwalk. Salak Kallid followed, coming to witness the scene. My body had fallen upon the sleeping bag, and Anastasiya now sat huddled over it, grasping at my neck.

"He's alive," she said. "His thread has gone back to its usual strength."

"What does that mean?" Simone asked, climbing down the ladder.

"The tea has worn off, I suppose," the Russian girl said. She stayed kneeling by my body.

Simone came by my side to inspect. Anastasiya's evaluation was right – I was breathing, and my heart was beating fine. It seemed as if I was sleeping.

Simone became worried.

"Will he wake up?" she asked.

"I'm sure he will," Anastasiya said.

"But his thread returned to normal, and he's still not awake," Simone protested.

"It didn't return to normal," Anastasiya said. "It's slightly different."

Simone looked at my sleeping face. She sighed.

"He'd better not have killed himself," she said, "and I'm damn serious."

"He will wake," Anastasiya repeated.

"Fine, I believe you," Simone said. She stood, and pulled herself towards the ladder. "I'm going back to training. would you call me if he wakes up?"

"Of course," nodded Anastasiya. She pulled out her bag of rocks again, now sitting by my side to sort through them. Simone, satisfied yet still worried out of her wits, clambered up the ladder. She turned the corner, through the portal and into the temple's main cavern.

Simone had been training with Salak Kallid in one of the temple's off-shoot rooms on the opposite side of the lobby. She stepped towards the cavern's centre, rounding a giant support column and coming into the ray of the great, bored skylight.

Figures stood in the mouth of the temple, like shadows against the midday sky. The leading silhouette had a T-shaped slit on their helmet face, glowing with white, divine light.

"You picked a good hiding place," the White Witch said into the temple before her. "But I could find James anywhere."

Episode 2

Cliff-Hangers – a Story about Grand Reunions

Chapter 8
The Wandering Soul

My eyes opened. I stumbled into the world.

"You're in for it Natalie!" I yelled, throwing myself off the cold, metal ground and into a fighting position. My arm screamed at me as I did so, and yelled worse when I flicked it to summon my staff. The pain was intense, but not nearly as bad as it was before my journey to the Void.

Natalie wasn't here. In fact, *nobody* was here. I was alone in a cramped room of blue and grey metal, one strongly resembling the cell in Hesslik's research centre in Melbourne. There was no carbon in the room. There was, however, air, and my ability to control it was unimpeded. I'd kept my thread, amazingly.

Why would Hesslik leave me with my thread? I pondered, dropping the stance and wandering towards the door. The fact that I had my thread was a cause for celebration – but celebration was quickly overtaken by other, more pressing thoughts.

I just became destinyless. I realised. *I just came back from the Void…hell, I went to the Void, and I came back. And it took me so long to get back, that I missed being abducted and imprisoned.*

This was not good. If I couldn't easily make my way in and out of the Void, then it would be a dangerous place to visit – and I needed to return to save Natalie. Then again, I wasn't sure that I'd ever make it back. I needed the flower's tea to get there in the first place. Somehow, I'd used the power of its thread to gain additional connections, in the most mind-blowing way possible. Without those connections, I didn't think I had the power to return. I'd cured my own attachment to the will of the black holes, but how would I help Natalie?

Screw Natalie, part of my brain seemed to say, *she's long gone now. She could have just stood in the way of us stopping Hesslik, but she went and destroyed history and kidnapped you. She's way beyond saving.*

I stood, pacing. That thought was jarring, but I didn't necessarily agree with it.

She's being manipulated, I reasoned. *Who knows what justifications she's being fed. Stay strong.*

I needed to save her from destiny – to show her that I'd found a way to solve her problems. There was no use sitting in this room, waiting for whatever was to come. I'd only just pulled myself out of the Void, but I had to return.

I sat down on the bed. *Just like inducing a vision*, I said to myself, forcing a smile. Then a terrible thought hit. *What if being in the Void was just a vision, and I still have my destiny?*

I gulped. I couldn't have known the truth, nor whether my mind was guided by my own compulsions to think it, and not by the god at the end of my thread.

I'll never know until I try to go back, I realised. I lay back on the uncomfortable bed and closed my eyes. If it was through healing meditation that I saw the vision of the Void, then it was through healing meditation that I would return, I reasoned. I tried to relax.

I commanded quatra to flow into my arm. I could feel already that it was much better than before I'd drank the tea - it couldn't demand nearly as much quatra as it once had. Still, the warmth spread through my back, and then throughout my entire body. The warmth soothed me, calming my senses, and I could feel my thoughts slipping. I didn't know if I was going to the Void, but I was going *somewhere*. I teetered on the edge of consciousness - a vast cliff along the ridge of the brain. I let myself fall over its edge.

Maiki! A voice yelled inside my head. My eyes crashed open, my heart racing in surprise. I was still in Hesslik's cell. I sighed, then grunted. *Damn it.* I groaned. *I was so close, too.* I closed eyes again, letting myself drift away.

Maiki! The voice cried once more. My ear felt full – a droplet of water was lodged in its canal. When did that happen? I banged my ear and looked around the room. There was nobody else in here but me.

Maiki, it's me! The voice said. I stood, backing myself against a wall. The voice was recognisable. It had a very distinct accent and pomposity to it. But, it couldn't be...

"Boekidin?" I asked aloud.

Yes. It took you long enough, he said in my head.

"It took me long enough because you're dead," I remarked. "Hesslik announced it just over a week ago. You died without leaving a ghost."

Then again, I wasn't sure why I believed Hesslik's word. One of my missions right now was to prove to everybody that he's lying to them all.

Yes, that's the right train of thought, Boekidin said, appraising the thoughts which I forgot he could hear. *Hesslik killed me, just like he killed Kuvalik. I assume that Iva told you about that, right?*

Yes. Hesslik cut him down with plasma, I agreed in thought. *He did that to you, too?*

Whilst I was in his mind, he cut me down. But Maiki... he said, his voice running breathless, *you were right about everything. He is planning to destroy the threads.*

"Ha!" I laughed aloud, then coughed to cover the sound. *So, you believe me?*

I felt the memory, Boekidin said. *I can't see memories, I feel them. There was so much shame and guilt in the thought, but then so much triumph. He switched so suddenly between the two.*

But the proof was there, right? I asked. I was once again aware that I'd never *proven* what I believed Hesslik's plans to be. I'd seen visions, and inferred his plans from the Empire's current endeavours, but never recovered actual evidence – not that a lack of proof stopped Natalie from joining him.

Yes, there was proof, Boekidin said. *He absolutely had the conviction to remove the threads, and he has been planning it ever since.*

Ever since? I asked. I moved myself to lie down on the bed – as was more comfortable. The Void could wait. *You stayed in there to investigate more?*

I was trapped, Boekidin said. *He killed me and kept me in his mind. I've gone Natasvoul. Clearly, my thread is still out there, but it's not with my soul.*

Ouch. I groaned. Natasvoul, I remembered from one of Natalie's many lessons, referred to a wondering soul – a *Kidin* whose mind and soul had travelled too far from their body to return.

But I had time to look at the full history of Hesslik's memories, Boekidin said. *He is making demonstrable steps towards the Suneva soul-genocide. But I found something even more disturbing.*

What? I asked.

I found the distinct moment when his demeanour changed, and it wasn't due to his own convictions.

Wait...what do you mean by that? I asked.

Something switched in him, Maiki, Boekidin said. He hushed his voice, as if we'd be overheard. *It was the day he killed Kuvalik. The memories from then on are clouded – touched by quatra. They're much more difficult to read, but I had lots of time. Killing Kuvalik wasn't his own idea. It was planted in him.*

By whom?

By destiny, Boekidin answered. *Before that day, Hesslik had honest care for the state of the Empire and the people. He didn't realise that his vision wouldn't work out, it was a thought planted into him. Amasos manipulated him.*

To what extent? I asked. *How much of the thoughts are his?*

A significant amount, Boekidin said, *but that doesn't matter, his mind has been changed. Thoughts which were planted as his have now become his. The control isn't overt, it's* subtle, and manipulative. But every time that he has a thought against his current actions, it's beaten out of his subconscious. Hesslik is under control.

This is exactly what Natalie thought was happening, I said, *her Yamitse too. It's why Natalie changed sides.*

No, it's not, Boekidin said. *Her change came just before her transformation into White Witch, but it was nowhere near as subtle as Hesslik's. Natalie has been fed serious propaganda by Amasos for a long time – she was very touched by destiny. However, her control of white quatra has left her open to greater pushes. I think she's being forced to believe that her actions are protecting her, when they're really opening her up to greater manipulation.*

This is awful, I said. I couldn't even comprehend what was happening inside Natalie's head. Would these effects manifest somehow in the Void? Surely, they would appear some strange way in the realm of quatra.

It's not just Amasos, though, Boekidin said. *I've been going through many heads. Everybody has switched recently. The black holes are exercising greater control.*

That's not good, I uttered.

It's not all bad, Boekidin said. *Although, from what I can tell, Amasos is trying to rile sympathy for Hesslik. They want the Suneva gone.*

But why would they want to give up their only control? I asked.

I don't know, Boekidin said, *but Veritas is gearing Suneva up for a fight. They're being selective about who they're choosing to affect, and I believe I'm one of them, and surely Iva Argol must be too.*

And what about Nerios and Omercronius? I asked.

Nerios, I don't know. There's been change, but I couldn't discern the aggregate, Boekidin said. *And Omercronius is just as elusive. They're both doing something, but I can't be sure what.*

I hummed aloud. What was Omercronius trying to achieve with me? I thought of my search, and how Omercronius had led me to the right scriptures, to the Omercronian flower on the spire, and finally to the Void, where I shed destiny. It felt to me that Omercronius was giving me the tools to undermine Hesslik - and therefore Amasos.

Omercronius did what? Boekidin gasped into my head. Of course, he could hear my calculations clear as day.

I'm destinyless, I said. *Could you see it in my mind's eye?*

*I...*Boekidin hummed, and jogged somewhere in my mind. Without employing his usual subtlety, I could feel his rushed movements within my head, his feet stomping around. *Yes, there's the vision,* He said. *You went to the Void? I can't believe it.*

71

You know about the Void? I asked.

The Void is the next step up the pipeline, Boekidin explained. *The first removed step towards the black hole is the realm of the mind and soul, called* The Slip. *Beyond that is the realm of quatra. People have seen it, but I'd never believe that anybody has* been *there...*

Well, here I am, I shrugged, *I've been there.*

You're a Voidwalker, he said in my head. *Remarkable.*

And my first act will be pulling Natalie from the Amasosian sea, I said. *With her free from the pull of destiny, we can do anything.*

I agree with that, Boekidin said, *but I think there's more to it that just pulling Natalie out of destiny.*

Of course, I said. *There's temples in the Void. My dad told me they were important.*

At that moment, a key was inserted into my cell door's external lock. I heard it press against and activate the tumblers. *Stay with me,* I whispered in my head, and I received a grunt of agreement as the door swung slowly open inwards.

In my grip, I could feel the air beyond the cell which floated in the hallway. I held onto it with my soul connection, and pulled it into the room. My arm roared in pain, but not nearly as bad, nor for as long, as it usually would have.

Air blasted through the door, sending it careening open into the wall, and sprawling the entering Suneva across the floor. I leaped off the ground, blasting air towards the rear wall to launch through the doorway. I rode on a wave of air pressure – the new mass of air in the room pushing to escape with me.

I soared towards the exit, a breath away from the freedom of the hallway. I prepared for landing, setting my hands ahead of my body to blast against the coming wall.

A bolt of quatra smacked into my chin. It zipped straight to my thread, cutting off my connections. I plummeted towards the wall of the hallway, unsure of whether to extend my hands and tear my shoulder again, or meeting the metal with my face first. A wave of water swept up from under me, rushing over my torso and turning me upright. I fell into it, splashing softly against the wall and falling to my knees. An armoured hand grabbed my right, uninjured arm, and dragged me back into the cell. I lay across the floor, wet and hopeless.

The White Witch stood before me, the T-shaped slit of her ram-horned helmet glowing pure white. Her armour was darker than when I had last seen her – the silver coloured plating having turned charcoal at its edges. She let her armour melt away, revealing a stoic, tall Natalie.

Then I noticed her eyes. No longer the blue-green of our first meeting – no longer a gateway to the soul. They were clouded over, silver, looking past me and around me, not at me. I was reminded that the Natalie I knew was gone.

"Hey, just the person I was going to look for!" I squeezed out, remembering my objectives. "And now you're here, and I need to talk to you."

"About what?" she asked, pulling me to my feet. "What didn't I make clear?"

"Everything!" I threw my arms in the air dramatically. I wasn't sure if she could sense the gesture, what with being blind and all, but it was instinctive to do so. "You just ran off leaving a note, you didn't let anybody talk some sense into you. Now Chad's gone and run to the woods and Celeste is commanding an army."

"And you're living in mountain temples," she remarked.

"I'm finding *answers*," I said, stepping back from her. Even without using my thread, I could sense Natalie's power. It radiated from her soul, casting itself like divine light, strangling. "You didn't even bother to see what else was out there! You just accepted everything you'd been stewing over as an unchangeable quantity of the universe – destiny, the harmful nature of quatra, your own insecurities. I'm here to tell you that they *can* change."

She laughed a pretentious chuckle, throwing my retort aside. Stepping close again, she bore herself over me.

"I came here and received answers," she said. "Hesslik is helping me to keep destiny at bay. I don't know where he learned it, but he knows how to retain oneself against the will of the black hole when drawing immense power.

"But that's just the meantime," she said, striding away, towards a corner of the room. Her hands stayed fixed at her side, sensing the fields around her. "When the threads go, we'll be normal again. We won't have to worry about being safe from these insane cosmic forces. We won't have to worry about the safety of others around us, or whether our thoughts are our own. We will have free will and guaranteed safety. I'm sorry that you don't see it that way, but it's necessary."

. This Natalie before me was a shadow of the one I had seen only less than weeks prior. It was the same body, but the mind was absolutely altered. It made my blood boil. I could feel the steam rising from my ears. I could feel the steam rising from Boekidin's ears, deep inside my head. He was ready to tear my mind apart and yell at Natalie through my mouth.

"You're brainwashed," I uttered, and she turned to hear me say it again. "You think Hesslik is helping you, but he's making it worse. I can see it in your eyes, you're being manipulated by destiny. You're doing exactly what Amasos

73

wants! Why would you even trust Hesslik to be a teacher, anyway? Where did you learn that he gave such good advice?"

Natalie scoffed at my remark, avoiding the question. "I am stronger mentally now than I've ever been," she said. "How would you know that I've fallen to destiny?"

"I…!" I went to tell her about Boekidin – that he's been in her head, and that his state-of-living is more evidence to the mountain of reasons to distrust Hesslik's word – but he coughed loudly in my head.

Don't tell her about me, He whispered. *She'll tell Hesslik, then he'll* actually *kill me.*

"…I can just tell," I choked on my sentence. "You've changed. It happened slowly, but now it's in full force. You've embraced your transition, and it's dangerous. I know that you love being a Suneva, and I know that you wouldn't survive without your powers." My mind started running, I was onto a good point here. I had piqued Natalie's interest also, and she stalked closer.

"I mean, you basically pass out when your thread is blocked. Its senses are second nature to you. Imagine the blandness of life without them. And you'd be legitimately blind! No seeing through your fingertips."

"My sacrifice is a selfless one, to save others from becoming what I have," she rebutted.

"Your *sacrifice?*" I scoffed. "Natalie, if you really hated what quatra was doing to your life, you'd have just removed your own thread and agreed to help Hesslik on the side. The problem is that none of this is *your* decision. You just think it is."

That caused her to pause. Her mouth shuddered, like a robot trying to recover from an error. It seemed as if no logical argument would come to her to counter that point, and I smirked in my brilliance.

"I can't convince the Suneva to follow Hesslik without my powers," she said, finally thinking of a somewhat-valid justification for her bizarre actions.

"Why did you go to him anyway?" I asked. "If not to remove your thread, what else did he ever offer you which was anything like an answer to your problems?"

"I knew that he could teach me proper control of my thread," she stated.

"How?" I asked.

"Because he talked to me, just like he talked to you in Greece," she admitted. Guilt had strewn itself across her hard face, despite her willing it not to.

"That's how he knew my name when we went to his castle. It's how he knew what to taunt me with."

I was flabbergasted. Despite my shock, I felt a cold, seething grin come to my thin mouth.

"Well, my faith in you is entirely shattered," I said. "You made Celeste cry and even threatened to leave her upon her big admission, even when we really should have seen *that* coming. You gave me an equally hard time for something I didn't even set up."

"I know," she said. "I know that is was wrong to do that."

"I'm starting to think that you've lost your moral compass, Natalie Athanas," I said to her. "I don't know what to believe about you."

"Don't give me shit for it, James," Natalie demanded, parting with all pretence of guilt. "He came to me, too. It wasn't my fault that he knew my problems and how to solve them."

"Whatever," I said, dismissing her. I felt beyond betrayed that she'd assimilated our separate situations, but it wasn't worth arguing it with her, not now. "Look, you can follow that idiot Hesslik, destroy a part of your personal identity, and ruin it for thousands more because of your fears of fatalism, or you can join me."

"Why?" she asked, crossing her arms.

"Because I've solved destiny," I said, and her predatory, dead eyes narrowed on me. "Chad was right about the Void and the river of the universe. I went to the Void and pulled myself out of the flow. I effectively took myself out of destiny. I can do it for you, too."

Natalie was shocked. Her mouth hung open, her dead eyes looking in the wrong direction.

"You did what?" She asked, her mouth slowly turning to hang agape. Her glassy eyes, even though lacking connection to her soul, radiated not joy, but unending horror. She had to clutch herself to remain upright, and I was left beyond confused.

"You wanted this, didn't you?" I asked. "I just solved destiny. You can come home!"

"You went to the Void!" she scorned, a finger pointed to my face – or, at least, where she thought my face might have been. Natalie advanced aggressively, and I backed myself into the wall. "Pulling yourself out of place in realms you don't understand has dire consequences, James." Her finger was at my throat now. "Not only have you corrupted the flow of this world, but your soul will *rot* and *die* now that you have disturbed it. You've just doomed yourself – this is why we can't be trusted with the power we've been given."

"Natalie, I…"

"The place of Gods is not for us," she said finally, and raised a hand. It seemed imminent that she would hit me in her anger, but she turned herself away instead.

That last comment, however, I could tell was not her own. Her tone of voice changed to say it, her eyes glowing in a way that they did not before.

"Those aren't your words, or your thoughts," I declared, and her face flared red in offence. "My soul is fine. You're being fed bullshit to stop you from freeing yourself. I have your answers."

"You have nothing for me, James," she defended, walking towards the door of the cell. "To think that I let you keep your thread. You know that I saved you in the temple, right? You think I'm brainwashed, but I've been myself this entire time. I thought I'd kill your consciousness if I removed your thread mid-vision, but it seems that I could have stopped the greatest threat to the Suneva and society at large."

"And what's that?" I yelled. "Freedom?"

"A *Voidwalker*," she said, slamming her key into the lock of the door. "A Voidwalker could ruin everything. You're having your thread removed, James. You won't ruin this world for your selfish desires."

"Get out!" I commanded of her, as she had already opened the door. It seemed pointless to yell it – she was already leaving – but it made me feel as if I'd won the encounter. Natalie sneered as she left, and the door to the cell slammed shut. Still backed up against the wall, I leaned onto it and slumped to the floor. A tear came to my eye.

You did good, kid, Boekidin said. *It looks like she's worse than I thought.*

But how much of that is actually her? I asked. *That's what scared me most.*

I thought back to her face of red rage and offence, her adamance of her own sanity and free will. Was she being controlled, manipulated, or was she simply delusional?

I could not know the answer. I could only hope that in freeing her, the Natalie I knew would return. I could only hope.

Chapter 9
Night Dancer

Chad stared down from his penthouse lookout, deep in the heart of Chicago city. His tower overlooked the target – a squat building of reflective, black glass, not a single light glowing – which rose to the height of the carpark stacked next to it.

Despite the building's modest height, it was modern of design. Its full glass exterior mirrored the dazzling lights of the city, reflecting them back like the spangle of stars across the sky. There was no concrete to be seen on the exterior, with barely a visble crack between its panes, making it appear to be a giant, shining monolith.

Chad stepped back from the window, considering the mission. Tonight, he was *Lion's Foot*, Hesslik's remarkable agent – only, without Hesslik. This was a job taken as a mercenary, under his new master.

Master, that was what he called her. Nobody could know her identity, and if he even dared to think her name, any passing *Kidin* could eavesdrop his thoughts and find it. She would only be known as *Master*.

Her mission for *Lion's Foot* was simple – he was to infiltrate the building and make his way to the head office. Master did not request a stealthy mission, so Chad's plan was entirely to his discretion. Once there, in the first draw of the ornate head-officer's desk, there would be a device. The intended use of the device would be obvious, and *Lion's Foot* was to use it.

Chad was also to apprehend a certain Suneva. The mission statement told him of their blazing pink helmet, blue quatra, dark-crimson stomach plating, and *liktas* abilities. They were to be captured with their thread in tact, and brought to the head office to be left as a witness of Chad's actions until the morning. If anything, this kidnapping was intended to leave a spectacle, and Chad had no idea why.

But it wasn't his role to question.

He descended the elevator. It might have seemed brash to him, even a week ago, to be taking on another mission like this. However, *Master* had shown him that his worldview was narrow. Chad knew, as well, that he could be doing better things with his remaining time than sitting in a forest, only helping himself. Despite this, he wasn't sure that infiltrating Hesslik's Chicago tower was one of the things he *should* be doing with his time.

Nevertheless, *Master* had been adamant that this mission was of personal importance to Chad. She told him that upon completion of the mission, he may feel more invigorated to involve himself in the future of the Suneva.

Chad didn't currenty feel any compulsion to add to the fight, despite the proven fallibility of his *being the rock* philosophy. Chad liked his friends, but he did not want to fight any more wars. He did not want to feel that the fates of many rested on his shoulders, and that he would be accountable for their demise.

And yet here he was, prepared for a fight.

Chad had surmised that Nerios must want him to act, and that by not helping, he was fighting the current of destiny. Even though obeying *Master* wasn't an equitable inaction to sitting still, Nerios was *definitely* not pushing him down tonight's current trajectory. Chad could almost feel the arms of the divine as they struggled to restrain him. So many things had already tripped him up on the way here, and the knowledge of screwing with Gods made him smile.

He crossed the street – still occupied, but barely bustling at twelve-midnight – and walked past the compound's main entrance. Chad had seen the building schematics earlier, which had been made available by the Anderson leaks of Hesslik's computer archives, back when we escaped from his castle. The head office was dead in the centre of the building, on the central floor, three floors off the ground.

Of course, it would be a terrible idea to enter by the main door. Chad could sense through his fingertips that a quatra user was in the entrance hall, and through his feet, connected to the earth, he could tell their position. They were guarding the doorway.

Chad walked past the building, to the large carpark on its right side. It was a five-storey complex, made of ugly concrete, zig-zagging its way into the short sky. Chad stepped through the entrance, and started to climb a set of stairs.

Cause minimal damage until you find the device. He ran over his plan in his head. *Get to it quickly, use it, and run out. Save yourself.*

But the mission was made complicated by the witness – and not just any witness, but a specific Suneva. Chad planned to climb the carpark to the appropriate floor, then bust his way in, but he had no idea of knowing where this pink-helmeted figure would be. Chad hoped, for sake of ease, that they happened to be near the head office space. Perhaps they would be the one guarding it.

He wasn't sure, though, that he should be so optimistic.

After some flights of stairs, Chad found his way to the fourth floor of the carpark. He crossed the empty lot to the left wall, where the structure met Hesslik's monolith.

There was a gap between the two, and it was larger than he had anticipated. He also noted that the monolith's side was still glass, here where the view was less than interesting. Chad grumbled – he could maybe make the leap, but then he'd have to break through the glass, signalling his intrusion.

Chad then remembered he was a Suneva of iron, too. He rolled his eyes at the realisation and palmed at the iron chain hung on his hip. He sensed for iron within the structure of the carpark, and dug at it, drawing it towards him. He used this new metal to form a plank, which he ramed into the face of the concrete, creating a makeshift bridge towards the monoloth's glass exterior. Chad then created a sharp dagger with what iron he had left.

Examing the glass wall, Chad noted that each pane was held by a pin in each corner, and sealed with rubber around its edges. Reaching with his soul connections, he could sense some iron in the alloy of these pins. Chad grinned, and eased himself across his precarious plank, one careful foot at a time. Once at its end, he tugged at the iron in the pins, yanking them from the wall.

The window did not budge, the insulation holding it tight. Chad added the new metal onto the knife he had constructed, and used it to carefully slice at the rubber on the pane's edges. Slowly, he worked the glass free from the top edge down.

The last piece to slice was the bottom of the pane. Chad took care here – if the pane dropped away from him and fell to the ground, it would shatter with such a sound that he might as well have shouldered his way through it to begin with. He cut the rubber from each direction, making sure to slice evenly towards the centre. He rested the pane on his bulking shoulder as he kneeled to its bottom. His feet tenaciously balanced on the thin plank of iron, four storeys in the air. He started to sweat.

The pane lurched, and slid on his shoulder. Chad's eye bulged, and his hand whipped to catch the glass, dropping the knife. His shaking legs slid on the iron plank. The glass freed itself from the sill, and slid frighteningly fast. Chad pawed at it with his hands, but it was too heavy to stop with just the friction of his fingers. He grasped desperately as its edge fell past his shoulder, but his sweaty mitts were useless against gravity. It was freefalling.

Chad reached for the chain which furled over the holster on his hip. He yanked it from its place, and whipped it down. The links of the iron chain, under his command, zipped through the air faster than sound – must faster than the falling glass. They snapped around the pane and locked on, and the glass heaved against them.

The chain lost its slack immediately, tugging Chad down with a violent pull. His boots slipped, toppling him off the edge of the plank. Chad threw up his free arm, remaining cool as he fell, and commanded the iron plank towards his hand.

The plank, stuck into the concrete, could not move. The action instead brought *Chad* closer to the plank, and allowed him to grab onto it before his hand fell past. The sheet of metal flexed under his weight as he caught it, concrete cracking by its base. It sprung back to even, but Chad's connections flared in his panic, and his hand melted through the iron plank where he held it. Quickly, he scrambled onto the metal before his hand could destroy it. It buzzed under his body, vibrating about in its recoil. Once the plank settled, Chad wretched himself onto the carpark's ledge, and hauled up the glass which dangled from his chain. He settled the pane on the carpark floor, and coiled his stressed chain back onto his hip. Sighing his relief, Chad embarked on the plank once more, and leaped from it onto the fourth floor of Hesslik's building.

It was pitch dark.

Chad grinned – the darkness was helpful. He knew that Hesslik's men preferred to be seen in their armour, and so the glow of their quatra eyes would give them away as they patrolled. All Chad had to do was stay out of his armour, and dance away from the patches of coloured light. He stepped away from the widnow, into the blackness.

His eyes adjusted, and Chad found himself in a private office, behind a closed door. The office all was made of old-fashioned, varnished wood. The door was similar, with a window of obscured glass. Taking up the centre of the office was large, oak desk, like that of a lawyer. The whole aesthetic rung to Chad of a film noir setting. He creeped slowly towards the door – blackness through its glass – and crouched to the ground, listening.

Chad, as *Lion's Foot*, did not often employ stealth, as he was strong enough and skilled enough that a skirmish didn't matter. This time, however, he was far from the earth, and with only his iron chain. It reminded him of the mission on which he lost his leg, caught high in a tower by an Argol ambush. The memory caused him to shudder in his crouch, and his mind wandered to me. What a joy it would be to control *air*, he surmised, so that he could never be caught out of his element in any fight. Unless, of course, the fight happened underwater, but that

80

wasn't often. It was no wonder to Chad why Natalie had chosen to become a prolific witch, given the rarity of water near any given ambush.

He shook his head, throwing away the procrastinatory thoughts, and pressed his ear to the door and his palm to the floor. Although, the ground at Chad's fingertips was not earth, he was still able to detect the vibrations on its surface. He found this curious, but he'd always been able to do it, and had been advised never to question it. Chad listened closely through his skin.

There was a conversation being carried in the far distance, perhaps the other side of the floor. Feet scuffled loudly, although none of them were outside his door, or in the near vicinity. Chad waited for a whole minute, assessing the movements he could feel. Those holding the conversation did not seem to move, and there were no other vibrations to arouse suspiscion. Satisfied, Chad opened the bulky wooden door, and slipped in to the hallway beyond.

A dull green light, from some stand-by device, was all that gave luminescence to this passageway. This hall carried the same wood-varnish aesthetic as his entry point, and Chad could sense the iron in the nails and bolts which held the facades together, giving him a sense of the hall's shape into the darkness. It continued a short way to his left and to his right before turning a corner inwards at both ends. There were doors to offices lining both walls in either direction – it appeared that this floor would be made up of private offices. This was not what the floor plan for *any* of the floors had suggested – or, perhaps, he'd simply interpreted them wrong.

Chad decided to move left, away from the vibrations he'd sensed earlier. With light fading to this end of the hall, he took a firm grip on his chain, and held the loop of it in his fist. He stuck close to the wall, and rounded the corner with a careful step.

Around the corner, there was only true darkness. Chad wondered, briefly, how he would locate the correct office if he could not see it. Still, he knew it was on the exact centre of this floor – wherever that was in this maze of halls. He continued moving forward, taking note that he was stalking directly away from the carpark, towards the building's centre.

This hall must have run the building's length, for Chad had to sneak a long way down its run before he could take another right turn. He hoped that he did not miss the main office in any of the doors which he had passed – all without nameplates or indication of purpose.

Chad made the first available right turn. Suddenly, as he landed his first footfall into the next corridor, the atmosphere around him became heavy – like diving into a pool full of honey. He gripped tightly at the chain, still furled in his hand.

Dense quatra field, he murmured to himself. The darkness before him was advanced, and as his eyes adjusted to it, he noticed that the blackness danced, like air off a hot road. In the curves of its waving form came glistening specks, like confetti falling in moonlight.

That's how they're guarding this place, he thought, planting his foot solidly down. *That's why there's no guards. They send everybody into visions.*

Chad was grounded. In the riverbed of the world's flow, his feet were solidly planted. The stream could not alter him, although it would wear down his soul if he persisted to so resist it. He could not be trapped by the field's visions like others – although his mind *had* drifted in the catacombs, when caught in a much stronger field than this.

Chad took a breath, and felt the floor by his feet. Bravely, he stepped into the confetti-lit field, and he closed his eyes.

The river washed over him.

Waves churned overhead. The tendrils of the current brushed by his naked skin, streaming over his back and turning turbulent over his face. He was going with the flow, it seemed.

Chad reached for the ground and palmed it. The floor was not earth. It was silty, and grainy, but not earth. His feet were sunken into the bed here.

You're in an office, in Chicago, he told himself. *The floor is carpet.* He caressed the ground with his hands, but his convictions did nothing to abate the feeling of sand there. *Grainy carpet*, Chad told himself.

He was holding his breath as the water flowed over him. To overcome this vision, he had to act stupidly defiant, unwaveringly sure of his surroundings.

Breathe, he told himself. Against all instinct, feeling the water rushing at his lips, he did.

Air came in, and Chad opened his eyes. He was in the middle of the intense field, walking despite not telling his body to do so. He stopped, and planted his foot. Chad squatted into the shadow of the field, and palmed at the floor. He felt its vibrations through its fingertips.

He could feel his power heightened in the field – this, a place of strengthened connections, allowing him tighter grasp on his thread with Nerios. Through the floor, Chad could feel the same conversation he'd sensed earlier. He could also sense feet pattering on the floor only a few yards away, behind the closest wall. Chad squinted, digging further into the carpet.

82

His ability to sense vibrations through any floor was bizarre, he reflected as he scrounged for a stronger connection. However, he'd learned from the Native Americans of the reservation that quatra powers weren't so easy to define as the European Suneva seemed to believe. A connection to anything should just be taken for what it is, as questioning how it fits in to your understanding of your connections could cause you to lose it.

Yes, there was definitely a figure behind this wall, he concluded. Chad sleuthed closer to the wall, and touching his palm to the varnished wood, searched for a door. The metal name-plate of the room called to him, it's iron glistening. He ran his hand over to it, and felt for its indentations.

'Head-office, Tano Teralik Karr' It read. Chad grinned, and grabbed at the chain holstered to his leg.

He held the first link of it in his hand, but used his command over its iron to hold the whole thing furled in the air. Carefully, he moved his other hand to the doorhandle, and turned it slowly to check that it wasn't locked. The handle caught on to the latch, and slowly, with a final small twist, the latch started to retract. Chad held on tight.

One, two, three…

Chad twisted his hand and leaped through the gap, closing the door behind him. This room was much like the others, but alive with electric lights. Still, there was no time to scrutinise the surroundings, Chad had found the Suneva he had sensed, and they had not yet comprehended what was happening.

Chad whipped his chain towards them. The target turned their head to the commotion, stopping their pace by their elegant, wooden study desk. Their helmet was fuchsia pink, with navy eyes. Chad grinned, he'd found his man.

They reacted quickly. Their *shath*, a machete like blade, swished through the air with incredible power and precision. Their body swung through with their strike in perfect form. Their now red-hot blade crashed into the iron and shredded through the chain, cutting cleanly.

Chad surged the chain forward – he had enough of it to lose some links and still wrap his victim. Tano Teralik was cunning. With his free hand, he grappled with the remaining chain as it smashed into him. With a grin forming, a surge of electrical power roared through the iron linkages.

Chad's eyes widened. Usually, he could twist his feet into the earth and take the charge, however he could only do that as Ferrad, and could only do it safely when he was on earth he controlled. Chad would die now.

He tried to let go, but the deadly charge ran into his hands, seizing his grip on the chain. His legs straightened, causing him to jump. His mouth frothed in an instant, and his eyes rolled. His connections strained wildly.

His body fell like a logged tree, albeit, a violently spasming, incredibly pained tree. The *Liktas* did not give up, clawing at their connections to send Chad into a burning, blind agony. Chad's grip on the chain, electrically powered, was so strong that he threatened to break his own fingers. As he hit the carpet, his hands made a final seize. His connection to the iron flared, and the chain melted like putty in his hands, breaking away.

The charge roared out of the flaccid end of the chain, now held by the *Liktas* Suneva in pink and crimson armour. Chad seethed. That shock couldn't have been any worse than touching a power outlet, and he'd be fine, surely, but he was in shock. Still, Chad couldn't scream. Making a scene here would be deadly.

Teralik aimed his long knife at Chad, and Chad knew what this meant. Forcing himself with every fibre of his mental resolve, he pushed himself off the ground and onto his knees. A bolt of quatra wrung into the carpet where his body had lain, scorching it black and melting a ring of it.

Chad's brain swum loosely in the cavity of his skull. He blinked, attempting orientation. A bolt flew towards him, and he outstretched a hand to redirect it. Teralik, now angry, charged the knife, ready to strike with another arc of fury. Chad's chain was still stuck to the man's forearm.

Chad gathered the might of his connections into it. Controlling its movements, he whipped the chain's links around behind Karr. Their arm yanked unnaturally around their body, swinging their torso with it. An arc of concentrated plasma burst from Karr's weapon tip, tracing across the table as they spun, burning the beautiful wood surface to charcoal. Chad continued to pull the chain around itself, encircling his victim. They dropped their weapon, grabbing at the linkages to pull themselves free. Chad constricted the snake of metal, tightening it around Karr's struggling limbs. Iron melted into iron at Chad's command, and the chain turned to a solid, binding ring. Teralik fell to the floor.

"Good," Chad said, stepping calmly over the body to get to the other side of the room. Teralik kicked and scratched at the carpet with his spiked feet.

"Who the hell are you!" he yelled, clearly trying to attract attention.

"Ex-agent *Lion's Foot*," Chad said calmly, as he had been instructed. "Past personal-agent to the *Fara Hesslik*." He walked to the business side of the desk, turning on his heel to open the top draw.

"And who are you, *Tano Teralik Karr?*" he asked with a grin. This draw was empty, so he tried the next.

"You don't get to know that," Karr spat, still squirming. Chad did not react to the remark – he did not need to know who this man was, really. It didn't concern him. He opened the second draw, and his eyes glared upon an item he would hope to never need to use.

This draw held a fully operational thread-remover.

"Oh no…" Chad cringed. *Master* had warned that the use of the item would be obvious. Clearly it was not for himself – because *Master* aimed to convince Chad to join the cause of stopping Hesslik This fate was for the tied up Suneva, Tano Teralik Karr. Chad's hand drifted towards it, but he could not take it.

"Did you ever make an enemy of anybody, Tano Teralik Karr?" Chad asked. He was determined not to use the device, but his body and soul did not refuse to touch it. He grabbed it in his palm. Despite knowing of its amazing, devastating power to the soul, Chad did not feel that it was an immediate threat. This was his usual inclination, although he couldn't be certain why it had occured.

"What does any of this matter to you?" the man asked, rocking on the floor. "Nothing will matter to you soon. This place is heavily guarded. There's a bounty on your head, and you're not leaving my sight."

"Okay, it's a little wishful of you to command me," Chad said, trying to gather himself. The device he held should have buzzed with evil, but his inclination towards holding it did not indicate this.

"You're a traitor! You cannot ask anything of me!" Tano Karr said loudly. Chad groaned, he stepped over to the squirming Suneva with the gait of a cowboy.

"Hesslik tried to have me killed, multiple times. I had to run away. Of course, they don't tell you that," Chad said to the man. Through his helmet, Karr was sceptical. Chad had no time for convincing an idiot of anything.

"Look, I don't want to do this," Chad said, "but I want to know *why* you deserve this fate. Who the hell did you piss off?"

The man said nothing. He arched his back, then rocked his head forward in a convulsion. Lightning rained from the part of the helmet where his mouth would be. The hit was well aimed, striking Chad in the hand, and powerful enough to leave a burn. Chad dropped the thread device and instinctively grabbed his burnt skin.

"Not one for Hesslik's codes, are you?" Chad asked, trying to maintain his cool.

"I'm the head of Hesslik's public relations here in North America," the man finally gave a worthwhile answer. "Of course I'm a follower of the codes. How dare you accuse me of heresy."

Heresy. Chad almost laughed. Heresy was defiance of the church and the powers of God. Every Suneva was, by nature, a heretic. It was one reason why Stacy's father had hated Suneva so harshly.

"You follow the codes, yet you electrocute a man without armour?" Chad asked. "Did you even know I was a Suneva."

"You represented a reasonable threat, to which I have the *right* to use my God-given powers against."

"Right...okay," Chad grumbled. "You don't even think that's a *little* bullshit, though? I could have just been a guy with a chain. I'd done nothing supernatural by the time you'd grabbed it. What threat level is a man with a chain to you?"

The Suneva paused. "You're clearly a Suneva," he responded. "Any witch could tell that."

Chad rolled his eyes. The man *was* an idiot. A self-absorbed idiot who had bent Hesslik's rules for their own use. This was the kind of person who was a dangerous Suneva for the order of things.

"I say that you're just the kind of person who abuses powers to suit them," Chad said plainly to the man.

"What I've done is hardly wrong," the man defended. "I'm just protecting Hesslik's Empire. These are orders I was given."

"Yes, but you're shooting first and asking questions later," Chad said. "Patience is a virtue of all Suneva. So is understanding others. These powers come with responsibility."

"Why should I bother to understand you?" Karr asked, and he did so seriously. "Even before I knew you were a traitor, you were just a Suneva breaking in to a secure facility. You're to be treated as such."

"Well, I've heard enough," Chad said. He felt surely that removing this man's thread would only improve the pool of existing Suneva. However, he was still reluctant to use the thread removal device at all. He didn't feel he had the right to decide this man's fate, but he was ordered to. This would lead to a great truth, he was told. Although, he wasn't certain of that either - but he couldn't know until he'd done it.

Chad bent down to pick up the device. It felt neither comfortable nor wrong in his grip. The experience of holding it was indifferent. He walked around the man.

"Who ordered you to do this?" Karr asked in a blind rage, thrashing about. "What use do you have with removing my thread?"

"What use do you have for this device at all?" Chad asked Karr. "Why was it in the drawer of your personal office desk?" That shut him up.

Chad pressed the prongs against Karr's neck plating. There was a screaming from deep inside telling him not to do it. It wasn't a voice of destiny, or compulsion, like he had heard before. This was his own convictions plaguing him. He found them much harder to ignore.

Chad could not feel destiny pulling or pushing his movements, but he did sense the tension it left in the air. It was thick, and entangled, pure tension.

His finger lingered on the trigger. It was too late to turn back.

He pulled it.

An arc of electricity exploded between the red prongs of the device. Karr screamed, his body convulsing. His Suneva armour sublimated and smoked off his body, rising in a black cloud which Chad made an effort to avoid breathing.

A saggy, old white man was revealed underneath, still bound in iron links. His eyes rolled up into his skull, and he slumped backwards unconscious. Chad grunted.

Then the tides changed over his head, his breath sucked from his chest. His body, deep in the river of the world, was being flung in the current as it changed directions rapidly. Chad *needed* to help the cause against Hesslik. It was so apparent to him now that he couldn't believe he was standing still. The device in his hand screamed to him as pure evil. It was boxed danger with prongs on top. How had he stood to hold it? He needed to act, now!

Hold on, Chad halted his train of motivation, brakes grinding dead. *These clearly aren't my thoughts*, he paused, looking at the unconscious man in the room. He walked over to them, knelt down, and slapped the man in the face. Karr did not wake. Chad slapped him again.

"Bah!" Karr spluttered, and remembering his predicament, started to wrestle with the constraints. "You'll pay for this, you'll…!" Chad covered the man's mouth.

"Who was your black hole?" Chad asked him, and released his grip.

"Why would I tell you that?" the man spat. Chad smacked him again.

"*Who was your black hole?*" Chad ordered. "This has importance for *all* Suneva."

The man appeared less sceptical, although his answer was garbled, and reluctant. "Nerios," he replied.

"Of course," Chad stood, now realising what had happened. His sudden compulsion to act must have meant that Nerios wasn't pushing him to act before – in fact, Nerios was probably telling him to be neutral, and to feel good about doing nothing. It took the removal of a Nerian thread for the lazy God to realise he had to be involved in the fight. Nerios didn't believe in the power of thread removal – although now they had to.

"I'm an idiot," Chad said aloud.

"I'll say!" Karr agreed. Chad ignored it.

"I've been doing their bidding this whole time, convinced that it was my own idea…" he scratched his chin, considering the next move. If he chose to obey the call to action, he'd be doing just as they wanted. However, he was now aware that the black hole was sneaky, and could manipulate him into believing that ignoring compulsions meant he was defying them, when he was actually suiting their grand purpose.

"What would you do," Chad asked Karr, "if you wanted to do something, but your actions contributed to an ominous grand scheme which you could never know the nature of?"

Karr was perplexed, he tried to search for the proper way to respond.

"You'd do nothing," Chad adapted the man's silence. "So, I won't do that."

"Hey, that's not what I said!" Karr rebutted.

"See you later," Chad said, picking up the thread removal device, "and thanks."

"Thanks?" Karr asked, bewildered. "You better hope I never catch you! By my word you're dead, kid."

Chad closed the door behind him, and ran through the field. He would find his way out of this building and report back to *Master* with what he'd found. She could tell him where to go, now.

Simone confirms Natalie's story, Boekidin said to me. I sat stewing in my cage, having waited for him to return before attempting to meditate into the Void. I hadn't yet told him what I was planning. I'd only just thought of it.

In what way? I asked.

She says that Natalie ordered that your thread be preserved, and that she appeared to have actual concern for your wellbeing.

Well, that's a start, I grunted, *but it doesn't take back destroying historical texts.*

I stood and walked over to the door, pressing my palm against the crack by its hinge. I drew on quatra, and powered my connection to the air, sensing for movement in the hallway.

What about Annikida? I asked.

Simone said that you were all spread out when Zamelle stormed the library. Anastasiya tried saving Simone, but couldn't get to her through the fighting. Simone told her to save you instead, but you were already being handled and she was being attacked, so she fled.

But she's safe? I asked.

As far as Simone knows, she got free of the battle, Boekidin said, *and I'll add, by what of Simone's memories I could see, it's an accurate account. Anastasiya did try to save her first.*

What else did you see in the memories? I asked. I hadn't instructed that Boekidin investigate what Simone wasn't telling him. He had taken liberties of his own there.

Your sister is a badass, to put it plainly, Boekidin said. *She showed no fear in the face of danger, and did everything she could to fight off the White Witch, a Liktas, and two Sunesca. She seems to have an instinct for stealing energy to hinder an enemy.*

Good, I said. *I'm glad that she's embraced who she is. I was worried she'd reject being a Sunesca.*

It's absolutely the opposite, Boekidin said. *She trained with the demons whilst you were meditating. They must have taught her something really useful, because she's in a full straight jacket up there, tied to a board.*

Oh cheese, I cussed. I'd gotten Simone into this, and now she was stuck in the castle tied up. What would Hesslik's plan for her be?

I wouldn't get down about it, Boekidin said. *She seems to be able to steal energy without moving. She's tripping everybody who comes into her cell. She's having fun.*

Well, that was reassuring. I took my hand from the door, having sensed nobody nearing the cell, and sat back on the firm bed. Natalie would come soon to escort me away - away to have my thread removed in front of a crowd. I had no sense of time, and Boekidin had been unable to find Natalie again to determine how urgent my escape was. However, if I could depend on Natalie's morals, my plan could work.

What's this plan? Boekidin asked me.

Go into the Void, remove Natalie from the Amasosian sea, then do the same to Hesslik, I said.

I thought you said that you couldn't step into the water without getting pulled back in, Boekidin criticised my idea. *How do you think you'll get them out?*

Well. I cracked my knuckles. A smirk came across my face. *That's where I need a witch who can repair armour,* I told him. *The Void is made of quatra in the same way that armour is – according to the Guardian. All I need is a Suneva who can make me a surfboard and who will help me with the rescue.*

Okay, he quizzed, his voice perplexed, *that's even more complicated. How do you plan to get this witch into the Void?*

I avoided answering the question directly. *You're a witch of high acclaim, aren't you, Boekidin?*

Yes…

And you can repair armour?

Yes, I can, he agreed.

Then stay where you are, and listen to my instructions. This could take a while.

Okay… he agreed, albeit uncertainly, *but I hardly see…*

Shhh! I grinned. *I need silence for this.* I heard him huff, then sit down on something in my mind.

Boekidin said that the Void was *up the pipeline,* past the armour, the shath, and the mind, situated at the end of the thread. That gave me a basis for the sensation of travelling through the red and white tunnel of glowing pain, and gave me a sense of how to get back there. It also gave me an idea of how to get Boekidin there.

I relaxed my body, sitting against the wall on the bed. I drew quatra into my flesh, and I let it invigorate me. My arm stung as quatra set to heal it. I kept the energy coming.

I tried to remember the sensation of first finding my armour. Deep up *there*, in the thread, between myself and Omercronius. I reached for that spot with my soul. My eyes were closed, my mind travelled. Quatra flowed.

Up there. I climbed. I was travelling without moving, ascending past my armour, my consciousness flying further. I lost feeling of my muscles and body, my mind drifting, water in a pipe. My breath fuelled its movements. Breath, in and out, like the tide at the sea, the sounds of life. Formation to ruin, the cycle of existence. There was peace. I was at peace. *Breathe.*

I gasped, and I woke, lying awake in the ethereal sand by the plate inscribed by my late father. I scrambled to my feet quickly, and touched the surroundings. I pinched myself – this was no dream.

"Yes!" I shouted with joy. I ran through the sandy path of the dunes, jogging for the temple.

Its steps were not infinitely numerous this time, and I climbed them with ease, coming to the open room at the structure's peak. Curiously, the Guardian was not here, and I peered out over the horizon in wonder of where he could have been – although it wasn't important.

Okay, are you there Boekidin? I asked into my mind. Around me, the not-wind rustled the not-branches of not-bushes. I waited for his response, hearing the whistling of wind. I looked to my watch, to discover that it didn't work. I sighed, figuring that if I couldn't hear Boekidin, my plan would not work.

Yes, I'm here, he said finally, and I perked to his voice.

Great, I beamed. *Now, you've just got to leave my mind.*

Okay, he quizzed, *and go to whom else?*

Nobody else, I said. *Here. Exit here.*

Boekidin fell silent.

I'm not sure I can do that, he said.

Sure you can, I encouraged him. *According to you, the Void is one step beyond the mind. Surely you of all Suneva can get here.*

Yes, but one step is a huge difference.

And my mind or soul is currently in the Void. I reminded him. *Neither of us know how it works, so why don't you try it?*

I guess you're right, he feigned agreeance, *but I hope I end up where you think I will.*

In reality, I hadn't thought about where he would appear here, although it seemed that he didn't catch that thought of mine before attempting to leave my mind, or else I'm certain he would have turned back.

I felt him exit, like water finally dripping from my ear - the relief was ecstatic. Then the image of him, wavering, blue, like an old ghost on a cartoon, erupted from my soul-skull like a fountain, forming his eagle-raven body in front of me. Strangely, Boekidin wore his armour, whereas I did not.

His feet touched the temple's floor, his body expanded to its full size, and his image solidified, giving up its transparent blue sheen for his black, silver, and gold armour.

Boekidin's head shook as he became aware of his existence. He looked around, perplexed, examining his limbs and his surroundings.

"It worked!" he exclaimed.

"Yeah, mate, of course it did," I beamed, and went to high five him.

Our hands collided, and in that moment, his feet were torn from the floor.

I gripped on, and was tugged away violently by his body, which was being flung northwards. I managed, with my free hand, to grip onto a square column of the pyramid temple.

The force pulled on him. His armour was wet, water streaming off it and being sucked away towards northbound oblivion. The vortex was too strong for me to resist.

"Grab onto my body!" I ordered him. He did so immediately, sinking his claws painfully into my sides. Using both hands, I heaved at the column, pulling us away from the vortex. I lifted my leg up, and rammed it into the corner between the column and the floor. I hung there for dear life, refusing to be ripped away.

Air continued to rush past, screaming across my ears. Boekidin's talons gripped into me with their might, water grating at his armoured form in grappling streams. The rush heightened through its crescendo, our arms and limbs straining to fight, and then it died suddenly. The last gust of air tugged, and the last drops of water flew, the vortex shedding off and flying its keep back northward. We fell to the floor.

"It worked..." Boekidin said, exhausted by the effort.

"What was that?" I asked.

"That was the power of destiny," a new voice said. We looked towards the Omercronian sea, where, at the south temple entrance, the Guardian stood.

"That is how strongly the sea holds its Suneva," he continued. "Veritas did not want to lose you."

"I still can't believe that this worked," Boekidin said, almost ignoring the Guardian. "You do realise that we could be the only Suneva to do this, right?"

"We're not, though," I answered. "My dad left me...or, my sister...a message. Temples have been built."

"By the dead," The Guardian said, "although, you're not the first living to walk here." He quickly turned, not having even climbed the last step to the temple, and stepped down. I watched his head bob out of view.

"Weird guy," Boekidin noted.

"I don't know what to make of him."

"Do you think he just stood there, watching us struggle?" he asked.

"Didn't occur to me."

Finally, I stood, and helped Boekidin up after me. His wings rustled as he straightened his back. I stared westward, out over the dunes and desert.

"You were right about this place," Boekidin said. "It's made of the same quatra that armour is." He gripped at the column and tore off a chunk of its stone. With what appeared to be great effort and strain, he pressed the chuck into a flat disc, then pulled at tendrils of it, forming a nonsense shape.

"You said that you wanted me to make something, right?" he asked. I nodded, and led him over to the south lookout, over the Omercronian sea. I scouted the waves, then pointed.

"Look there," I said, and Boekidin tried to follow what I was pointing towards. Then he caught on, and flinched.

"Sweet Veritas!" he exclaimed. "Are those…?"

"Suneva," I said. Out in the sea, a body breached up to the surface over a wave, then crashed back under. Many floated that way, unconscious. "These are the flows of destiny," I said. "Or, it's a *representation* of what being trapped by Gods would look like."

"It's horrifying," Boekidin gasped. "This looks worse than when tourist groups try to surf. They all look dead out there."

"How would you save them?" I asked him.

Boekidin pondered, peering over the vast sea and its treacherous waters. He stroked his hook-beaked face.

"You said that we can't touch the water," he thought aloud.

"Not unless you want to be taken back in by destiny," I said. "Although, I don't know what would happen if you touched the water of another black hole."

He shifted his head towards me, his face suddenly null. A realisation had hit him.

"I'm destinyless, aren't I?" he asked.

"Yes, you are," I said, "but you're technically dead, right?"

"I'm not sure," he admitted, feeling at his arms and body. "I don't think I'm dead. I'm just *Natasvoul* without a body." And he looked back out to sea,

93

pondering. "I think we need to conduct an experiment first, before we make plans," he said, finally. "Follow me."

Boekidin led me down the temple steps to the water line of the Omercronian sea. He picked up a large, sturdy branch along the way, and used his power over its make-up to give it two large handles. He had me dig my legs into the sand just beyond the water's edge, right up to my knees, and hold on to one handle of the branch whilst he grasped the other.

As we both firmly held the long stick, he carefully lowered the edge of his toe into the divine water of the sea.

Nothing happened.

He lowered his whole foot in, and still there were no effects. He hummed curiously, and waded backwards down the steep bank until at his arm's full reach, where he was over knee-deep. Water rushed in and out around his legs, forming waves behind him which lingered out into the ocean.

"I wasn't expecting this," Boekidin said.

"What does it feel like?" I asked.

"It's just like regular water," he said, "which wasn't what I was expecting. I thought it would phase through me, or reject me, or maybe I'd walk on it."

"But, do you feel it pulling at your legs?" I asked him.

"Yes," he nodded, "it's a strong current, just like a rip. I wouldn't want to swim against it, but I can stand here just fine. It's nothing like getting pulled through a vortex in the sky."

He waded his way out, having to pull hard against me to escape the current. He sat down on the sand next to me.

"Let's see if it's any different for you," he suggested. "Of course, if you're uncomfortable doing it, don't."

I was uncomfortable. Stepping into the grasp of Omercronius could mean never stepping out again. I had to put my trust in Boekidin to hold me from my fate, but could I rely on him with that? I considered that Boekidin had put his trust in my word enough to risk his life finding answers in Hesslik's brain, and he was my *enemy* at that point.

"I trust you to pull me out," I said. "I'll give it a go."

Boekidin dug himself into the sand, and I, holding on to the branch with him supporting it, slowly waddled out towards the waterline. I tested the icy sea with my toe, then slowly continued once I realised it was okay. I waded out to my arm's length, out at knee depth. and stood there curiously.

"You're right," I said, "it's just like real water."

94

"Strange, isn't it?" he asked. "You'd think it would behave weirdly."

"Nothing here behaves weirdly, despite it all being a representation, and not a reality," I noted, and Boekidin hummed to the thought. "This could be more dangerous, though," I said. "If you feel the same as me in here, it means we could both become stuck in any of the black-hole seas."

"It does," he agreed, "and it wouldn't have mattered anyway – my initial idea was to create a fishing rod to fish people out, but standing here, looking over the vast ocean, that seems like a stupid idea."

I laughed, pulling myself out of the water and joining him on the shore. It took an impressive effort to wade out against the gripping current, and that set my heart to worry.

"My thought was to make a surf rescue board, and paddle out to save people," I suggested. "I've done it before – I used to surf-lifesave. But I'd be worried riding on these waters."

"That's right, you did mention a surf-rescue before you pulled me in here," Boekidin nodded. "You should be fine to ride the waves out, and from the board you can identify the floating people easier, it's smart."

"Although," he added, "maybe we could combine the fishing rod somehow, as a way to fish out the deep ones."

"So, you're an expert on surfing and fishing now, are you Boekidin?" I joked.

"I am," he said. "I surfed the whole North Island as a kid- and I fished it too."

"Okay then, you're the expert..." I shrugged a smile. "Well, I agree. Rescue board and rod. We'll get the both of us out there. Now we just have to find the Amasosian sea and build the boards on the way."

Boekidin turned from the Omercronian waters, stepping towards the temple. On his toes, he struggled to peer over the impressive dunes, but turned back to me fruitless.

"Which way?" he asked. "And how long do we have?"

"Veritas pulled you north," I said, recollecting the vortex tugging him out of the temple, "and this is Omercronius. So, it's either east or west."

"Exact opposites..." he commented.

"I have no idea how time works in here, but I think we need to act quickly. Still, I'm sure Natalie would have my thread removal put off until I wake up."

"Let's hope your faith in Natalie isn't misguided."

"No, I'm right on this," I said. "Either way, east or west?"

Boekidin held his hands out by his side, and put them into the peace-sign pose. He concentrated for a moment, letting them float in the field. "East," he said.

"How'd you reach that conclusion?" I asked.

"It's a guess," he admitted. "There are too many threads here to find any specific one, but I got a hint of something familiar in that direction." He pointed to the east, over the dunes and past the boulders that surrounded them. "I don't want to ruin this on a gut feeling, but that's all I've got."

"Then I trust it, too," I said. "Let's go."

We walked together, along the sand of the cove first, then up the rocks and dunes at the east end. We climbed onto what became a rocky plateau, which turned slowly to grassland. We trekked the grassland, continuing along east, until the ground turned to hard rock again. The stone here was different to that at Omercronius' cove, though. The ground was black and flaking, and cut into hexagonal prints which occasionally rose above the ground as sharp-edged columns. Dancing between the strange outcroppings, we fell into the scent of fresh sea air, and followed it to the sound of sloshing waves. At the end of a trail we were met with a sheer drop – a black cliff face plummeting to the dark sea. Peering over the edge, at least sixty-metres below, the sea churned and raged. Waves roared out to the ocean, but also crashed and wrestled with the volcanic shore. The water ran lethargic, as if thicker than a regular sea. It was dark, and dull grey, like everything else in this world.

Boekidin arrived at the ledge just behind me, holding the front of the board he'd been making. It was a very accurate recreation of a surf-lifesaving board from memory. I praised him on it.

"We've come the right way," he said. "I can feel Zamelle now, just."

"So, you can sense other Suneva in the Void?"

"You can't?" he asked.

"I've never been able to do it."

"Oh…" he quietened, "well, she's over this way." He pointed left, along the cliff face, and walked off. I followed.

The basalt shoreline continued around, forming bays and recluses, which jutted in and out across the line of the sea. The grasslands to the west grew more populated as we walked, bushes propping up, leading to a forest of short trees. The trees grew to tall paperbarks with bristly leaves. Mountains peaked in the distance behind them, just visible over the canopy.

96

The land's edge jutted back, forming a long cove capped by crumbled cliff faces, which had fallen into the sea and lay further out like ancient shipwrecks. In the cove, beyond the basalt heaps, stood proud rock apostles as tall as the cliff plateau, battered at their bases. There was no beach at the base of the fall, only a long drop into the oblivion of destiny.

And the sea churned violently. Its thick tendrils bashed at the apostles and the basalt cliff face. Water sprayed high, and rained down over the restless bay.

Scattered in the tumultuous sea were spots of vacant ocean – small cylinders of open air which water would swirl around instead of through. In one such space visible at the base of the cliff, the body of a Suneva lay on the sea floor.

"Something tells me…" Boekidin said, taking in the seascape, "that Amasos is enforcing tighter control over their Suneva."

"You don't say," I agreed.

Boekidin reached to the ground, clawing at it, removing material which appeared grey and lifeless in his fingers. He added it to the second board he had made – one for me, one for himself – sticking on the finishing touch.

"What's the plan?" he asked, looking down to the sea. "These will help, but not to get down."

"And not to get up," I added.

"We'll have to devise something else," he suggested. "Maybe a ladder."

"A ladder sounds good," I said, toeing to the cliff's edge, squatting to inspect the rock. Staring down to the water made me dizzy. I was so impossibly high, and the water so frighteningly violent. The sensation was mesmerising and horrifying. I palmed the rock, which despite its appearance, felt like it might give.

"The rock doesn't feel super stable," I said. "Anchoring a ladder here could…"

The rock crumbled under my feet.

My ass landed on the edge as my legs pulled me over, and I spun and clawed to stay atop it. Boekidin rushed to me, but not quickly enough. My hands slipped off the smooth stone, my haphazard efforts inadvertently pushing me off the cliff face. I flipped in the bay's wind, thrown head-first down at the churning ocean.

I screamed as I plummeted towards it.

Celeste had her troops mounted on a hillside, deep in the valley of Hesslik's castle, in the Olympus mountain range. From their vantage, shrouded by the cover of thick forest, they could see the ominous, ancient grey building rising from the foot of Mount Olympus. The lights were on in the main dome, although from the scout's reports, and what Celeste could see through her binoculars, most of the attention was centred around the building entrance.

Inside the keep, between the castle walls and the castle itself, sat an assembled stage. Lights, speakers, and a lectern were mounted on the concert-like setup, peering out over a muddy field to the gate. Suneva seemed to be making a pilgrimage into the castle grounds, all gathering to the stage. They walked a path not far from where Celeste and her Argol force hid, who were hushed quiet.

Celeste had taken a small team of good Suneva with her. They were twenty strong, but they would only need three or four for the main assault and abduction, anyway. Although, to neutralise and abduct the White Witch, these would have to be three or four *very* skilled Suneva, and Celeste had brought an entire entourage of such talent along.

Yvon, a *Kidin* boy from her childhood, was acting as the main scout. LeGrand had come along to support, as he would not be needed on the insurgence team. Michael Richard, despite his insolence to her cause, had been appointed as sub-leader of the mission. He would not infiltrate the castle, but led the scout teams and defended their forest base. Celeste was reluctant to appoint him this role, but the entire team she bought seemed to trust his judgement. Giving him this power would probably subdue his fractured ego, also.

A young man trekked through the undergrowth near the camp. All fell silent, and Juliette Leroux stalked out to investigate. She came back with young Yvon.

He discarded his black cloak on the baggage pile – a repurposed Sunesca garb used for disguise by the scouts. He jogged over to Celeste, stumbling over the sitting and lying members. His eyes were worried, his stance tense.

"What is it?" Celeste asked, sensing the shock in his aura.

"You won't like this," he stuttered in his thick Marseille accent. She shot her hand out to take his, and the boy's shaking calmed. His aura mellowed.

"What is it?" she asked again. "Did you find out the purpose of the stage?"

"Yes," Yvon said, "and that's what you won't like. Hesslik is making a public thread-execution. He's doing it to deter immoral and unethical Suneva."

"So, those who oppose him," she snorted. "That's disgusting."

Other important members had started to gravitate towards the conversation. Michael listened in with interest, as did Celeste's mother Juliette, and Alexis LeGrand.

"That's not the bad part," Yvon continued. "The thread they're removing, it belongs to Maiki. They're doing it within the hour."

Celeste's gasped. A small pink flame, heavy with rage and worry, nursed itself on her fingertips. Looking to Michael, it was clear that he felt indifferently towards this news.

"I don't suppose you want to change the plan?" Yvon asked.

"No, it's perfect," Michael declared. "We're striking within the same time frame. The crowd and guard – hell, even Hesslik himself – will be distracted by the execution. We can run in unseen without any effort at all."

Yes, that was of course the practical answer, Celeste realised. That was what her father would have done – save Argol men, do the mission, support Suneva kind.

"She's the one doing the execution," Yvon rebutted. "We have to change our approach – either another time, or another way."

Michael sighed, and stroked his stubbly chin.

"We can't let the execution happen," Celeste said finally, and all eyes fell on the young leader.

"And why not?" Michael asked. Of course, he had his own inclination as to Celeste's motivations, and she would not give him the satisfaction of being correct.

"Because it's a travesty to the community," Celeste emphasised. "How can we let Hesslik decide who keeps their threads and who doesn't? Doing this will set a precedent. It will confirm that he *has* this kind of power."

There were nods of assent, even from the uninvolved group members, who now all gathered to listen to their leader and second-in-command quarrel. Michael gave a sly smile.

"And what if the Suneva on the stand wasn't Maiki?" Michael asked. "Would you be so willing to charge in there and save their thread?"

Celeste huffed. The fire on her fingertips licked with reignited vigour.

"Yes," she said determinedly.

"Really?" Michael asked, and stood back, making sure that all could hear him. "You would lead a group of good Suneva into the middle of Hesslik's castle, where a huge number of officials and other Suneva would be gathered, where *Hesslik himself* and the *White Witch* would be within metres of the target, to save somebody you didn't know from execution."

"Yes," Celeste said again, although she now realised the major flaw in her plan, and knew exactly where Michael would take this line of thought.

"You would risk each of these good Suneva to capture, for the sake of one stranger's thread, just to prove a point?" he squinted, although his soul was grinning – she could see the triumph painted across his aura.

"As you should hope that I'd do the same for you," Celeste stated. The crowd was silent – nobody giving praise to either side.

"Oh, but I wouldn't hope," Michael said. "You see, I'd think it rather *selfish* to risk the capture of my people, and the removal of *all* of their threads, just to save mine."

There were groans of agreement for this statement, with other opinions staying characteristically silent. It seemed that others were slow to back Celeste up – they'd rather see how she fended for herself. She sighed.

"Then I should hope that other Suneva see past your selfless sacrifice to save you, if they didn't want to give Hesslik the *right* to impose the same fate on them later."

"I'll hand it to you," Michael said, "your argumentative skills have improved, but you still can't hide the fact that you want to put us all at risk for Maiki. You're acting selfishly – all of your plans so far have been in your own self-interest. I just want you to see that."

Then he'd won them. Yvon and LeGrand shuffled closer to Celeste, showing their support, but even Celeste's own mother seemed to shift to the other side. The circle widened.

Yvon turned to leave, pushing past the gathered Argols. The fires on Celeste's fingertips fizzled. She didn't want to admit to this group that her motivation to save me was, indeed, selfish – although she was able to argue some good intentions for it. They'd already seen past her. What would she do?

Yvon returned a moment later with a lit candle. It was the kind that Argols traded between each other for favours. These candles were made with a special wax that was imbued with the quatra of a Suneva. Every Argol knew the purpose of these candles – they gave luck and inspiration. He placed it in the centre of the circle.

The mood of the gathering mellowed almost immediately. Celeste felt her anger and shame dissipate, falling away from her soul. However, her resolve to save my thread remained, and, in fact, it strengthened. She felt more determined now than she had before to not let this atrocity happen. More candles would help – they always did. Celeste turned to collect her own.

She returned with the candle her father had gifted her upon handing her the Argol organisation. Celeste hadn't pictured burning any of it so early into her reign, but here she was. Her pink flame bubbled the wax quickly, and she set it down with the two others which now joined Yvon's. Lirralik, the *Liktas* agent whom was part of the insurgence team, went to light their own candle. Almost all at once, the whole group turned to Lirralik, and in unison gave a strong whisper of a '*no!*'. Lirralik was taken aback, but put their candle away.

Those candles in the centre were made of red wax and orange wax – Veritan and Omercronian respectively. The candle held by Lirralik was blue, so would have been of Amasos. Once lit, candle rings would emit heavy compulsions, uniting a group towards a decision. They radiated luck to those who stewed in their bask. It was not well understood how they did this, but things seemed to fall into place for those who worshipped the candles. The effect would last under an hour, but often this was enough.

The candles also seemed to radiate innovation. Those near the candles would have their best ideas brought to their own attention. One could be led down a train of thought which drew them to an often fruitful conclusion. The candles had decided that the addition of a blue candle was a bad idea, and this had to have been significant. The blue would conflict with the generated aura.

Celeste stewed in their light, the idea to save my thread bubbling and boiling in her mind. She thought that the candles would dissipate it, in favour of a more selfless re-evaluation of the situation, but they did not. In fact, she felt confident that her logic about Hesslik setting a precedence was more important than even her own thread. It was a dangerous thought.

She glanced to Michael Richard, and felt nothing. She had expected rage, or hatred, but these compulsions had been mellowed. If anything, his unscrupulous stoicism to save his men was probably what the team needed right now.

In a way, they were both right. Celeste's dedication to saving me was selfishly driven, but required if Suneva rights were to be preserved. Michael's dedication to his men was what made him a great leader and planner. He picked his battles well, even if it narrowed his field of view and limited him from helping the entire Suneva community.

In the end, there was only one decision to be made.

"I'll save Maiki alone," Celeste said. Her mother gasped, but Michael nodded with a grin. "Michael is right, it's not up to me to put you all at risk for something so clearly selfishly motivated – although I beg you to see the wider implications of doing this. Maiki is not just a friend: he is *family* after all that he's done to help me. I know my father might have had stronger resolve than to be this foolhardy, but we can all agree that the Argols are about family."

"You can't!" her mother said. "You'll never get out of there with your thread."

Celeste ignored her mother's comment.

"I'm putting Michael in full charge of the mission. And, in the case that I don't come back intact, the Argol gang." There was a collective gasp, although Michael seemed the most surprised of all. Gone was his greasy grin, replaced with what appeared to be real admiration for Celeste. "He is always capable of making decisions in our best interests, and seems to reflect my father's wishes."

"I'm not my father," Celeste continued, "and I'm sorry to have not been as selfless as he, but I've got to save my friend, because I couldn't live with myself if I didn't."

"I'm coming with you," Yvon said, standing by her side. Michael grunted, although did not stop the lad.

"I will too," LeGrand said. "Maiki is a promising young Suneva."

"Anybody else?" Michael asked to the gathered group. Juliette Leroux stepped forward and joined her daughter, although her hesitation marked her reluctance.

"You've got a death wish," Juliette whispered to Celeste, "but if I can't stop you, I have to go with you."

"Okay, this is good," Michael said, "we can work with this."

"I know you'll make the right decision," Celeste said to the man, and bent down into the circle before them. There, she extinguied the candles, dampening their strange auras.

Celeste gathered her small party and stalked with them to the edge of the woods. There Celeste, Yvon, LeGrand and Juliette donned the scouts' Sunesca robes, and slunk through the undergrowth to the clearing before the castle.

Now, they would wait.

Chapter 12
Lifesaving

It wasn't the height that frightened me most as I plummeted down the cliff's face, but the speed. The black rock soared past my belly, gently swaying further away, as I *accelerated* into the violent waters below. I would hit them faster than I could even comprehend, my face would surely melt into my neck on impact.

I reached hopelessly for the air around me, to have some effect on this fall, but I could not connect to it in the Void. The air was just a representation, nothing tangible, leaving me with no options. The water churned to meet me, and I raced to meet it.

A board sailed past my face, thrown faster than I could fall. I squirmed — thinking about falling atop of *that* instead of the water — when talons sunk into my shoulders, then arms to meet them, grappling me like a parcel. Boekidin pulled my back tight against his underside, his impressive wings extending to their full span and catching the wind.

We jerked up instantly, his clawed hands ripping at my underarms, drawing me up with them. It was only a short reprieve, however, as our combined weight proved too much for Boekidin's wings to parachute. We succumbed to the remaining short fall.

The two boards splashed into the water ahead of us, and Boekidin threw me aside as we neared impact ourselves, saving me from being crushed under his body. The sea, denser and more viscous than regular water, reacted like custard as we slammed into it. The surface stiffened against my body on impact, and I was winded by the force of it on my head.

Stunned and motionless, the water broke quickly for my still body, and it consumed me. For a moment, I couldn't act, I could only wallow in shock as my head sank under. Waves rolled overhead, their rip tugging me down as they roared above. I could see myself suffocating in here if I couldn't act quickly.

Shaken to my senses, I tried to swim for the surface. I reached for what light I could see through the murky waters, pushing down desperately. Yet with each push down, more sludge-like water rushed in to replace that which left. The thick liquid choked my body, forcing me under. I struggled harder, only to sink further. I hit the sea floor.

Panic struck me, but struggling only made the sensation worse. A wave rolled overhead and swept me off my feet, tumbling. I was running out of breath

– any longer and I'd pass out here, in the sea of Amasos, and wake up in the real world.

I planted my feet when they found ground, and prepared for my last effort. Squatting low, I held my hands in a peak above my head, and leapt as hard as I could for the surface. My body was streamlined, but the water was still too dense, and just as I came to see the light, I was ground to a halt by the weight of ocean over me. Using my hands now would bog me further down, so I kicked instead. The water rushed to fill each gap made by my feet, but the custard-like currents could only push me up, away and towards the surface.

I breached it finally with a red face, tearing a thick film of water from my skull to breathe. The air was glorious to my lungs, and with it I could finally think clearly. I lay on my back – which was easy with the density of the water – and stayed there to catch my breath.

The new greatest threat became apparent to me – waves. Two roared towards me from separate directions, a desperate attempt by the sea to hold me down. Thinking quickly, I freestyled towards one, flying up its face just before it broke. I surfed down the far side of it, to see a vacant life-saving board bumbling on the water's surface. I swam towards it.

The effort was dizzying. My legs fought drowning as the thick liquid pulled them down. My arms sweated just to break the surface after each stroke. It was easy to keep my torso above the waterline, but the effort required to part the dense sea and move through it was immense.

Waves battered me. They came from the shore, pushing through the board and towards me. Their rip pulled it away from me, and their force surged me backwards. It seemed almost impossible to reach it, but I couldn't give up fighting.

I didn't come to the Void just to get trapped by destiny again.

I pushed through the immense pain. I was Maiki, the Voidwalker. The sea of Amasos could not hold me from my goal. It had no power over me. I shouted these words, and swam on.

The admission of my power fuelled the ocean's outrage, and in its anger came chaos. The waves spurned from its rage were frighteningly tall, but not as well timed or aimed as those which came before. One of them crashed over my head roaring inland, and tumbled me closer to the board. I surfaced, and duck-dove under the next I could see, only to be washed out again. I surfaced closer to the board than I had been before the tumble, and I pounced towards it.

I grappled it in one hand, and let out a whoop of victory. I flopped my body over its surface, and almost fell off the other side before righting myself. I got to my knees on the board and collapsed from the exertion. The waves rolled under me, but for now, they could do nothing to force me about.

I spotted Boekidin in the swell, further north along the cliff face, struggling to reach his board. I leaned down, shins planted heavily on the board's deck, and plunged my hands into the water. I forced the water behind, but found that my great push was reduced to no more than a sharp shove. Paddling over the ocean's surface was akin to dragging the board across sand. To find Zamelle through this slush would be a tremendous effort.

Boekidin flailed in the sea, not yet noticing me. I crested the waves coming towards him, riding off the far faces to reach his board. I straddled my mount, adopting a position to lift his board from the water's surface. Once I reached it, I threw it towards him.

He grasped it with his long, black claws, and pried his armoured body onto the deck. His wings were slick with the gelatinous water, and he shook them dry like a dog, sticky water flying. I paddled over to him.

"I can't believe we survived that," I said to him. "Thank you."

"You're welcome," Boekidin said. "Thanks for helping me up. This water is insane, it's like custard. I thought I was a good swimmer, too."

"Maybe not in armour," I teased.

"Maybe not," He frowned beneath the helmet.

"So, do you think you can find Zamelle in here?" I asked him., and he gave me a hard look. "We're already down here, we might as well try."

"I can find her," he affirmed. "She sticks out in the field like a sore thumb. But, don't you think it's a bit risky? We weren't prepared for *this*." He gestured all around – the sheer, black cliffs, the tall, proud apostles, and the gnarly waters swirling between.

"I know," I said, "but I don't think there's another choice. If I can't save her from destiny, she *will* remove my thread. I don't know whether that's hours or days away, but it is *definite*. I have to save her."

Boekidin's brow furrowed beneath his black, predatory helmet.

"Is this about you, or her?" he asked, and then braced to his board. I followed, just as a wave tore past us from behind my head, rolling under the boards and into the cliffs. "Not that it's easier to risk my soul for either cause."

"I...of course it's about..." what was this about? It was hard to think clearly with the sea churning and rocking beneath us, and with time so valuable. The two facets choked at me, wiling me to just paddle off instead of answering the question. I *had* to go and save Natalie, that's why I was in the Void, and why I had come here now. Hesslik could not be stopped without her, and this was the last chance to free her mind from its possession.

The last chance, because my thread was going to be removed, and Natalie might also be the only slim chance capable of stopping that. If my thread fell now, there would be no voidwalker to free the White Witch. I doubted that I could coach another Suneva to come here to the Void either – my first journey was luck, the meeting of an injury and a strange flower. Mine and Natalie's joint survival were intertwined, and rescuing her from destiny was the first step to saving us both.

"It's for her," I said. "Of course it is."

"So, it's selfless, then?" Boekidin asked. "For the good of all Suneva?"

"Yes," I said. "If we don't get her out of this sea now, before Hesslik removes my thread, there won't be any other voidwalkers to do it. You'll never get back here on your own, and nobody else will."

"And we couldn't come back later?" he asked. "We could make better preparations, and attack with a plan."

"I don't know that there *will* be a later." I gulped. "We can't bank Hesslik giving us more time."

"Okay," he nodded. "It's a risk, but a required one. Follow me."

Boekidin got his shins to the deck and arched his back, digging into the sea. We paddled off together, following the waves and hectic swirling current outwards. Boekidin led me towards the closest apostle. It rose like a lumbering giant, towering above the raging ocean. Moving the boards across the custardy sea was exhausting, and it tired our whole bodies, but we eventually drew close to Natalie. I could sense her now, with what little field sense I had.

We followed our feelings, close to the foot of the giant stone tower. Then I caught a glimpse of it – raw power. Two bright lights, the headlamps from a deep-sea vessel, shone through the dense water. Natalie's eyes pierced the darkest of seas, forming two solid beams which jutted out of the water, breaking the light sea mist which had formed at the apostle's landing.

As we came closer, I could see pollution churning in the waters near her body. Murky liquid bubbled to the surface, swirling on the waves like oil. There were two distinct factions of the pollution swirling concurrently – one pool of bright orange muck, and one of pure white.

"She's leaking quatra," Boekidin pointed to the sediment. "Isn't it funny how it's represented here."

"In what way do you mean *funny*?" I asked. The clouds of oil *were* indeed coming from her. They appeared to rise in plumes from the same place as her eyes.

I paddled over to hover atop her body. The light from her eyes, mystically, seemed to pierce through my board and through my body. The beams of white rose to the sky, into infinity, separate from the grey dull which was the rest of this world. Waves rocked and lapped around me, and it was hard to stay anchored above her when caught in the sea's angry vortex.

"Do you want to pull her out?" Boekidin asked. "I'm not confident about falling back in there."

I sympathised with the man's plight, but wasn't confident in my own survival odds.

"Sure, I'll do it," I nodded grimly, slumping to plunge my arm into the murky depths. I could see the shadows of Natalie's fingertips as they swayed past her glowing eyes. Her hands hung above her head, lamely coursing with the water's flow. I palmed for them blindly, but failed to get a hold. I felt the clock ticking, pressing faster action.

I held my breath, then launched my shoulder and face into the sea. The water lapped at my hair, tugging it down over my eyes. Despite that, I could see Natalie's fingers now through the slick oil of her quatra, still suspended deeper than my reach. I breached for a breath.

"I'm going to have to get in," I told Boekidin, dread setting as I said it. "Hold my board."

Boekidin winced for me, and paddled over to grab the board. I clutched at the ankle tether holding me to the it, tugging the rope tight against its mount to check its sturdiness. The board creaked as I yanked it, but I chose to ignore the sound. Bestowing the line with my faith and fears, I slid from the liferaft.

I grappled the board's nose and threw my head under, down into the misty-dark water. The streams of it lapped around my body, gripping in like tendrils of the God, trying to pull me away. I closed my eyes to their touch, and palmed blindly once more, thrashing through the white-polluted sea.

My hand hit something. I grasped on instinct. I had Natalie's wrist – or what felt like her wrist. I pulled against my board, bringing myself up to the surface.

Only, her body wouldn't rise.

My arm was tugged straight just before my mouth breached the water. Panicking, I yanked harder at her writst, aware that if I let go to breathe, I might not find her hand again. Then arms grappled at my head, heaving to pull my lips clear of the water's surface, straining my arm behond its full extent.

"What's wrong?" Boekidin asked, holding me up. I could barely hear him with my eyes and ears submerged.

"She's stuck," I spluttered.

"Check if she's caught on something."

"I…" that would involve letting go of the board, and I didn't know that I trusted the tether *that* much. "Alright. Let me go." I ordered, and Boekidin nodded solemnly, releasing my face.

Natalie's arm, a spring set stretched, immediately recoiled, towing me into the depths. I was hauled through the water, crashing into her body with a thud. Surprisingly, her body shifted with mine – it had risen by the force of its own spring against me – and now ground to a halt as I bashed into it.

I released Natalie's hand, climbing down her anchored body to her toes. From her trunk to her furthest extent, Natalie's body was free of binds. Perplexed, I dragged myself back up her limp body to her hand. Once there, I gave her arm a frightful tug towards the surface, raising her body more than enough to surface my whole head.

"Not bound," I said to Boekidin, "just hard to move."

"Destiny is keen to hold her," He noted, sliding my board to my awaiting hand. I grabbed it, flopped my legs over the thing, then pulled my torso onto it with my free hand, careful to keep Natalie's wrist in my grasp. With my chest against the knee-holds, and my shoulder submerged at my arm's length, I heaved.

Boekidin paddled over, palming the white-murky water for Natalie's other arm. He found it quickly, and joined in my efforts. We heaved on each count of three, drawing the girl closer to the surface by the inch. Soon, we had her hands waving above the water line, but held down by a thick meniscus. I clawed and stretched at the film of water that gripped her, but it refused to break.

"Amasos *definitely* doesn't want to let go," Boekidin coughed.

"It doesn't matter," I said. "We can pull her out at the cliff face. Let's get her to the rocks, first."

"What's the logic in that?" he asked. "Will it be any easier to get her out by the shore?"

"I don't know," I said. "Pulling her *up* and *out* of this water seems too hard right now. It might be easier to move her *through* the water. Keep the God happy for now."

"Sure, let's try it." Boekidin hummed along, although a sunken lip revealed his anticipation. "Let's take a wrist each and kick her along."

I nodded, and lay myself flat to the rear of the board. Legs hanging out, I kicked myself along by Boekidin's side. We motored away, the action of dragging Natalie under the surface proving much easier than pulling her up from it. Waves and currents thrashed into our faces, fighting their way out to the abyss of the far seas. The sea was angry – either at us or by its own accord. We wrestled its rip with vigour, fighting Amasos' tendrils against a ticking clock which we could not hear.

We bobbed and thrashed in the undulating sea, our limbs growing tired. However, without any physical body in this realm, it was difficult to understand *where* I was feeling the fatigue, and it was easy enough to push myself through it.

We came close to the cliff, after the effort of paddling wooden planks across stones. Water rushed at the vertical, basalt face, spraying high and raining over our heads. Only few sharp rocks survived at the boundary between land and ocean, and waves crashed onto them violently, throwing the thick sea into the spikes with reckless abandon. Otherwise, the waves crashed up against the sheer face, rising and falling against it, sloshing forcefully. Neither the spikes nor sheer face appeared to be a safe place to land. However, a look between Boekidin and I suggested that we'd rather be crushed against the sheer face than against the sharp rock-bed.

We steered our way towards the exposed cliff edge and waited for a break in the waves. Boekidin sat up on the board, reaching into the sea with his free hand and solidifying the water. He created two sharp daggers, and handed them to me.

"For you to climb with," he said, and peered up to the cliff's top edge. I followed his gaze, staring up to a ledge impossibly high.

For the meantime, it seemed that the waves were drifting out, rather than coming in and up against the rocks. We perched ourselves on the boards, riding closer to the rock face, and dug into the wall with our free hands – Boekidin with his claws, myself with a dagger. It gave me a solid purchase on the cliff.

We looked down to the submerged body hanging by our wrists, then nodded to each other.

"Three, two, one…"

We heaved at her arms, lurched downwards by the pull of the sea. Natalie breached clear of the surface, but the thick water stuck over her skin like a membrane. The unbreakable slime, stretched at capacity like a loaded spring, towed her back under.

I was thrown from my purchase on the wall and ripped from the board, sucked down into the sea. Boekidin dropped her wrist as he saw me tumble under the tide.

109

As I gained my bearings, holding onto Natalie for dear life, a wave rolled in and crashed against the black pitch. I gripped my arms around Natalie's whole body, holding her close as I blocked the impact against the sheer wall. We tumbled under the meniscus, and eventually I surfaced. Waves rolled dangerously in the distance, coming our way. Amasos knew what we were up to.

"Quick!" I shouted, tearing towards Boekidin and my board with one hand. I got within arms reach, and he pulled me in. I wrestled with Natalie, finding her second wrist and throwing it at Boekidin. Finally breaching the water for the board, I palmed the dagger which I'd driven into cliffside. Natalie bobbed just under the surface. Waves came fast towards us.

"Slower this time," I said, "and with heaps of strength."

"If you pull as hard as you can," Boekidin said, "I'll try to break the surface tension with my claws."

I nodded to his plan, and heaved upwards.

Natalie slowly rose, the amazing surface tension of the water bogging her still. Boekidin had planted his clawed feet into the cliff wall, giving him extra purchase as he pulled. He then surprised me, extracting the foot closest to Natalie, and casting its talon to the meniscus covering her hand. With careful dexterity, he traced a line down her arm, splitting the goo. With the force of our pulling, the membrane quickly fell away. Succumbing to its own spring energy, the tear propagated down Natalie's body. Suddenly, she flung out of the water, pulled up by the full strength of both of our arms. My eyes lit up, we'd done it!

The sea disagreed. A violent wave, the highest I'd seen in the Void, rolled its weight into the cliff like a freight train. In the face of our victory, the wall of water swept us from our handholds, flinging us up the basalt face with ease, and dropping us into the sea below.

I hit the water with the full surface of my back. It stung, and I was dazed. Natalie landed atop me, and I grappled her tight. I was mad now, but with resolve. The surface *could* be broken, and we could tear her from it easily. With vigour, I kicked towards the cliff's edge, to where Boekidin now hung from his board. He heaved himself from the heavy sea. I crunched my spare dagger into the rock near him and yanked myself out of the water from its purchase, grabbing the dagger I'd left in the wall above it. I handed him one of Natalie's arms once more, and we eyed eachother with weary faces. We were tired, but far from broken.

Pain.

I felt it in my left arm, the pain of it being held, and pulled. However, the sensation wasn't on my immediate body. The arm I had now, which held a dagger in the basalt wall, was fine. The pain was distant, but connected. It called to me through my soul, and subsequently, from everywhere in the Void at once. I winced.

"Oh no…"

Thunder cracked in the sky. Boekidin didn't seem phased, he didn't even seem to hear it. I looked up to the source, the south sky. I could see a snippet of it from here, peering from behind the imposing, black cliff. I caught the image of an arm around mine, tangled in the dull, low clouds. It pulled me up. It belonged to Natalie.

My eyes darted down to her helpless body, which dangled limply from my arm, asleep here. Despite her soul's helplessness here, I could feel her power, which exceeded all imagination.

"Boekidin," I called to him. "They're taking me! We have to get her out *now.*"

"What?" he stammered.

"They're executing my thread!" I yelled. "Quick, we have to get her out!"

He glanced to Natalie's body, then back to the cliff face.

"How will you climb when holding her?" he asked. I felt pain again, and my gaze snapped out to the sea, whose huge waves rolled towards us.

"What's it matter?" I asked. "I'll figure it out, just *lift!*"

I tugged desperately on her arm, and Natalie came free of the body of water, still thick with the surface meniscus. Boekidin didn't pull with me. He had a guilty look strewn across his face.

"Rip the goo! God damnit!" I yelled, but Boekidin released Natalie's wrist.

"There's no time!" he urged me, and pointed to the cliff's top. "They're going to take your thread, and you want to climb this whole thing carrying her in one hand before they do it? No chance. *Climb.*"

I choked Natalie's wrist in my grip, my face flying into a rage.

"She's the only chance for the Suneva!" I asserted, pulling her up. My arm, in this realm, was dead tired of holding on.

"*You're* the only chance for Suneva," Boekidin rebutted. "Nobody else can come here to the Void. You're the only hope."

"And if I don't save her," I enunciated, "then my thread goes. They're intertwined events. I need to save her for her to save me."

"You don't get it," he huffed, frustrated. "Save yourself!" And he started to climb the cliff, urging me to follow. "I know that if you get to the top of this cliff, and return to the world, you will save yourself. Your thread won't be removed."

"And how do you know that?" I crushed Natalie's hand in mine. A tear started to tread down my face. I couldn't let her go. I'd come so far.

"I *feel* it," he said. "I'm a Suneva, it's what I do. *Feel.*"

"How?" I yelled. "There's no destiny for us anymore. There's no coincidence. We can't be saved by these cosmic forces. It's just us against all of this…" I gestured out to the sea, to its destructive power which tracked towards us. "It's just us and our actions."

"So, make them count," he growled. "We can't win this fight here and now, but you *can* win the one in the real world. I *believe* in you. There's a whole black hole over there backing you up, letting you see visions! We need to come back here with better preparation, and the only way to do that is to survive what's happening to your body. Come on and *move!*"

He descended the cliff, stretching his arm towards me. A wave was coming fast, which would reach us by the time he got to me and wash us both away. Natalie's hand rested in mine. Her body was comatose, peaceful, *beautiful.*

Natalie was a force of this world. She was loyal, and powerful, and opinionated, and passionate, and caring, and she would never let me down. But she had let me down now, and I couldn't deal with that. I couldn't let her go like she suddenly did to us. But I had to.

I had to let her go.

I dropped Natalie's hand, and she sprung downwards into the dark sea. I wrestled for the second knife, which lay under my foot, and stabbed it above the old. Boekidin, seeing my turn, reversed, and stuck his claws back up the rock. I stabbed the old knife ahead of the new, and clambered up the face.

As we worked our way up, the series of tidal waves crashed into the black rock below. Water sprayed all the way to my ankles, it's tendrils of destiny threatening to hold me and drag me back. I could fight this abyss, I would not bow to Amasos.

And I would not bow to Hesslik.

I powered ahead of Boekidin, surprising him with my swiftness and my intent. My arms ached, both real and their representations, but I forced them on. I was Maiki, I was the Voidwalker. I came here unprepared, expecting an easy fight, but I couldn't have expected to battle a *God* and win on the first round. This would be a long campaign, but it was only over if I gave up.

I was the master of my own destiny.

I made the final haul, lifting myself, and the board hanging to my ankle, onto the hexagonal rock surface. I rolled across the black stone, exhausted, yet still clawing my way towards the forest. I would not suffer a slip and fall after coming so far.

Boekidin came not long after, launching off his talons and swooping towards the forest. He stood tall over my laying figure.

"Get in my head," I told him. "We're going back."

"You made the..."

"Shut up," I ordered. "And thank you for believing in me. Now, get in there, and don't make a sound."

He nodded, sullen. He then evaporated, puffing into a twisting mist which flew into my ear. The feeling was of a slight uncomfortable clog, as always. I let it happen, drifting into exhaustion.

My eyes closed to the crack of thunder. I fell into darkness.

Chapter 13
Execution

Vast, white light came back to me. Was I dead?

No, surely not. My eyes came into focus slowly, and I wrenched my arm up to rub them clear.

Pain, firstly, shot down my shoulder. It was just noticeable, like a static shock rather than a knife through the muscles. Time in the Void had healed me well.

Secondly, I couldn't move my arm. This was not for the pain, rather it was bound to something. The fright woke me up fully.

My head bounded out of its rest, my eyes bulging open. I was being driven down a stone hallway, bound to a rolling chair by my ankles and wrists. I wriggled my legs and body, but there was no way to break free.

"Ah, you're awake!" Hesslik said from behind. I flung my head against the rest, and wretched my eyeballs to get a look at him. His head came into view, bearing over me with a large grin between his yellow helmet and cyan partition.

"Good – for you, that is," he said. "I was going to remove your thread asleep or awake, but you being awake makes it look more ethical, so that saves me some paper work." He stood tall again, chuckling at his quip.

I stared down the hallway, which would soon open to the outside of the castle. In front of me walked Zamelle in full armour, wheeling something on a dolly.

"Amasos has you, Zamelle," I called to her. "I saw it in the Void. You're stuck in their sea of thick mucus, being forced about."

She stopped abruptly, swivelling to face me. I saw now that the dolly carried a person, bound like a mummy. It was Simone, struggling in the bindings.

"Shut up, James," she stung, pointing a long, armoured finger at me. The slit of her helmet shone with Amasos' white fury. My only reaction, in my surprise, was to subconsciously summon my armour. It crawled over my body, and somehow did not break the binds. With thinner joints, I had more room for play in the restraints, but the thick armour was so wedged in the chair that I was otherwise more stuck than before.

"That's *Maiki* to you…" I quipped. Zamelle's eye slit flushed brighter and I sunk into the chair.

"You're working against the best interests of Suneva and humans worldwide. Just shut up and accept your destiny."

"You're acting against your own best interests," I retorted.

Zamelle stamped over to me, her finger still pointed. It came between both of my green, glass-like eyes.

"You will *never* know my pain, Maiki. *Never.*" She stepped back, re-attending to Simone. "Don't you *dare* pretend to know what my best interests are."

I shut up, and the cavalcade started again. I could have gone on, but further argument was pointless when Zamelle was incapable of changing her mind.

Sound roared at the hallway's portal. Lights shone out from some kind of deck, lighting the faces and helmets of a sea of Suneva and humans. There was an uproarious cheer as Simone and I were wheeled onto the stage. The set-up was beyond anything I'd have imagined for an event like this. The scene was that of a music festival – we were rock stars strutting onto the giant black stage, with speakers and lights bolted along the silver lattice of a scaffold gantry. The crowd, intoxicated on the love for the performance tonight, gagged and cheered, moshing in the pit to get close to the stage. Their *Fara*, the act for tonight, stepped out to the platform's edge, and greeted his field of fans.

The sea of onlookers continued from the stage all the way out to the castle's defences, at least one hundred metres away, across what might have been a grassy field, but was now a muddy mess. Storm clouds covered the full moon, but plenty of light met the fans and stage, pouring from roaming spot lights. This really was a show, although I couldn't discern who the attraction was – Hesslik, or me.

I was wheeled to stage right of the centre stage, with Simone parked behind me to my right, resting against the wall. I twisted my head around to her, to find her serenely calm. She was calculating something, or merely concentrating. Zamelle joined Hesslik at centre stage, and Hesslik donned the microphone.

"Hello all. Hello all," he said in his perfect Liktan, sailing his hand across the audience. They gave a sheer as his long, grey fingers passed by them. His black cape, caught in the breeze of their excitement, flapped behind him, bearing the large, white emblem of the Mark of the Black Sun.

"Welcome to a special event," he said, and the audience drew to a hush. "Tonight, I display the power I have created to police extreme cases of Suneva behaviour. The show here, tonight, will be a grand gesture to all countries of the world, that we take the actions of Suneva very seriously, and will not tolerate unethical peoples amongst us."

Another cheer roared from the crowd. He had them lapped in his words, wrapped around his tongue. Despite Boekidin's belief in me, I hardly felt that I was getting out of this spectacle with the thread of Maiki intact.

"Tona and Tano, hands together for *na Ocras Quatrona*, Zamelle Menas." He gestured to Zamelle, who stood stoically on the stage. The crowd was unsure how to feel about Zamelle – it was not too long ago that she was captured at a grand dinner within this very castle.

"After becoming the White Witch, she felt compelled to reform, and join us, to make the Suneva people strong. She has been instrumental in her short time as an agent of the Suneva people, having captured the grand terrorist Maiki, and his entourage." He pointed across to Simone and myself, locked in our restraints. The crowd knew exactly how they felt about this revelation – with cheers rising from every corner of their packed being.

"I think it's important that the first Suneva to receive this treatment publicly – and hopefully the only to do so – is such a prolific wrongdoer and threat to the future of all Suneva. He will make a strong example to others, that opposing peace and prosperity for our people – in favour of selfish endeavours – will *not* be tolerated."

"Prolific wrongdoer…" I snarked under my breath. I wriggled in the restraints for a way out, but it seemed that Hesslik had thought about this. The sharpest parts of my armour couldn't reach the straps – not even my fingers.

"Would you like to hear a list of your offences?" Hesslik asked. He'd directed the question towards me, but still held the microphone to his own helmet. The crowd hushed.

"Yeah, I feel that I should, if you call this *justice*," I remarked, and he smirked.

"Of course," Hesslik smirked wryly. "This is justice, after all." A guard came – a regular Suneva who had covered parts of their armour in navy blue pieces bearing the symbol of the black suns – and handed Hesslik a sheet of paper. As Hesslik examined it, the guard walked over to me. He produced a small lapel microphone, and pinned it awkwardly into my chest piece.

"As this is a ceremony of justice, Maiki will of course be given the right to defend himself against my allegations."

"I'm surprised –" I said, and my voice boomed over the crowd. I winced in the shock of it. "You don't think that anything I could say would be slightly incriminating, Hesslik?"

"Only to yourself," he quipped, and a chuckle rose amongst the audience.

"Now, Maiki. You have many charges lain before you. The first is criminal breaking and entering of my compound in Melbourne, and the destruction of my library storehold and my scientific documents. Five years of research lost to a fire which you started on the warehouse floor."

I gulped. This was the truth, although it's not how I would have put it. "It was during a fight for my thread!" I said. "Vestas was going to…"

"*After* you broke into the premises?" Hesslik interrupted.

"Yes…"

"And *after* you'd made yourself a threat to my officers and scientists?"

I was compelled to say no, but this wasn't true. In both cases, it was our party who had attacked first – Vestas even insisted that no fight was necessary. We were stepping into traps a year before their consequences would prove themselves.

"Yes," I responded, head drooped.

"Then the count stands," Hesslik smirked.

"Secondly, you *stole* works from my library – a *public* library, open to all Suneva. Is this true?" he asked.

"A public library in a closed warehouse? I certainly wasn't allowed in," I smiled, thinking I'd made a point. Hesslik stooped his brows.

"Did you steal the book?"

"Which book?"

"The book of Suneva tales by Salak Nolver."

116

Oh, Kuvalik's book. Yes, I did steal that.

"Yes," I answered honestly, "but you'd stolen –"

"And you used the information gained from this book to subvert my plans to bring the Legendaries back to the Suneva, yes?"

"That's quite a stretch," I moaned. "I mean, it was *our* plan to find them, and..."

"Did you stop Boekidin from finding the Legendary Suneva?" Hesslik snapped.

"No, we helped him find them – we basically handed them over," I rebutted.

"But your intention was to undermine his mission."

"Yes," I groaned, "but his team blinded my friend." I gestured to Zamelle with my head.

"Did his team ever act unethically?" Hesslik asked, and I rolled my eyes. It was the cat, Vassi, who taught me about Suneva ethics, who apologised profusely for hurting me.

"No," I grumbled. Hesslik smiled.

"And finally," he continued, "you subverted one of my agents, and conspired with Naxaer and Iva Argol to aid your terroristic mission to undermine Boekidin. Is this true?"

"Hey, I didn't subvert *anybody*." I would have thrown my hands in the air, if they weren't pinned to a heavy, metal chair. "You did that by trying to get rid of him."

"Did you conspire with those who subverted my agents and..."

"I never conspired with *you*," I interrupted cheekily.

"Please, let me finish," Hesslik growled.

"Let *me* finish," I insisted. "I get to making good points, and you cut me off."

"I'm not the one on trial here, Maiki." Hesslik avoided any sense of confrontation, and marched on. "Did you conspire with the Argol family and a subverted agent to undermine Boekidin."

"I conspired with those characters, but *not* for the sake of you, or Boekidin," I said, truthfully.

"Then, we'll leave it to the audience, but I think the decision here is clear..." he said, turning to the crowd. Their faces were excited, grinning, gnawing at the gates.

"If you take my thread, there will be war and consequences," I said, suddenly mustering stoicism. Half of the crowd booed, securing my fate, but I didn't quite care. To hell with them, thinking that could grant the power to destroy a man's soul. "I am the Vochduhvlad, heir to the ancient throne of the *Kiin* King."

"Of course you're the *Vochduhvlad*," Hesslik laughed. "You're the *only* Vochduh."

I growled, ignoring the comment. The crowd laughed. "You charge me for destruction of information, yet your agents who captured me, led by Zamelle Menas, destroyed my ancient library of texts.

The crowd gasped. Hesslik idly turned his helmet to mine. "Do you have evidence of this, Maiki."

"Do you have evidence that I destroyed your stores?"

"Several witnesses and security cameras," he said flatly.

"I have many witnesses of your crime, too," I said. "One of them escaped capture, one of them is my sister, behind me. One of them is the White Witch, Zamelle Menas. The others, I do not know."

"Well," Hesslik dismissed the claim, "I hardly see-"

"Is there a *Kidin* in the audience?" I asked. The faces in the crowd looked uncomfortable at the mention of the power. "Go into my…"

Not your own head, stupid! Boekidin rasped. *I'm in here!*

"…into my *sister's* head. She witnessed the events."

Simone glared death towards me. I winced.

"James!" she growled.

"What?" I asked.

"Why not your own head?" a man asked, coming to the front of the crowd. People were giving him a wide berth.

"Because I was unconscious at the time," I explained.

"Hmmm…" the man hummed. He closed his eyes, and sat on the ground, disappearing from sight behind the stage.

"Gah!" Simone exclaimed, and wrestled with her binds. Clearly, this man was a *Kidin*, and in her mind. Hesslik watched on with intrigue and a blank expression. He didn't appear nervous, per-se, but he was deep in calculation.

"Oh my…she's *Fairysmog*," the Kidin man said, leaping to attention. The crowd around him stiffened in shock. A whisper of the rumour spread like a wave, rippling through the field in an instant.

"No! You idiot!" I yelled at him. Simone growled behind me – I was dead. "That doesn't matter, did you-"

"Not only do you conspire with Argols and subvert Hesslik's men, but now you're working with the most prolific Sun…" The man was cut off, although his mouth continued to move. Wind billowed from the restraints which held Simone down. Her eyes, like ruby fires, sparked with hate for everything.

"I gave that up when I discovered who I am. I *renounced* it. I closed that section of my life," she roared. Silence settled all around – although this time, not by Simone's hands. Even Hesslik was taken at the magnitude of her ability – stealing sound without movement.

"Don't you dare hold that against me to incriminate us," Simone boomed. "What did you see about the library, you slimy idiot?"

"Well, I didn't see…"

"Bullshit!" she blasted. "What did you see?"

He went to open his mouth, but Hesslik gave him a stare somehow more threatening than Simone's. We waited in silence – who was this Kidin more afraid of, an unprecedented Sunesca or the *Fara* of the world's leading Suneva nation?

The man stayed silent.

"It appears," Hesslik continued, "that there is no evidence to suggest that I desecrated the *Vochduhvlad's* property…"

"Go into Zamelle's mind!" I urged into the crowd. "Not this fool, he's just been intimidated out of his honest answer. If any of you care about justice, do it! There's got to be a *Kidin* amongst you who wants to fight for justice!"

"That's enough, Maiki!" Hesslik ordered. The audience shuffled, although the tensions were now too high for anybody to utter a noise. I slumped in defeat. Hesslik had won.

"You've delayed this long enough. For your crimes, and to set an example for all who *think* to do the wrong thing by our people, your thread will be removed."

"Hypocrite!" Simone blasted. Hesslik ignored the comment.

"Zamelle, if you'd do the honours."

Zamelle was handed a small black box by her guards – made of matte plastic, with two protruding prongs and a large, red button. The crowd stiffened in anticipation. The sound of Zamelle's clawed footsteps across the wooden stage echoed long out into the valley, audible over all else. It seemed impossible – this would be the end of Maiki.

I still believe, Maiki, Boekidin said.

I don't believe in miracles anymore, I thought back. *It's just up to me now, and I failed.*

119

Then there was a miracle.

The gates to the outer wall of the castle burst open in a roar of pink, purple, and orange flames. Quatra bolts exploded from the scene – well aimed, spraying across the stage. People screamed, the mosh pit revolting into absolute chaos. Suneva were caught in the crossfire, their threads disappearing and their grunts of pain crying out.

"Everybody evacuate!" Hesslik called into the microphone. "Side exits!" he demanded. The entropy of the crowd, spilling like a turbulent fluid, made some semblance of a current towards the side exits. The seas parted from their centre, giving the attackers a straight channel to the stage.

Zamelle threw the device at me, landing it on my lap – it seemed that she never really needed her sight, after all - and took aim towards the attackers. Each bolt of quatra the invaders fired from that moment was met with an orange one from Zamelle's summoned swords. They whizzed through the air with frightening precision, drawing the bolt-fire to a standstill. Hesslik joined in, summoning his jagged blade and firing upon the intruders.

I could make them out now – four brave Suneva in the mosh. The first Suneva was bug-like, yet elegant, and with a pink flame – clearly Tona Iva Argol. The next was a Suneva with golden gleaming armour the shape of a phoenix – LeGrand. The third had a semblance of Iva, but armour of pale pink and indigo – I thought they might have been Sanavaer, Juliette Leroux. The fourth was a Suneva in charcoal grey armour, with a flat faced helmet and a mean mace. I did not know them.

It's Celeste, I said to Boekidin. *She's saved me!*

She always does, He responded – and he was right.

Hesslik's royal guards vaulted down from the turrets above the castle and pushed into the fray. They surged through the crowd, and although slow going, would be upon my saviours soon. I had to act.

Carbon - I felt it now in the straps of my chair. They were leather. How didn't I notice it before? I must have been too stressed to even think of it. This was a huge oversight by Hesslik – too big of an oversight to be an accident. Did Natalie install a trap to save me?

I tore at the element, and the armbands dissipated into fire and dust. I did the same for the leg bands, and broke free, leaping to my feet. I summoned my dual-prong sword-staff, and let the magnitude of my connections grow within me.

I made a sweeping attack, summoning a vortex of air from behind me and blasting it towards Zamelle and Hesslik, who still stood on the stage. The force of my attack was strong – stronger than any vortex I'd ever made. They lost their footing immediately in the wind, falling across the stage.

Then I ran for Simone. Her face was a mess of emotions, no single one looking to act. I was glad for this – as long as her hatred of me for exposing her secret would stay under wraps for now, we'd get through this. Using my sharp carbon blade, I sliced down the outside of her body, cutting each strap. She wriggled, and I grabbed her hand, pulling her free of the tangled mess of cloth.

Simone pushed past me, grabbing at the forces she could control. Zamelle had just regained herself on the stage, and as soon as she had stood and redirected her first bolt, her limbs were ground to a near stop. Simone ate the White Witch's energy, exhausting it as a wild wind from her palms. Zamelle now moved through the air like tar, only a flick of the finger away from being totally locked in place.

Bolts still flew towards her, though, and I added one to the onslaught. They plunged into her armour, one at a time, and I rejoiced, realising that she would finally be free of her thread – free to live her own compulsions and follow me home.

But, *somehow*, each bolt was redirected without any movement from her body. Zamelle's willpower over her quatra pathways was just that strong. I stood in awe – had Hesslik taught her that? I doubted the *Fara* could muster such a feat. Zamelle was *just* that good.

Beyond the stage, the crowd had pushed out to the clogged doorways. The guards, at least twelve in number, were closing in on Iva and her Argol invaders. Hesslik stood just off the stage, shouting directions at his men. With Zamelle being held captive, the Argols had a chance to fight back, but they were already desperately redirecting attacks, they needed my help.

I whipped my staff at the ground, blasting off the stage on a jet of air. I soared high and far, gliding off my arc to land in a skid atop the mud and dirt. I ran up to the rebels.

"Maiki!" Iva shrieked.

"Thank you!" I yelled, blasting bolts of quatra towards the enemies who enclosed us. Mine were easily redirected by the elite guards, but offered some small distraction. Hesslik's men closed in slowly - against the heat of Iva's pink reign – as a circle surrounding us.

"Cover the bolts," I called to the four fighters. "I've got an idea." I pushed outwards, by only a few steps, and gripped at the carbon in the earth before the ring of guards. I spun on my foot, tearing the black element from the ground in a circle, and spraying it outwards towards the enemies.

Many moved to cover their helmeted eyes and faces – by meaty, sweatbag human instincts – as the graphite flung upon them. From the ground where the carbon was torn rose a wall of flames and steam, as oxygen and hydrogen violently reacted. Iva, catching onto my plan, gripped into her own connection – that to heat – and intensified the flames tenfold. Guards shielded themselves now from the roaring fire, instead of the meagre debris, stumbling away from the light. For my final act, I spun around myself, collecting a whirlwind of air which I ejected outwards in a gust. Flames spurted radially from the ring, engulfing guards. They fell back fast – although some bravehearted called the bluff, and jumped through the wall of fire.

A shriek pierced my ears. Bolts of quatra rained upon us, orange and white. Dust and dirt bubbled and sublimated, craters forming where white bolts impacted. Looking to the screams, I could see Simone cowered on the floor of the stage, Hesslik over her, an arc of electricity connecting them.

Don't you dare.

I leapt from the mud into the air, back uphill to the stage. I blasted once more whilst soaring, giving myself a second kick, which saw me to the stage's gantry. I swung off it, onto the stage floor, and blasted a bolt of quatra at Hesslik.

Zamelle turned at lightning pace, smothering the bolt before it had a chance to hit. Hesslik spun to face me, his dangerous arc following.

The current coursed through my body, hot and painful, cooking my nerves. I felt my body roast helplessly under the current, with nothing I could do to fight it. My eyes rolled in my helmet, like they were swimming in a stew, unable to focus. My ears rang with the zap of static. I plunged to the ground, and avoided a bolt of quatra by spastically producing a gust of air to push me off the stage.

Simone cried, but had Hesslik moved on from toasting me, leaving me to rot in the mud. Instead, he reinvigorated his resolve to butt-out the flames of Iva Argol – his direct political enemy. To his stride, Simone's eyes burned with a kick I'd only seen once before – in the soul of the demon who haunted us. She grabbed onto the forces of the world, and drained all that she could. A disc of air billowed from the stage. Zamelle once again was stuck into place – although Hesslik hadn't noticed, and he yelled orders to his royal guards.

I pulled myself up to peek over the stage lip, locking my gaze with my sister. Seeing an opportunity, I aimed my hand at her, and glanced between my palm, her body, and Zamelle. I couldn't be sure that she'd caught my message when I acted, but she soon would.

I leaped to the stage, over the head of Zamelle, and fired a bolt at Simone. Her face went to shock – her head would quite literally explode into bloody powder if I'd misaimed.

Simone caught the bolt through her hand, and for an agonising moment, it didn't appear from any of her limbs. I'd killed her. She'd absorbed it.

No, it came finally, out the other hand, and it was well placed. To redirect, she'd had to let go of her hold over the White Witch, but it didn't seem to matter. The bolt landed perfectly at the base of Zamelle's neck.

Zamelle shrieked. It was a cry of unholy agony. It called to the most desperate, soul breaking, inconceivable pain that anybody could ever experience. It pierced the valley of the castle, bouncing off the great mountains surrounding.

All combat stopped, all stared towards Natalie, as her armour shattered across the floor like glass. Her face was red, as if about to melt, and steamed the tears which rolled down her high, defined cheeks. She fell to the floor, screaming in agony. And with the thump of her body, not a single Suneva or Sunesca in the battle moved. Not a breath was taken.

"Don't stop, get them!" Hesslik ordered to his men. Then kicked back into action in an instant.

A bolt of quatra came from my right, where two guards stormed from the hallway I was wheeled down earlier. I deflected their attack towards Hesslik, and gave a vortex of air to sweep them from their feet.

The first guard threw at me two strips of metal, which, commanded by his connection to them, wrapped around my wrists and threw me through the air, out of the way. I landed square on the dust of the mosh pit. I tore at the strips with my long, sharp fingers, but they wouldn't budge.

On the stage, the guards grabbed Natalie and stood her up to walk her out. Simone, having none of that, stole from their movement. Hesslik swooped back, his cape towing about in Simone's breeze, and shocked her again. The guard holding Natalie ran now, hauling the White Witch towards building. The second guard stood his ground, staying to fight.

I got to my feet and launched through the air. If I could get out of this battle, no matter how desperate it seemed, I could do it with Natalie. I soared over the second guard – not even bothering to attempt to neutralise him. I wanted the White Witch.

Then my momentum changed midair. No longer was I moving forward. With a great whiplash, my armoured body jerked back. The metal strips around my wrists tugged me away, high above the stage. I smashed horribly against the stage-

123

right gantry, and found that I couldn't move despite any best efforts. The second guard stood below me with outstretched and posed hands, magnetically holding my wrists in place.

Out to the field, Iva and her company were truly surrounded. The twelve guards there had formed in, fighting their way through her hot flames. They appeared worse for having tried, but with the sheer number of bolts they set upon Iva and her friends, there was no way that Iva could maintain her defence.

Then LeGrand was down. The golden phoenix cracked like glass, shattering to dust. He held his arms up in surrender, and ducked to avoid the heat of flames.

There was a sudden uproar, and all heads turned again towards the castle gates. At least twenty Suneva stormed through the entrance, led by a man in gleaming silver armour. Quatra bolts crashed into the wall-side of Hesslik's guard, dissipating the threads of at least five unsuspecting fighters. Suddenly, we were on the up.

Hesslik roared, capturing the attention from the break in. He held his lightning-bolt sword high to the sky, and thunder cracked to the command of his posed hands.

Then lightning struck.

Not lightning like Tallik the Space Cowboy used to make, *real lightning*. It reamed from the sky, the ancient force of Gods, of Zeus. It drove into the ground at the footfall of the new wave of attackers. Men flew back from the force of it as the bolt ripped a schism in the battlefield. In its wake, scorched earth, one Suneva dead, and a jagged tear which ripped through the earth.

Hesslik held the position again, raising his sword high. One brave Argol kicked to his feet, standing tall amongst his fellow men. He was of indigo armour, with a copper staff of a *shath*. Thunder cracked, and when the lightning fell he caught it.

And he redirected it.

His arm seemed to fry by the action, but he'd saved many lives. The bolt – which came through his right arm, through his copper staff, left through his other, straight towards Hesslik. The *Fara* leaped from its path, and the direct hit from the storm crashed into the castle wall behind where he stood, blasting stones outward in an explosion of rock and rubble. The guard holding me tight, miraculously with the vigour of a man scorned, stood his ground.

Hesslik groaned with rage. He held his sword by his side now, and seethed through his helmet. The weapon sparked violently, and arced randomly. The bursts of electricity grew more dangerous and frequent, until they coagulated into a single, thick snake of red plasma. It broke through the stage, sublimating it.

Hesslik trudged off the platform, down the field, dragging the plasma whip along the ground.

Mud bubbled and burned in his wake, creating a path of black scorch and dusty flames. The sound of bubbling and burning faded as Simone kicked off the ground with a gust of wind. She leapt after him, stealing the sound from his great whip.

"*Cheese*, No!" I called after her. The guard turned to see where she'd gone, and lost momentary concentration. I tugged on the bracer around my left wrist, and found that I had enough strength to move it. I pulled it off the wall, and in the split second before it collided again with the gantry, fired my bolt.

It raced through the air, smacking the guard in the chest. He didn't have the reflexes to redirect it, and I felt my hold to the scaffold immediately tear. I fell to the ground, narrowly avoiding squishing his human body.

Simone vaulted from the mud, one foot out, ready to give Hesslik an airborne roundhouse kick into oblivion. It was foolhardy, and it was incredibly brave, but only in the stupid way.

Hesslik wasn't dumb, he felt her coming. His body flicked around and his hand came to meet her foot. Hesslik tugged Simone out of the sky, slamming her towards the ground to his left. As she bounced against the mud, Hesslik backhanded her with a closed fist.

The ridge of his gauntlet cut her face. Blood flung from her cheek and brow and she slammed on the ground, hard. I shrieked the shriek of a true Suneva warrior, half ghost, half man. It was haunting, it was real, it was powerful. I leaped after Hesslik.

His guard were falling fast, but it would not matter. Hesslik wound his arm, flinging the red-hot plasma whip around with glee and abandon. The flat-helmeted, charcoal Suneva – whom had entered with Iva and LeGrand – came bravely to the dictator. He swung his mace at Hesslik, blasting a bolt of quatra which missed – only just. Hesslik broadly gleamed beneath his helm. His hot whip flung, and it sheared through the charcoal Suneva's arm.

From the pauldron down, the severed limb flew, red hot on its burning end. The mace shattered like glass, crashing into oblivion. Hesslik held out a pointed foot and kicked the foe back. They stumbled onto the cold earth, shrieking as I did.

Simone clawed herself up, her resolve far beyond her pain. I was almost upon her, having leaped to glide through the sky. I yelled for her to stop, to preserve herself, but it fell on deaf ears. Simone stole the power of the man's shriek to propel herself upon Hesslik. She grabbed his cape as she flew across his back. The shock of being tugged caused the *Fara's* concentration to fault, extinguishing his plasma whip. Hesslik landed on the ground in a pile with Simone.

As he stumbled up, shuffling aside of my sister, two Argol soldiers came from the fray with a large, metal post between them. They threw it horizontally at the standing *Fara*. It collided with his gut, and he grabbed at it to throw away.

The two Suneva then pushed in unison on the magnetic field, and Hesslik was violently flung backwards by the bar, across the muddy, dusty ground. His arms flailed in surprise as his body slammed against the castle wall, right where the lightning had struck.

In the same moment, the last of his guard fell.

"Run!" Iva screamed to her forces, and they dashed for the gates. Iva rushed to Simone's side, where I now knelt. She and I grabbed Simone like a log and jogged for the exit.

Iva Argol had saved me from Hesslik's grasp – like she had done many times already.

Boekidin was right. The Voidwalker would live.

***

We recuperated at the crest of the hill, in the Argol basecamp. Suneva didn't have a large need for medical supplies, as injuries to armour did not often affect the body, but there was enough there to repair Simone. She lay dazed on the ground as Juliette Leroux brought to me bandages and antiseptic. I washed her wounds, and applied the medicine. Simone gasped in the pain of it – she was awake, which was good. Juliette Leroux helped me to wrap the bandage.

"*Cheese*, you were brave," I told Simone as she looked towards me, "and not in the good way. That was stupid. Stupidly good, but still stupid."

"I saved the day," she said, half conscious.

"Yeah, you did," I smiled.

"And you let that slimy *Kidin* into my head." Her memory came back, my face dropped in dread. "James, how will I fight for the Sunesca if they think I hate them?"

"We'll work it out," I said. "For now, lets just try to stay alive."

126

"Yeah, okay," she grumbled. "What a dickhead that guy was. Do none of them care for justice and morality?"

"They're all blinded," I agreed.

Celeste stepped over towards us, coming to stand tall next to me. I rose to meet her. Standing nose to nose, her hot breath once again on mine as our adrenaline pumped, I was reminded of the many times we'd been caught intimately like this just after facing danger. Her lips near my face, I was reminded moreso of the intense lust I felt for her, and the time in America we'd spent hot in eachother's embrace.

I leaned in, and instead of a kiss, we fell into in a long, deep hug.

"You saved us there, Simone," Celeste said over my shoulder. She released me just as quickly as she'd held me, standing back formally.

"You saved us," Simone corrected her. "We couldn't have saved ourselves." Although, something told me that Simone rather didn't like being saved by the *Argols* – especially Tona Argol herself.

"Thank you, Celeste," I said, my blush showing. "Seriously. How did you know I was going to be there?"

"I didn't," she said. "I led my men here on a mission to rescue Natalie, when your execution derailed the plans. What happened to you, anyway?"

"I was also trying to rescue Natalie," I said, "but she found me first."

Celeste hummed, then smiled. "Great, we're on the same page, then. Rescue Natalie, break Hesslik." Her mind was whirring, tactics flying in her skull. "Simone and yourself should join me on the next raid on this place. First, we'll need to find Chad..." I raised my hand in objection, but Celeste ploughed on, oblivious to my concerns. "There have been reports that *Lion's Foot* is back, ransacking Hesslik's bases – so Chad's stopped moaning in the forest and come to his senses. Rumours of his next hit will leak soon. We'll intercept him, and convince him to help us out. Then, with his help, we can come back here and break Natalie out."

Her tirade was met with an awkward silence. My lips stumbled to break it.

"I'm still not sure that I want to work for Argols, Celeste," I admitted, weakly. "Maiki has a reputation, but I don't want to appear to be an Argol colluder, you know? Plus, Simone hasn't got the brightest opinions of the organisation."

Simone blushed, looking away guiltily. It was unlike Simone to drop her stubborn guile.

"Oh," Celeste's cheeks went red. "No, no, this wouldn't be for the Argols. I realised that I can't sacrifice Argol lives to rescue my friends. This is a small insurgence team, independent from my day job. That's why we need Chad."

"That's selfless of you," Simone noted, with a genuine smile.

"I'd be vouching to bring Chad back, anyway. He could have turned the tide out there," I pointed to the concert pitch. Celeste nodded eagerly. "But there's one problem with your plan: We can't simply drag Natalie out of the castle."

"What? Why not?" Celeste asked. "Hesslik's using mind control. Just remove the device, like you did for my sister."

"This isn't basic mind control, this is *cosmic* mind control," I said, spreading my hands over my head for effect. "Amasos is directing her thoughts, Celeste, and Hesslik's too."

"How do you know?"

"Boekidin told me."

"*Boekidin?*" she snorted. "James, he's dead."

"His body is dead, but *he* is *natasvoul*," I said. Celeste stared blankly. "Boekidin trusted us, Celeste. He went into Hesslik's mind to find evidence of what we were saying, and got killed for it. He spent his dead weeks in minds, seeing the effects of destiny. Everybody is being manipulated, but Amasosian Suneva are being led to the demise of threads. Amasos wants the Suneva dead.

"And I went into the Void, too. I removed myself from destiny and saw Natalie's connection to her own destiny. Amasos has her bound. I tried to save her, but ran out of time."

"Hold on." Celeste rubbed the bridge of her nose. "You're working with Boekidin, now?"

"Yes."

"And you trust him?"

"He died trusting us."

"Okay," she sighed, "and you've removed yourself from destiny, too? Doesn't that seem wrong to you? Having a destiny is part of being a Suneva."

"Proving that one could defy destiny was what would bring Natalie home," I argued. "It was the main reason she joined Hesslik, so I had to do it. And it *will* bring her home."

"So, you think you've got a better plan than mine, then?" Celeste asked me.

"Better, but almost the same." I nodded, combining Celeste's ideas with the general plan I'd had lying in my head. "Boekidin and I need time to prepare a rig to fish Natalie out of destiny. In the meantime, we should find Chad and assemble this team you wanted to create. Boekidin and I will remove Natalie from destiny, and then the team can break in to Hesslik's castle and rescue her before Hesslik realises anything has gone wrong. She'll come willingly once removed from the control of Amasos – I know it."

Celeste rubbed her chin. Simone smiled, through her pain.

"I'll gladly join an insurgence team," Simone said. "It sounds like a good plan, as long as we do it under our own name."

"It is a good plan," Celeste agreed. "I can leave the Argols in Michael's hands for a bit longer. But, it will all depend on us getting those *Lion's Foot* leaks…"

As Celeste played with her bold, red lips, deep in thought, a figure walked over behind her, his arm hanging limply from his shoulder. He was young, with a half-shaved haircut, and scruffy clothes. His face was non-chalant, with an attitude to it.

Yvon, Celeste's childhood friend.

He snuck up behind her, a hand to her waist. She turned, initially offended to be touched, but smiled immediately at the sight of him. She wrapped her arms around him, and they nudged noses.

Then they shared a passionate kiss.

It was only three weeks since we shared out last kiss.

My heart sank.

Episode 3

Boekidin's guidebook to love

Chapter 14
Don't Give Love a Chance

White furniture, white walls, black carpet, brown floors. Adam Leroux boiled a chicken soup in his white marble kitchen.

White tiles, outdoor courtyard, where we danced on Christmas Day. But Celeste did not dance with me, she danced with *him*. Yvon.

They lounged on the white sofa opposite me, gathered around the T.V, their arms interlocked, their limbs amok. I seethed through my teeth.

It had been somewhere in the span of twenty days, as it was mid-February now, that Celeste and I had last kissed and snuggled and bonded, yet she had already moved on to the next man.

My face shrivelled at their happy, disgusting sight. I'd observed her and Yvon on the journey here, always one hand deep in embrace. He used a frilly, cutesy name to describe her, and she blushed to it each time. They were abhorrently cute, and it had happened so fast. How did she abandon her feelings for me so quickly? How had she come to so quickly accept the advances of this man, when we'd spent up to a year toeing between the idea of a meaningful kiss at all? I felt betrayed on many levels, even if I didn't have the right to.

I turned to Simone, who was reading next to me, somehow undeterred by the television. The book she held in her hands looked ancient, but it wasn't *that* old, maybe just twenty years or so. Anastasiya had taken Simone back to the Vochduh temple, where she'd left a marker stone, to collect this book from the demon Salak Kallid. He'd written it for our dad, although Dad never returned to the temple to collect it. It was a translated works about the energy transformations of Sunesca – a personal account of the five demons themselves.

Anastasiya walked in to the living room, having just loomed over Mr Leroux as he prepared the food. She had come back to us as we left the mountain range of Hesslik's castle, quoting her fear of being caught by the White Witch and Hesslik as her reasons for not breaking us out. Legendaries seemed to be a funny lot in that way, although it's what I'd come to expect. They hated being around figures of power.

Which made it stranger that she admitted her powers to Celeste Leroux – *Iva Argol* – the empress of a vast Suneva gangland. Despite this, Anastasiya still showed incredible reluctance to let Celeste's father or mother – or any other Argol, really – know of her abilities.

"This feels odd, James," Simone said to me, turning from her book. "In all of my life, I never expected to sit in Argol's house, with him cooking me dinner."

"Did you expect that they'd be two separate events, then – you sitting in his house and him cooking you dinner?" I joked monotonally. Even in a bad mood, I couldn't help but joke. Simone gave a defeated look.

"Yes, funny," she said. "I'm just surprised that he's not such a bad guy. He's a lot like Celeste, actually."

"She's like him, you mean," I said. "And, having your life's joy taken from you probably takes your edge off, you know?"

Simone frowned, staring towards the man. "That's grim."

"At least he doesn't have to die to see his daughter lead. There's his positive," I pointed out.

"I expected backlash from him," Simone admitted. "Me being *Fairysmog*, and all."

"I don't think he knows… and I wouldn't tell him."

"You practically told the whole Suneva world," she grumbled.

"I'm sorry for that, I didn't think it would go that badly."

"You weren't thinking at all," Simone groaned.

"I know," I admitted. "It seemed innocent enough, but I should have considered whether you wanted a guy running through your head."

"You should have."

"Anyway, let's just be thankful the guy didn't have a microphone. *That* would have been a disaster."

Simone nodded, and put her head back into the book. Demon handwriting, I noted from here, was the eloquent writing of a trained royal.

My eyes wandered back to Celeste, who stood, passing Anastasiya to get to the kitchen, and kissing her mother on the way through. Those thick, red lips. Those deep, brown eyes. Trapped in my mind, in my memories.

You should probably talk to her, you know, Boekidin said, ever the voice of reason. *No use sitting on her couch complaining.*

Yeah, but…

No buts, Boekidin said. My attention was turned to Celeste's butt as she walked, and Boekidin slapped his own forehead. *Look, man. You're not going to feel better by sulking. Get her to explain the situation to you, and, even if you don't like her reasoning, it's better than just projecting.*

132

I sighed, because he was right. It just seemed so difficult – from her single move, I didn't know where I stood in her eyes, or whether I had any authority to question her on it. Would she open up to me at all, or pass me off?

You don't know until you just go up there. This is what you're finding out! a voice in my head said, and for once, it seemed like it was my own. I stood from the couch, face determined, and strode over to Celeste. She hung over her father's shoulder, watching him add ingredients to the broth.

"Come to watch, too?" Adam asked me. His face was a jolly melancholy, stuck between enjoying life, and despising his new existence. Somewhere in this house, his thread still hanged.

"Actually, I was wondering if I could have a private word with *you*, Celeste," I said, hand resting on her shoulder. She regarded me, and her snarl was sour. There was guilt in there, but it was caged, and plastered behind a façade.

Adam seemed puzzled. He wouldn't have known – or at least, for the continuation of my soul, I pleaded for his ignorance – that I had been lightly involved with his daughter.

"Please," I asked her. She flicked my hand from her shoulder, as one would swat away a fly.

"My room," she instructed, pushing off from her father's arm. She trudged through the kitchen, then up the stairs before me, commanding, rather than guiding. I followed.

Celeste stormed into her high-ceilinged, white bedroom. The window shades were closed, leaving a blue-grey darkness to settle over everything. The door banged shut behind me, and she drifted over to one of the single beds, leaning against it with crossed arms.

This room was full of memories – of butterflies in stomachs, of an *almost* kiss.

"What is it, James?" she asked, although I could tell that she know *what*. Celeste was smart, she wanted me to play my cards first.

"It's Yvon," I said, and she nodded as if that was the answer she knew was coming. This fuelled my disgust. "It's been what, under three weeks? And you're already deep in each other's arms, using cute names, blushing and holding each other."

"And?" she asked. "I'm happy."

"*And?*" I scoffed, my anger bubbling slowly. "I'm sorry Celeste, I just didn't expect to get left behind so quickly after what we built. Did I mean nothing to you?"

She quizzed my anger, her brow furrowing. "You own me, do you, James?" she scorned.

"No, I…"

"What exactly did we build, hmm?" she asked, drawing closer. I was backed into the dresser by her advance. "I asked if you wanted to be casual. You know, just intimacy for the sake of it, nothing else involved. *Lust.*"

"And that meant nothing to you?" I asked, nervously drawn to a whisper.

"No, that's the point of *casual*, James," she concluded. "That's what you agreed to."

And she was right, it *was* what I had agreed to, I'd even been the one to say that I didn't want to get romantically involved. Seeing her and Yvon together though, it made me forget myself. What about the two of them pissed me off so much? I scrunched my face, thinking of it. Then it came to me.

"You were the one who wanted me, though," I said, pointing the finger, "and it took us *so long* to get anywhere. It took a year of back and forth, misinterpreted flirting to land even a meaningful kiss, and you can throw away that buildup of anticipation and lust in such a short time, that less than three-weeks after the fact you've found a new love?" My question didn't make much sense, and Celeste only raised an eyebrow to it. I huffed. "I mean, you took so long with me, and I thought we might have had something, no matter what we said about it, then it takes less that three weeks with this Yvon guy to fully abandon the idea of us and build a relationship. What gives?"

Finally, I had a well worded question, and Celeste drew on the bed's column for support as she mulled an answer. A satisfied grin formed on my face, I might have won this argument, and I wasn't sure why that was important to me.

"The answer might hurt, James," she said, finally.

"It can't hurt more than what you've already done," I shrugged.

"Oh, it *can*," Celeste warned, her eyes pleading, *begging* me not to ask for the answer.

"Just say it," I grumbled. "I asked because I wanted to know."

Celeste sniffled, and she went to speak, but stopped herself, trying to gather the correct words. I waited with my greasy frown.

"You were *convenient*, James, but I liked Yvon," she said. "He was my childhood crush, I saw him at *Imeres Avoul*, we connected over the week we spent here. We kissed, we did more…" I felt my legs wobbling under me, my hot lungs breathing smoke. I slammed my hand upon the dresser for support, but I barely kept myself standing. "Why did you have to bring it up *here*, of all places." And she gestured to the room, where I was trying to stop myself imagining them in certain acts all over it, but couldn't.

"Holy *shit*," I spluttered.

"Then it was just you and me, and I liked the attention you gave me, James, I always have," she continued digging her own grave, complete with an offshoot for my trampled heart and guts.

"Why did you have to do that to me?" I asked, and tears were now growing heavy in my eyes. "I have a heart, Celeste. I even *pushed* you away, first."

"That made me want you," she burst, and she was now crying too – crocodile tears against her soft skin. "Your rejection made me *need* you, I couldn't stand it."

"It was for your ego?" I growled, my fist balling hard, tapping at my thigh. "I'm a real person Celeste, not a self-esteem boost!"

"I'm sorry!" she burst, now really crying. Her hands covered her face.

Momentarily, I could see the scene in third person – me, tall and angry, towering over a crying, cowered girl at the height of her emotions. I felt a pang of guilt all of a sudden. How had I done this to her?

Then I remembered that she was the one who screwed me over. I might not have initially been justified in my sour-attitude towards her and Yvon, but knowing the truth, I had every right to feel emotionally betrayed. Although, Celeste didn't see herself as being in the wrong here, however concerning that was, and I wasn't in the mood to convince her of it right now.

"*Cheese*," I cussed, calming myself somewhat. "You know what, it doesn't even matter."

"What?" she asked, appearing from her ball of emotion like a scared sunrise.

Goodness, I could see the remorse in those huge, brown eyes. Remorse for having to come clean, no-doubt, but also for playing with my heart.

"I said it doesn't even matter, Celeste." I turned from her, towards the door. "You can't take it back, anyway."

"But I can say sorry," she spluttered. "I'm trying to!"

"That doesn't matter, either," I said. "You didn't know what was going to happen before you started – fine…" I turned to her, meeting her gaze. "But don't you dare do anything like that to this poor boy's heart – if you really like him."

Celeste nodded, her face alight with great, amazed shock. She'd just gotten away with it – her face revealed her sullen glee. Did I just let her get away with it? Did that destroy any lesson to be learned?

"I won't!" she said. "I promise James. I hate that I've put you in pain. I wouldn't want to do that to anybody again."

"Then don't treat love like a self-esteem game," I said, finally. "And *cheese*, don't tell the boy that we were intimate. I know that I won't."

Celeste nodded gravely, slumping onto the bed, exhausted from her emotions.

"I have one last question," I said, and she raised her tired head. "What does this make us?"

"Friends," she said. "Friends like before."

"Fine," I agreed. "I'm okay with that, now that I know where we stand."

A knock came to the door, and we shared a glance. The door opened without response, Yvon tripping into the dimly-lit scene. His eyes were excited, although his spirits soon were crushed by the mood of the room. He lowered his posture to meet it.

"Celeste…" he said.

"Yes?" she asked, her face red from tears. He shot me a daring look of suspicion, and I chose not to be threatened by it.

"There's news about Chad," he said. "Reports say that *Lion's Foot* is heading to New York."

Chapter 15
New York, Old York

The world broke around me. Anastasiya disappeared from sight, her huge, hulking, armoured hand splitting into six images, and rocking past me on all sides.

The tunnel.

Teleporting wasn't instantaneous. We had to travel the distance, even though it was always much shorter than the real distance between the two points. Around me, the world soared in strange images, reflections of itself in every direction, cross sections of flying objects breaking apart, warping, bending over me. With all the flashing lights and pure darkness, the experience was enough to make you throw up.

Celeste and Yvon had flown ahead of us, carrying the onyx stone which would guide Anastasiya to our destination. She sat in the Argol house in Marseille sensing its movements – her hands connected to the vast quatra field.

Quatra is four dimensional, Anastasiya told me. The peace sign pose is the proof of it — three directions of the fingers, yet the bolt of quatra comes out at forty-five degrees to them all. It's orthogonal, apparently. Anastasiya could sense this four-dimensionality, and could use it to track quatra trails this way over vast seas and great lands. Adam Leroux was amazed by her senses, even if he believed her to be a simple witch.

I could see light now at the end of the tunnel. Blackness gave way to an ocean, parting like the red sea in front of me and closing behind my head. Then came a city scape, rushing by in its amazing cross sections. I raced towards the light. I was a train in a tunnel, so close, barrelling towards freedom.

I plummeted from the tunnel's exit.

I had an amazing landing, I should think. In one instance, I was flying, barrelling, with great *momentum*. Now I was still, on my feet when I could have been sure they were behind me, and that I was going to land on my face at high velocity.

I brushed myself down. I was on a street — a busy street. The road was several lanes wide, sidewalks guarded by sprawling oaks.

Cars stood still on the roadway, their colours black and dark, beautiful mattes. Their circular headlights stood on stands from elegant fenders, ahead the sweeping, chrome grilles.

I stood before a building adorned with gold and silver railings, which formed the texture to its curved faces. It was covered in windows which fit snugly in the depressions of its brick, sunset orange exterior.

"Thank you…for your help today. Olomb," a man said to me in a thick, French accent. I stopped gawking at the building to see who had addressed me.

I might as well have been staring at another skyscraper - the man towered over my figure by at least a foot. He was built like a barrel of whisky ready to burst, wearing an old-style, red pinstripe suit. Next to him, his young son held an ice cream and admired the little birds at his feet.

The man took a tin from his jacket pocket, and from it produced a fat cigar. He rammed the trunk of it into his mouth, and clicked his fingers at its end. A burst of yellow flame cracked from his hand, lighting the cigar.

"Thank you, Tanivaer," I said. Tanivaer Argol was a Suneva of questionable conscience, and was just as brash as the rumours would have you believe. His son, Seros Argol, seemed so sweet. I wondered if he would grow to have half the temperament of his barrel-chested father.

"You're a good man, Olomb. And, I might add, I did not know that you had such power." Tanivaer waved his hand at my up-and-down. I looked to myself in a mix of confusion and admiration. "I *can* thank you for your help, but the *people* don't get to. I feel like a Suneva of your status should be doing more for the people! What happened to the great Electric Nation?"

I supressed a smile. Not one of happiness, but one of bother.

"Patience, my friend," I said. "I will make my move when the time is right. Destiny has a hand to play here. You believe in the power of destiny, don't you?"

Tanivaer removed the cigar and nodded his fat head.

"When the cards of destiny fall into place, then the time will be right. The world isn't ready for us yet."

"You say that," he said, twirling his cigar about his gross mouth, "yet here I am. The people *do* need somebody to lead them. You think because Suneva haven't been prominent for centuries that they don't need guidance, but they do, and I'm the proof."

"Well, then, you can hold onto them in the meantime, until the time is right. Then I'll be back to guide."

The man snorted, chuckling and shaking his head. He ashed his cigarette by his side – embers just missing his son's face. "You think you'll win them back?" Tanivaer snorted. "There is no 'mean time' here. If you don't act now, I *will* be the leader of the Suneva world. You can't just take them back after that. They are ready, now."

The truth was, Tanivaer wasn't charismatic in the slightest. I knew that he would not gain followers as quickly as he promised. Unless he planned to coerce them, which I certainly knew he did.

"I'm not worried about Suneva being ready, I'm worried about everybody else," I corrected him. "This kind of operation can't be internally focussed. Leading Suneva into the world requires the cooperation of the world."

The man huffed. "They don't like us. I can already see that."

Because the time is wrong.

"You're wasting your time waiting, *abandoning* everybody. People will never change, but Suneva are out there, waiting to be told who they are, and who they should be!"

I couldn't deny this fact, so I derailed the train of thought.

"Look, they'll come to me. You'll see," I said. It wasn't my strongest argument, but I couldn't accept defeat to Tanivaer Argol.

"I shouldn't take your word with such an immense grain of salt," Tanivaer admitted, reaching for another cigar. "I mean, you're what? Fucking ancient. You've seen many years. You know people."

138

"That I do," I smiled smugly.

"But, please, consider joining me," he said, and I was taken aback. He'd never bought up such a thing – not even today when I confronted him, *giving* him my help without request.

"Look, you're useful, Olomb, and despite what you've done to the people, they trust you. You're a martyr to them. If you join this movement, you'll give it legitimacy, *and* you'll save your soul. You owe it to all Suneva!"

Save my soul? I shook my head, grinning. What an implication.

"I know what I have to do, Tanivaer," I said to him. "This is your movement. I owe it to stick to my plans, *you* owe it to be a leader, if you so feel like it."

His eyes grew frustrated, shaded by an angry brow. Lines formed on his temples.

"Okay, fine," he said, "I cannot convince you." He snuffed out this second cigar, and grabbed his boy by the hand. Seros dropped his ice cream in the shock of being touched. Tanivaer turned towards the skyscraper.

"I wish you hadn't failed us," he said finally, before taking his first step. "I always thought you were a hero."

I smiled. Tanivaer was too impatient – to untrusting – to see that great plans required long planning. I turned from the scene, looking down the street.

I outstretched my hand, as if grabbing for the tree in front of me, but it was much too far away to latch onto. I made a fist.

My arm was knocked by an invisible force. "Watch it, weirdo!" some man called in a heavy Brooklyn voice. He stormed off, a greasy look following me. There were people everywhere now, and certainly no Seros nor Tanivaer. The building was no longer art-deco, but a modern, all glass sensation, rising high into the sky but barely competing with the surrounding towers. Modern cars filled the road ahead of me. I was now in casual clothes, not a mid-thirties suit. My hand was outstretched to a tree-stump.

I am not *Olomb*, I groaned, shuddering in rage. I kicked the tree stump, and realised that I must have looked insane.

Well, you are insane, I realised. Most people did not tackle an invading personality and memory set in their head. I grumbled, stalking towards the lobby.

It was beautiful – a spacious, marble masterpiece, with a grand chandelier of mirrors hanging forcefully from a high roof. Each corner of the lobby sat at an angle not quite right, creating a dizzying effect.

139

In its centre stood Anastasiya with Celeste and Yvon. Before I came within hearing distance, she extended her arm beyond herself and pulled through reality – disappearing into a sphincter in spacetime.

"Everything alright?" Celeste asked me.

"Yes, I'm fine," I grumbled. "Seeing *his* memories, is all."

"Oh…" she understood immediately, and did not question as she led me to the elevator.

I guess this all makes sense then, Boekidin said from inside my head. He sounded deeply satisfied.

What makes sense? I asked.

Well, the second city in your mind, made of neon lines, hanging to the ground like a balloon on a thread. And the way that in the most recent of your memories, the names Kuvalik and Olomb are punctuated by annoyance and shame.

How would you know about my other *memories?* I asked him.

I'm just trying to get to know my host, Boekidin said, his tone implying a wink. *And what's this about a city?* I asked.

Ah, well, the mind is like a city, you see, he said, as if he'd forgotten that nobody else could know such a thing. *But you've got parts of a separate, distinct city just shoved in here. I didn't want to bring it up, in case I freaked you out, but I was left wondering for a fair while.*

Well, there you go, I said.

How the hell did it happen? Boekidin asked me. *I mean, I just saw his bank tip over, and memory orbs fall out of the roof into yours.*

Memory bank? I asked. *What a lame pun. Why would memory storage look like a bank?*

Why not? he asked. *Anyway, you're avoiding the question. How did this happen?*

Kuvalik gave me his thread, I said. *He melded himself with my soul, I think? I honestly don't know* how *it happened, but he did it.*

Boekidin went silent. I waited patiently in the elevator for him to reply. The awkward silence in here didn't seem so bad when he was chatting. I had no idea to which floor Celeste was taking me, either. If she was talking, I wasn't listening.

James, he gave you his thread, Boekidin repeated, stunned. *James, you have his powers. You have to learn them.*

No, I don't, I rebutted quickly. *I'm having enough problems with him taking over my thoughts. Our minds are already melding. I'd do anything to stop the process. I don't think embracing him is the right answer.*

140

But maybe it is… Boekidin suggested.

And even though it sounded stupid, I hadn't thought of that before.

The elevator doors opened, revealing a grand penthouse with a view of the surrounding Manhattan skyline.

And my lord, what a view it was.

I stumbled out of the elevator, perplexed by the immensity of the city through the window. The grand entrance to the penthouse was luxurious – paved in black marble and the finest carpet, walls hung with the most tasteful of artistic masterpieces. The fireplace to the left, made of beautifully carved cobble stones, bubbled and spat with a flame which turned from orange to pink as Celeste stepped towards it. Sprawled on the couch, by the fire, was a man reading a book in his evening wear.

As the fire changed colours, heat intensifying, he shifted. He turned over, abandoning the book and dropping the glasses. He gave an excited, sly smile.

"Tona Argol," he greeted, standing and stretching, "nice to be graced with your presence. I didn't expect to meet you personally this soon in to your rule."

"Celeste is fine," she corrected him, stepping towards his position, "and of course I'd come here soon. New York is one of our most important strongholds. Thank you for letting us stay."

I was blown away by the sheer volume of the man's voice. It perplexed me that anybody with such dominating timbre could find a career in a mob. There's a reason for the tight-lipped stereotype.

Another man emerged from a room beyond the panoramic window and fireplace. He closed the door neatly behind him, shifting his glasses on his lean head. He had in his hand a toolbox. It hung from a strained arm.

"Ah, Tona Argol. *I* was, however, expecting you," this new man announced.

"Yes," she smiled, "I did call ahead."

I sauntered into the room and sat at the bar near the elevator. Our host – the loud man in his eveningwear, lingered over, coming around the bar to rummage at its drinks.

"Tano Merinar Serar," he said, standing and stretching a hand over the bar. I took it, and shook.

"Tano Maiki Leukess," I greeted back. "Thank you for having us. What a place you've got." I gestured to the surroundings.

"It's modest." He nodded. "Now, what would you like to drink?"

Something to drink? Well, it would drown the lingering disappointment of Celeste abandoning me for the guy she told me not to worry about. That, and failing Natalie.

"I'll just have your favourite drink, sir," I said. He smiled wryly.

"You're a smart man, Tano Leukess," he grinned, and leaned under the counter to pull out an array of metal mixers and glass bottles.

"Now, just take a seat here, and get out your armour," the lean man with the glasses said to Yvon. He had Yvon sit at the dining table, upon which he splayed his collection of tools and parts.

Yvon let his armour consume him, with its flat face, bulky definition and charcoal finish. His arm was missing, as Hesslik had sheared it through with a rope of red plasma.

The lean man inspected the wound hidden by the pauldron, and nodded. He pulled out a plate and piece of metal tube from a pile, which it looked like he'd prepared earlier, and started to smooth metal pieces together like clay.

"Riskidin is your name, right?" he asked the armoured version of Yvon. His voice was majestic, ringing as the smooth American spoken by cowboys in the black-and-white westerns – a relic of an American accent.

Yvon – or, Riskidin – nodded. The Argol man then extended his hand for Yvon to shake. "Henry, or *Sarastelek*. I've been Naxaer Argol's armourer for a long time. You're in good hands."

"So, how soon will this all function again?" Celeste asked Henry. He held a square tube, melding its base onto a circular plate. He, with some form of grace, rammed his finger through the centre of the plate, and pulled through it a tube.

"It depends. Recoveries differ," he said. "The soul has to regrow over the metal. That takes meditation."

"What kind of meditation?" Riskidin asked. "The kind when I let my soul wander?"

"No, no, not like that," the armourer dismissed, melding a joint onto the lattice which created the forearm. "It's the meditation needed to heal a wound. Just like healing, it takes a lot of time."

Henry continued to work. The hose seemed important, as he made certain to weave it between the structures, yet didn't allow it to be crimped in the metal braces. On the arm were actuators, which connected to the hose through junctions. The hose continued down to the end of the arm, and was pulled through the final plate at the wrist. Henry set the whole arm aside, and searched through a small box on the table. Metal rattled on metal.

"Interesting, huh?" Tano Merinar quipped. He slid the finished creation across the bar to my hand. The drink was a deep blue, in a short glass.

"Yeah, very interesting," I said. "I wonder how he learned it."

"It's as old as Suneva cutting eachother's arms off," Merinar said, "and that's pretty old. The tech only gets better, though."

I inspected the drink in my hand. There didn't look to be anything too exciting about it. I wafted the scent towards my nose.

It smelled of pure petrol.

"Heavy drink of the Croatian Suneva," he grinned. "Go on, give it a sip."

Reluctantly, I raised the blue concoction to my lips. It passed into my mouth, then down my throat. It was smooth – pleasant, even. There was a slight burn, but nothing to what the smell or ethnic origin indicated. I smiled dumbly.

"Good, right?" Merinar chuffed. "Always fools the first-timers."

"Yes, it is good. Thank you," I said. He stepped off the bar, and I took the opportunity to join the conversation around the amputee.

Carbon, I immediately sensed as I drew closer. Not in the metal, which Henry was masterfully controlling, but in the tube. It was a form of carbon that I had never weaved, an advanced composite of some kind. I pulled up a seat nearby, and watched the armourer work.

Riskidin's shoulder looked ghastly. The pauldron remained in tact, but just below it the arm was severed. Inside the cross section of his arm, cauterised by the hot plasma, was no flesh or bone. The organic tissue was made of quatra, I could only assume, like the armour plating itself.

Whilst the plating was black-dusted charcoal, the inside appeared as a deep violet, writhing mass, like vines or snakes grasping and slithering. It was disgusting. They seemed to hold the plate to the body, but must also have acted as the muscles. I was repulsed.

The armourer finally found what he was looking for, and held it high with a relieved sigh. It was a hand, moulded of metal and full of pipework. It didn't appear to have any actuators for articulation. The fingers must have moved by other forces.

Henry screwed the hand onto a joint protruding from the wrist-plate – which also appeared to have no mechanical means for articulation – and tugged the hose taught. He held it to the severed quatra pipeline in Riskidin's writhing, violet shoulder.

"This is the hard part," Henry said, closing one eye. "You've got to bond the pipe just right, or else the soul won't take to it. It's harder with these new

143

grapheme ones – an advancement from Anderson's leaks. But, this material is better for aiding flow…"

He attempted to butt the two ends together. The carbon hose would fit to the inside – although, to me, that seemed counter-intuitive. Quatra would flow against the seam, pushing the prosthetic away, right?

"I can help," I said, leaning in. Henry gave me a bemused look.

"You know about this craft?" he asked.

"No, but I'm a *Maikess*," I said. "I can control the grapheme."

"Ah, okay. I will be able to do it though, it just takes time."

"I know," I said, "it just seems that it would make more sense to have the joining pipe on the outside of the old one, right?"

"It would," Henry said, an annoyed tone taking his voice, "but you'll displace the muscles by doing that, and we want them to grip on."

"So, I can *meld* the carbon tube into the natural tube. There'll be no flow interruption."

Henry hummed, rubbing his chin. Riskidin seemed suddenly anxious, having his arm's fate fall out of the expert's hands.

"Give it a go," Henry said, smirking. "I'd like to see if this works." And he shifted away, leaving the open gash facing me. Riskidin's eyes peaked with fright.

This job was easy. It was hard to make forms of carbon, but not too difficult for me now to meld them whilst holding their connections. I let the atoms work their way over the quatra casing, gluing the whole thing together on the micro scale. I stepped back, and marvelled my work.

The armourer tugged on the pipe, and almost pulled Riskidin off his chair. Satisfied, he gave me a nod.

"Good work, kid," he said. "You ever want to give me a hand again, you let me know."

"Thanks," I nodded. "It's nice to be a help."

"Thank you, James," Riskidin said to me. He tried to lift his arm, but it hung limply off the moving shoulder. He frowned.

"Time," Henry reminded him. "The soul has to grow over it before it will ever work."

The armour of Riskidin separated, running off the skin and back into Yvon's thread. The new arm seemed to simply disappear – phasing out of existence as his actual arm took its place. That arm hung limp, and it reminded me of my own limitations. I'd spent so long in the Void, that I'd forgotten my arm even hurt.

I tested it, pushing it down to lift myself from the seat, and was met with familiar bursts of pain. I wasn't better yet, but it no longer pained me constantly.

I strolled back over to the bar to fetch my drink. Tano Merinar had made his way around me to the table where Celeste was seated. I took another swig of the drink. This would put me out of action quickly.

"Any ideas on how to find Chad, James?" Celeste asked from across the room. I turned on a dime and made my way back, this time, drink in hand. Merinar had fixed up a blue concoction for himself, and we shared a smug glance.

"Well, couldn't you just sense him here?" I asked. "I mean, Boekidin could track us, and Natalie could sense his team. Chad can't be harder to find than Legendaries, anyway."

"He might be harder to find given your lack of destiny," Celeste remarked.

I had briefly considered this truth whilst hanging next to Boekidin on a void-cliff, hauling Natalie by the wrists, that a lack of destiny meant everything was up to *me* now. No helping hands would come along. I hadn't, however, considered that this would affect the mundane things I'd taken for granted, such as the small compulsions I'd relied upon for well over a year. In finding Chad, I would have no guidance – either physically or mentally. A good plan was on my own merit.

"And no, we can't just track him," Celeste continued. "That was something only Fisira and Zamelle could do – the two candidates for *White Witch*."

"Oh…" I hummed, frowning. This truth I *hadn't* considered. "I could try something in the Void, if we have no ideas," I suggested. "Maybe I can get Boekidin into Chad's head, and we can tell him to meet us."

"I'd rather not be putting Boekidin in people's heads," Celeste said. "We can use that as a last resort."

"Fine," I agreed, "but we'll have to get back in the Void anyway. Boekidin and I have to make preparations for saving Natalie. It's not an easy job."

"Sure," she waved her hand, "whatever you need to do. Are you sure, though, that you don't have any other ideas."

I've got one, Boekidin said.

"What is it?" I asked aloud. Everybody looked to me, and my cheeks flushed red.

Nice one, he commented. *Looking through your memories, it seems that Stacy told you she studies Law at NYU.*

Really? I asked. *Gee, that sounds exclusive.*

I've got no comment on that, Boekidin said, *but she's probably in the city, and it's likely that Chad would be visiting her, right?*

145

Sounds good to me, I thought.

"Stacy studies at NYU," I said, finally, to the gazes which were upon me. "We could find Chad visiting her there."

"It's a thin chance," Celeste said, "but it's good. Once everybody is finally here, we'll try it out."

Chapter 16
River's Convergence

I woke in the Void, covered in black dust atop a rocky ridge of a cliff face. As I rose, the three apostles of the Amasosian bay came into view. They stood tall, like grand sentries guarding the sea.

Under the dull grey sky, beneath the tumultuous waves, Natalie's body waded, inundated. I could see the plumes of white and orange smoke pooling around her as she drifted towards the impressive rocks. She was trapped by the God who had purchase on this water and all life in it. I *would* save her. I'd made that resolve.

My body ached to throw itself headlong back into that sea and save Natalie with brute strength. Waiting was a waste of time – even if it was my own plan. I needed to help her. She couldn't help herself.

Boekidin's claw rested on my shoulder. I jerked in surprise.

"We'll get her," he said, "we just need to be prepared."

"What should we do, then?" I asked. "A rope, probably, and a safety line, too?"

"I've got some ideas," he said, "although the alarming weakness of the rock will make them hard to achieve." He kicked at a hexagonal column of black rock. A small stone broke apart at his toe – the kick hurting his foot more than anything. Boekidin yelped in surprise.

"My dad left me a note by the Guardian's temple," I told Boekidin. "It said in it that there are more temples in the Void. They had to have been built by Suneva, right?"

"The Guardian told us that the dead built them, remember?" Boekidin quizzed.

"I don't buy it," I said. "The demons in Vochduh city said that Suneva have come here before. They *had* to have tried to get others out of the seas, and they *had* to have left their ideas and inventions somewhere."

"You think they left them in these temples?" Boekidin asked. "That might be true, *if* anybody truly has been here before you. Why would temple-builders be associated with rescuers, anyway?"

"Fine, fine," I huffed a void response, "but *somebody* built the temples, dead or alive, and they wouldn't have done it for no good reason – they would have had *some* story to tell. I think these sites are worth investigating."

"I think you're right on that," Boekidin noted. "Let's hope they left some mechanisms for me to work with, whilst they were at it." He rubbed his beak, then turned to walk due westward, towards the Omercronian sea we had come from. It took me a moment to tear myself from the image of Natalie, wrapped under the eyes of the apostles. Eventually, I pulled away, and scampered to catch up.

We walked together, back over the rock and across the grasslands which bordered the thick forest. Eventually, we climbed over the jaggered earth which capped the Omercronian cove, and stepped down off the plateau, into the vegetative dunes.

We sifted past the temple and the guardian who rested at its crest, then rounded the corner into the under-brush trail. I was able to lead Boekidin back to the stone slab written by my father. I handed it to him.

"For *Simone?*" he asked, furrowing his beady eyes.

"Yeah…" I blushed, "long story."

"Do I have permission to look for it in your head?"

"It's not *that* juicy of a story," I said. "I have Simone's thread, is all. I thought you'd have known that."

"Never saw that in your memories," he scratched his head.

"This path only goes one way," I said, moving on. "Should we just follow it, and see if there's a temple at the end?"

"Seems a little…misguided to me," Boekidin hummed, staring to the sky. "The first temple could be anywhere in the whole Void."

"Well, the tablet alludes to *many* temples, and it was left here – potentially a sign," I noted.

"Potentially," Boekidin said, then sighed. "I guess we have the time to wander. Anyway, you could be right, and we'll never know unless we walk the path."

"That's the spirit," I patted him on the shoulder. "Build a case on loose clues and follow the thread. Let's see where it takes us."

He smiled at me, rolling his pink eyes and chuckling. I left the slab where I'd found it, and led Boekidin on the sand track in the gulley of the dunes.

A lifeless area of wild vegetation was an oddity. The thickness of the dune scrub, and the types of plants which clawed their way up its lose soils, reminded me of the ocean beaches back home. Walking those tracks would lead you to birds, and lizards, and possums, and spiders. Here, though, there was nothing, and the silence between Boekidin and I led me into a hypnotic state, letting my mind wander.

"I'm still pissed off at Celeste," I said, finally. The sand underfoot had now given way to gravel, crunching under my footfall. "I just don't get how she could string me along when she had feelings for somebody else. I know she didn't really owe me anything, but still..." and I trudged at the gravel, kicking up dust with an annoyed foot. "She owed *Yvon* something, at least."

Boekidin sighed a laugh, tutting from behind his helmet. "Ah, James, you got caught up in a tricky romance. The two of you were never *really* into each other, anyway. It was just lust – that much is obvious from the memories."

"You *saw* those?"

"But it was simple attraction. It's a shame that she acted on it when her head was somewhere else."

"I know it was just lust," I admitted, more annoyed by the fact that the situation still had a hold over me, rather than the situation itself. I just wanted to be over it, but the emotional manipulation bit hard. "It still hurts to be treated that way, though."

Boekidin hummed, his metallic hand falling on my shoulder. "Head up, kiddo," he said, and although he wasn't intending to sound condescending, that's certainly how it felt. "Don't beat yourself up for getting caught in a sticky romance, either. Although, did you expect any different from Celeste, after how much the two of you had been stringing each other along for a year?"

"I expected a year of stringing along to have *some* emotional impact on her..."

"But you told Celeste yourself that you didn't even want *her*, that you just wanted the physical side of things."

"I did."

"Then what did you expect, that she'd dig her claws into a fiery romance after you?" he hummed, and I slumped in my step, unsure of wat to say. "I say it's better to be burned now than from anything more serious, right? You need to think about how you want to be treated, and what you actually want in a romantic partner, if you're still seeking it. I can guarantee you that your ideal woman isn't the cute girl claiming to be an international fugitive, who happens to rock up to your friend's movie night."

I laughed, kicking at the dust. The whole situation was ridiculous, wasn't it?

"And look," Boekidin continued dishing advice to fill the silence, "I think what's really at the heart of your hurt is that Celeste always had it her way. She kissed *you* every time it happened, she made the rules for your brief fling, regardless of the input you had. She crafted the relationship her way, and was knowingly doing wrong."

"How did you hit that nail so squarely on the head?" I asked, chuckling to the bird's psycho-analysis. He ignored my question, ranting on, through the valley of the dunes.

"What you should look for is somebody who truly respects you. Somebody who you rely on, and who you care deeply for, no matter what your dick thinks. There's somebody out there who would walk across the hot sands of the desert for you, and for whom you would do the same, just for their happiness. You might not find them soon, or you will. I, personally, am losing hope for my own love." He had a nervous chuckle with himself, then steeled. "Not having a body kind of ruins that now, but there are plenty of minds to see, and clearly I can still change the world."

"That's rough, buddy," I nodded, suddenly thankful for my living state. "But your advice is solid. How do you know so much?"

"You forget that I'm living inside your mind, James," Boekidin turned his head towards the sky. "It's not boring in there with all of your experiences to live through."

"Right..." I cringed. "Well, I can't complain with the end product...I guess. Thanks for the help."

"It's what *Kidin* do," he smiled, patting my back. "We know people better than they know themselves – at least, this is the role of the Shiverman."

***

149

I spotted it from a while away, as we crested a large dune. A glint of sunshine reflected into my eyes, beaming off a brilliant white surface. Marble, standing in the distance, past a maze of valleys.

We emerged shortly after from the sandy knolls and scrub, into the desert proper. The vegetation had been slowly dying, leaving nothing but vines which tangled over the sandy hills and held them down, like netting to the earth.

We had found a temple, here on the border of beach dunes and desert, and it was very unlike the other.

Its architecture was almost Florentine – a grand, columned entrance under a peaked awning, leading to a rectangular room of stone, roofed with a giant dome.

The structure was beautiful, but sculpted of bland, sand-coloured stone. It would have blended into the desert which it bordered, were it not for the silver details adorning the carving on its entrance peak. They shimmered in the light of the bright moon above, calling to travellers.

Past the desert, I noticed, was a grand mountain range. The peaks were much higher than those we'd witnessed by the Amasosian cliffs to the east, but might have been connected to the same range.

"What a temple," Boekidin said. "Somebody had an appreciation for fine architecture."

"Well, maybe not just an appreciation," I said. "This building might have been *modern* to the Suneva who built it."

Boekidin nodded, rubbing his beak.

We climbed the entrance steps, onto the stone plateau which spawned columns like a forest of marble. They stretched high – higher than they looked from the distance. In fact, as I looked to the roof, I saw that the columns rose forever, slowly converging. The peaked awning of this place was the sky. There was no more void, or temple, only a thick jungle of marble. Racing towards the evermore.

"We're not getting anywhere soon if this place keeps throwing us curveballs," I laughed, but there was no response. I glanced around, then did a full sweep. Boekidin was not in sight.

Then I saw a light – shaped like a cut doorway. The entrance, surely. I ran towards it.

Boekidin and I converged, stumbling into the door at the same time from opposite directions. We fell off each other, crashing down to the stone floor inside the entrance and almost sliding off the ledge within.

The inside of the temple was cylindrical, with a large domed roof and skylight. We lay on an annulus platform, which ran the perimeter and separated the basement level from the ground level.

It was an exact replica of the *Vochduh* library, complete with books.

My mouth hung agape. Boekidin had to pull me up, as my body refused to move in my excitement.

"Hey, this is your library, isn't it?" he asked.

"Yes!" I exclaimed. "My god…it's…how?" I ran off like a madman, caressing the tomes which occupied its many layers. They weren't how I remembered them – their spines were blank – and my heart sank quickly. I halted my jovial, madman skipping about the circular deck, and stopped by one of the blank, nameless books. I grabbed it off the shelf.

The spine name appeared as I held it in my hand. It coalesced from nothing, forming a name in English. *Biography of King Deoshan*.

Although, strangely, I was astutely aware that no such thing had happened. The words weren't in English, really. There weren't even words. As I flicked the book open, a similar phenomenon occurred. Words formed, and I read them, and whilst they read like words, and the experience was the same as reading words which I understood, I had the acute realisation that I wasn't reading.

Somehow, these books were holding *meaning*, rather than words.

"Boekidin, this is incredible," I said, my glee returning. "A whole library, and I can read it all!"

Although, when was the last time I'd actually read a book? Reading wasn't generally my thing, was it?

"Who do you think put this all here?" he asked, admiring a tome. He picked it up, and too, was blown away by its ability to give itself meaning.

"The monks, obviously," I said, remembering the blue and green robed men from my vision – not unlike the Guardian. "The demons said that some of them did beat destiny – but it was hundreds of years ago."

"They've made books out of pure connection, it seems," Boekidin said. "Either that, or *everything* is this realm is an interpretation, even *man-made* things."

"Well, you'd have to wonder what it is that they've really *made*, you know?" I said, palming a few more volumes. Now that I'd experienced my first connection to a book, I felt that I could gauge my interest to tomes by sight alone. I wondered what it was that my soul thought I was interested in? I grabbed a few, just to be safe.

I descended the ladder, tossing the books to the ground below, and gathered them by the lectern. I started to read.

***

I found quickly that reading ancient texts could be boring, and time consuming.

Save for the fact that I just had to look at a page to understand its meaning, the concepts were, at times, difficult to comprehend, and removed from my world entirely. These men wrote from a perspective now hundreds of years lost, before even Olomb brought them the war which would cause the downturn of Suneva Empires as a power in the world. Their social constructs were beyond my understanding, their ideals alien to our own.

But we had one thing in common – a way of thinking which purveyed time and class – our understanding of ethics and morality.

Sure, I'd learned Suneva ethics from Kuvalik, and maybe some of my thinking came from his mind fusing to mine – but these scholars understood honour, and what was right and *just*. I expected a society of hypocritical, war-mongering enslavers, riding their high-horse about their ethics and scholarship, to be totally unrelatable, but they were not. These scholars had a deep understanding of the way things should be, and how people should be treated. The warrior clans of the Vochduh Kingdom were a necessity, or so the king said, but not something which the scholars enjoyed.

In fact, more often it was the captured and integrated Suneva who fought on the battlefronts through their own volunteering, protecting the Kingdom and its cities from invasions.

The articles I was drawn to spoke highly of Sunesca – although the time for using this information was long past, as I was already in the Void. I managed to find the piece written about Salak Nolver, a review on his ability to draw enough energy to make plasma arcs, and his inability to hit a target with them whilst blindfolded. This, to the scientists, was a great test of free will.

I, however, couldn't find anything on plucking Suneva from the void-seas of gods. This was puzzling.

Boekidin, on the other hand, sat outside the temple, amongst the retreating vegetation of the dunes, taking the hands-on approach to preparations. He was scavenging vines which grew here naturally and twisting them into thick strong twine. This, he coated in a paste of mystery quatra substance to give it bulk.

I joined him when I became bored and defeated, with a piece of text in hand which I wanted to show him.

"What'ya doing?" I asked him, stepping forth from the temple. He regarded me, then continued to stick his head down, braiding.

"Making my own preparations," he said. "To get Zamelle out of that bay, whether or not anybody reports doing this, we're going to need a crane, and a ladder." He held his twine up to me, gesturing for me to inspect it. I held it in my hands.

It was thick, and felt sturdy enough, but I couldn't be sure. I didn't have a good intuition for things like this – except when I made them from diamond.

"I'm an engineer by day, you know." Boekidin smiled. I sat down next to him, ass to the grainy sand, and watched him continue. He had three long vines between his fingers.

"I didn't know that," I said.

"Ah, yes…" he blinked. "You don't go in my head... well, I'm a mechanical engineer, although the job has lost its art."

"How so?" I asked. I was curious – Boekidin was a Suneva, second-hand man to an Empire, and he had a day job? How did he fit that in? Meanwhile, I couldn't possibly tell him what real-world job I wanted. I was so removed from that now. It hadn't crossed my mind in a while.

"Engineering used to be hands-on, like this," he said, starting his story. "Back when it became a field, and men melted iron and made tools, and built huge machines which they knew every part of. It was crude, but the beasts they made were *alive*. Things breathed, and parts moved and buzzed. Hell, if you looked at a plane from the first world war, it looks like goblin technology with the sheer number of ingenious cranks and shafts they had to use for transferring power and system response.

"Now we've lost that magic," Boekidin grumbled, braiding faster as emotions ranted. "Computers have taken over control systems, you see. And men now sit in offices designing parts on screens, instead of by hand, or by the lathe, or the drill, or the smeltery. We're not connected to what we make anymore. I design parts, but I don't make them, or assemble them, I just tell others how to do it. The machines aren't my own, anymore.

"I wish…" he said, looking to the sky. The vine section he was working on ran out, so he tied more in, with a knot I'd never seen before. "I wish that I was born back in the days of iron, fire and steam, James. I've been into old bastards'

153

minds. I've seen the end of it. How glorious it would be to be a man who *really* worked with machines."

Boekidin smiled at me, expecting an input, although I really had nothing to say.

"I didn't know there was this side to you, Boekidin," I said. "That's amazing."

"Not many Suneva do," he said, continuing with his work. "Most just see a *Kidin* with a mean face. A bird, not a man. They refuse to know me. I appreciate that you're so trusting, James," he said. "I'm glad that I went into your head in Hesslik's castle – I was considering not doing it, that you mightn't have believed my story."

He smiled, and it was genuine and wide, almost coming out the sides of his beady, evil helmet. I felt sorry for him – his soul's projection of itself, his armour, was so uninviting. But beneath it, he held a smile like a princess.

"Hey, man. I'm glad you're here, too," I said. "I need more insight in my life. It helps having you around, and I'm liking the company up here." I gestured to the great expanse, out to the mountains distant. "And clearly, I need an engineer, too. What is your plan?"

"Ah, well." His pink eyes beamed – probably the only vibrant colour in this whole realm. "I'll make a hand-cranked crane, and a harness to be attached to its hook, plus a ladder, a blunt knife, and a better board. My plan is that you climb the ladder with the board, with the harness on, and ride the waves out to Natalie. If you get into trouble, I'll reel you back in.

"Then, you get to her, and put the second harness on her, which you attach to the board's tow bar. You swim her back, and attach her to the crane. This is the dangerous part for you, but you'll need to stay on the board, and cut that weird membrane off her as I lift. Then, I'll keep her in the air, and get as much lifting done as I can as you climb the ladder, but once you're at the top, you can help me out."

"Gee man…" I said, imagining the scope of it. "That's a well-designed plan, but how long will it take you to make?"

"Not long," he said. "I've already got the frame of the crane, the spool, and the mount." He gestured to my left with his wing. On the dune stood a trestle crane, made of harvested wood, solidified and bound with quatra. "All I need is more rope to make the ladder, the harnesses, and the *rope*, funnily enough. We can reuse that initial board for the meantime."

"Wow," I uttered. "That's fast work."

"Hey, what's that tablet?" he asked, palming the slab of stone which I'd brought out with me to show him. I let him take it from my hands. It was made of the same stone as the one my dad had left for me, but written in a different hand.

Although, the writing wasn't the purpose of this tablet. It was, rather, a map. A map of the Void.

The land was vaguely rectangular, surrounded by four seas with many coves, beaches, and outcroppings on each face. The map marked the spots of temples – of which there appeared to be six, each represented stylistically at their points – and depicted four rivers, one flowing to each sea. They appeared to originate at a single point, somewhere in the mountain range which I could see past the desert.

"Temples?" Boekidin asked me.

"I think so," I said, pointing to the tablet. "There are two markings, here and here, which are the two we've seen so far. I could only assume, anyway."

"And what about this?" he asked, pointing to the rivers' origin. "We haven't seen any rivers here."

"We haven't crossed them, yet," I pointed out, tracing our path to the Amasosian cliffs across the stone map. "The only ones around here are further west and further north than we travelled."

"That convergence point seems significant, anyway," Boekidin scratched his metal head. "Do you want to try and find it."

I grinned at him. "We've got time, and I like the meditative aura of this place. Think you can twine rope on the way?"

"I can try," Boekidin suggested. He put aside the pieces of mechanisms he'd already constructed and scavenged for long strands of vine. He wrapped them around his shoulder, and we set off, leaving the map in the sand.

***

I walked ahead, the vines around my shoulder like a spool. Boekidin trailed, pulling the strands back to twist them into twine. Lagging behind him was a train of set rope, dragging along the ground.

We walked north east to find the river, across the vast sea of sand. The desert was neither hot, nor exhausting, as I had expected. Here, in the Void, everything was as dull as the greyed-out landscape, including bodily feelings. The sun – which, rather, was a moon, and also didn't exist – did not beat down hot, and the winds did not draw a chill. Only pure neutrality could be experienced here.

The river bisected the sands cleanly. A short beach, patched with low shrubs, formed the banks. The flow of water was slow, and the stream not much wider than a creek. Despite its narrowness, it appeared deep. And, curiously, it flowed inland, toward the mountains.

"The seas feed the origin?" I asked as we inspected the flow. "That's unexpected."

"Clearly, then, it's not an origin," Boekidin stroked his beak.

"But, why wouldn't streams run off from the mountains?"

"Why would they?" he asked. "It doesn't look like it would rain here."

"Huh…" I quizzed, looking up to the sky. It was constantly grey, but never had it once drizzled on me. "Maybe there's a stranger significance to this central place, then, than I thought."

Boekidin nodded. We picked up the twine, and started to walk along the banks, following the stream's flowing.

Desert sands gave way to pebbles, and rock to boulders. The land became a barren waste of smooth stone, hard and unforgiving. The stream carved it – the knife of time – setting a canyon in the brown-orange earth. Ridges of stone tracked down the slowly-forming cliff sides, as mountains rose from the dry, flat rockscape to loom over the river banks. Strata, layers of colour in the earth, danced and swayed down the rockface – all headed towards the stream's end. To the centre.

Boekidin and I tracked along the canyon's edge, along the hard and unforgiving ground. Below us, the stream cut further into the Void's mantle. Boulders – protected from winds and erosion by the ever-growing mountains – blocked our path, and several times we had to navigate our way dangerously around ridges and crevasses.

One mountain conquered the sky above all others. Its peak could have been seen from the lowest valley in the barren range. The river carved towards it, bisecting mountains and leaving tall cliff faces to line the scar in the Void it created. In passing one such mountain, who's peak had been cut and toppled, Boekidin and I had to scale down into its canyon to pass. Boekidin crafted me claws to hold on, but the journey was dangerous still. A ledge of stone, no wider than a foot, and more brittle than salt, was all to support us. It withered under our feet, turning to powder with too much weight. I hung onto the claws through my grip, although that was fading fast, and we couldn't have reached the other side soon enough. I slumped onto the grey rock.

"I don't think it can be long now," I huffed, pointing downstream. "We're at a clear line of sight to that mountain."

"And to think you came in here just to get some ideas," Boekidin said. "They've probably found Chad out there by now."

The land came rugged towards its centre. The stone of the ground burned red and orange, with black marks streaking across mountain faces. As we clambered close to the singular peak, canyon stream in sight below, we found that there was no single highest peak. Instead, three other high peaks appeared, behind the body of the fat, bulging mountain we'd been following.

And behind those peaks, in the far sky, were revealed three more moons which hung above the thin clouds. Four moons in total, each casting light onto the land, each observing their own quadrant of this place.

Near the base of the mountain, the canyon started to roof over. It bored under the stone monolith, leaving it to stand proud and undivided over the whole realm. Boekidin and I scratched our heads. Other mountains had toppled to the stream, but this one stood.

"I'm not going in there," Boekidin said, pointing to the building darkness. "Even if we lose the trail, there's no telling how tight that tunnel gets."

"You don't need to convince me," I agreed. "Maybe it'll emerge again back over the mountain."

"Why would it do that?" he asked.

"Why would it tunnel? That doesn't make sense, either," I pointed out, and he frowned. "Things don't need to make sense, here. Rivers don't flow inland from seas."

"Except tidal rivers."

"Sure," I said, and hauled a completed section of vine-rope over my shoulder. "Just follow me."

I examined the tunnel, plotting its trajectory in the map of my mind by the assumption that it flowed true and straight – which it hadn't done properly it's whole course, but I could only hope.

I trekked around, over the roof of the canyon, to follow the base of the mountain. It was incredibly tall, and rugged. Scaling it was not an option, so we stuck to the valley, running the circumference of its base just before its lowest point. It was obvious, from the lack of erosion and pathways down the slope, that no water flowed from these hills. It did not rain in the Void. This concept seemed easier to accept than the alternative – that it did rain, and the rain represented something.

"What do you think these rivers *represent?*" I asked Boekidin as we circled the valley, finally meeting the foot of the second great peak.

"Who knows," he mulled. "Some destiny or control, surely – knowing this place."

As we rounded the valley, we came to see that it converged with four other valleys, meeting at a central point between the four, huge mountains. Visible next to each other now, we could see that each mountain was built from a different hue of orange stone, with unique and vibrant strata layers marking their faces. The tallest mountain appeared to be the one in the west, the one which shared the valley we'd been walking around.

We walked towards the central point of the mountain range, under the short shadows of the looming stone giants. At the convergence of the valleys, in which no water seemed to have ever flowed, was a break in the rocks. The gap formed a dark cavern, with mysterious tangles of light dancing around its lip. Boekidin and I edged over to the cavernous drop. Light beamed into my eyes, blinding me momentarily. I held my hand up to my face, then, nervously, peaked through.

The light shifted and swirled, twirling along the walls and roof of the rocky cave. It was light reflected off the surface of rippling water, far down below. I dropped to my knees, crawling to the edge and peering into the abyss.

An underground lake.

"Damn," I said. I lounged over the edge and tried to dip my head in to see past the rock floor. There was a short column till the cavern proper, and my neck was by no degree long enough to give me a better look down there.

"Must be where the rivers meet," Boekidin said. "Although we couldn't know without going down."

"I wonder why, though," I said. "There's got to be something important in there."

"There must be," Boekidin agreed. "Something important enough to draw the seas to it and carve through the landscape of stone. Perhaps it's better left *without* us disrupting it."

"I still think we should investigate," I said, eagerly. "Just no touching."

I noted that I held the correct tool for the job – a rope. Grinning, I looked for something to hitch it to. The rocky ground had many sharp protrusions and loose boulders, but none appeared to be a great anchor. I paced around the gash in the void-earth, inspecting its banks.

"There," I said, squatting low by a large protrusion. It stood slimmer at the base, tapering to a bulb. I flung the end of my vine-rope about it.

"You know any good knots?" I asked over my shoulder. Boekidin stalked by slowly, careful not to slip on the cavern's lip and fall. He squatted next to me, taking the rope from my hands.

"You want to lower yourself down?" he asked. "That seems dangerous to me."

"It will be fine," I said. "I'm good at climbing ropes."

"Really?" he asked, turning from his knot to gesture condescendingly to my physique. My offence caused me to flinch back.

"You think I'm weak?" I asked, aghast.

"Man, I was bigger than you at twelve," he said, eyes back to the rope.

"Well, you could properly condescend me if you had your regular body here," I teased. "Right now, you're a thin-jointed bird guy."

He grunted, making a final pull at the rope. Satisfied, he found the other end, and threw it around my waist.

"I'm tying you to the other end of this," he said, "just in case your puny arms give out."

"Alright, mate," I joked along.

"No, I'm serious," he said, his pink, beady eyes glowing. "I'll stand up here and hold onto the other end. We can't take chances for this impulsive adventure."

"Okay, you're right," I admitted, and I let him tie the twine around my waist. The rope was smooth, and didn't irritate me like the vine could. With a hard tug to either side, he'd secured me to it.

"Now, take your time, and don't get too cocky," Boekidin added. I nodded my head, and crawled towards the gash. Holding dearly onto the rope, I lowered myself backwards over its edge. I stood, my body horizontal to the waters below, and shuffled my way backwards down the rocky wall of the irregular column. As my feet moved, I let my hands slip over the coil of rope. Boekidin stood above, vine clutched in both hands, watching dreadfully.

The column soon gave way, setting back to the walls of the cavern, and allowing the darkness to take it. I let myself hang from my hands, and gradually lowered myself as I found the strength.

The cavern glowed a deep, aqua blue. The walls and roof were painted in yellow, dancing reflections of the moons' rays off the surface waves, trickling across the rock structures. The cave was serene, deeply peaceful, calming. I felt that if I let go, I'd be in no danger.

This place was deeply familiar.

Although, it was not that *I* had seen it before. Somehow, something that *I* had not seen was sitting in my memories. How was this? The cave *was* homely. Perhaps I was just tricked by its inviting aura. Still, I *knew* this place.

I craned my head down, peering between my knees to see the water below. It shone brilliantly under my shadow in the clearest of crystal blues. I couldn't see any of the river mouths in the cavern – the edges were so dark that its extent was unclear, and it seemed that they might have been below the surface, anyway, bubbling up like a spring.

The one thing I could see below me, in the centre of it all, was a body floating. A body of a dark-haired man of musculature, face down, bobbing in the water. Although I had never seen this man before, I could sense one thing. I shared my body with him.

Kuvalik.

Chapter 17
Will of the Worlds

I awoke from the void-dream in my bed in the penthouse, where I had put myself to meditate. I checked my watch – it was already the next morning.

I slammed the watch to the desk. *The next morning?* I jumped from the bed, checking that I had enough clothing on before bursting through the door.

Voidwalking could replace sleep, it seemed. I felt refreshed, as if I'd spent my time in the bed passed out. I hoped dearly that my experiences in the Void weren't merely my sleeping, because that would seriously set back any chance I had at saving Natalie.

Everybody was gathered in the great, open area of the New York penthouse. It was pouring with cold rain outside the window. The city, under the dull grey sky, appeared a wash of smeared lights and blaring horns through the panoramic glass.

Simone lounged on the black couch by the fireplace, reading. Anastasiya hovered by Celeste, talking to her and Yvon. Most eyes fell upon me as I burst into the room. I paused.

"Finally, you're up." Celeste waved a hand, not bothering to look. She, Yvon and Anastasiya were eying a map of Manhattan island. "Any ideas come to you in there?" she asked. "Because if not, we'll go with the 'visit Stacy at NYU' plan."

Finding Chad, right. I remembered, stepping forward.

"Did you find him in the Void?" Celeste asked. I froze. Had I said I was going to do that?

"Forgot to look for him," I admitted. "Instead, I found something of cosmic importance. Although, I don't know what it means."

Simone chuckled at the comment. I could almost hear her mutters as she returned to her reading.

I think what we found is specifically important to locating Chad, though, Boekidin said. I furrowed my brow.

"How?" I asked. Eyes fell upon me, and I realised that I was talking to Boekidin aloud again. My cheeks flushed red.

Kuvalik somehow found Celeste, Chad, yourself and Natalie, despite you all being spread across three continents, Boekidin explained. *The power to find Chad is right there. You just have to open yourself up to it – to his thread and its destiny.*

Open myself up to it? I stammered. *Haven't I opened myself up to him enough? He's already invading my memories.*

You haven't yet opened up to his thread, Boekidin said. *It's there, but it's not feeding you.*

Great, I smiled, *and it's going to stay that way. There's no way I'm going to sabotage my sense of self any further.*

I walked towards the kitchen to scramble up some breakfast. I fumbled inside a cupboard coated in black marble.

You saw where Kuvalik was, Boekidin said. *He's connected to everything. Using his thread must be important. You can't deny that.*

Sure I can, I insisted.

You certainly shouldn't, he warned. *Plus, you could learn liktas. You could defend against electricity.*

That's tempting, I replied, *but it won't convince me.* I put slices of bread into the toaster, and waited on them eagerly. Now that Boekidin had mentioned the thread of Kuvalik, I could feel it there, just off the base of my neck. Power pooled at its end, leaking onto me. It *begged* me to use it. It made me nervous.

Kuvalik didn't entrust you with his destiny for it to be left behind, Boekidin said. *It's clearly an important destiny. All of the black holes contribute to it. I know it will help you find Chad.*

How did he know? The toast popped, and it caused me to jump back.

Do you think I'll lose myself? I asked.

I don't know, Boekidin said, *but you can always close the thread again.*

Close the thread? I pondered. That was what I needed. I supposed, toast in mouth, that trying it once couldn't be so bad. If it helped us find Chad, then it had to be worth it. Even just a little.

I could feel the thread calling to me anyway. I knew how to open myself to its power, just as I'd opened myself to *my* thread's own power. All I had to do was give in to the great release. Let it power me. Let it in to my soul.

All it took was one deep breath.

Power.

There was a great rush of absolute energy. It surged through me, from quatra veins deep into my bones, then all around. My mind raced, expanded. This made the King's Flower seem dull. For then, upon drinking the tea, I merely got an impression of being air in the temple. Right now, I was the whole world.

Connections. I was connected to everything. Nerios, yes, as Kuvalik had always claimed, but I had eyes in all of the black holes. I had no control over the sensations, but I had a feeling of everything, of all tendrils of the Suneva.

The black holes had thoughts, which had *velocity.* These raced through quatra-space, unstoppable forces, thrashing with speed and direction. These thoughts, in their grand momentum, crashed by each other, around and under, up and through, weaving into something bigger and more unstoppable than their whole. It was a lattice of thought, squirming, writhing, forming the fabric that was space and time. The scope was impossible to perceive. An idea beyond things. Larger than a universe, packing into my brain, trying to compute sections of itself at a time.

These thoughts coalesced as forces outside of the physical. Celeste had forces crashing into her skull. So did Yvon, so did *everybody* – except me. I could barely sense all that there was – there was simply too much to know and see. But it was all there - time and space, destiny and occurrence, the velocity of divine thought - wrapping in my brain.

I needed to find Chad. Did he exist in this web of the mind? How good of a witch was I? I held my hands, in the peace sign pose by my side.

The world was vibrant with quatra, as if this beauty had been there this whole time. I was a man blind to colours, finally given eyes through which to see them. Was *this* what being a Suneva was meant to feel like? There was quatra everywhere, on every Suneva, smeared across every surface. Remnants of powers used and energy spent. Yvon's arm, where his soul was healing, leaked a cloud of bright yellow energy into the field.

But Maiki was gone – I could tell as my sense of space diminished. I had switched, shutting his thread out to call upon this one. Air was just floating gas now – something I could barely notice. But for this sacrifice, I was given a world of pure delight and vibrancy.

There was a new sensation in my fingertips It buzzed, and cracked, and rode my nerves like a giddy cowboy. Electricity was in everything, working. It streaked through cords, burning in light bulbs. I felt that I had the ability to do grand things with it, but I was a veteran Suneva in the body of an amateur. I would have to relearn what I already knew. There were high levels of power here, in these hands. I knew it.

Good. Good! Boekidin itched with delight. *Now, Chad. Can you find him?*

Can I find Chad? What did Chad mean to me? I pondered on him. His blonde hair, impressive build, infectiously friendly nature, positivity. Was he there, in my memory? Where did I first…

He was my student. Trekking through the forest. It's a hot day. Connection to the earth, he's learning it. Soul through the ground, not the other way around. Quatra. I can *taste* it. That's his scent. *Red*, burning red, of deep passions, of loss, and love lost. Of hopelessness and hope. Anguish. I see it in his eyes. We sit around the fire, across from a man. A huge man, with red, lined skin and an eagle nose. He is a handsome man. The fire tells all, of future present and past.

Chad's quatra. It's scent. One of the four, connected to the Legendaries, each with a leg in a distinct corner of destiny. Natalie, the most frightening. Her power is wrong. I would not have chosen her, but it is her path. The time has come.

The time *already* came. I'd done that. I bought them together.

Then where is Chad? I can feel him…

"That way!" I shouted, pointing. My toast fell from my fingers and splatted to the floor. The room stopped, and all stared with wide eyes. The voices I heard – the thoughts with *velocity* - were a tempest in my head, but not in the real world. I couldn't have been sure anybody was making any noise out there at all before I burst.

"Chad is…that way." I held my finger, letting it wiggle. It pointed beyond the window, into the centre of Manhattan island. The stares drew more confused, but my resolve didn't wash away. I stood tall.

163

"How do you know that?" Celeste asked.

"I opened up to Kuvalik's thread...and...boy, I can't believe this is what the quatra field is meant to look like..." I took another moment to appreciate the variety of it. Colours were so alive, swimming, swarming. The field truly lived, and I'd never seen it.

"Kuvalik's thread is powerful enough to single out Chad from here?" Celeste scratched her head.

"No, his destiny is interconnected to *everything* – especially us," I said. "I know where Chad is. I'm being led there."

Celeste smiled slyly, as did Anastasiya.

"Trusting destiny, now, are you?" she smirked. I grumbled.

"This is different. Kuvalik is a key destiny. He can sense the movements of all of the black holes...I found out just now."

"Right," Celeste kept her smug face. "Well, James, lead the way, then."

***

Umbrellas over our heads, the rain came down. I kept a hold of Kuvalik's thread, powering my soul through it.

Was it my soul I powered, or his soul? Was my soul Maiki, or was Maiki separate to me, just as Olomb's consciousness seemed to be separate to Kuvalik's thread? I supposed I'd never know this answer, but it did haunt me. I had no idea what I was doing to myself, or what the consequences would be.

The streets were slick, and slippery. People passed in a bustle, like a great river of flesh, moving as a single, hive-minded organism.

An organism of great chaos, yet great order. The individual was erratic; a bead in the sea of entities a variety of speeds, heights, and aggressions. Men pushed between each other, skipping around slower walkers, bursting at the chokeholds to the flow. Yet, as a whole, the crowd moved together, uniform, within specified bounds. It was bounded entropy.

The roads were much the same, a symphony of rage and desperation. Horns blared in every direction, for no reason but to create noise, blending with bike bells and testosterone shouts into a cacophony of disturbing intensity. It flowed too, although much more slowly. This city was alive, but inefficient.

I dodged around corners, following a deep, burning compulsion to which I had attuned. I was scared that if I switched my soul back to Maiki, I would lose it, so I stayed, despite my fears. The world was empty now, though, of my usual delights. No wind passed me by, no breezes to dance on the fingers. No carbon, giving a fullness to everything, making me feel safe.

Instead, the city was alive with buzzing. Everywhere there was a flow, deep and hot, of electricity. It was portable, it was in wires, it buzzed between shoes and ground in static shocks which were harder to perceive. Beyond that, the world seemed smaller to me now. Everything was closer, as if at arm's length. One reach and I could smack the fat, rude man across the street. These sensations were surreal.

And under it, a deep, throbbing rhythm of compulsion, spurring me on.

Scenes were familiar. It seemed that I had been to New York a few times in the past. As I turned corners, brushing past men and women in their morning rush, the world would switch. One version of the city was flat, and dusty. Horses drew carriages between beautiful old buildings on a paved, chaotic streets. The street was for everybody, with no rules to apply. Men wore hats, and suits, or begged in tattered rags. Women dressed in full decency, with skirts below the ankles, dragging in horseshit, laughing despite the tragedy of their situation.

Then there were more modern scenes, a time of golden facades, rounded shapes, dreaming of tall buildings to brake the skies. Deep oranges, and stained, rusty reds. Men wore suits with a wicked smile, strutting on streets with a cigar hanging limply from their mouths. This world was dangerous, and poor. Woman were more provocative in dress, no longer walking as an accessory, but with their newfound control and freedom. Hairstyles were newer, bolder. Makeup was sleek. Everybody was a master of their own destiny.

At least, those that were rich.

A great schism roared its way between streets in this world I glimpsed. There was extreme poverty, and sky-reaching extravagance. A world of bubbling differences, guns in hands.

Most disturbing of all, I felt a pang in my heart, as if I was unfulfilled. This pain I knew was old, hundreds of years old. What was I missing, which I surely must have felt this whole time?

No, you dickhead, that's not your pain, I reminded myself, but it was hard to resist feeling it as my own. Of course it had to have been mine. Where else did it come from?

We swept across main streets, strolling south down Fifth Avenue with increasing urgency. Like true New Yorkers, we joined the fray of the confined chaos, becoming a part of this place's natural flow.

Then I saw her face in the crowd, across the street. Her tan, soft skin, framed by thick, chestnut hair. Her eyes, which shone as portals into a far cosmos. They would show me my place in the universe. They were how I learned to love. *My love.*

She held a map in her hands, surveying the tall buildings like a lost child, eyes searching with wonder. I paused, mesmerised. She was the hole in my heart.

A man passed her by, and the face which emerged behind him was not the one I'd been staring at. I recoiled in confusion.

You don't bloody well know them, my sanity called forth. *You are James. You have never been to New York. You have no long-lost love.*

I am James.

"Are you alright?" Simone asked. The group stopped behind us.

"No," I said. "I hope we find Chad quickly. I don't like what Kuvalik is doing to my head."

But would it ever leave me, now that I'd let it in?

We crossed quickly over the road, into Washington Square park. Our feet tracked along muddy snow, squelching. I trudged desperately across it. Chad was near, he...

I could feel his scent.

"He's close," Celeste said, just as I'd gone to speak. "He's around here somewhere."

We paused in place, feet set into the concrete by the arch, each reading the field. I begged for this madness to be over. I wanted my thoughts back. I needed my *soul.*

"So, the rumours were true," a man approached from the mist, wearing a hooded jumper, soaking wet without an umbrella. He pulled back the damp cover, to reveal a fresh face of blonde, boyish hair.

"Chad!" I exclaimed. "Oh, thank *Nerios,*" I praised.

Thank Nerios? I growled in my head. *Boekidin, I'm going to need you to pull me back into reality when I start seeing weird things.*

I'll try, he replied, *but I'm not sure we're always seeing the same scenes.*

That was concerning, but I tossed the thought aside. I leaped for Chad, holding him in an embrace. We let go, and he made his way around the group.

Just as I'd felt the calling of Kuvalik's thread to me, there was my own there, *wherever it was.* My own soul, it thrummed with a familiar rhythm. My rhythm. That was me. I reached for it, letting it consume me.

And then it overtook me. Maiki. My own thoughts. The air sloshed around, thick between my fingers, affording me the awareness of my entire surroundings at once. The field of quatra dulled to nothing - its colours in all of their glorious multiplicity vanished to a near distant memory. Locked, almost phased out, but present.

I was overcome by calm resolve.

Olomb had to live like that, I said to Boekidin, *but I get to choose. How could he live with somebody else's soul screaming at him?*

Maybe that *is why he had so many identity issues,* Boekidin suggested. *I think you've been making a mountain of a molehill, James. In order to lose yourself, you'd have to expose your soul to his continuously.*

I think you're right, I hummed, feeling Kuvalik's glow in my neck. *I mean, I hope you're right. It would be useful to use his thread more often.*

With that level of power, I think you should, Boekidin agreed.

Chad finished with his rounds of greeting, and Celeste buzzed about him with an umbrella and a finger held to the sky. The mud had climbed up Chad's boots, soaking his feet, and he seemed content without the shade, so he politely refused her.

"No, I'm not offering the umbrella," Celeste said. "I'm trying to ask you something important!"

"Oh, right…" Chad coughed, chuckling.

"What *rumours* did you hear?" she asked. "What are these 'true' rumours?"

"Right, well, I heard two things, Celeste," Chad said, stepping from his mudbed and twirling his way around her. "The first wasn't easy to find through Hesslik's propaganda machine – although I happened to be in the exact right office for it – but I heard that you overturned James' thread removal concert. And, I see that it was true." He paused to wink at me. "Secondly, I heard that Iva Argol had stepped foot in New York, and I'm glad that it's also true."

"Where did you hear that?" Celeste asked. "How easy are my movements to track?"

"I've got a well-informed *Master,*" Chad noted, tapping his temple. "That, and you bought a plane ticket in your name. MarsieLe to here. Couldn't have been more obvious."

"I…right…" Celeste blushed. "I'm surprised that you *wanted* me to be here, though. I never expected that you'd want to see me again after you ran off."

"Well, I never expected to run into you here, either. I was going to try and find you just now, so we could track down James together… but it looks like you beat me to it," he laughed, and pulled the two of us close to pat us both on the back.

"How did you find me?" Chad asked, to all of us now. "In all of the world, why did you come here?"

"I was told by my information scouts," Celeste said. "When I heard news of Lion's Foot attacking Hesslik's bases, I wanted all of the information I could get."

Chad's face paled, then turned to nervous chuckle. He released his grip on Celeste and I, letting us wade back into our small crowd. He twiddled his fingers.

"Well, I guess that's what happens when you attack the propaganda head office," he winced, "but, I'm glad that you're here, I could use your help."

"With what?" I asked. Chad smiled at me, rubbing his palms and raising his eyebrows in rhythm.

"Oh, Jimmie boy. Don't you worry. I'll get to the details."

Chapter 18
Freedom

The idea of destiny had been weighing on Chad.

"When I removed the guy's thread," he said, "my whole world just shifted under me." Chad swept his hands across his field of view, accompanying it with a vocalisation of crashing waves. Split gargled from his mouth. "The guy was Nerian, and, I don't know. Maybe Nerios didn't believe in the power of thread removal?"

"That doesn't make sense, though," Celeste said. "Kuvalik was Nerian, and he knew to gather us."

"But Kuvalik's destiny is something different," I said. "Believe me, I *lived* it." My eyes stung, haunted.

"What about Vestas?" she quizzed, and we gave her a curious expression each. "I'm sure he cursed to Nerios before. He *invented* the technology. Nerios *had* to have known."

"Then there's more going on here than we know," I said. "Boekidin only deciphered Amasos' and Veritas' plans. He didn't know about the other black holes."

"These are some seriously mixed messages," Chad rubbed his forehead.

168

We gathered on the black, penthouse couch, coffees in hands, wet clothes hung by the fire. Stacy was with us – although she remained quiet after saying her first hello. Chad was visiting her between her lectures when we had found him, and he had asked to bring her back with us. The girl's eyes still framed Chad in a lusty gaze, although she held herself back, their shared father enough to deter any action on either of their parts. Either way, Chad talked openly with us about a girl he was courting – somebody he'd met on one of these recent missions. He refused to give away details, shrouding her in mystery.

"The feeling was insane, though," Chad continued with his previous train of thought. "It was like a tide shifting all around me. I felt the world turn inside out. I felt my own desires get *beaten* into a new shape. I thought…I thought this whole time I was resisting the pull, but I've been doing *exactly* what it wanted me to do."

He rested his chin in his palms, not regarding his drink, sitting despondant.

"So, to fight it, you played as Lion's Foot?" Simone asked. "That would have roused Hesslik and rocked the anti-Suneva news, but what else?"

"What? No," Chad shook his head. "No, I thought sitting in the forest looking at flowers was fighting Nerios. No. Somebody came to me and employed me, promising answers, and they were right."

"Who?" I asked. Chad chuckled, but did not break.

"Shouldn't tell. Shouldn't even *think* of them. That's breaking a code of trust."

"It's not Hesslik though, right?" Simone asked. "Because, that wouldn't be ideal."

"No, gee!" Chad winced. "Not Hesslik. *Master* sent me to remove the propaganda head's thread, and now they've sent me to crush Hesslik's factory in Brooklyn, which makes the thread-removal devices."

"It sounds like you could use my help," I said. "Boekidin and I…"

"*Boekidin?*" he asked, as if he didn't hear me drop the name just before.

"Long story," I sighed. "Anyway, *Boekidin* and I escaped destiny. I went to the Vochduh temple, and by accident found myself in the Void. You know that place you talked about, the *river* of destiny? Well it exists as the realm of quatra called *The Void*. I got Boekidin into it and removed him and myself from the flow, and I could remove you from destiny too, if you'd like."

"You can?" Chad lit up. "But, I don't know. Then I'd have nothing to rebel against," he laughed, sipping his warm drink.

"Oh, how could you live?" I exasperated. "I'd take it you're in, then?"

"Absolutely, James," he smiled. "Give me the free-will I *thought* I had."

Celeste and Anastasiya stirred to the comment. The legendary of teleportation rose, even, walking out of the room and into her own quarters.

"Take me with you!" Yvon blurted to me, then, when all attention fell to him, sat tall with regality. "You said you could take a *Kidin* with you."

I nodded.

"Then take me. I want to feel the difference. You can always reverse it, right?"

"Yvon, I could give you the destiny of *another* black hole, if you wanted it," I emphasised. "It's reversible."

"Good, then I'm in." He smiled subtly. In his glee, he was composed. His sharp features striking, his determination shining through stony eyes. In a moment, I was encapsulated by the charm Celeste must have seen in him. Although Celeste didn't seem happy with this outburst. Rather, she eyed him with a greasy stare.

"So easy to throw aside your destiny?" she asked, although he didn't respond to it.

"Can two *Kidin* get inside one mind?" I went to say, but I was too late. Yvon's face went blank, his eyes rolling up, and a bucket of water splashed over my face.

Subtlety is the way of the Shiverman, James, Boekidin reminded me.

***

The final drops of water – a thick, gargling meniscus – flew off Yvon into the southern sky, over the dunes. Boekidin and I had to wrap ourselves around a marble column of the library to keep him from being whipped away by Omercronius' pull. The Guardian watched on from the shade of the vines, his eyes piercing. He turned away as the last drop flew, stalking back into the dunes.

Boekidin eyed him too, but said nothing.

The great force of suction subsided, and Yvon dropped out of the sky, landing on the hard marble. He groaned, and took Boekidin's hand to pull himself to his feet.

"What on Earth was that?" Yvon asked, grabbing his head to stop its spinning. He brushed himself off, spraying water over the dusty floor.

"That's the pull of destiny," I said. "It's stronger than you'd think."

Yvon heard my answer, but didn't acknowledge it. His eyes drifted, wide, admiring the dull sights.

"The *Void*," he exclaimed. "I'll admit, I'd never heard of the concept until you brought it up." His focus shifted to the black, raven-like Suneva who stood by him. "And I can't believe I'm meeting Boekidin – working with the Shiverman himself."

"Nice to meet you," Boekidin stared with his beady, pink eyes.

"So, what do we have to do?" Yvon asked.

"Pick up something from the pile over there." Boekidin pointed beyond the steps, to a pile of drab-grey machinery. "And I'll show you."

We trekked west, quickly coming to the river between Kuvalik and Omercronius. It was shallower and wider here, closer to the estuary, than downstream, and we were able to wade carefully across the flow. The water still had a gnarly pull, however, and it swept hard at the ankles, threatening to upheave us and drag us to the Void's centre.

Across the bank and through the sands, the desert gradually turned to grassland. A vast meadow of grey-green stalks sprouted to the eye's limit. The fields rolled across the horizon, undulating slowly, like the rhythm of serenity itself.

Beyond it all, the gentle sound of a splashing ocean yearned for us, urging us onward. The grasses grew thick and weedy as we followed the calling. The undulations steadied, forming flat lands which eventually sloped down together.

Finally, we reached a cliff at the end of the plains. Beneath the tall cliffs – shorter than the ones by the Amasosian sea – was a thick strand of beach made of compact sand and infrequent boulders. The cliffs themselves were sandy too, with gorges cut into their faces where falls of sand had broken like rivers.

We stumbled through the loose soil over to a sandfall. Without proper wind to erode them, and with such a wide beach before the calmly crashing ocean, the sandfalls stood tall as a series of loose ramps to the water's edge. I put the equipment I carried – part of the crane and a riding board – over my shoulder and leaped onto the slope.

I coursed down it, drifting on my feet like a snowboarder on a run. I leaned this way and that, kicking up sand on the eternal formation. The structure shifted and moaned under the eroding pressure. Yvon made his way down similarly. Boekidin chose to leap from the cliff and glide on his giant, black wings.

We each touched down on the long sand of the beach. Waves, more like ripples in a pond than drowning surf, plodded away from us, out to sea. The cove was peaceful, serene. Not a sound emanated but the gently lapping water.

A large boulder was moored close to our footfall. Boekidin climbed atop it, and used the vantage to survey the sea. He dumped his equipment on its surface.

"We'll set up the crane here," he said. "This is a practice run, boys. We've got a few chances, and truth be told, this looks *much* easier than the other sea, but let's get it done in one go."

***

Simone stepped out on to the New York city streets.

Walking alone in New York city, as a young, foreign woman, was an ill-advisable activity, even according to Argol Dons. But there was one thing Simone had which others, not even an Argol mob-boss, did not.

Simone was a *God.*

In the city, an eternally turning mechanism propelled by hundreds of threads of destiny and the velocity of thought, rain continued to pour. Simone walked with an umbrella above her head, catching the torrent. Around, horns blared, people screamed, feet shuffled, tyres screeched.

People zipped by, recklessly. Pigeons swooped for scraps in the bucketing weather. And worst of all, was the water itself.

As a God, Simone could make it all *slow down.*

Energy surrounded her, visible to her senses like wild streamers waving in the wind which served as a constant reminder of her abilities, which had woken her up to her own reality. She could draw from those ribbons of red and grey – from kinetic and sound. There were others, though – orange, white, and black. Two of these would be for heat and light, which she could not draw on, yet. The other – the black one – was the energy of quatra. She could see the black hole's wills being exacted around her, and that frightened and excited her.

Air billowed from her knuckles. Exhaust. She picked the most piercing sound nearby, that of a man talking loudly into his phone. The grey ribbon of his voice was thick and billowing, stretching towards her as she passed. Simone drew the energy through her elbows, letting it pass through her palms and fingers as exhaust air. Power sucked from his throat, the man's voice broke into a hoarse whisper, and his eyes bulged in surprise.

A myth amongst Suneva was that a Sunesca could only draw from one source at a time. The Order of Salak let it be perpetuated, as it benefitted them to enforce the false rumour. In reality, one could draw from multiple sources if they had the concentration for it, and if they could feasibly convert as much energy as they took. Drawing many sources of the same type was much easier than trying to take a variety of energies.

The man's voice was low energy. Converting this much power was easy now to Simone, and she could convert more than this at once. To draw at this power level from multiple sources, however, Simone just had to train.

Salak Kallid had praised Simone upon her return to the temple. He had not expected her to pick up sonic manipulation so easily, and handed her his book in reverence. The book was a guide, written over millennia by high-ranking demons in the Order of the Salak, on what it means to be a Sunesca.

"How do you get this text to *all* of the possible Sunesca?" Simone asked Kallid upon receiving it. It was an easy task, according to him, as there were only fifteen living Sunesca, and enough dead ones to make two hundred.

Two hundred? The prospect was so odd that Simone had trouble imagining it again. Kallid explained that destiny is powerful, much more so than anybody would believe, given that the black-holes' power is so concentrated in only the Suneva. It is truly a feat to be a Sunesca, as to do so is to break their will, and that is *incredibly* rare.

This left Simone in a puzzling situation, and she pondered it through her lonely adventure into the raining streets of the big apple. If there was already a book telling people how to be a Sunesca, and an organised group of them – the Order of the Salak – what was her role as a leader alongside myself, and my movement? Being in the eventual limelight of our success or defeat, what message would she give? What importance would she present to the world?

And no, it wasn't as simple as being a cog in the team. Simone had always striven to make a change in the lives of the misrepresented and underappreciated. What could she add to the Sunesca?

Freedom. It was the one thing that Kallid's book preached more than anything else. Being a Suneva is about peace, and being a Sunesca is about *freedom*.

Suneva had to deal in peace, because they had a duty to fulfil destiny. For them, there was no choice. They gained powers and had to be damn okay with what they were going to do, and had already done, with them. They only had peace and justification for themselves.

Sunesca had freedom. They had powers which could take away the actions of destiny. They were the fighters who doused the flames of cosmic oppression brought by the four Gods. They saw themselves as the peacekeepers amongst untouchables. A necessary cog in this magical society.

But what about me, and my achievements? Simone pondered on it as she passed a man, soaked, begging for spare change. It was a shame she didn't have any with her, and her only thought was to curse a black hole. Somehow, through some convoluted turn of events, one of their orders had led to this. They'd never foresee it, but they created all of the hardship in the world, as well as all of the good.

I had surpassed destiny. I was either given the opportunity to, or conjured the ability myself, and I had now rescued other Suneva from destiny, too. Some Suneva now powers without their duty to obey, granting free will. Did this mean that Sunesca were redundant? That Simone had no reason to advocate to be a protector?

No, of course not.

A business man fumbled with a few coins near the beggar's hat. Simone stole the motion of his fingers, causing him to drop the money all at once into the starving man's cache. His eyes lit up, beaming with hope.

This was what the Suneva couldn't do, she realised. Suneva could create energy, and dance around with powers, having limboed under the cosmic contract to obey their masters, but they could never *take*. They could only give.

And, Simone realised, to change the world, one needed both. Where a Suneva could only step up to the bad guy and punch him in the face, Simone could strip the enemy of their ability to act out their desires. This was the difference between treatment and *prevention*.

To *freedom* from oppression, and the strangle of will, these new destinyless Suneva were but anarchists. They were angry teenagers, biting the hand that fed them. They were running around spray painting trains with the money their parents gave them, and calling their teachers bad names because it felt like they were rebelling. It wasn't true freedom, it was kicking the toes of your masters. Annoying, but ultimately ineffective.

Simone could affect change, and this made her smile. The world *did* need her – Salak Nera.

***

I rode out to sea, harnessed to the crane's winch, paddling my rescue board furiously. Boekidin held a pointed finger in Chad's direction, not the way I was going, and I had no choice but to follow. He was the witch, after all.

Bodies bobbed and splashed in the calm sea. The water, despite the low waves which churned its surface, was crystal clear. This made the rescue experience terrifying, as my hand slipped past the limp backs of drowned Suneva. I was surfing through a sea of the dead.

Apart from the lifeless, hanging bodies, this section of ocean was rife with submerged boulders. Some of them broke the surface, standing as short ledges and plateaus to be covered by the incoming tide. Others rose proudly from the water, but with their surfaces smoothed.

The rolling tide was gentle as it rocked under me. In the direction of Boekidin's pointing, however, I could see a swell. Waves churned over a breaching rock, grinding against its sides. The current thickened, sliding with an increased ferocity. The activity disturbed the sand seabed, which mixed into the tumultuous mess. Strangely, visibility was still high, despite the silt.

It was there, in the stronger currents that I found him. Nestled in the channel between two breaching boulders, in a constricted stream of water which raged at high momentum, Chad flailed in the current like a tree in the wind.

I navigated into the channel, and tried to park the board over him, but the strong undertow dragged me away and out the other end. It was hard to stay put between the boulders.

I looped around the large, flat rock and approached again from the up-current side. I let myself slide into the gap between the boulders, then drifted left, beaching the board atop the left slab of earth. My vessel slipped on the surface, cracking its hull across the stone-face. I cringed to the sound, but used my weight to flip myself over the board, onto the rock. I flopped atop the plateau it provided.

I crawled closer to the edge, hanging my head over the channel of fast water. The rock proved to be a slippery platform during this low tide, as a membrane of water clung to it just as the Amasosian sea had to Natalie. From the ledge I could see Chad. I extended my hand towards him.

And, of course, I could not reach him.

I huffed, and analysed the situation again. Boekidin yelled something, although I couldn't hear it, and raised my hand to shut him up and let me think.

The current pushed through the squeeze between the rocks in one direction. It was a fast stream of water, so hovering delicately over Chad would be impossible. I couldn't reach Chad from this rock, and it looked like I couldn't reach him from the other side, either.

If I rode the current and tried to grab a hold of him, I ran the risk of flipping forwards over the board and bashing into the rocks on my way out. I didn't want to abandon the board, in fear of being flung and tumbled by the currents and grated on the boulders, so there seemed only one other way to do this.

I had to lean out the back of the board, riding the current backwards.

I walked my board to the upstream mouth of the current and threw it out onto the water, just beyond the pull of the channel. When it landed, I leapt atop it, and faced myself towards the beach, away from the current's path. I checked the ankle strap securing me to the board, and seeing it was tight, threw both of my open hands into the water. The surface parted over my body, running slick like oil. I threw my head in after my arms, opening my eyes and preparing for the sting of saltwater.

Although none came – just like the colours of the Void, the sensations here were dull. With my open eyes, I could see Chad anchored between the rocks, flailing in the current, his arms straight up to sunlight and his head cocked the same way, straining for freedom.

I would deliver it to him.

I shifted myself into the influence of the great pulling water, and rode it towards him. My head upside down, eyes staring through silt, I lined up my open palms to his. They swayed about between the two rock faces in the tide, his body flailing like a flag to the wind. I raced towards him fast, and I could only hope for the best.

My hands met his, and I grabbed them.

My whole body was jerked, held back at Chad's arms' extent. His body was solidly stuck, holding against the current, built into the ground. My board flew from under me, washed away by the strong current. I fell into the turbulent flow, and was stretched out by my ankle as the board's strap tried to tug me away. Why was Chad stuck? This water didn't have the same *pull* as Amasos to hold him back from me.

He's too grounded. I remembered Chad's own words. As he had described it, he was grounded in the river and its flow, resisting the pull of destiny. I was spiritual, floating near the surface, always being sifted away.

What did *grounded* even mean, anyway? I couldn't see Chad's feet, so I couldn't tell what was holding him down in his strange spiritual state. I'd need to investigate. I surfaced myself, catching a lungful of air before taking the plunge once more. I worked my way down his body, like I had done to Natalie before, evamining it for Nerios' hold on him. As I climbed further down the huge man, the ankle strap tugged and whined, gnawing at me like a dog.

I reached his knees. Sediment which flew from the seabed sprayed into my eyes, obscuring my vision. I tried to gasp, but realised I had no air. I needed another breath.

But did I? This was the Void. Did I need to breathe here? The urge was desperate, I didn't want to risk it. I clawed my way back up his body, holding tight to his hands, and gasped for fresh, dull air.

Yvon had paddled onto my position. He waded by the other side of the rocks, avoiding the stream.

"Looked like you were struggling," he said. I gagged for air, forming a response.

"He's…he's stuck," I spluttered. "I hardly have enough breath to see what's wrong."

"Need help?"

"I don't see what you could do," I said, analysing the situation. It was hard to do whilst grabbing Chad's arms. "Look, I'm going under again. I might have to ditch the board to get a better idea of what's going on," I said, and got a hand to my ankle to mess with the strap. "Go around to the exit of the stream and catch the board. Throw it to me when I come back up."

"Okay," Yvon said, digging his arms into the water and paddling away. I disarmed the strap, letting the board drift free through the low canyon.

I plunged back into the water, making great leaps to reach Chad's shins. I ran into the problem – his shins were submerged in the mud - his feet were nowhere to be felt. I cursed, and pulled myself to the upstream side of his legs, so I could rest my weight on him. I dug with my hands, shifting sand. I couldn't see much through the dust, but it seemed that for every handful of mud I moved aside, another handful would slide in.

This isn't just sand, I groaned. *This represents something about his soul. It can't just be moved aside.*

I jetted for the surface, taking in another breath. I couldn't shift the sand, so what would I do?

*Just try harder…*I resolved. I gritted my teeth and plunged back under.

I squatted quickly by his feet, digging my heels into the sand and grabbing tightly to Chad's knees. I prepared for the lift, then heaved with all of my might.

My muscles strained and groaned. Bubbles coursed from my taut lips, my fingers and forearms burning from the force of my grip. Chad shifted in the sand, but refused to budge.

"Just, let go!" I said aloud, voice muffled by the water. I tugged at his legs once more. "Let go, man. Let me take you!"

177

A wind whispered past my ear – curious, as I was underwater. It carried on it a small voice, a meagre sigh travelling on the vast, cosmic stream. *Let go?* I thought I heard the voice ask.

"Chad?" I bubbled from the mouth. "Yes, let go!"

There was no voice to respond, no whisper, and I was convinced I must have imagined it. I was forced to surface once more.

As I plundered for breath, holding Chad's arm, I had little motivation to try again. The task seemed futile – Chad wanted his fate in the mud. Yet, as I was prepared to give up and float over to Yvon, hope gripped at my heart.

It coursed up through my hand, emanating from Chad. Touching objects in this realm was…odd; books you touched imbued you with meaning, things you saw were soul interpreted, souls you touched, you *connected* with.

Chad was ready to let go. I dove back under.

How many times had I tried to pry him out? It didn't matter, this try was the charm. I squatted low, hanging off his shins with a nuclear grip. Aloud, I counted down. "One, two, three…"

On the third count I heaved, and the mud shifted. I was thrown from the sand, blown away by the force of Chad breaching the seabed. I soared on his body, rocketed to the surface by my own impressive squat.

We crashed out of the water, splashing onto the surface. The current pulled us along, down to where Yvon was stationed with the board. He threw it towards me as I approached, and I grabbed it with one hand. Yvon helped me wrangle the body, which still flopped limp, and threaded the harness around it. Once Chad was strapped up, we connected him to the back of our boards, and connected the noses of our boards through a special knot to the winch that Boekidin operated. We swam against the weak current, driving back to shore.

Boekidin cranked the handle, drawing us in towards him, keeping our course. It made the job of fighting the sea-wards currents easier, but didn't seem necessary in these waters. The crane still moaned to the effort of dragging us along.

And finally, it snapped – shearing at its base pivot point.

Under his helmet, Boekidin's face burst into red. He scrambled to collect the pieces of the crane, but they fell from his fumbling grip in a waterfall. He huffed, gave up, and started pulling the rope by hand.

"So, clearly, estimating this stuff's stiffness as wood was no good." He saved face as we beached, dragging Chad's body to the broken crane's boulder. "I'll have to do some proper tests on it."

"Plenty of time for that," I said. "We shouldn't be striking Hesslik's castle for at least a week, I'd have to imagine."

I settled down on the sand, ready to nod off and wake up in the real world. Boekidin hauled me back to my feet, pulling me from my suddenly restful state.

"Not now," he scolded. "Let's get this stuff back to the library, and let's get Chad somewhere safer than five metres from the ocean. Look at those cliffs." He pointed behind him to the sandy walls. "It's clear that when the tide comes in, the water goes to their edge – or, at least, to the edge of the sandfalls."

"Alright, you're right," I said, preparing myself for the long journey back., "but how do we carry all of this stuff *and* Chad?"

"Oh, I don't need the broken stuff," Boekidin said, kicking the pivot and base off the boulder. They fell in a heap across the beach below. "Poorly designed. We just need Chad, the boards, harnesses, ropes, and part of the crane I'm carrying now. It's almost *less* than we took."

"Alright," I mumbled, tossing Chad onto the boards. "You tell yourself that."

Yvon and I picked him up like a stretcher, and Boekidin piled a few more items around him atop the peaceful body. We walked east, back up the sandy cliffs and across the plains, towards the library.

Chapter 19
The Bust

The subway train rattled through its tight, dark tunnel. All sorts were packed into the flying tin, bouncing around the underground network. All sorts, including us, likely the weirdest of them all. Chad, Celeste, Yvon, Simone, Anastasiya and myself – a multilingual, multiethnic, rag-tag team of Suneva, off to destroy a warehouse of goods.

We stepped out at our destination station, close to the water on the border between Long Island and Brooklyn – an industrial suburb called Willamsburg. Water flushed down the subway steps, bouncing over drains to form a murky waterfall from the street level. Consigned to wet feet, I plodded helplessly through it, cursing to the cold, chilling wind which followed once on the street level. Where the rain had been persistent, yet weak, for the past few days, the skies had finally culminated tonight into a vast storm. Rain pelted the concrete - so much of it that the inner-suburb streets around the subway entrance were totally devoid of life. Lightning screamed overhead, painting the silhouette of Manhattan island, just visible over the brief Williamsburg skyline, into a flash of black against blue. We each ejected our umbrellas, which grew from short handles like our shath weapons. Under their shade, we walked into the storm.

Chad strode westwards, leading us towards the Hudson river. According to his follow-up intelligence, Hesslik's thread-cutter factory would reside in a warehouse not far from us, one overhanging the giant river on a dock. We trudged on, through the heavy weather, the cold wind biting at our faces. Usually I liked the wind – it could make me feel powerful, and afforded me connections – but tonight it was a nuisance, wearing me down and chilling my bones.

"Huddle around me," Celeste instructed to the group. "I'll try to keep us warm." And we did, moving to butt up to her hot body.

Anastasiya landed in the huddle next to me, sitting tight under my umbrella as we waited for lights to change at a crossing. We were coming towards a main drag of shops now, neon lights pouring into the rain-swept, empty street.

"Do you trust this plan?" she asked me, her eyes pointing to Chad.

"Why wouldn't I?" I asked, curious. "Chad's an old friend and a great agent for planning missions. If anything, it's his source that could be questioned."

"Well, that's what I mean," Anastasiya huffed in her small voice, "and this source is leading us to a specific place, what if his *master* was compromising us? What if they're selling our location to Hesslik?"

"I...hmm." I hadn't considered this. I trusted Chad well enough to believe in the intentions of this *Master*, but it was strange that he couldn't disclose their identity to us. Who was this person to whom I'd given my trust?

"It should be fine, I trust Chad's discretion," I resolved, moreso to end the conversation than due to any faith in the mission.

"Oh, *Master* is trustworthy," Chad chimed in, having heard the fuss. He spun about just as the light changed green, and strolled backwards across the wet road to face us. "You'd like her – *them* – actually, Anastasiya. They've only delivered me to Hesslik's destruction so far, and they're keen to take down his institutions. Hell, I just went on a mission to de-thread Hesslik's propaganda head."

"Why do they, or more importantly, *you*, believe that this mission is crucial, then?" Anastasiya asked, and she had the attention of everybody now.

"You don't want to destroy thread-removers?" Chad mused. To his left, we now passed several bars, this road heading in a straight line for the shore.

180

"It does seem pointless, actually," Simone piped up, emerging from her umbrella. From her fists extended a small gust, and around her the falling rain paused – the water's energy stolen before its drops could land near her head. "If Hesslik is already going to destroy all of the threads in about two months, what's the point of us worrying over a few little hand-held devices?"

"I'm more concerned with what he's going to do with a factory of thread removers, given his confirmed plans," Chad said, spinning back to the river. "If he's destroying the threads anyway, he's got to have *something* in mind for these newly constructed devices. There's some stunt ahead, and it must be important that we stop it."

I nodded – I hadn't considered that the devices' redundancy could cause a more immediate danger.

"That makes sense," Simone nodded, "although it's ominous." And everybody agreed, walking in silence towards the butt of this street. I could see now, at its end, a set of warehouses hanging over the swirling river. Lightning stuck the city behind, throwing the dock's silhouette over us.

"How much do you trust this *Master* not to double cross us?" Anastasiya asked again, and I could hear Simone and Celeste grumble in unison to the objection. Chad spun with a patient smile. "Iva Argol knew that you were going to be here, and I just don't see how that's possible unless *somebody* is leaking your whereabouts. It's a long chain of Suneva to get information from America to Iva Argol."

"That's true…" Chad frowned, and stroked his chin. "Celeste, who's your source?"

Celeste turned to her lover, snuggled into her shoulder. "Yvon, who's your source?"

Yvon turned white, frightened under the pressure. "Uh, one of Merinar's men," he squirmed. "It came from inside our organisation."

"Right," Chad hummed. "Well, given *Master's* inclinations, it makes sense that they'd give my whereabouts away to Iva Argol. They wanted me to join this group again."

"And you don't think they'll give your location away to Hesslik?" Anastasiya squeaked. "You don't think that *anybody* along that chain from *Master* to Iva Argol might have sold that information?"

"*We* didn't even know where Chad was, except for in this city. We even needed Kuvalik's thread to find him," Celeste grumbled. "It's fine, there's no double-cross, heist-style bullshit here. We'll be safe."

"I'm sure of it," Chad added, coming to a stop before a small road. Across it, looming into the dark bay, were a set of warehouses lotted behind their barbed gates. Chad pointed to the central one, a beast of rusting corrugated metal and concrete, rising some three storeys tall from the road which it abutted. The building was long, starting on dry land but extending long over the river, held above the water on sets of petrified stilts which groaned in the storm's tide. Behind the barbed fencing lay a roller door to make up most of the façade, with a clear side entrance visible under a spotlight. The rest of the building, including the fence by the roadside, was held in the darkness of the storm.

"This is the place," Chad noted. "Creepy looking."

"It's not very big," Anastasiya noted, then peered to the whole group of us present. "Have we got too many people for a stealth mission inside a building this small?"

"No," Simone huffed, and was almost about to step away, not elaborating, but stopped to explain. "You don't trust my powers, but believe me when I tell you not to underestimate them. I can make this a silent entrance." And she marched across the road, pushing up to the predestrian gate before the warehouse. She gestured for all to follow, and Chad jogged quickly to her tail.

"No cameras?" he asked, an undirected question.

"I see two." Celeste pointed to the distance, near the side entrance. "One above the side door, and one above the roller."

"Right," Chad nodded. "According to the floor plan, that side door is the best place to enter by. James." He turned to me, "can you take down those cameras?"

"Sure," I nodded, and extended my palms into the peace-sign pose. At first, I found it odd that Chad had chosen me – what would I do, blow the cameras away? But I found in extending my soul that the plastic sentries were full of carbon. I amassed my connection to the shells of their bodies, coalescing them into diamonds and drawing the gems towards me.

Lenses and circuits rained from the cameras' mounts, shattering on the floor.

"Good work, dude. Any more?" Chad asked, and through the carbon heatmap splayed at my fingers, I couldn't sense any similar anaomalies in sight.

"I think we're safe," I said.

"Good," Chad nodded, and threw his palms to the metal wire fence before us. Grappling into his connections, the metal melted under his touch, and he ripped apart a one-man-wide space to walk through. We followed him through it, one at a time, Chad leading us down the side-alley between the ajoining factory and towards the side door.

The light atop the side entrance shattered before we reached it, Celeste pulling a white chunk of oxygen from the raining glass before letting it dissipate. Once in front of the door, a dark and corrugated metal slab, Chad pressed a hand to the ground and an ear to the wall of the factory, listening. I could see Annikida next to me dropping her hands into peace-sign poses, and every other member of the party seemed to be doing their own checks for life inside. I twiddled my thumbs instead, not wanting to add another chef's hands to this broth, and let the rain press down over my head. The amount of noise that the storm generated on the tin roof here was frightening – I wasn't sure we'd *need* stealth for an easy entrance.

"No movement inside," Chad noted, rising finally. "Lots of rain though."

"I couldn't sense any Suneva inside," Annikida noted.

"I felt *one*," Celeste said, "although only for a second. Maybe there's just one guard."

Chad made an effort to count all of our heads, then reported. "Six of us can take on one man, although it would be rude to do so." He reached for the handle of the door. "Cover me, Simone."

Simone pushed past me, idling behind Chad. The Suneva of iron and earth pulled metal from the door's deadbolt, freeing it. With a careful hand, he nudged the thing open, and Simone acted, drawing at the sound to eliminate its swinging creak.

Beyond the door was a dark, yet short hall, with a low roof. We piled in, Simone grasping at the energies of our footfalls on the concrete, creating a silent entry. Ahead of us, towards the front of the building, was a door which took the width of the hall. There was an office behind, and half-filled posterboards lining the walls.

Chad gestured towards the door ahead with his brow, and led the group towards it. The silent footfalls were magical, I noted, as even the hardest press of my boots was dampened to the buzz of fresh air from Simone's hands. Still, the storm rattled the tin walls to our right, nullifying the Sunesca's effect. Beyond the door, too, eminating from its slits, was the further onslaught of the rain's white noise. Water was gushing and pouring somewhere inside or around the building, only audible now that we were in it.

Chad came first to the door, squatting to press his hand to it and the floor. "That Suneva you sensed, Celeste," he whispered, "must be beyond here. They're not making a sound." And he then let the armour of Ferrad take his body, extending his *shath* weapon, a great battleaxe. We each took the hint, deploying our own Suneva *alis* forms to meet Ferrad's. He then held his bulky, armoured hand to the door's knob, and slowly turned.

The door burst open, much to Ferrad's surprise, and slammed fast towards him. Simone jolted into action and drew from the door as it swung and stole its energy, stopping it right before it smashed into the wall and gave us away. She missed, however, the cause of the door's opening – water. Standing all the way up to a person's ankles, a lake of water cascaded from the opening. If it weren't for our already wet shoes, I was sure that somebody would scream, but we each remained silent. The torrent rushed in from the room, never ending. In the light of the factory floor that I could see, the full deluge of the storm was splashing down onto the ground inside.

I pushed past Ferrad, stepping bravely against the current into the strange scene before us, the green quatra of my eyes lighting the way. This door opened up halfway down the length of the factory, facing towards the roller door. As I turned, I could see that the hall we had come from formed a section of shelving hanging onto the side of this factory.

The remaining factory was a strange mess. Holes had been ripped through the ceiling, their edges charred, as if caused by a fire – although the tears themselves were almost perfectly round. Blue light drifted to the factory floor through the gashes, along with thunderous rain and several falls of rusty water. The back of the warehouse, beyond the holes and light of night, was shrouded in pure darkness. The floor was empty, devoid of any machinery for making thread-destroying devices. The place seemed abandoned.

"This can't be right," Ferrad gawked, staring about the space. "I think I got the address wrong, maybe if I…"

Lightning cracked in the black sky, blasting the scene full of white, divine light. With each corner illuminated, five obvious figures presented themselves in the previously dark back of the room. Two young men, sharing a single face, two Suneva in blue and silver augmented armour, and one Suneva with a T-slitted helmet and ram-like arrow horns. Zamelle Menas, the White Witch.

Her slit glowed white upon her command, as if she was waiting for our moment of realisation. Zamelle stepped forwards, perched on the raised stage towards the factory's rear. She stopped under the moonlight, and her hench-crew followed – the Sunesca twins she had taken to the temple, and two royal guards.

"I knew we shouldn't have trusted this!" Annikida whined.

"How did you find us?" Iva ordered.

"Easy," Zamelle said, the weight of her divine authority silencing the room in a single word. Even the rain hushed to her command. "I told Chad's sources about this factory, I told you that he'd be here, and I assumed that he'd pull you all along on a mission. Easy, right? No coincidence, no destiny, just logic and a good plan."

"Good plan, alright," I shouted, "because you didn't think of it! You're still being controlled, Natalie. This is what Amasos wants."

"Controlled, am I?" she asked, leaping down from her perch to stroll towards us. I stumbled away in fright of the woman, who now stode and spoke with the air of a God. Around me, weapons were readied, but none fired. Zamelle parted the curtain of a waterfall, whipping it around herself through her connection to it, stepping into our line of sight.

"I don't think so, James. I have control over my thread, finally. None of you knew I was in here, did you?" she asked.

"Iva sensed a Suneva," I suggested, although Iva shook her head.

"Not the *White Witch*," she grumbled.

"That's because my thread no longer leaks," Zamelle smiled through her divinely glowing eyes. "I have taken serious measure to control my quatra. I have trained tirelessly, and gone through rigorous exercises of self-control and self-understanding, and now Amasos cannot control me like you claim they do. My actions are my own, and my thoughts my own. I can resist their impulses."

"But that's what they want you to think!" I yelled. "I mean, *cheese*, who's even talking? You sound like a comic-book villain! Where did Natalie go? What did destiny push you to? I can save you."

She sighed, drawing her famous twin swords. Water danced as she did so, compelled by her mighty, everpresent connection.

"James, you are not advanced enough in quatra and self-control to meddle with the powers you are currently toying with. The consequences of your recent actions are beyond you, and will be devastating. You're doing *shit all* to combat destiny. The Void is tricking you – surely you can tell it's an untrustworthy place," Zamelle said, calmly. "You *cannot* cheat Gods, James – and that is exactly what you're planning to do. You *can* train yourself to be mentally strong, and resist impulses. You *can* train yourself to control your thread, and preserve your soul. You *can* achieve nirvana in self-understanding, and understand when decisions are yours and when they are not, but you *cannot* cheat Gods. You *cannot* do what you're doing without repercussions. Only Sunesca have the freedom we're seeking – and you can have it too, once your thread is destroyed."

185

Rain roared through the silence, pelting at the lake-floor of the factory. I had no response for her. Natalie was gone. Through her white T-slit, hungry eyes raged the fire of her soul. She was an animal, a pawn of a God ready to exact its vengeance. Water whirled at her feet, magnetised by her startling *power*.

"Have you got nothing to say?" she asked, and all of the rain in the factory pulsed to her question.

"Maiki, save her," Iva turned to me quickly. "Run. Find somewhere safe. Go into the Void, and *save her*."

"What?" I stammered. "I don't know that we've got stuff ready, I..."

"I believe in you," Iva snapped, shoving me towards the door. "Just get it done. *Hurry. Run.*"

Zamelle raised her twin swords to the air, and with a shifting, insane grin, churned a tidal wave the height of the factory roof. I shrieked, and it *surged* towards us.

Iva Argol combatted it with an invisible force, boiling half of it to steam. I leaped from my place, pouncing on a jet of air, streaming towards the door. The two guards rushed to follow, but were knocked clean off their feet by a hunk of concrete thrown by Ferrad.

As I fell through into the hallway, chaos erupted behind me in a sea of quatra bolts and elemental forces. I sprinted for the side exit and threw myself around it, bursting onto the alley between the warehouses.

I ran for the compound's exit, but beyond that, there was no plan. I had to find somewhere safe to meditate and fall asleep, but where would that be in this part of the city, on a wet and rainy night?

The pubs, Boekidin urged. *Go to the pub.*

"This is no time for beers," I said, stopped at the street. I peered over my shoulder, eyeing the twisted metal of the warehouse roof which danced in the light of quatra and pink flames. The sounds of battle radiated and echoed.

Just go, man! Boekidin growled, and I came to my senses. A plan racing to my thick head, I eyed off a set of neon lights just a block up from where I stood. I ran towards them, tearing away the armour of Maiki.

I screamed through the front door of the first establishment I could reach, staring at the bar staff before an empty sitting area. The wood panelled, long shop lined with kegs would have been just David's kind of place, and I would have sat for a beer if the time wasn't more pressing.

"Mother of God, do you have a toilet?" I yelled to the attendant, whose face fell to shock. I ran over to the bar with frightening intent, slamming a ten-dollar bill onto the counter. "I'm *desperate.*"

"Yeah…dude." He pointed a hesitant finger to the rear, illuminating a short hallway. "In there."

"Bless you!" I coughed, and blasted off a jet of air, flinging myself in the direction of his finger. I rounded a corner, stumbling through a dark bathroom, covered floor to ceiling in lame graffiti and skate stickers. Spotting an unlocked stall, I faxed myself through the door's opening and launched my ass onto the toilet seat. I locked the door, then sat in silence.

A toilet? Boekidin quizzed.

I've fallen asleep on one before, I replied. *Now, dickhead, let's get up that pipeline, into the Void. Now!*

But I couldn't relax, I couldn't find that pipeline – my mind was a racing mess. If Boekidin said the mind was a city, then mine had a traffic jam of drag racing cars, stuck infinitely at each intersection, doing burnouts around corners to euro-trash beats at one hundred miles per hour.

Calm it, man, Boekidin's voice broke through the fuzz of my smoggy mindscape. *Don't think of the situation. Listen to my voice, my smooth voice,* He lulled to a beat. I closed my eyes. *Listen to your heart beating. Slow your breathing. Align the two. Feel the pulse. Sync. You are going to be in sync with yourself. Control your heart.*

I could control my heart through my breath, and my breath was all-powerful. I felt my relaxation through the throbbing of my pulse. It became infrequent, my blood fresh.

Slowly, I calmed.

And then I meditated.

Chapter 20
Churning Sea

I awoke in a heap of sand and clutter, under the shade of the Vochduh library's grand awning. It took a good moment to comprehend where I was, my body rolling, my mouth groaning, and my eyes adjusting to the dull, grey light.

The Void. I scrambled to my feet, my heart growing to a race. We had to run, *sprint.* Everybody's livelihoods were on the line, including my own. I stalked

187

about frantically. Which pieces of equipment were important? Where was Boekidin? I raced around the columns of the library entrance. His body had to be here.

"James!" he yelled. A large, mechanical hand gripped my shoulder and swung me around, to face out to the desert. There Boekidin was, beady eyes glowing on that glorious, raven face.

"Quick...we have to run!" I stumbled to the pile of equipment and knelt amongst it. "What's important?"

"Okay, hold up." He hauled me to my feet. "Give us time to think. We can't afford to make mistakes." He pushed me out of the way, and knelt himself in the pile of machines. He grappled with the pieces, tossing half of them aside by my feet.

Boekidin shot up, finally. In his pile were broken members and an assortment of the crane. By my feet were the winch wheel, part of the winch mount, a pulley attached to part of its mount, the ladder, both harnesses, and a single board. Boekidin analysed the heap again with his beady eyes.

"Winch drum with rope, mount, and pulley to act as the crane..." he spoke his thoughts aloud. "Ladder to get you up and down. Harnesses to keep you and Natalie on the safety line. Board, to swim on."

"Rope for Natalie?" I asked, grappling at the bare towbar of the board.

"Ah!" Boekidin raised a finger, and pounced back to the previous pile. He pulled from it a short rope with two crude carabiners on either end. I secured it to the board.

"Okay, good, lets..."

"No, wait!" Boekidin ordered, examining the assorted equipment I was about to scoop up. He played with the winch, rolling it in its bearing by turning the crank. I could feel the sweat oozing from my real pores, soaking my wet clothes and the dirty toilet seat. I was experiencing an out-of-body level of stress. I bounced on my toes.

"Okay, looks good," Boekidin said, finally. I stumbled into one of the hardnesses, then grabbed as many items as I could and tangled them in the rope ladder. I threw the ladder about my waist, tying it there. There was no time for Boekidin to protest the ill-treatment of his wares. He grabbed the remaining items – the board and the pulley.

"Good, let's run!" I said, and immediately kicked off. A length of parts and pieces trailed me, hanging from the waist-secured ladder. I sprinted east, over the desert sands, towards the Amasosian sea.

Simone sat at the edge of the battle ground, by the escape hallway. Bolts of quatra were flung in the warehouse carelessly, redirected without thought, most met and destroyed by an orange bolt of Zamelle's. They skimmed near Simone's face and body – any single hit, not redirected, could kill her instantly, blowing apart the affected limb in a shower of blood and flesh. Simone's eyes were alight, her senses alert.

They had to be. Simone had been given the ability, by her Sunesca biology, to see and redirect quatra, but not to sense it. If she didn't see a fatal blow coming, she would die.

Elements flung through the air too, and Simone might have had a remedy for that, given the kinetic nature of waves of water, but this was not something she could stop. Any movement whose propelling source was quatra could not be stolen from – at least, not unless Simone was a demon.

Still, she could steal the movements of armoured Suneva, and she did so. Zamelle was her target.

A ribbon of red energy buzzed from Zamelle, whipping its form through the stale storm. Simone reached for it, drawing the kinetic energy of the White Witch towards her elbows. Converted through Simone's soul, the energy escaped her palms as a jet of exhaust, disturbing the water at her feet.

Zamelle came to a near stop, her waves spluttering and dying in the calm of the ankle-deep water. Quatra bolts flew freely now that Zamelle could not stop them – many towards her. One of Celeste's hit, a direct shot to the chest, and whilst for any regular Suneva this would have flagged the end of their battle, the blue bolt emerged from the White Witch's little finger, streaming towards the ground. Each bolt that collided with her body in the following flurry was redirected elsewhere. The White Witch didn't need motion for redirection. She was beyond that level of connection to her own quatra pathways.

This didn't deter Simone, however. She kept her foothold on the red ribbons which snaked from the White Witch as they appeared, grinding their motion to a trickle just as they went to move, removing them from the battle.

Then Iva Argol grew still – halfway through a redirect, her arm hung stuck in place, pinning her body with it. She seethed and growled her frustration, flames licking from her lips and red face. The rest of her body was stuck, too, and she flashed the warehouse hot pink in her bubbling rage.

Riskidin also slowed, Simone noticed. He struggled, but his power wasn't necessarily diminished by a lack of movement – *Kidin* abilities didn't require movement to be effective like other *quatran* did.

Two Sunesca, two targets. Simone groaned, looking to the twins across the room. Tall, dirty-blonde hair, dark eyes, the both of them. From one, electricity sparked off his palms. From the other, tendrils of flame danced.

"Fire at them!" Simone pointed, instructing Annikida. Simone looked to plea with Ferrad also, but he was busy picking up the slack of a downed Iva and Riskidin. He grunted, forcing a column of earth to burst through concrete, blocking an arc of liquid electricity from one of Hesslik's guards.

Ferrad then surged forward, throwing the stump of rock towards the *Liktas.* They dodged from its path, rolling through the swampy water. A sleek, silver arrow, fast and true, ran its way through the rock, splitting it through its centre. The *Vastas* Royal Guard, tall, and of similar silver armour, had repelled it through the boulder. He pulled another from his quiver, setting it to a barrel on his left arm.

Annikida finally nodded her white, antlered head to Simone. She shot one bolt of pink quatra towards the right twin, then reached after it, pulling herself through time and space. She disappeared into a break in the universe, remerging behind the left twin. Using one huge, spiked hand, she shoved him off the stage. The Sunesca spun to shower her with a lick of flame, but it was already too late. He tumbled onto his ass, yellow flame following, and Annikida ripped herself another hole. She appeared again across the room, and fired a volley on the remaining Sunesca.

Iva was able to move again, and roared in delight. She let an angry pink flame soar towards the *Ivaer* Sunesca. They dropped to their knees, sealing themselves flat into the water as flames roared overhead. Riskidin tripped over himself as his leg stamped into the water unexpectedly. He stumbled to stand, and joined back in to the quatra fire.

"Forget Zamelle!" Simone shouted. "I've got her. Keep those twins distracted!"

***

I heard another snap from behind – another rung broken on a snag as I ran. It had to have been the fifth now - climbing this ladder was going to be dodgy business.

My mind urged me on, but my spiritual legs and lungs had given up – my soul wearing itself thin. I jogged on, through the rough, tall grass of the meadow bordering the forest before the cliffs. I could hear the water churning now – the desert was well behind me. Boekidin ran by my side, undeterred by the rigorous soul exercise.

Black rocks ahead, my heart leaped, my veins flooded with vigour. I could see the heads of the rock apostles poking up beyond the ground, like watching sentries, spying. Waves crashed against rock, sending jets of ocean spray up, beyond the line of the cliffs. The dull ocean scent drifted towards us.

My feet touched basalt rock, and the edge was just ahead. I sprinted towards it and pulled up, coming to a stop just shy of the ground's end. The ocean was angry today. It boiled, toiling at the rocks, blind in its own rage. Natalie was out there somewhere, and peering over the sea Boekidin spotted her by the middle apostle. In just a few days, her body had drifted back out – now even further than last time. She was caught in a particularly rough swell, which tore and crashed over her body. In it was a thin fog of leaking quatra – much less pollution than the other day.

"Okay, now, calm down, take a break," Boekidin urged. I flung the rope ladder from my waist and collapsed onto a hexagonal pile of black rock. I wheezed. My soul enflamed, recovering.

"No time for relaxing, man!" I spluttered. "Who knows how much trouble everybody is in."

"It doesn't matter," he said, carefully untying pieces. He picked up the winch drum and rammed its mount into the ground. As if like clay, he smoothed the rock onto the base, hammering the structure in with his metallic arms. "If they're in trouble, that's it. *You* could be in trouble, but whilst we're in here, we have time. It might not matter if we lose the battle, as long as we win this war and free Zamelle."

"Hmm…" I huffed. "Lose the battle…win the war." I rolled over on my black, dusty grave, and peered out to Natalie in the sea. I could see the glow of her white, blind eyes peeking through the fog. She was ferocious. This wasn't a *'lose the battle, win the war'* situation. We needed to win this battle, or else we could be *removed* from the war entirely.

I turned back to Boekidin, who was tying the rope-ends of the ladder around a jutting piece of hexagonal rock. He smoothed the cable into the rock, then threw more quatra-essence at it, like a man throwing mud on a thatch house. The stuff ran like wet sand, and he bashed it into the structure with slapping hands.

191

"Veritas, this is sketchy," he cursed. "I don't know that any of this will hold."

"Don't tell me that," I said. "Tell me it's perfect, and strong."

"But you already know it isn't…" Boekidin rubbed his beak, then leant down to a spare structural member he'd bought along. He jammed it into the winch drum's stand at an angle, giving extra support.

"There, now it's strong…er," he hummed. "I'm going to need a few more members, though. Damn, I *really* wish I had more time to understand this material."

"Alright, that's it," I said. "I know you want to take your time to make this right, but I say we have no time." I stormed over and plucked the board from his feet. I took the rope end from the spool and clipped it in to the harness I was wearing, then clipped the second harness to the board's towbar.

"What are you doing?" he asked, shooting up to grab my arm. "You saw this all fail in the lightest current as it currently is. What makes you think *half* of a crane will do any better without serious improvement?"

"I'm not an engineer, I have no idea what will and won't work." I pushed his hand away. "I'm going out there. You've got until I get to her body to make this strong enough to lift us."

"Maiki, that's not going to happen!" he said, flustered. "We can't afford to be impatient here. I only want five minutes to strengthened everything. I'm just going to slap mud on it all, give it some bulk…"

"Battles don't last five minutes, not with Zamelle."

"And what if the rope fails as you throw yourself down that ladder? We don't even know if its long enough yet."

"I'll just have to put my faith in hope, and you," I said, stalking towards the edge. I kicked the furled-up ladder over it, watching it fall into the sea mist.

"This is no time for hope!" Boekidin growled. "You gave up hope when you gave up destiny. This is down to *us* now, and everything we do. No handouts, no luck, just planning. I only need five minutes, man!"

"Can't I put my hope in you?" I asked. Below, the ladder landed with a splash, and I watched it stir in the wild waters. I grinned – it *was* long enough, Boekidin shouldn't worry so hard.

"And put some faith in yourself, man." I pointed downwards. Boekidin cautiously stepped over to the edge, watching the ladder's end swirl with the current.

"What if it fails?" he asked. "What's plan B?"

"Secure the rope, and I'll rope climb."

"If the security breaks?"

"Then hold on like *my* life depends on it. Everything could break, but I don't think it all will. The ropes seemed strong enough."

"I still think you should wait." Boekidin planted his foot firmly. "This is brash."

"And I have to disagree. Have that winch ready to lift, we don't have time to waste."

I wrapped the board's strap around my ankle and slunk over to the edge. I stepped upon the first rung of the ladder, which creaked loudly, setting my nerves alight.

"Knife!" I remembered quickly, just as the board threatened to tug me over the edge. "I need the knife to cut the membrane, quick!"

Boekidin's eyes rocked alight, he scrambled for the pile. "See, we can't rush. We have to be careful and meticulous."

"Yeah, okay mate." I waved my hand. "Just hurry!"

"You're lucky we packed it in," he said, rushing over. Boekidin tucked it into my harness for me. "That's because we took our time to see what we needed."

"Yes, good preaching, good job," I stuttered, and Boekidin grinned, although the smile dripped with nervous anticipation.

I finally lowered myself down the ladder.

With each rung of descent, I could hear the sea thrashing more violently below. In my proximity it raged and swelled, water churning to meet me. Halfway down the cliff I was bombarded with heavy spray that threatened to throw me to the air. The rungs became ever more slippery and my grip grew exhausted, more weight resting on my feet. They lost their hold easily on the wet rungs, and a few times my heart stopped as I found myself falling through breaking wood, holding on by one hand.

I stopped to rest at the ladder's bottom, the swell churning and rising over my body. I held for life, peering out to the sea as waves crashed with vigour around me. They were ready to swallow me whole, to drag me into their depths, to control me. I steeled myself, and leaped from the ladder. Holding the board, I rode it like a missile rocket.

I crash landed, bouncing off the craft upon impact and rolling under the waves. Winded, I was churned under the tumultuous surface, until I regained my senses. I hauled on the ankle cable, fighting my way back to the sky.

I clawed my way onto the board, flopping over its face. Once there, I shot to my knees, and paddled away furiously. The waves were tall, marching in their swell – a military force. What appeared to be an angry sea from above turned to a bitter, vengeful goliath at eye level. White caps rocked all in directions. I could just see the tip of the middle apostle peeking over the high reaching walls of water. I pushed desperately towards it.

I crested one behemoth, and slammed down its far side, gaining serious speed. The water surface, despite its odd thickness, was slick to a fast-moving object. I rode the wave, its momentum coursing me halfway up the next, mad crest.

And even though I had made incredible ground, as I crested the next wave, I saw that I was still so far away. Already exhausted, I contemplated giving up, tugging the rope, and getting pulled in.

But Boekidin and I hadn't established any tug signals. *If only we'd prepared more...*

This was it then, no giving in. I had to have been near halfway. I buckled down. All or nothing, success, or thread death. This was a last stance, and it would take everything I had. Gritting myself, I hit the downwards slope with mad arms, riding it with style and catching air over the next slope.

I splashed back to the waves. My soul was invigorated, alight with courage and power. Amasos was trying to hold me down, but I could not be held, not by these waters, or any waters ever again. I was the Voidwalker – a Suneva free of destiny, here to save the Suneva society and the one friend who I bought into it unknowingly.

She was the White Witch. *How crazy is that?* I thought as I thrashed over and between the boiling, toxic water. The sea hissed at me, attacking with heavy limbs of thick liquid. I dodged and ducked, sailing on my two palms and board.

Who would have thought, from a night at an eighteenth birthday party, that the White Witch and a Voidwalker would meet? That we'd be so intertwined? What act of destiny had two future opposing forces meet?

Beneath my board, a trail of white fog hung in the water. A bubbling cloud of grey pollution, sifting in the fluttering tide and rip. Natalie was close. I could see the source of the smoke just head, in the shadow of the rock giant which loomed over me. I struggled towards it, the tides stronger now, the water burning with blind rage, slashing at my board.

I came to the source, a grey, bubbling depth in a wash of waves, with no Natalie in sight. I checked the buckle on the harness, and gripping the board with a strained arm, peered up to Boekidin. His head was barely visible, just bobbing over the black cliffs.

I was secured to the line, and to the board. I jumped in.

194

Simone recoiled in shock, falling across the wet floor.

She'd gone too far on that one streamer of energy, drawing in all that it could give, extinguishing it. A backlash jolted her body, braking her connection to the source and delivering a spasm of pain.

Simone grunted, scraping herself back up off the ground. As she rolled, a bolt of quatra impacted where she just lay. To this she growled and yelled. She was meant to receive cover to allow her to slow down the opponents, but this battle was raging on without sense. *Where was my rescue effort?*

Simone moved her way around the perimeter of the room. It was draining now – Ferrad had busted through the concrete a few too many times, letting the rain seep out into the river below.

Still, the waterfalls fell as desperately as ever, threatening to fill the room at the same pace it drained. The sky did not let off – a constant stream of lightning illuminating the battle scene between the electric arcs of *Liktas* Suneva and Sunesca.

Simone was annoyed at herself, she realised as she redirected a blue bolt from the *Vastas* royal guard. She was annoyed at her lack of control in stopping Zamelle – drawing too much energy had zapped her with pain, and she thought her skills were more refined than that. Leaving some energy in the ribbon was just about the second thing *Kuul* had taught her. Simone honed back on to Zamelle's movement, drawing it in. This time, she wouldn't get so greedy.

But, what if…

Simone had to let go again, of both Zamelle and her train of thought, dodging another hit.

Ferrad and Iva were caught again by the Sunesca of flames, and the Magnetic royal guard threw bolts at their slowed bodies, but missed. Then the Sunesca's electric twin joined in, doubling down the effort to constrict Iva Argol – clearly she was the biggest threat to them. This left Ferrad with an ounce more freedom to move, and he took it by the reigns. Ferrad strained a singular finger towards the Salak of Fire, and unleashed a red quatra bolt upon them, forcing them to free Ferrad from their grasp. Meanwhile, Annikida buzzed about the *Liktas* and *Vastas* guards, doing very little but annoying them.

She's a legendary, Simone grumbled, *surely she can do better than jumping around the place. Drop them from a great height, or something. Teleport them away, even?* Simone was about to yell it, but she had to save her breath for better things.

Iva growled and roared a pink flame from her near-frozen position. She would be hit any minute – just as Riskidin had been taken out of battle earlier, taking a hit of quatra. This brought an earlier idea to Simone's mind.

What if I stole the last remaining enery from Iva, and rolled both me and those twins over the edge? She thought, gripping into that tiny tangle of a red ribbon that danced off Iva's body. Simone pulled that weak link towards her, drawing at it.

The ribbon snapped.

"Gah!" Simone shivered, pain gripping her body and dropping her to the floor. Across the room, both twins were thrown off their feet, stumbling to the floor. Simone eyed that Salak of fire, whose head seemed to roll limply in shock, and then ran towards him. She wanted to drive a fist through his ugly, fat head. Her knuckles could be the thing to knock him out of the battle, because none of these Suneva would.

But the momentum of her run was stolen, consumed, and converted into arcs of electrical power. With all of the Sunesca drawn together, there was nothing to hinder the quatra fire in the heart of the battle, and the warehouse was thrown into a dizzying display of colour and magic. Danger bubbled through the roof's holes, the fight being given *velocity* by all parties. Everybody was unhinged, and enraged from having lost control of their bodies.

Simone didn't need to move to steal energy, so she stole the energy of the asshole holding her. He grinned to her tug, enjoying the imprisonment. Then, he halted his will to move, and the ribbon of energy diminished in Simone's grip. She did the same, and had to let go of the ribbon she held before its energy backfired on her.

"What are you fighting for?" he asked. His voice was oily, and dual pitched. It reminded her of the demons she'd talked to.

Do I sound like that? "Freedom," she answered flatly.

"You want freedom?" he slicked. "Then join us. Cut the threads."

"So, you know about that?"

The Salak of electricity nodded. His brother went to rise, and quickly was under assult by Ferrad's red bolts. Simone considered stealing his energy, but knew that they were being handled.

"Do they know?" Simone darted her eyes towards the royal guards. The Sunesca looked after her.

"No," he said. "They wouldn't want that freedom. They're after peace."

"I guess you *are* an asshole, then," Simone uttered under her breath.

"Tell me," the Salak said in his wiry, double voice, "what kind of freedom do you think you'll find on your current path?"

"Freedom of choice," Simone said. "To *choose* to have a thread."

"So, you're after the freedom of others? Even if it's at the sacrifice of their free will?"

"They will have their free will – my brother is working on that," Simone retaliated. "What will you gain from the destruction of the threads? Without destiny to fight, how will you bring freedom? How will you be useful as a Salak?"

The man smiled a grimy, long grin.

"You think we're better with Gods to get in the way?" he asked, his greasy mouth dancing as the words twirled out. "You must have an idealistic vision of the Salak Order. If the order worked, then destiny would mean shit-all. We're all only human, Salak Nera." He licked his teeth. "Without Gods in the way, we are *truly* free. We run our worlds."

"That's bullshit," Simone growled. "Without Gods to defy, you're just taking the actions of free people. You'd become the next oppressor!"

"And yet you're happy to let your brother wipe away destiny, if he can?" the man asked. "Because, your stealing of energy in a post destiny world is exactly the same as what I plan to do. It's still stealing from those who aren't controlled by destiny. I don't think you've thought this through."

Simone hadn't thought of this *at all*, in fact. She *wanted* to help me, and turn the tides to defy destiny. She wanted to become a herald of freedom, a face for the Salak and the Order in the new Suneva world. But, this realisation turned the goal on its head. Would she stop being Salak Nera as soon as the last destiny was removed?

"Why do you think the Salak Order drove the Suneva underground?" the man continued. "Why do you think they drove the public belief in demons and the supernatural into the realm of crazy? They wanted to contort reality without being disturbed, without people finding out they were manipulating them."

"Okay, I'm done here," Simone held her hand to the man, or she tried to, but he stole the motion with an oily smile.

He went to talk again, but Simone stole his sound. Two could play at this game.

Iva Argol shouted for her help, and Simone diverted her attention, away from the greasy, asshole of a Sunesca.

I swam down into the thick brine of Amasos. The water licked around me, sweeping me off kilter in it's white, foggy churn. I lost my bearings quickly as I was thrown about in the current. Up and down would have been lost too if it weren't for the ankle tether.

I flailed my limbs about, hoping one would crash into Natalie, but none did. I opened my eyes, and the water stung. It tried to crawl into the space between my eyes and skull, with thousands of tiny tendrils. It ran its hands through my ears, biting at the drum. It writhed into my nostrils, keen on latching itself around my brain.

My arm hit something. I squealed, driving the water to retreat, then grasped at the darkness. The sensation was gone, the object had moved. I was hungry to feel it again. I swam in its direction, manic.

I hit something else, this time with my foot. I fishtailed, bending around on myself, lunging through the smokey water. My finger tip touched it again and I grasped. The object was skinny enough to wrap my arm around. It gave as I held it, allowing me to squish it slightly. It had stretch, like skin.

It had to be Natalie. Object held in hand, I swam for the surface.

I rose, sucking in sweet air. The board knocked my head as a wave rolled over me, sending me spinning. I finally had a chance to look at what I held. It was a hand, fingers poking above the surface.

It wasn't Natalie's hand.

I cussed, throwing the body aside – I didn't have time be wrong. Where I had discarded the body, the fog was less dense, but it was thicker towards the rock apostle. I freestyled that way, then dove under again.

I opened my eyes, and fought the feeling of the sea gripping my soul. Amasos could try as they might, I would not fall to them. I swam on, into the deep fog. Its clouds stung my senses – a deep, divine energy. Divine, yet clearly evil. There was no orange fog here - no sign of the true Natalie.

Yet glowing eyes broke the haze. I darted towards them, but was yanked upwards by my ankle as the board crested a wave. I countered it with grit, charging towards the glowing set of eyes.

I grappled the head in my hands, it's thick hair falling around and between my fingers. It was Natalie's face between my palms, and it was lifeless, yet commanding. It hung with austere authority.

I was running out of breath, no time to gawk. I grappled under her armpit and forced myself upwards with one hand. Only, she was stuck in place, as I should have expected. I changed strategy, using the ankle line like a rope, to heave us to surface.

Her arm breached the waters, the rest of her body refusing to rise - Amasos would not let her see the light of day, their grip on their vassal was much too strong I unhooked the second harness from my belt, and gasped a final breath, ducking under the waves. I fumbled with the loops, running them tight around Natalie's limbs one at a time, but I finally had her. I took the time to secure her right - there would be nothing worse than losing her now.

Once I had checked the last of the straps, I clipped her carabiner to the board's tow bar. I mounted the board, and fought the rough current to get her back to shore.

***

Annikida bounced around in circles, pulling herself through space, between all members of the fight. She would fire a bolt, then zip off through a tear in space, reappearing elsewhere before anybody could retaliate.

Simone burned red at the cheeks.

Teleport those Sunesca away! Her rage boiled below the surface. *Have you ever been in a battle? How stupid can you be?* She'd tried yelling directions, but her words were constantly being stolen. She couldn't get *any* messages across.

Zamelle was regaining her movement steadily, fighting Simone's ability to steal it. The will of Amasos was strong – too strong for Simone to fight alone. She couldn't bring this girl freedom. She couldn't bring anybody freedom – she realised. Simone brought fortune to herself and friends at the expense of the free will of others. Her purpose as a Sunesca was a sham.

The *Liktas* guard fired a bolt, and Zamelle, with what movement she had, jumped into its path. The action was so unexpected, that Simone let her go, allowing her to fly into the quatra.

The White Witch redirected the quatra blast, throwing it straight to the neck of Iva Argol. It coursed through the girl's thread, shattering her armour across the water like raining glass. Her flames died in an instant, and Celeste LeRoux was born from their ashes.

For the second time in anybody's memory, Iva Argol had been bested in a battle.

Celeste roared, and launched herself at Zamelle.

***

Boekidin had cranked hard on the winch drum, drawing me in across the waves. At the base of the cliffs, I unclipped myself from the line and connected it to Natalie's harness instead.

"Raise her up!" I shouted at the top of my lungs. A thumbs up, borne on a black, metal hand appeared over the cliff edge. Soon, Natalie started to rise from the water. The movement was slow, and the rope was strained. The membrane on her skin trapped her with its immense surface tension. It stretched tight over her whole body.

I produced the knife from my harness belt and clambered to Natalie's head. Under me, the waves thrashed and gnawed – this would be too difficult from any other vantage point to get right. I raised the blade to the tip of her skull, then waited for the next wave to wash over us. As the water settled, I cut a line in the membrane down her face and over her chest. The gelatinous layer split, and with a frightening burst, Natalie's body shot up from the water, propelled by the taught rope.

I flailed, falling back into the swell as Natalie sprung up from under me. I swam to the ladder resting nearby, and began to climb. The board, hooked onto my belt, trailed me, scraping along the cliffside.

An onholy churn growled and roared behind me, and without the confidence to look, I braced myself close to the cliffside. A wave ran up the rocks, blasting me from toe to head, flying up my nose and into my eyes. The ladder and I were thrown in an arc away of the cliff face, and I could do nothing until the both of us crashed back into it. My hand crashed into the black rocks, fingers throbbing alight. My only instrinct was to let go and recover, but I couldn't obey it. I had to climb this damn ladder, *fast*.

Natalie hung limply in the air ahead of me, like an actor hanging on a line. The last bit of membrane still clung to her foot, pulling her taught against the winch's efforts. The water had tentacles. They each gripped obscenely into her skin, threatening to control her.

I heard a snap.

"James!" Boekidin shouted. The rope surged from the cliff face, snapping out to sea elastically. Natalie hung for only a moment, before her body was torn from the sky by the force of the tendril at her ankle. She zipped downwards, past me.

I pushed off the wall, one hand on the ladder, one hand extended.

I caught her wrist.

Natalie twisted, hauling to a stop. My shoulder stretched, my body jerking at the force. The rung I held broke instantly.

I caught the next one, miraculously. The force drawing Natalie down was strong – stronger than any of Boekidin's calculations could have accounted for. This second rung groaned, straining under the immense pressure. I clipped my feet into two lower rungs, spreading the weight evenly. Suddenly, things seemed calm.

I needed the knife to cut that last bit of membrane, however, I couldn't let go of either Natalie or the ladder to perform the cut. Beyond that, a glance at my belt told me that I'd lost the knife in the last second – it had probably fallen as I jerked.

There was another option. If I could clip Natalie to my harness, I could then use a free hand to drive off the controlling tendril of water. However, without any sign of the knife, if I dropped her, that was it. I'd never free Natalie once she fell back down. The clock was ticking.

"Are you okay?" Boekidin yelled over the edge.

"No!" I called back. "I need a third hand, man!"

"I'm coming," he called.

"What!?" I screamed.

"I'm coming down," he said.

"But…this ladder won't hold three of us. It's barely holding me now!"

"Who cares," he said. "We do this now, or we lose the war. Even you told me to have faith in myself. And I do. This ladder will hold."

What have I done? I winced. I *could* fall to Amasos now. This was truly frightening. Still, there was no time to think beyond the present. My soul was stretched to its limits, defying a God, holding a rung and a girl I had to save. My soul strained, and I could have been sure that my real body was crying. I could feel tears stream wet on my face. I was in real, emotional pain.

Boekidin lowered his skinny, metal ass down. Waves washed into the cliff, spraying me with water, not reaching quite high enough to grip onto me and pull me down. My arm screamed in pain again, as if this ordeal had ignited the tear once more. I bore down, gritting through it.

With each of Boekidin's steps I could hear the ladder screaming, too. It was made of quatra, it too had a soul, and it's was torn to its very limits. His talons scratched at the rungs, his claws threatened to cut the cords. I could see it giving way, I could see myself falling. One final groan, and it would all snap, it would...

Boekidin stepped off the ladder, digging his claws and talons into the rock wall. The soul of the ladder recoiled, and in my mind, I could hear its weak sigh of relief. I did the same, panting in exhaustion. Boekidin lowered himself past me, producing a knife from the folds in his wing.

"See," he said, reaching for the tendril holding Zamelle's foot, "you were right. I just needed faith in myself."

A wave, larger than any seen today, gathered its will. It surged suddenly, violently, careening towards us. I tried to yell, but realised that I couldn't yell fast enough. As Boekidin brandished his weapon, the wave crashed into the cliff, and roared up to meet us.

Boekidin was launched up the cliff face, soaring high before plummeting past me, landing in the sea at the cliff's foot. The wave rocked me, dousing Natalie, attaching more tentacles of destiny to her body. My hand slipped on the rung, which creaked like death, but I managed to hold. Although I couldn't hold this much longer.

"Fucking climb the god damn ladder Boekidin!" I screamed. "Do it! Please!"

I could feel my soul coming apart. It was breaking at the seams faster than I could stitch it back together. In the real world, I knew my face was drenched. Sweat and tears covered me. My ethereal being was tearing. Boekidin fumbled in the rip below.

***

Zamelle was unstoppable. No bolt of quatra made its way past her. She doubled down in ferocity, washing a stubborn Simone away in a fast and dangerous wave of water. Simone crashed up against the factory's roller door. She was dazed, and bruised, and she couldn't heal like a Suneva. She felt like giving up. She didn't even know why she was fighting anymore.

A bolt flew – Simone barely had time to register the colour. It hit Ferrad square in the head, and his armour cracked, shattering. Chad slumped to the ground.

Annikida paused, stopping between portals, then looked to Simone. Simone wrenched herself up, stumbling to her feet. She stared at the enemy, five strong.

Fuck.

***

Boekidin climbed the ladder.

My soul, which I'd worked so hard to repair after my arm was injured, was on its last tether. I could feel it, a single strand of my existence, a singular straw to a wicker basket, holding myself to the ladder.

A pang shot through my being, I gasped.

***

"Zamelle, *resist*, please!" Simone cried. She was finally allowed her words, but they would do her no good.

"I am resisting. With every inch of my soul, I am resisting the pull. I am the master of my destiny," Zamelle called.

She held the thread removal device to Celeste's spine. The two Sunesca stole the French Girl's energy, pinning her down. She tried to scream, but they stole her cries too.

Zamelle's finger reached for the trigger.

***

Natalie flung back towards me – the pang I felt marking her ascent from the sea.

I was okay. My arm held the ladder, in fact, it felt stronger now.

I am okay. I gaped with amazement. The load on my soul became light. I was flooded with elation. I could feel my being reknitting itself, drawing on the ancient power birthed within this realm.

Natalie hung limply by my arm, no longer pulled down by the water. Boekidin pushed her arse up to me.

"Climb, quick!" he yelled. In the distance, another wave rolled in.

"Hold her!" I ordered. I fumbled with the clip at my belt, but eventually got it undone, dropping the life board. I clipped myself to Natalie now, and let go.

The rope held. Her weight pulled snugly at my waist. I set aside my pain, and I climbed.

***

The device dropped from Zamelle's hand. The White Witch stumbled, armour falling away at her intoxicated command. She wheezed, clutching her chest, before her eyes rolled back in her head. She collapsed onto the floor.

Everybody in the room stopped, gawking.

"For fuck's sake, teleport them away!" Simone yelled, pointing to the two Sunesca. As if a lightbulb struck Annikida's thick head, she seemed to shoot into action. Simone could not see the emotion under helmets, and this unsettled her. She'd just have to assume that Annikida was unfathomably stupid.

***

I slumped over the cliff's top face, crawling from the edge, dragging Natalie behind me. Boekidin offered to help, but I struggled on alone until we reached the grass. I unclipped her, laying her face up on the void-meadow. I proceeded to collapse next to her body. Huffing heavily.

"James, I think we just made history," Boekidin said, exasperated.

"You and me, man," I coughed. My soul had already healed physically from its ordeal, although I was beyond exhausted from the efforts of the day.

"The White Witch is free of destiny. This is a strange new world we're stepping in to."

"Let's not think about it," I moaned and rolled over, facing Natalie.

Her chest rose and fell. Chad's had not done that when he was rescued here.

"Huh?" I quizzed. Boekidin squinted, squatting for a closer look.

Then Natalie's lips parted, opening for a breath. Suddenly her body gagged, drawing in a lungful.

"Natalie?" I yelped. I flipped up, bearing over her body as it spasmed. She coughed, then raised her hand to her eye, rubbing it.

"Natalie?" I shook her shoulders. Finally, her eyes opened.

They were beautiful – a deep blue, deeper than the cosmos itself. In them, I saw the vast expanse of space. Life beyond destiny – an ever present infinity of the universe, tangled with stars. And, unlike last time, as I soared through her beauty, there was no black hole. There was only peace, and freedom.

Natalie smiled at me deeply, those blue eyes staring into mine. Those hands which they commanded wrapped around my neck, and drew me in faster than I could think. Her lips wrapped around mine, her arms tight on my body, and we kissed passionately.

Our souls collided, crashing into each other, a wreck of emotional velocity. Breath and words escaped me. Goosebumps spread to every inch of my physical body as I rocked with emotion. Kissing in the Void, I found out, wasn't just touching lips, it was the unity of our beings.

We combined. Two worlds, two souls, two vast, striking cosmoses falling into each other. Passion more powerful than stars, alive in flame. I saw her past, present, and felt her sensations. Her emotions flooded my being, smattering across the vast sunset of the universe. We flew together, hand in hand, through a nebula of green and orange light, spewing elation in a fountain of connection.

Natalie *loved* me. I could feel it. I had a deep soul connection to her, and I knew it. I'd always known it, since I'd first seen her. It was my connection to her, above all else, which kept me going as a Suneva. The air could not compare to this woman. It suddenly became clear, magically, like fireworks.

When Boekidin talked of the person I would cross the world for, who I would risk it all for, I had no idea that I was in the middle of doing just that for her. I *loved* her, and I knew it.

I knew it.

Episode 4

The Happily Never After

Chapter 21
Coming Home

We pulled from the kiss, after what felt an eternity of raw, undying satisfaction. In my entire life had I never felt more fulfilled and confused at once. I loved Natalie Athanas. I loved her. I could yell it to the whole word, but what would I do with this love now?

As I pulled from her face, I could see her starry eyes wet. Her mouth quivered at its ends, and she couldn't hold it from bursting. Natalie fell into tears, finally, after years of strength. She hugged me close again, pulling me into the grass.

Even with my nose squashed into the dirt behind her head, I could tell that those weren't tears of joy. Natalie was in absolute emotional distress. Over the Europe trip I'd tried to convince Celeste to console in me, although she had mainly just held a hand or confided in herself. Now that the girl I liked finally did pour her emotions onto me, I had no idea what to do!

That one-month relationship with Sarah when I was fifteen did *not* prepare me for this.

Natalie hugged me tightly, holding my soul to hers as her emotions swirled. I could feel them, tumultuous in my own being. Then she released. Her face was wet – my shoulder was now wet too, and I pulled us up to sit face to face. The dress she wore in this void – orange and summery – also lay wet and tattered, although Amasos was to blame for that. Natalie's mouth quivered, but her eyes contained so much *joy*.

"James…Thank you!" she wheezed. "I knew you'd believe in me. I knew you'd save me. I knew…" She pulled her head up and kissed me on the lips again. Magic.

"Wait, so you knew you were being manipulated?" I asked, perplexed.

"Yes!" she wheezed. "Yes, I was trapped! I had thoughts, but they kept getting strangled and set aside and I couldn't do anything with them. I was so scared of it happening, James. I was so *scared*." Her mouth shook again, and it took a moment to steel itself. I reached for her hand and grabbed it, and she squeezed mine back.

"Why didn't you tell us what was happening earlier?" I asked.

"I thought I could face it alone," she said. "I didn't want to scare anybody. I didn't want to believe that I was falling, and I didn't want you to think that I was mad. I didn't want to show anybody my pain. I could be strong," she sobbed, "but I wasn't strong. James. I wasn't strong enough on my own."

Natalie strangled my hand to the point that my fingers could have broken. I wasn't sure of the consequences of broken void fingers. Still, the situation we found ourselves in was intense, and insane. What would happen between us? I'd have to man up and have that conversation, rather than leaving it and being disappointed.

"Bullshit, you *were* strong," I whispered into her ear. "You didn't get to see what you were fighting out there, but *cheese* if you weren't giving it everything. You are so strong.

"But it takes strength to admit weakness," Natalie retorted, sobbing. She strangled my body tight, bearing into me for her release. Secretly, I loved this, and a smile came to broadly dance across my face at the thought that I was a great emotional support. This might have been easier than I had expected, and I held Natalie strongly to my shoulder, cradling her over the grass.

"Thank you, James," Natalie repeated into my ear. I smiled more dumbly than before.

"You're welcome Natalie. I'm so glad to have you back."

I abandoned the embrace, and stood tall, offering her a hand up. She rubbed her eyes, then took it, weakly.

I pulled her to her feet, where she stood shakily. It took a moment for her legs to lock into themselves, but then she stood tall, back arched.

Natalie stared out to the horizon, over the violent sea and the three sentry-like apostles. She spun, gaping, taking in the various sights – the forest, the grasslands, the black, hexagonal rock columns, the churning sea. A smile formed on her face as her eyes grew wide.

"James, this is *beautiful*," she said, grabbing my hand. "It's so…vibrant! Look at all of the colours. It's insane." She pointed to the stalks of tall grass, waiting for my equal reaction. "How could grass be this *green*. You've been walking around in here?"

I squinted at the grass. It was barely green, rather, it seemed to be the kind of green you'd get when you left a plastic toy out in the sun for twenty years. I flicked it with my hands.

"What do you mean *vibrant*?" I quizzed. "Everything is a washed out grey. Even the sky." I pointed up, and Natalie gaped in awe.

"It's a pink and yellow sunset right across the whole thing!" She pointed to the vast expanse. "You call that dull? How many amazing sunsets have you seen?"

"Wait…" a realisation clicked in my mind, and I spun to her, pointing at her eyes. "You're blind!"

"I…I am blind." Natalie cocked her head. "But I can see here. It's all so beautiful, James. This is too much."

"But…but…" I stammered, turning back to the white-grey clouds. "I get your excitement to see, but its…it's just an overcast day. There's not even a sun! How can it be a pretty sunset?"

Boekidin took his chance to chime in. He strolled, just having detached the winch drum and pulley system from the rocks. "I think this is just another symptom of your thread, James," he said, and winked. "This place has been consistently mesmerising."

"*Boekidin!?*" Natalie spun, and stepped ahead of me defensively. I felt a slight pang for my manhood, even though it made sense – we both knew that Natalie was the more capable combatant.

"Hey," I calmed her, grabbing her shoulders. "He's a friend."

"I didn't think ghosts would have their armour in the Void." She squinted. "At least, the ghosts who have seen this place didn't say that."

"He's not a ghost," I said calmly. "He's Nazaseva. He came here through my head."

"But, you're dead." Natalie pointed at him. "I've seen the body. You were decapitated."

"I was in Hesslik's head at the time. I lost my body, but not my soul," Boekidin explained.

"Boekidin trusted us enough to risk his life," I added. "He saved your life here, too. He did all of the preparation for me to leap to sea and rescue you. When you're ready, I'd be giving him a huge thanks."

"Well…" Natalie coughed, flustered, "I suppose I should do that now." And she stepped up to the imposing bird-man, his beady, pink eyes bearing upon her. She extended her hand.

"Thank you, Boekidin."

"It was my honour, Miss White Witch," he said, making a bow as he did so. "Now, if I can add, we should probably get out of here. You–" he pointed to Natalie, "–are probably unconscious in a battlefield, and you, James, might be in danger."

"Yes…yes, of course," I said, regaining my head. There was a whole other battle going on in the outside world that I'd forgotten about. Who knew what danger I was currently in – or Natalie was in, passed out in the middle of it. "Let's march this stuff inland and make camp."

"Make camp?" Natalie asked.

"Yeah, have to fall asleep to get back," I said, "and we're not doing it this close to the cliffs. Amasos is tricky."

Natalie nodded. Boekidin handed her the winch drum, then picked up an assortment of other bits and handed them to me. Notably, he left the ladder where it was.

We walked into the nearby forest, further out from the cliffs, towards the Void's centre. Natalie struggled to keep up, dragging the drum behind her heavy head and tired legs. The forest we trudged through backed onto the mountain range which ran to the origin point, where Kuvalik's body floated peacefully. The trees here provided security and cover, so we scattered our belongings under their canopy, not forcing Natalie to walk any further.

She staggered past the pile, collapsing to her knees. "I don't think I'll get to fall to sleep," she said, and I rushed to her side, laying her down gently, "I'm going all dizzy. I don't think I could stay here if I…" and with that, her eyes closed and she collapsed. I let her body melt across the dirt here.

"I'm not sure this realm is for everybody," Boekidin said.

"Not even the White Witch?" I asked.

"I'd take it that's the only reason she woke up at all," he said. "Not many Suneva see this place. I never did until you convinced me I could make it here."

Boekidin saluted, then disappeared. My mind became thick again.

I wanted to think about what he'd said, but there wasn't time to waste. I lay down on the pulley wheel and let myself drift off into meditation.

***

Simone seemed despondent as she recalled the tale of the battle to Natalie and I. Celeste sat in a far corner of the penthouse, traumatised. She'd never come so close to having her thread removed. She'd never had her cries for mercy silenced before they could be vocalised. She had never had her faith in destiny so powerfully challenged as to see the shift in Natalie in just a single moment. Celeste did give me a great big hug for saving her soul, but she had not said much more to me, or anybody else.

Chad seemed to be on the up. The boy didn't internalise defeat, and it could be reasoned that weak moments happened to us all. It was only a matter of time before he was bested in a heated battle like that – and like Celeste, he'd only ever fallen to a white-quatra witch. He was just happy to have the group back together again, for his thread to still exist, and for us all to be back on the right track. He was hopeful.

"…and then Anastasiya teleported the Sunesca and the Royal guards away. Just like that, she picked them up, and moved them *somewhere else*," Simone said it with resentment, although I thought the idea was genius. What a perfect solution to clear a battle scene – just move the enemy *somewhere else*.

"Right, well, good work team?" I quizzed, shrugging my shoulders. "I can't believe we did it, really, but we just defied the will of an angry God *and* didn't die doing it. There's not much more to say except good job and let's rest."

"Rest *where?*" Celeste asked. "We can't stay here. Hesslik will want his White Witch back."

"Let's go home," I said, pouring myself another drink. "Back to Melbourne. I did promise Natalie's dad that I'd bring her home."

"Are you sure that's smart?" Celeste asked, pacing towards me. "Surely Hesslik knows where we're based. Do we really want to bring our operation to the most obvious place? There are plenty of Argol hideouts we can use."

"I vote for going back to Melbourne," Chad said, smiling. "There's good food there. Have you had Maria Grey's gnocchi? Plus, my favourite bed is in Kuvalik's house. Hesslik will find us anywhere we go, anyway. We might as well be somewhere that's comfortable, homely, and full of family."

Celeste wasn't pleased, although everybody else – Simone most enthusiastically – agreed.

"We need to go back there even for just a few days," Natalie added, finally. "If I feel a threat, we can pack up and move. I just think that a few of us need to be at home for a bit, even just to relax after everything we've been through. Whilst we're there, we can make our plan for the next two months, then go out and execute it."

Celeste nodded. "Yes," she said, and turned away, as if to add nothing further. Although she finally did speak. "I need to relax."

***

A plate of sweets was placed before me on the long coffee table. Unlike last time I'd adorned this leather couch, I was not sinking into it through high social discomfort. This room was full of smiles, from Natalie's dad, to her Yamitse Tess, to Natalie herself.

Both Natalie's father and grandmother had thanked me profusely at their front door – her father hadn't expected such a quick rescue, and he hadn't expected that I'd be the one to deliver it. I received hugs and kisses akin to what my own Mum would give me – although, I hadn't gotten those just yet. I'd come to the Athanas household before going home myself, just to be sure that Natalie made it home safely.

For me now was a plate of pastries, and I bit through a hulking handful with extreme gusto.

"You know, Yamitse, James can do the same for you," Natalie explained, bringing her Grandmother a herbal tea. Natalie took the seat opposite me on the couch, with her dad, Nick, hovering around the kitchen. "I'm *destinyless*, just like the ancient Vochduh monks."

"That's very impressive, James," Tess said to me. "Your father tried for years to do what you've done. He never got there."

"He didn't have a strange connection, or his sister's thread," I said smartly.

"Or," Natalie continued, sitting next to her Yamitse. Goodness, she was beautiful. Her thick, long hair, sharp features, bold nose and high cheeks. *Far out*, I smiled dumbly, *I'm doing well for myself.* Although, the eyes would take some getting used to. They used to be a beautiful blue – and certainly, I saw that in the Void. In the real world, they were greyed out, with only a glimmer of the blue that once enchanted me.

"Or, I still have one of the devices from Hesslik," Natalie said, and I recoiled in surprise, spilling a bit of custard-stuffing from my mouth. "I can take your thread away, if that would make you feel better."

"You kept one?" I tried to say through a full mouth. The message came across, just.

"Personal issue weaponry," Natalie said. "I *was* his operative. I'm not giving it back."

"I don't trust *cheating* the Gods," Tess said, staring through my eyes. "Although, I can't know if that's me talking, or Amasos. Your procedure is reversible, isn't it, James?"

"I assume so," I said. "I'd just have to throw your soul off a cliff and into the sea."

"I see," she frowned. "Well, it couldn't do harm. If you'd save my soul, I'd be grateful."

"Consider it done," I smiled at her.

Nick strolled up behind the couch, resting his meaty palms on the upholstery by my shoulders. He leaned down on my left, bearing over me, and whispered into my ear.

"Can I talk to you in the hall?" he said. It was not question, despite the fact it was asked as one.

"Of course," I gave the only allowable response, my hand shaking. I stood from the couch, and made my way calmly to the right of the kitchen, into the bedroom hallway. The door to the hallway was closed behind me, and darkness set over the stout room.

Nick leaned against his mother-in-law's wall. I stood brightly against the opposite side, uncertain as to my fate. He looked me in the eye, an eyebrow raised. I smiled, awkwardly, until the man lunged forward. My heart raced as his arms flew for me, but they grappled me instead in a warm hug. I spluttered my relief, falling into the strong embrace.

"Thank you," he said.

"That's…that's alright," I wheezed from the shock. Nick pulled away.

"I don't understand what you did, or what happened initially," he said, "and I probably wouldn't if you explained it to me. But, James, do you think this will happen again?"

"Will it happen again?" I pondered, there was a *long* timeline to think about here. I was confident that for the moment, Natalie would be safe and free from destiny and Suneva who would hurt her, but forever? I couldn't tell what the future would hold.

"For now, Natalie is safe," I said, honestly. "But she *is* the White Witch, a very powerful and important Suneva. How far in the future are you talking, here?"

"I mean for now, James," he clarified with a roll of the eyes.

"Then yes, she'll be fine."

"And can you help to protect her?" he asked. "Can you make sure that she stays safe?"

"I think more often she's keeping me safe than the other way around," I joked, although Nick's expression soured – deprecating my manhood was not the right direction for a gag.

"She's blind, James," he said, his lips drawing to a purse. "I don't think she's as capable as you think."

"I…I know," I admitted, "but she sees in other ways."

"And you'll help her through it?"

"Yes," I said.

"You're a good kid though, right?"

"Straighter than a mason's pole," I said.

"Apart from the magic shit."

"…Apart from the magic shit…" I agreed.

"And, you have feelings for her?"

"Yes."

"So, you'll keep her safe, then?" He held my shoulders in his meaty grip, bringing us eye to eye.

"As I said, she is much better at saving my ass than I am hers…" I repeated, and his gaze soured, displeased. I shut up.

"You brought into her that spark of confidence and happiness I haven't seen for the last few months, *and* you went across the world to bring her home. I think you're selling yourself short."

"Maybe," I agreed.

"Good," he said. "Despite what I might have said before you left, I think you're good for her. I'm also surprised that you brought her home before the police did."

"What did you say before I left?" My heart sank. I didn't remember the conversation.

"Don't worry about it," Nick patted my shoulder, then stood me up tall. "Just be yourself and don't break her heart."

"Yes, sir," I said.

"Just call me Nick, please."

"Yes, Nick," I said.

He straightened himself, then walked over to the door to lead me back to the leather couches.

***

"Did you ever see this happening?" I asked Natalie. We swam in her bed, covers up to our chins, bodies interlaced. The door was closed, her folks were in the other room. Our combined heat sweated the bed, but it was a beautiful warmth. Holding her made sense – my hands and arms fit where they needed to, her smile fit into my soul. This was a stark change from her trying to apprehend me and my friends

Natalie smiled a cheeky grin. She tugged her ragdoll body from the sea of bedspread and reached curious hands for my mouth. When she found it, she kissed me full of the lips. I sank into it, my mind going numb to logic or sensation.

"Yes," she said. The long, loose sleeves of her top wrestled about her wrists, dangling over my cheeks. "Although, not at all."

"Those are two opposite answers," I pointed out.

"I know," she said. "It's just…I don't really know. When I first met you, I think I had you figured out wrong. I was sure you were coming on to me, and I was getting ready to let you down."

"Ha," I chuckled, "it's funny, because I was trying so hard *not* to make it look like I was coming on to you. I just wanted a friend."

"Same," she said. "But…I don't know. You filled such a big space in my life. There was a week in there where I think I started to like you, but then it went away. I saw that our friendship was really beautiful, you know?"

"Yeah, I know," I said. "So, when did it change?"

Natalie paused, pondering. Her hands gripped around my face, admiring my features, fingers hanging out of the loose long sleeves of her top.

"When I woke in the Void and saw your face," she said. "That's why I said 'I don't know'. It just seemed in that moment that I'd always seen you like this, and hadn't known it. Admitting it to myself felt so…liberating. I feel free."

Her eyes couldn't hide her feelings, which resided in the deep expanse of her soul. It was still visible to me in the floating cosmos, even though the colour of her irises had blurred away.

"What about you?" she asked.

"The same, really," I said. "You've always just been a friend, but I knew when I first saw you that we were connected deeper than that. Either way, I've always had this affinity to stand by you and make sure you're okay. Maybe that's what friends do, but it's more than I felt for anybody else. It wasn't like with Celeste, where I wanted to help her to make myself feel good, I just wanted to be there for you because it was you. It really just made sense when you woke up. I didn't expect a kiss, but it changed my world."

Natalie laughed a cute, surprised giggle. Her body wriggled closer into mine, and she pecked my lips.

"I'm glad it 'just came to us', then," she smiled.

"Me too," I said, giddy with red cheeks.

"But…what does that make us?" I asked, my face turning serious. Natalie met my expression, even without seeing it. "I mean, we should both be on the same page, right? It just feels so fast."

"Let's see where it goes?" she asked.

"That's what I said to Celeste, and she just abandoned me."

"Do you think I'd abandon you?" Natalie asked.

"No…but…I don't want to leave my happiness to chance," I resolved.

"What do *you* want *us* to be?" Natalie asked, caressing my nose.

"I want you to be mine," I said, "but I don't want to call it anything yet…if that makes sense?"

"Then I'm all yours," she said, "and you're all mine."

***

"Is that Captain Numbnuts?" Mum called through the house as I slipped through the front door.

I could only assume that *I* was Captain Numbnuts. "Yes?" I answered, flinging my suitcase down by the study's door. Mum peeked her head around the corner of the kitchen, then pulled herself around it, trudging up the carpet towards me. I was immediately set to fright, and pinned myself to the front door as it closed.

"You're mad?" I squeaked, although the woman appeared confused, and her shoulders dropped.

"No, no, I'm not," she said, and grabbed at me, pulling me in for a hug. I wasn't sure what treatment I was expecting this time, after my third grand Suneva trip against my mother's wishes. It certainly wasn't this.

I stood awkwardly as she pulled away, waiting for her to say something so that I wouldn't have to incriminate myself. After a moment of staring, she finally spoke.

"Thanks for calling during your two weeks away," she said, squeezing my shoulder.

"Oh, that's okay, I…" *You didn't call her, you idiot.* "Oh…"

"Yes, *oh* is correct," Mum nodded with her biting smile. I tried to shrug away, to phase through the door and back out of the house, but it wasn't possible, and I was left to my awkward devices. "Luckily your sister calls me, James. Even Celeste rang to say you were all okay."

"She did?"

"Yes," Mum said, and finally let me go. She turned and tracked towards the kitchen, her step inviting me to follow. I did so, but against all available survival impulses.

"I know what happened with Dedo," Mum said, taking a seat on a barstool. I leaned over the countertop, still stiff as a frozen carrot. "You found out that he had passed on your first day away. I know that this trip wasn't just to see him."

I gulped, but kept my lips stiff, urging Mum to fill the silence. That was the story I'd told her, wasn't it? – that we were going on a trip to see Dedo and Baba, to give Dedo some of Dad's stuff.

"I know everything else that happened, too," Mum continued, setting my eyes alight with fright. "I know about that ancient temple that your dad visited, about the battle in a castle, about going to New York, and fighting in a warehouse."

I had only a cough as a response, my brain falling solidly out of its case. I searched for exits, any temporary relief for what was to come, my palms grappling at the air in the room. Simone wasn't home, was she? She'd already told Mum everything, her grave would be dug in the backyard. I thought I could see it through the window, the meagre cross pressed in atop compacted earth. I turned white.

"I think I'd rather know these things, James, is the point," Mum finally said, and my brain short-circuited, attention returning to her.

"Excuse me?" I stammered.

"What you're choosing to do with your free time is frightening, and you won't stop for me," she said, and her voice was calm, not demanding or imposing. "It's important to you, I can see that... it's been apparent for a short while now. But lord, James, hearing every few days that you're safe, *knowing* what's going on, it made the difference this time. You can thank your sister for that."

"I can?" I gasped, still lost for a proper response.

"And your dad," Mum said. "He left me a letter that Simone found just now. I think it was written after he died..." And she gave me a look, some search for confirmation. I nodded to it, not sure how else I was meant to reciprocate. "He was involved in this magic shit, too. I mean, I *have* to believe that now - the man came back from the grave, he lived in the fucking attic." And she shook her head, trying to make sense of her own words. "Still, his letter was an assurance that all of this magic is safe, and that you've been left in good hands."

"The letter wasn't about Simone?" I asked.

217

"It was, but Simone told me that he meant for it to be about you," Mum hummed. "Although maybe he was right all along – Simone is level headed, and you're a numbnuts with no gauge for sensibility."

I chuckled to the remark, finally finding myself again. "Maybe he was right," I joined along, "but I appreciate the trust."

"Don't get me wrong, my trust is with Simone," Mum said, cold. I stiffened again, nodding to her. "She's at least let me know what was going on. If you can do the same, James, you've got my trust."

"Okay, okay," I nodded. "That's easy."

"But tell me that these crazy adventures don't go on too much longer," she sighed, standing. "Because I just want you to have a long, stable life, James. I don't want you to throw away these years that mean so much. You *or* Simone."

"There's only…" and I had to count it on my fingers, "two months of the *real* crazy stuff left, Mum." I said. "Then real life comes back. Real life, but different."

"Right…good," Mum nodded, huffing. She seemed satisfied, and I was amazed. "I'm not going to be mad at you," she continued, and my concern grew, "but just tell me everything that's happened so far. Simone told me you guys travelled through wormholes, that you talked to demons. I just don't want to be ignorant anymore. Tell me everything."

And so I sat down next to Mum, and that's what I did.

Chapter 22
The Planning Stage

I walked under the railway line, through the cobbled alley, passing under the shadow of the track-bed. The sky was clear and blue, another vibrant day in the falling weeks of summer. It was hot today, almost unbearably so. After our meeting at Kuvalik's house, I was thinking of suggesting we go to the pool.

The sun hit my skin again. A hot, impatient breeze danced through the underpass, and I felt its energy in my hands. The wind – my deep soul connection.

Simone, Natalie, Celeste, Chad, Yvon and Anastasiya were all waiting for me, in my house.

Kuvalik's house. I reminded myself, gritting my teeth. I hated slipping like that. I'd caught myself doing it twice since I'd come back from New York, and in

218

the most inconsequential of moments. The mundanity of the identity crises was the most worrying part to me.

The size and calibre of the guest list today was also surprising. Little could I have known, some weeks ago, dashing into the woods with a near-broken arm, that I could have gotten the group back together. Even slimmer the chance I would have guessed that the group was *bigger*, and more prolific than when it disbanded. Our tiny movement had gained support. Things were looking up, and I smiled towards the shining sun.

Impressively, in that small, once dilapidated cottage to which I walked, would be some of the most important figures in the Suneva social sphere alive today:

Zamelle Menas, the White Witch, historical spiritual leader of the Suneva people. Iva Argol, matriarch of the most influential Suneva group of the past century. Boekidin, the *Shiverman*, a feared and powerful *Kidin*. Annikida, the Legendary of Teleportation. Ferrad, the infamous operative *Lion's Foot*. Simone, *Fairysmog* and now *Salak Nera*, influential blogger and now budding Salak. And finally, what I brought to the table – Maiki, the Vochduhvlad, and Kuvalik, the ancient *Liktan Fara* and owner of the super-connected destiny.

Needless to say, the cause to stop Hesslik, having started over a year ago, had found itself in unsuspectingly good hands.

I shortly came to the gate of the late Olomb's house. The energy of threads buzzed inside it, just detectible through my posed fingers. I reached around to the latch on the gate, fumbling with it, before finally getting the damned thing to open. I came into the yard, peering at an overgrown hedge by the blossom tree. The dark, grey sky sat ominously in the backdrop.

"When was John Grey coming around to help me with that hedge, again?" I said aloud, trying to remember.

I looked to the house, which was wet still with the rain from this morning. *It didn't rain this morning,* I quizzed. *And John Grey is* dead.

"Damn it," I mumbled, my vision sifting, rising like hot gas off a road's surface. The sky was its deep, vibrant blue again, although the hedge was still overgrown. Frustration whirred inside my head. My gears ground, and I stormed up the veranda, towards the inset front door.

I don't think that one was useless, Boekidin cut through my heavy head. *The old man just wants his garden looked for. Your dad probably left a few gardening tools behind.*

"They're in the shed," I responded, pushing open the thick, wooden door. "But I'd rather not have my identity stripped for gardening advice. You said this wouldn't happen"

I said no such thing, Boekidin stammered. *I didn't claim to know anything — all I said was that the thread could be closed once opened.*

"Sure…" I agreed.

But I don't think it's going to get much worse up here, he chuckled. *There doesn't seem to be any harm in using his thread any more than you already have.*

"That fills me with hope," I groaned sarcastically.

Come on, man. Boekidin smiled — his expression soaking into my mind. *Put a spin on it.*

"I'll try," I agreed, my response snapping. I tried to steel myself as I trudged down the hallway. If I could regain my jolly optimism in time to face the group, perhaps this meeting would go well.

Chad had gone to the shops and purchased new beanbags, it seemed. Now around the couch-side coffee table there rested an armada of soft seats, ready to house a conference. Chad hoarded three for himself, lying across them like a daybed. Celeste took centre stage on the couch for herself, with Yvon tucked up next to her. Anastasiya sat on the beanbag next to Natalie, sitting behind her long blonde hair and flushed cheeks in reverence. *To think that a* Legendary *is excited to be in Natalie's presence.*

Simone perched herself next to Chad, taking two bean bags. Her Sunesca robe had been torn badly and ruined in the battle to save Natalie, although that didn't stop her from wearing it. It draped over her like a night gown, hood up, covering her face to the mouth in shadows.

"Right," I said as I strolled into the room, brave face on. I set down the book and pens that I had brought with me onto the coffee table, and turned to the kitchen. "Would anybody like tea?" I asked.

"I would, please James," Natalie said first. She said it with the slightest of smiles given in slightly the wrong direction. I found it endearing.

"Is that *you* talking, James?" Chad asked. "I've never heard of you brewing the tea."

My eye twitched a nerve. I was so certain that it was me, but Kuvalik could talk aloud through my body — he'd done it just a few metres ago. What else was I saying aloud that wasn't in my own words?

"Tea just seems like the right thing to do here," I spoke the truthful answer – the reason I'd suggested tea in the first place. Chad smiled, nodding. He was just looking out for me. "Anybody else?" I asked.

"Just make one for everybody," Celeste said. "You know we all want some. Tradition is tradition."

Celeste didn't say it with any attitude of facetiousness, although her bossing me around still made Anastasiya blush. The Legendary made a hand as if to teleport to my side, but I shooed her gesture away, turning to the kitchen.

I was taken aback. I didn't remember the kitchen looking so good. It was pristinely clean, coated in fresh crème paint. Yes, there was some dust, as there should have been, but not much. John Grey must have come around this morning and cleaned it after the gardening. Strange.

I reached up into the top cabinet, where I always kept the tea. The box felt light, and my heart sank. There wasn't another box there either. Surely I didn't leave myself with low supply. I'd never do that. I pulled the box into sight.

This was not the box I put in there. My tea box was a yellow tin. This was an old Manchester breakfast tea box. When did I drink *that* tea?

Who was I making tea for again?

"James, can I have mine with no milk?" a voice asked. The voice of a young girl. Who's James? I turned to my living room, to see a crowd of young people gathered here. Amongst them, those *white*, shining eyes, glossed over. Eyes of evil.

But with such a sweet smile.

The girl you love. It clicked. *I'm James.*

"Oh, fuck me!" I cursed aloud, grappling at my face. Anastasiya almost fell off the beanbag in fright.

"Sorry," her voice whimpered, "I…I should have asked before, I…"

"You're fine," I fussed. "No milk, that's okay. That's not why I'm mad." And I spun back to the kitchen, still clutching the box of tea. "Sorry for scaring you. If ever I randomly shout, it's because I thought I was Kuvalik." I pressed the button to let the kettle boil. There was dead silence from the living room.

"I'll take no milk, too, James," Chad said, breaking it. "Or, we could call you emperor. You're sure to respond to that no matter what, Mister Vochduhvlad."

"I…" I didn't quite have a response to that on my tongue, although it made me smile as I lined up the tea cups with bags. "Yes, that would actually work, wouldn't it?" I said.

"Well, does the title of *Emperor* speak to your soul?" he asked, standing from the impressive bean-bed. "You've got two identities, and they're both Suneva world leaders."

"*Outdated* Suneva world leaders," I added.

"*Irrelevant* is probably the word you're looking for," Celeste chimed in. Chad snickered as he walked into the kitchen next to me. He shooed my hands off the mugs.

"I'll take over this," he said. "You're traumatised enough. Take the beanbed-*five-thousand*." He instructed, pointing to his monstrosity.

I stammered. "I...I've got this, man." I said.

"Nonsense," Chad smiled, pushing me gently towards the group. "*He* had me make tea by campfire. I can manage this. Sit."

"Thank you," I said, resting a hand on his meaty shoulder. I stalked away, towards the sitting area. Pulling up a beanbag between Natalie and Anastasiya, I finally sat, letting my hand rest on Natalie's leg.

She jolted in faint surprise as I did so, but reached to grab it anyway. That gave me a moment of bliss.

"Anyway," Celeste continued, "whilst Chad makes these teas, let's start this meeting."

"Agreed," Chad said, clanging a spoon to the mugs.

"What details do we know?" I asked. "We should make a timeline of things."

Natalie perked up on her low perch. She stared ahead with grey eyes, ears alert, not choosing to look anywhere.

"We've got until the seventh of May," she said. "It's the twenty-first of February today. That gives us just under eleven weeks."

"What do you know about Hesslik's plans?" Simone asked. "You were his operative, after all."

"I know a bit, but not everything." Natalie continued. "I know where he's planning to host the gathering, but I didn't find out where he would place the energy device."

"Why would he move the device away from the castle?" Celeste asked. "It's smarter to keep it where he can guard it, right?"

"And it'd be too big to move out of the castle anyway," I interrupted, looking at Natalie. "I saw it on New Year's Eve. It wasn't finished then, but it would have no chance fitting through even the laboratory doors."

"He doesn't have to move it," Natalie said, "it stays where it is. Ideally, it can transfer the same current globally. Technically, he doesn't even need the gathering; he's just fool-proofing in case he's wrong about its range."

"Then why would the gathering and the device be in separate places, given that logic?" Celeste asked.

"The gathering isn't at the castle," Natalie said. "I should have made that clearer."

"Where, then?" I asked.

"He's hired out a whole block of streets in Thessaloniki," Natalie said. "I've seen the layout – he took me to it. It's *massive*. And, well, it has to be if he wants to fit the Suneva free world into it."

"Where?" Chad asked, his ears tingling to the conversation. The last spoon rattled against a tea mug.

"Thessaloniki, the main city streets. It's the second biggest city in Greece, just north of Olympus," Natalie said. "I mean, lots of space, but he'll need it for all the Suneva there are."

"How many Suneva are out there?" I asked.

"Half a million active," Natalie said, "by his latest census."

"Sweet *Cheese*," I cussed, "half a million? No wonder he's rented a whole city."

"There's a strong enough Argol presence in Thessaloniki," Celeste said. "It's a risky place to set up an Empire event."

"Not anymore," Natalie said. "He had me convert them."

"What?" Celeste choked on her tongue. She sat bolt upright. "How did I not hear about this?" she asked, rage boiling. "I am *Argol* for Veritas sake."

"I don't know," Natalie said, "they cut communications. It's more likely you just heard *nothing* from them."

Celeste's ears steamed, her cheeks flushing. Chad brought the tea down to us, and was extra careful to put Celeste's somewhere far from her hands, which twitched in a fit. He took his place finally on the bean-bed. I sipped my tea.

"I can't believe that," Celeste griped. "They accuse me of losing loyalty to the Argol name, but shit like this is happening right under my nose?" She picked up her tea with a gnarled hand and, reluctantly, sipped it delicately. "I refuse to believe that my organisation is broken."

"I guess that's what happens when your dad tries to control gangters with hugs and kisses instead of violence," Chad said. "Didn't he ever watch those mafia movies? You've got to kill a few people for loyalty."

The comment was made with a grin, although Celeste was far from laughing along. She turned to him, cold.

"I don't run a *gang*," she snorted. "I'm the leader of the *Suneva Free World.* The *only* one we've had for the past century."

"And, in a free world," Chad continued, "people get to choose who they follow."

"I…I…" Celeste stammered, attempting to grapple onto an argument. Stubbornness consumed her. "Why would they go to Hesslik?" she asked.

"Because he's reasonable," Chad suggested with a shrug.

"He's an idiot!" Celeste seethed. "The only thing he's promised is to bend over backwards to sign away our rights so we can 'fit in' with society. Screw that. I'm not giving up my rights."

"Okay…" Simone interrupted, stealing the attention. She let a silence linger before leaning in to the circle. "I think this is all fairly indicative of a greater issue at hand."

"Which is…?" Celeste snapped.

"Nobody can agree of what the hell we want," Simone said plainly, and faces fell blank. "Think about it. We're sitting here devising plans to stop Hesslik's great gathering and destroy his device, but what then? He'll probably make another one, use it at another date, and we'll just keep chasing him around. We could try to defame him, but then the Suneva would split into splinter groups or rally more strongly to his cause. If we just take him down now, without knowing *what we want*, then we do nothing. We don't stop him. Our goals are short sighted."

"What are you suggesting?" Chad asked.

"We need to create our own nation – or religion, whatever it is. We need to give the Suneva something to follow in the fall of Hesslik. Something that satisfies everybody yet fulfils nobody entirely. An amalgamation of all current Suneva ideologies. Something for everybody."

I nodded, thoughtful, sipping my tea. Chad seemed to agree, as did Natalie.

"When did *you* become an expert on Suneva politics?" Celeste bit.

Simone gave her a dry glance, and chuckled. "I was *Fairysmog*, honey," she met Celeste's tone. "I knew what each Suneva influencer ate for breakfast and shat out at lunch. I wrote about their every decision and slandered them into the ground. I know what the Suneva factions are up to. I was once your enemy. Don't forget that."

Celeste grunted, and sat back in her chair.

"That's a great idea, Simone," I said, "but we've only got eleven weeks. How do you propose that we rally support from the entire population in eleven weeks?"

"That's not the idea," Simone said. "We just have to be the best option when Hesslik falls. They only have to know about us."

"And who would join us, with our notoriety?" I asked. "I don't think half of the Suneva population would follow Maiki, or Fairysmog, or the defected agent *Lion's Foot*, or Iva Argol…"

Chad gripped at the sides of his beanbags, holding on for dear life as his mind took him on a lightbulb-moment rollercoaster. His eyes lit with fantasy, realisation, and abandon. He turned to me in shocked glee.

"Yes, they will," he said, a finger to their air.

"Huh?" I stumbled.

"A fraction of Suneva *already* follow Iva Argol, the bearer of the pink flames. A fraction of Suneva follow us, because they hate Hesslik…" his mind rocked his body, throwing ideas at him through a mesh screen, "and even more Suneva would follow the White Witch, because she's basically the Suneva Jesus. Many more would follow the Vochduhvlad, because they distrust the black holes and have an ethical inclination. Many would follow the Shiverman, or a Legendary Suneva of teleportation…"

"And what about all of the Suneva who would rather follow *Hesslik*?" Celeste asked with scorn.

"Then we offer them the Suneva that Hesslik claims to stand for. The poster-boy of Electric Suneva nations. The one leader who threw the world into the modern Suneva era. We offer them Kuvalik, the golden *Fara*."

"*What?*" I objected. I looked around the room, pleading for sense.

"Chad's right." Simone said, jumping aboard his thought rollercoaster.

"Just imagine…" Chad took me by the shoulders, gesturing to the far horizon of the kitchen wall. "Kuvalik and the White Witch roll up onto Hesslik's stage, tell the world of his device and defame him. Then, Iva Argol comes from the crowd, with her army, and pledges to join them. It would rock the world."

"No…" I stammered, "I can't do that. I don't want to use his armour. Do you know how much that could screw with my head?"

"And you think that it will look realistic if I just up-and-pledge allegiance to Kuvalik?" Celeste asked. "*That* will need some work."

"Look, James," Simone said, locking her gaze, "Kuvalik gave you his thread because he couldn't enact his plan as a ghost. He couldn't have the influence."

"Those weren't his words," I asserted.

"It was the gist, right?" she sighed. "What *were* his words?"

"I don't remember!"

Her gaze averted, her stare intensifing. She looked past my eyes – not into my soul, but into something else entirely. A way I'd never known anybody to look at me.

"Kuvalik, what were your words to James?" she asked.

"I said that I died too early to bring my plans into fruition – that I felt my ability to influence the world fade before me," my mouth ran, drawing words from his thoughts, pushing them into my brain. "My plans would fail if I didn't pass on the destiny that was given to me."

"See?" Simone smiled, her vision correcting to focus on *me*. I snapped back into reality, fuming. "He couldn't enact his plans as a ghost because he couldn't be *present*. This is the chance to use his social power to create the change he always wanted to make. This is fulfilling his interconnected destiny."

"Don't you *dare* do that again," I threatened. "That's *horrifying*."

"I'm sorry, I had to prove the point," she said.

"And how do you know this is what he wants?" I scorned. "You didn't ask him."

"We could…."

"*Don't!*"

"Okay," she said, resting her hands in her lap. "I just think it seems in line with his plan."

"It's *very* in line with his plan," Chad continued. "Maybe he didn't gather us to find the Legendaries after all. I mean, we haven't even included them in our plans. Maybe he just *knew* that we'd represent the perfect mix of ideals going forward into creating this new world. He picked three Suneva world leaders, and then me for some reason. This seems like it was *exactly* his plan from the go."

"Oh *cheese*," I uttered, then composed myself. "Fine, fine. I be Kuvalik to get the people into the nation – then what? I can't be him forever. I refuse to do that."

Simone raised a finger as if to make a point, but retracted it. She caressed her chin. Deep in thought.

"Maybe that's part of the appeal," Natalie suggested. "Kuvalik has risen from the dead to unite the people, but he'll return to death when it's done. Resurrected for a brief purpose – and *you* were the Suneva he chose. That's *powerful.*" She smiled at me – or close enough to me. I liked the solution, but I was still nervous. I was glad she couldn't see my face.

"Yes, that's good," Chad waggled his finger.

"Well, for this to work, I'll need to have all the support I can get," Celeste sighed. "I'll need to build the Argols back up. I'll especially need to win back those Thessaloniki Argols who changed their allegiance. Having Hesslik's festival in an Argol city would give us good leverage and penetration."

"And the circumstances seem perfect, even," Natalie said. "If your defectors really do like Hesslik's vision, they'll like Kuvalik's – especially if it's the halfway between Liktan, Argol, and Vochduh ideologies. It will look like you were really listening to your people in siding with Kuvalik."

"Yes…that's actually a great point," Celeste smiled, finally, "but I'm still not convinced that *I* am on board with this mushed-up ideology."

"We'll all have to compromise," Simone said, "but I guess that 'Kuvalik's' new nation is as much yours as you argue for it to be. We'll have to decide the rules that it plays by."

"Okay, good," I said, "this far-off plan works. What do we have to do to achieve it? We've got eleven weeks."

We each returned to our own heads to ponder. Yvon, who had been keeping minutes, unnoticed, reviewed his piece of paper and started to write dot points.

"Firstly," he started, "you'll have to find out where the big device is being held – although, you'll need to go to the festival regardless, because you've apparently decided to shut it down on *the* day…"

"To give Hesslik no time to fix it," Chad smiled.

"Yes, right," Yvon squinted. "Should we leave this intelligence job to Natalie? She was an operative, after all. You did get access to the computers, right?"

"I can't see," she replied plainly. "I can't use a computer anymore."

"Ah…" he twitched, turning red from embarrassment.

"Wouldn't Simone be better for that?" Celeste asked. "Fairysmog had her connections, right? You told *us* that Anderson was responsible for Hesslik's leaks."

"Yeah," Chad agreed, waggling a finger, "Simone, could you find us information? Just pull the *Fairysmog* card on your old friends."

"I could try," she said, "although it might be difficult if the news of me being Fairysmog has spread."

"Let's hope it hasn't," I said, feeling a pang of guilt.

"I could probably help, too," Chad said. "I'm good at information. Plus, I was also an operative of Hesslik's. I know his systems."

"Great," I said. "Yvon, what else?"

"Well, Celeste has to convince those Argols in Thessaloniki to follow her...then convince them to abandon her for Kuvalik."

"Easy," Celeste said. "Anastasiya can come with me. We'll be in and out in a day." She smiled sweetly at the meek girl, her bold, red lips inviting. Anastasiya recoiled in shock, but nodded her head to the idea.

"Then James and Natalie," Yvon said, "you've got to dress up as Kuvalik and the White Witch and go spouting rhetoric in public places."

"Sure..." I frowned. "Easier said than done."

"I'll find some key dates," Natalie said. "There's got to be a public spectacle soon."

"Then," Yvon continued, "we'll have to find the time of Hesslik's announcement and the planned thread-death. We'll need to gather an Argol force to split the crowd and get us to the stage..."

"Shouldn't be difficult," Celeste added.

"And we'll need to get a further idea of what people actually want, if we're going to offer them a better solution than Hesslik's Nation," he said, "and personally, I think that's a job up to me and the Shiverman."

Huh...I heard my name? Boekidin rusted in my head, knocking over a pile of incorporeal thought objects. He stumbled to his bird-feet. *Sorry, I wasn't listening.*

"Review the memories later," I whispered to him. "But that sounds good," I said aloud to the group. "I mean...it sounds like a good plan, not that it sounds enjoyable..."

"I agree," Natalie said. "It sounds tough, but we've got eleven weeks."

So much time, I mused. *I don't know that I can impersonate Kuvalik for that long.*

"Good," Celeste said, taking the final sip of her tea and standing from the couch. "Now that we're clear, let's get to it."

Chapter 23
Festival Crashers

The Void was beautiful, even if it was dull.

There was no confusion in the Void. I was Maiki. He was my soul. He was my mind. I had freedom.

No powers, no complication, no ability to manipulate the world. Just me, the dull sand at my feet, the strange plants, and the insane, tumbling seas.

I spent three weeks dreaming in the Void. I would fall asleep in a meditative state and wake up on the dusty, stone ground of the void-library. In the first week, I would oversleep as I couldn't hear my alarm – it would take Simone rattling me to realise I had to be somewhere.

My alarm's persistence to scream at me come morning, however, meant that soon it became a feature of the Void – echoing over its deserts and through its vast canyons when I had to be up. I didn't miss appointments, now.

Boekidin sometimes came in, too, to build and invent, but otherwise he was out on his own missions, collecting information for Natalie and I. He was scanning minds of Suneva, jumping from soul to soul throughout the city. He could be gone for days – torn too far from me to return easily, taking his time to slowly trek back, learning about people.

He would find for us what the Suneva wanted. What would a perfectly represented Suneva ideology look like? What would convince these people to join Kuvalik and the White Witch over the impressive orator and manipulator Hesslik?

I played in the realm of the spiritual, rescuing friends from their ties to destiny. I took my surfboard out to the seas – all of which Boekidin and I had visited and set up safety measures to allow me to do this alone.

Of particular interest was the Fara Hesslik. If I could find his body out in the sea of Amasos, then I wouldn't even need to play around as Kuvalik. Once I pulled him ashore, his mind would be his again, and he would realise that he didn't actually want to get rid of all of the threads, and that he was being manipulated.

Or, at least, even if he *did* want to destroy the threads on his own, it would be easier to persuade him otherwise without a God spewing words in his ear.

But, his body wasn't there.

I spent a whole night of sleep searching the coast. I rowed my new row-boat out, past the apostles of the Amasosian cliff bay, right out into the swell of high seas where one or two unfortunate souls were harboured, strangled in the rough waters. I scanned the cliffs and their coves, under the eyes of tall, black rocks and the dark, thick sea. It crashed against me in its aggression and spite, trying to rip me from my mission. Hesslik was nowhere to be found.

And strangely, neither was Anastasiya in the calm, clear sea of Nerios.

I spent many other nights in the Vochduh Library reading the works of ancient monks. The secrets to flight were contained in these books, I could feel it as I touched them – connecting to their meanings, words, and authors. Many tomes lay scattered about the lectern as I scanned the open one – it's words forming just as I looked at them, then dissolving away into obscurity.

All of the ancient Vochduh could fly, or, at least, they seemed to do so in all of Olomb and Kuvalik's memories of the temple city. The books which I read described hundreds of ways to do it. One hundred different mindsets to be in, one hundred different perspectives to think of your relationship and connection to the air around you. Are you a user, or a commander? Is it command, or communication? Is the connection not simply *being* the air, or is it greater than that?

I'd felt a deep level of connection once, right before I came to the Void the first time, when high on the King's Flower. The only problem was that I couldn't possibly remember or articulate it. If I wanted to replicate that connection, I'd have to find the right description of it in one of these texts. I spent countless mornings with my head stuffedbetween fages, re-enacting the styles of long dead monks in the hopes to levitate. None had worked yet, but one would. It would be out there, in the vast library.

Today, Natalie and I would be attending a cultural event in Melbourne's grand exhibition building. Built for the world fair held in our city, it was an old, beautiful building with a high central dome. Today was a Slavic and Greek food and dance festival. Chad had found that many of the dance clubs attending were Suneva affiliated, and that most of the crowd would be Suneva too. In fact, it seemed that Melbournian Suneva used this festival annually as a cover for their own meetup and celebration. The timing was a little late though, leaving us with only eight weeks to really build a rapport, but it was better than having no festival at all to launch our campaign.

I walked over to Natalie's house, where Yvon would meet us. I had been pulling her into my dreams over the past weeks. I had found through Chad that the Void had empathic qualities - touching souls would allow me to connect to their emotions. Touching Natalie's soul, however, would bring her awake.

Each time her blue eyes awoke to stare into mine, it became apparent how the Void could be known as heaven. Her smile was always so wide, her soul so alive, to see, and to see all of the vibrant colours of quatra. She skipped through the fields I found dull, grabbing my hand and dragging me along. We would kiss in the temple, our souls pushed up to the walls, emotions swimming together in the stream of time.

It was the ultimate form of connection - two souls intertwined through a different realm., two people which became one through their intimate touch. It was a blessing to feel – and a reward at having cheated the Gods.

Natalie could never stay long, and despite her elation at waking to see me and the vibrant world, she urged me not to either. As she drifted off, her mind would run, and she would mumble that the Void was dangerous – that she was in danger. I worried that I was letting her slip into nightmares, but always accepted her will to fall away.

I hadn't *actually* seen Natalie in the flesh for something over a week. She was busy – down visiting her Mum by the beach. She had invited me, although I had my hands full too. And secretly, I was nervous to meet her mother – a woman so devoutly repulsed by Suneva that she divorced her own husband, disowned her own mother, and drove her daughter's meltdown.

Natalie answered the door, pretty as ever. Her hair was misstyled – although I'd come to expect that – and her greyed eyes stared past mine. She reached for my face, and held my jaw in her palms. She smiled, then she kissed me.

"Ready to go?" I asked. "I'm not. I'm still nervous."

"So am I," Natalie agreed, and stepped back into the house, leaving room for me to follow. "Come in first," she insisted. I did so quickly.

As she turned to lead, she drew her twin swords. I jolted in alarm.

"Yvon, get your stuff ready," she called into the house before I had the chance to ask what she was doing. "We'll be leaving soon."

"Natalie, why with the swords?" I asked as I stepped up to the kitchen bar. She walked past me, towards the right-hand door to the hallway.

"To see," she said, and pointed to her face.

"That's…"

"It's fine," she interrupted, and went to walk into the hall, straight into a closed door.

I jumped into her path off a blast of air, leaping across the kitchen to grasp the doorknob and throw the door open. She paused in shock of my sudden movements, then frowned.

"I'm not sure they're helping," I said, joking. Natalie scowled harder.

"They are," she insisted. "What the hell is that door made of, anyway?"

231

"Wood?" I questioned, feeling for carbon.

"There'd be hydrogen in it then…" she groaned, pushing past me.

"Are you alright?" I asked, jogging in her tail. She tapped her swords to the toilet door, then reached her hand for it. She fumbled for the knob as her weapons vanished.

"Look, I'm here if you need a hand. You don't have to act all strong in front of me," I said, and grabbed her arm, moving her hand to the knob. Natalie sighed heavily, accompanied by a sniffle. Her hand begrudgingly turned the knob, although her grey eyes turned glassy.

"Oh, hey…I didn't mean to…"

"I need more help than I'm willing to admit, James," Natalie turned to me. "Without destiny, it's hard to see. I'm trying my best, but there's a *lot* of hydrogen, and water, and souls, and…it was all much simpler when I was being led by compulsions. I think I'm going to have trouble today in the crowd. I don't want to admit it, but it scares me."

"Then I'll help," I smiled, resting my hands to her jaw.

"But what scares me more, is becoming dependant again," she said, and removed my hands. "Just…I'd like you to hold my hand *today*," she added. "Maybe just this once, I'll ask for help."

"I'll be there."

"Thank you," she smiled, and went into the lavatory, closing its door behind her. I sauntered out to the living area, where Yvon had just arrived, and was preparing his bag. Natalie joined us soon after, and we walked all together to the station.

***

The crowd was large, spilling into the Carlton gardens and the museum beyond.

The masses were building, bubbling around the smells of ethnic smoke and spiced meats. Natalie reached for her swords first, then reconsidered and chose my hand instead. At least I'd made the list of considerations. I had to afford Natalie the choice to ask for help, and I was glad to be chosen.

I held her hand tightly as I lead her through the grass, towards the exhibition building. The skin of her hand was tough, but her fingers were slender. They fit nicely between mine. Her eyes didn't bother looking straight ahead.

232

Instead, they rolled around, shifting, seeing through her free hand which held the peace sign pose. Natalie analysed the energies of the crowd.

"So, what are we going for?" Yvon asked, scanning the amassed community through mirrored sunglasses. "Do you want me to find the mood of the crowd now, or after the speech? I mean, have you written what you want to say?"

"Kind of," I said as we came to the fountain before the exhibition building. People gathered around it, posing for photos, winding their cameras. "I've written *something*, but it won't do us any good if Boekidin's intel doesn't match the attitudes of *these* people."

Live updates, maybe? Boekidin suggested.

"Yes, that sounds good," I said aloud, then frowned, remembering that only I heard him. "Boekidin said he can live update us."

"I can do that too," Yvon smiled, determined. "I'll just need to look asleep in the corner of the room…"

There was a lot of Suneva energy here. I could feel it on my fingertips, as I'd always been practising and failing to do. All this time, and I still couldn't connect to the field properly, but I'd have to be stupid not to feel the massive presence all around. Kuvalik's thread itched at me. *It* could read the field in all of its depth of colours. It was begging to be used.

"How will *you* approach this, James?" Natalie asked me, squeezing my hand. "I know this will be hard for you."

She was right. Today, I would have to let Kuvalik in. I would have to adopt his armour, stand on the stage, and hope that my brain lasted long enough to run through the entire speech I'd prepared.

"I guess I'm just going to have to toughen up and get on that stage. I need to be Kuvalik," I said.

"Yes, but I mean technical details," she clarified. "Are you Kuvalik, or did Kuvalik give himself to you?" she asked. "It's a card you can play now, or later. Redeem Maiki as Kuvalik's chosen Suneva, or leave that aside and bring it up later."

"I…" I hadn't considered that. Why did Natalie only bring this up *now?*

Show the transformation, Boekidin said before I could make my reply. *Bringing it up later will destroy the trust you'd gained. You have to be honest upfront.*

"I'll have to show them now," I said. "I think it will help me, too. Maiki first, chosen by Kuvalik second."

"Okay," Natalie smiled, "if that's what you think will work, let's go with it…"

"Yes, I agree," Yvon chirped, almost cutting Natalie off. He made his way to the front of the group. "From what I've seen, Kuvalik turning out to be Maiki would be much, much worse than Maiki turning out to be chosen by Kuvalik. It's like a redemption arc, versus finding out that Suneva-Jesus is actually the face of Suneva anarchy and terrorism."

I groaned at the insulting explanation, but took it for what it was. I continued without rebuttal.

We walked up the steps and through the huge, grand doors of the exhibition building. Light bounced off every surface, coming in through the windows of the great dome and the clerestories in the roof. The space was holy, like a marvellous, wooden cathedral. The eastern wing had been cordoned off and set up as a stage. The western wing had a display of archaeological finds, of all things to display in this mixing pot of a fair. On the stage danced performers from one of the represented countries – although to me all the costumes and dances looked about the same, I really had no connection to my parents' cultures. A sizeable crowd watched, but was nowhere near as numerous as the one gathered outside.

"This might be the wrong place to make your stand," Yvon said, noting the stage. "The atmosphere in here is right…almost religious… but the crowd is out there." He pointed out the doors, to the smell of wafting spit-roast smoke and sweaty people.

"There wasn't a stage out there, was there?" Natalie asked. "I didn't feel one."

"No," Yvon rubbed his chin, pondering. His soul-severed arm obeyed him well now – his spirit had reknit into it. My own injured arm was fully recovered now, too. I was now able to summon by staff again without becoming Maiki.

I followed Yvon's gaze, up to the mezzanine level of the grand hall. That wouldn't do as our stage either, it was still inside. If only there was some kind of platform on the face of the building, which looked over the fountain and the festival.

But there *was*.

"I've got an idea," I said. "Follow me."

I led the group out through the doors again, fighting past the gaggle of festival-goers amassed by the steps. I backed up towards the fountain, peering up the building's façade. It had an inset arch over the doorway, but the face rose to the total height of the roof, with a section of flat roof between two low towers.

"Up there." I pointed. "On the roof."

234

"Oh, right, yes, I see, on the…" Yvon followed my finger, up to the place between the two towers. "*On the roof?*" he stammered.

"We want a spectacle, I think getting up on the roof is as good as it gets."

"That's *illegal*," Yvon persisted.

"So is hijacking a stage," I rebutted.

"Yes, but it's considerably less illegal. Hijacking the stage is 'get escorted off the premises' illegal, not 'go to jail' illegal."

"Usually I'm not the one to think of something this bold," I admitted, "but if I'm going to have to use Kuvalik, I'm going to make it a real spectacle."

"So, how do you want to get up there?" Yvon asked, then crooked his neck to see inside the grand hall. "I'm sure there's an entrance way in there through the mezzanine. There's got to be some way for…"

I leaned down into Natalie's ear.

"Become Zamelle," I instructed her. She obliged, letting the blue and teal armour take her body. I allowed myself become Maiki, the armour locking into place over my skin.

"Oh no…" Yvon yelped.

"Now, hold onto my back and don't let go," I told her. Zamelle was no longer in need of my assistance to see, not with the quatra skin covering her body, enhancing her senses. She found her way around my armoured body easily, and latched on.

Already there were gasps from the crowd, most of whom could sense the change when a Suneva adopted their armour. A slow radius cleared around us, becoming a trickle and stream as I ran the steps towards the building. I threw my hands to the floor, blasting down a jet of air.

It was much harder to haul the extra weight up. I'd only made it about half of my usual height before landing on the building's face with my long claws. Heads and pointed fingers honed on Zamelle and I as I made my next leap. Gathered people looked away from their souvlakis and chevaps, gazes affixing to me, *Maiki*, carrying the White Witch to the top of the exhibition building.

My claws sunk again into the intricate stonework, and I felt a pang of guilt as details were ripped off. I'd have to leave a diamond behind to get this fixed. It wouldn't have been so bad if I didn't need to carry Zamelle.

With one final leap, I soared over the side tower, touching down on its tip and pressing off to land on a cloud of air, amid the centre of the roof on the front façade.

The roof slanted down towards the crowd, and when Zamelle disembarked she stumbled on the slope. Her feet fumbled, her body leaning over the building's edge. I caught her arm, blasting air outwards and yanking us back to the dome of the building. She caught her feet in my arms, and stood carefully upright on her own.

We stood before a silent sea of people, gathered to stare, gawking. Where the festival before was lively, with shouting and music, I could now hear the scraping of my metal foot across the roof tiles.

Then somebody screamed.

"It's the White Witch!" one voice said.

"Is that *Maiki*?" another asked.

Soon more voices joined to shout and point and scream questions towards us.

Zamelle summoned her right-hand sword, the slit of her helmet glowing in glorious white light. She titled her head back as she raised her sword to the sky, and shot a brilliant bolt of white quatra into the clouds. Silence reigned again.

I took this as my signal. I let go of the armour of Maiki, letting it retreat to the thread. My face to the crowd, like it had been in front of Hesslik's crowds, like it had been exposed many times before, I searched for Kuvalik's thread. It was calling to me – easy to connect to.

I hesitated.

Stunned faces met mine. I had to do this, but could I be Kuvalik? Could I be the *Suneva-Jesus* that Chad and Yvon so eloquently described? We had an idea of what these people wanted, but was it arrogant to pretend I could be their leader? That I could present them with a future they would follow? This was a lot of pressure.

You can do it, Boekidin told me. *Be the hope for these people. You've got it in you. I've got it in me*, I repeated.

I opened myself to the thread. Its armour pressed at the gates, eager to envelop my body, ready to be my soul. I wasn't sure how I felt about that, but I didn't have time to feel anything much longer. It quickly rushed over me, locking into place with a divine, golden glow.

Senses. The field was mine, in all directions, over all distances. The crowd was littered with colour, vibrant, all souls holding a place in the cosmos. The mood was electric. Charge hung everywhere.

"Suneva of the crowd, listen to what we have to say," Zamelle boomed over the gardens. The sound echoed between trees, flowing between ears like a slick breeze. "I am Zamelle Menas, the White Witch, historical spiritual leader of the Suneva people. This is Kuvalik, leader of the first *Liktan* Nation, the thread which powered *Fara Olomb.*"

"That's Maiki!" resounded a cry from the audience.

"Olomb was murdered by Hesslik, and my ghost was formed," I spoke. My voice was ancient. It trumpeted on golden waves of sound, reverberating with wisdom and friendliness. It encapsulated all that was caring, and all that was generous. The voices of objectors snuffed to fall into reverence of it.

"I have given my thread to Maiki Leukess, rightful *Vochduhvlad*, leader of the *Kiin* people, my student, my friend, and capable leader. He has allowed me to be here today to speak to you through his body, to spread my cause, with the help of the White Witch.

"Hesslik has failed you by killing me and rushing my vision. His impatience has cost us the prosperity we could have had in our re-emergence. We *need* to become a part of society, to create a visible community for Suneva, to preserve our traditions, to ensure our safety, and to ensure the safety of others.

"Hesslik has not created unity for Suneva, but has rather drawn a rift between us. Being divided through this time in our history will forever separate us as the years continue. Ideologies will draw further apart, until we become unrecognisable from each other – until we lose what it is to be a Suneva, and this coming-into society becomes an effort in vain.

"Hesslik, in adopting the parts of Olomb's vision he liked, has left out the largest Suneva community – the Argols. He has ostracised them by promising to give up the rights they hold dear – rights we should all hold dear. He has alienated and branded Suneva who speak against him, which will only lead to extremism.

"There will be sacrifice to be made on all sides. In order to become the community we wish to be, we will need to forfeit some of our behaviours to hold true our promise of peace. We will need to conform to ethical values to guide us and show that we are serious about being members of society. If we do this right, we *can* be accepted for who we are. We *can* hold those accountable who abuse power for personal gain.

"If you choose to support Hesslik into this great gathering, know that your thread *will* be taken from you. Hesslik is a coward, who believes that the only solution for our integration is to take away that which makes us different. This solution is too easy. He has given up on you, but I have given my power to deserving Suneva for thousands of years to ensure that we continue and thrive.

"Unite under myself, the White Witch, and the *Vochduhvlad*. Unite to be the strong community you deserve. Unite to have your voice heard as we re-join this uncertain world, and to be the driver of your own destiny. Together we are Suneva, and together, we can be ourselves and thrive without fear. Believe, and unite."

I had stared into the eyes of a man recently dead and drawn his words. I had been engulfed in bright, violet light which roared through the vast expanse of cosmos in the basin of four black holes. It was a collection of words decided upon long ago, an ideal to be spoken by whomever held this destiny. Kuvalik was bound to this mission. He had seen hundreds of years of Suneva society. Now he had allowed me to see it, and channel it.

I finally came to from the trance I was in. I still wore his armour, but I felt that I had my mind back. *That wasn't so bad*, I thought to myself. I had lost control, but I'd only done good in doing so. I looked over to Zamelle, smiling through my helmet. She was in complete awe, almost at the point of dropping her swords.

Jaws hung amongst the onlookers. It was a crowd stunned. Some had fallen to their knees in reverence, whilst others – hopefully the regular people amongst them – had chosen to run. Their footsteps, however, could not be heard. A thick blanket of silence had censored all but the birds, and even they had stopped their chirping.

"Far *fucking* out..." a voice coughed. This caused another man to laugh hysterically.

I...I think you nailed it, man, Boekidin said. *I have notes on their thoughts...but we can look at those next time. This was almost perfect.*

"Kuvalik said it all..." I admitted, just a whisper. "I don't even remember what I just said. It just, sort of, came out."

"Unite!" Zamelle shook the lull, capturing attention. "Suneva and Sunesca, of all beliefs and of all backgrounds must unite if we are to preserve our identities. I urge you to spread the word of our movement. I urge you to be the change you want to see."

Zamelle raised her swords to the sky once more, holding them above her head for a long moment. *Shaths* were drawn in the crowd, and held high above heads, a field of silvery weapons glinting in the strong afternoon sun. I shook my left arm to draw my own weapon, but found that Kuvalik's would not form there, and nor would mine. Instead, I raised my arm to the sky.

Zamelle shot a bolt of white quatra to the heavens, and suddenly the gardens erupted with energy. Hundreds of bolts, of all existing colours, in all of their vibrancy, roared straight upwards, lagging behind the faster bolt of white. They dissipated halfway to the clouds in a fireworks display – their colours bleeding to meet the vast sky.

Zamelle looked to me, urging me to make the closing statement.

"And…" I scanned the audience in their hushed solidarity. "Enjoy your festival. You will see and hear from us again."

Chapter 24
Search for the Right

"Am *I* the bad guy?" Simone whispered aloud to herself, sun shining down through the clouds to spite her mood. She walked to our old house by the freeway, her mind a mess.

"Surely not," she resolved, although she wasn't certain. That electric Sunesca of Hesslik's, *Salak Dickhead*, as she had lovingly coined him, seemed to believe that creating one's own freedom was only a means to restrict the freedoms of others. He seemed to enjoy the idea that he could manipulate the free will of those around him to give himself an advantage.

Simone had always seen herself as a harbinger of freedom. From her first steps into social justice with university, to volunteering work in women's health groups, to fighting for the future rights of ordinary people in a Suneva dominated society. Now she was given the power to create freedom, but it was a lie.

Simone couldn't create freedom, she could only oppress others on a scale far worse than anything she ever fought against. She was censorship itself.

It was almost a comic-book level of villainy. The kind of ironic villainy which caused a bad guy thinking they're doing the right thing to turn the world into some homogenous, giant, diesel-punk factory where it always rains and the sky is black. And then there'd be some hero, some strange, unempathetic nice-guy who *'cares about nobody'* and fights with samurai swords, who would have to take Simone down.

Was this the future *Salak Nera* was creating? Was censorship all Simone could do with her powers?

She attempted to calculate excuses, her pace growing even more lethargic, until she realised that she barely did *anything* with the power she took. Simone stole energy, the expressions and free-will of people, to turn into exhaust air. She'd spent the last few weeks learning air-manipulation from me, in an attempt to use the exhaust air for something useful, but it was still just an excuse.

Although, she thought, *when James learns to* fly...*well, then it will be useful.*

She continued her trudge towards our old house. She needed to talk to Salak Kuul, her original demon mentor, and our childhood tormentor.

Simone needed to ask him questions about his purpose, and the goals of the Salak Order she had become a part of. According to *Salak Dickhead,* the Salak Order orchestrated the fall of Suneva society – they were the ones who had forced Suneva underground, in order to spread disbelief in the supernatural and forge the Salak advantage in society. It seemed preposterous, but she remembered that Olomb, the leader of the Suneva at the time, *was* Salak Nolver too. He could have easily orchestrated the whole thing by himself. Simone would not stand for that.

Finally, she reached the entryway to our old house. The garden was still a mess, the same as it was over a month prior when she had first come back here. Vines crawled down off the walls now and started to cover the driveway floor. From between bricks, mortar turned to clay, which became dirt, and vibrant ecosystems sprouted from the nutrition-deprived cracks.

Simone stepped her way carefully across the drive, up to the rotting, wooden back-gate. A car went by on the street, although not as fast as the driver would like, as Simone stole its energy to blast off a cloud of air, high over the gate. She stole its energy again to land safely, and tip-toed her way down the side-path towards the shed.

The lock was still broken on the shed's tin door. It perplexed Simone that the current owner hadn't figured this out yet. Then again, it wasn't all that surprising. A demon lived in their shed, that was reason enough to never come into the back yard.

Simone palmed the door open and stepped inside. As always, the space remained incredibly dim even with open windows. Dust flung into the air before her, yet crawled to a stop at the top of its arc, refusing to fall, sitting in the strangled light like dead glitter.

A shady mist waned in the corner. It spun around itself, stealing shadows from behind the tool rack and the tall, metal cabinet. Black, writhing ribbons danced in it all amongst a cloud of soot, collecting the fragments of shadow into one being.

"Salak Nera, you return," the demon croaked in his deep, split voice. "How were my brothers?"

"They're...how did you know that I saw your brothers?"

"You went to the Vochduh temple. It's a Salak Order outpost," the demon chuckled, and Simone accepted this answer.

"Salak Kallid seemed the liveliest," she reported, satisfied. "He taught me how to steal sound."

"Ah, *good,*" the demon growled with bared teeth. "Yes, Kallid is a good teacher of the sonic arts, But *I* will be the demon to teach you light. That is my specialty."

"I'm glad," Simone said. She walked to the left of the room, and pulled herself up onto one of the work benches, where she sat staring at the ribbons of black dancing in the dark, sooty mist.

"But I don't know that I should continue this anymore," she said, finally.

"What?" Kuul snapped. The shed plunged into darkness – real, pure darkness, blacker than a moonless night in a cave. Simone shuddered, squirming towards the wall.

Dull light slowly oozed back in, like thick honey through a filter, it had to force its way past the demon. Simone was almost too shocked to talk, although she managed it.

"I don't think I can continue to be Salak Nera, because in creating freedom for myself, I limit the free will of others," she said.

"…Oh…" the demon sighed. His darkness quickly faded, leaving just the ribbons and their small ball of mist. "Well, that's stupid," he chuckled. "You really think that the freedom you create is freedom for yourself?"

"I…wait, what?" Simone stammered. "If course it is! I steal the energy of others to allow myself to do things."

"You steal energy for exhaust."

"Which is why it's almost villainous!" she protested.

"No, you never created your own freedom," Kuul clarified, his ribbons spinning smugly through the shed. "Sure, you *do*, but that's never been the aim of how we use powers. When you steal energy, you take from the black holes. Even when you take from people, they are a hand for the Gods. When we limit destiny, we give this world agency."

"Yes," Simone rolled her eyes, "I'm fine with *that*. I just…when there is no more destiny, aren't we just tyrants, like the Gods?"

"And when would there be no more destiny?" Kuul asked.

"When Hesslik removes the threads."

"You believe that you'll fail to stop him?"

241

"We might," Simone admitted, honestly, slumping back onto the wall, "and James is already pulling Suneva from destiny. What if he finds a way to do it en-mass? Then when we steal, we're just taking from the free will of others."

The demon paused, his writhing ribbons slowing their dance, fluttering like seaweed in the tide. Now Simone wore the smug face – her concerns were warranted enough to make an ancient being scratch their head.

"I don't think this changes much," the demon finally said.

"What?" Simone asked. "Why not?"

"Because, our job is to provide freedom," the demon said. "To ourselves, and to others."

"And without destiny, we're just taking the free will of regular people," she argued.

"So, don't take from regular people," the demon resolved.

"Then who am I taking from?" Simone quizzed.

"Same as you've always wanted to, *Fairysmog*," the demon grinned, "those who control others. Those who seek personal gain. Your fight has never been with Suneva or black holes, in its essence. It was always with inequality. Go out there and tip the scales to the layman."

"I…" Simone slid off the bench, standing again on her own two feet. "That makes perfect sense," she said, the realisation flooding her like hot blood. Excitement came to redden her cheeks. "Impede the powerful to defend the less fortunate," she smiled. "Break the untouchables…"

Possibilities came to mind, of endless situations resolved by censoring those who have had too great a say over outcomes that affect others. "*This* is real justice," she thought aloud, "real *fairness*. I can break the boundaries of privilege to give *fairness* to the world. Kuul, this is an amazing realisation…Thank you!"

"Justice…" he smirked. "Of course the sister of the Omercronian Vochduhvlad is concerned with justice and fairness."

"Justice and fairness," Simone pondered. "Ah, that's my other question." She raised an accusatory finger to a ribbon of the demon. "Did the Salak Order orchestrate the fall of the last Suneva Nation?"

"Yes," Kuul answered without further prompting.

"Wait, really?" Simone squinted. "Why?"

"Personal gain," Kuul said flatly. "We sought freedom, we made our own freedom. All it took was widespread disbelief in our powers and the suppression of Suneva voices."

"You had a part in it?"

"Absolutely."

"Did Nolver?" Simone asked. The blood which flooded her with hope now started to turn sickly, boiling.

"He didn't know it was happening at the time."

"And what are your thoughts on it now?" Simone growled.

"It gave us freedom to do whatever we wanted, and, ironically, removed our freedom to act in the public eye unless we wanted to reinvigorate belief in the supernatural," Kuul said. "In essence we condemned ourselves to create freedom in small spaces. It backfired, really. I don't care for our decision much, which is why I'm training you now."

"Thousand-year-old demons weren't capable of *that* much forethought?" Simone quizzed.

"Time doesn't really matter to the eternally living," Kuul responded. "I waited, and now the solution has come, just as Nolver said it would."

"Right…" Simone crossed her arms. "So, you all basically caused this whole modern mess and fracture of the Suneva community."

"Yes," Kuul agreed, "although, by either incredible genius or unwavering coincidence, we've never been closer to defeating destiny and delivering freedom to the people – the whole purpose of the Order. So, really, it seems like we did the right thing all along."

"Of course," Simone sighed, and rubbed the bridge of her nose. "Right, well, I'd best be going, now that I don't hate myself." She pushed her way through the dark fog of the room, towards the rusted door. "Thanks for your help, Master."

"I'll always help my star apprentice," Salak Kuul called. He picked up a wrench from the shelf with his incorporeal being, and waved it back and forth for a goodbye. "When you're ready to learn light, come back to see me."

"Will do," Simone said. She opened the door, and stumbled into the piercing daylight.

***

On such a nice day, when the birds sung and the wind carried sounds and screams of children splashing into pools, the best activity that Simone and our dog, Errol, could think of, was to curl up in the study and sit by the computer.

Just like the sun, it had light. Light that projected over your face and gave you headaches for staring at it too long. Just like the beach, there was a bank of grainy mystery-objects to get stuck under your fingernails. Just like discarded toys in the sand, you probably should wash your hands after touching the computer. And just like playing outside, there were no friends here to play with either except for your imagination, so the computer really was the ultimate machine of a summer well spent.

Simone did something she had not done in a long time – and probably would have never considered unless she'd realised her true motivations – she logged in as Fairysmog.

Her mission in life, she realised that morning, was to help those who needed it. Simone would liberate the oppressed from their oppressors – and right now, the Suneva required her liberation. Their freedom to be themselves was on a thin line, tensed, and with scissors to its midpoint, held by a madman who threatened to take away their identities. Hesslik could be stopped, and Simone's part in all of it was to find where he was hiding his electronic transmission device.

The group was right to suspect that Fairysmog had her connections, many of which could still prove useful. And they were, indeed, correct to assume that Fairsmog had connections to *Anderson*, the codename for the hacker who stole Hesslik's entire library of computer files on New Year's Day.

Simone hadn't visited the site in a while – she just left the community to its own devices. *Although, perhaps*, she wondered, *this would have gone over better if I moderated it properly, and changed these people's opinions*.

She scrolled down the feed to see the kinds of things which were being said, and immediately found an article about James and Natalie's spectacle at the ethnic festival, which spoke in a confused tone about the situation. On one hand, the author wasn't sure whether to believe that Hesslik would lead to the downfall of the Suneva threads. On the other hand, they harboured an incredible hatred for the White Witch, and would not resolve to stand by either Suneva side.

Interestingly, a lot of the topics of conversation were technology based, and most of them were posted and controlled by Anderson. Although posts were anonymous, Anderson chose to have his own flair, and his posts attracted the most interest.

As Simone scrolled, her eyes straining and red in the dark room against the bright screen, a message window popped up.

When did I install instant messaging? Simone quizzed, her mouse zipping. *Must be some scam ad they've put on for revenue…*

Her pointer zipped to the title. It read *Anderson*.

"When was this a thing?" Simone asked aloud, stroking Errol who had curled by her feet.

Glad to see you're back. Anderson's message read.

Simone recoiled from the screen in her surprise. She closed the window and reopened it, just to make sure that he really had messaged her. As she expected, the tab was still there when she refreshed the page.

Hello Anderson, she wrote on the heavy keyboard, *glad to see that you've been looking after things well.*

Yes, a bit of sucking up would go a long way, Simone decided.

Why did you leave the fight without a word of warning? he typed back. *You were the leader this cause needed. You were the pioneer for Suneva awareness.*

A pioneer of social justice, at the age of twenty? Simone chuffed to herself, and blushed. She had to force down the compliment to stop it racing to her head.

I was confused, she typed, honestly. *I think I led people down a path that was way too hateful to be useful. I had to leave it.*

"Damn it, this is already going poorly," she cussed to Errol as she anxiously awaited the next message.

You turned out to be a Suneva, didn't you? he replied. Simone winced.

No, she said, *I have Suneva biology and senses, although I avoided destiny by dodging a thread. I am not a Suneva.*

This wasn't a lie, but it certainly wasn't the truth. Oddly enough, as a Sunesca, Simone had very limited Suneva senses. She could see quatra due to her biology, and redirect it, but she could not sense it at all.

I see, Anderson replied, *well, you always believed that you were given the ability to see Suneva for a reason, right? Didn't you say it was to help others get through the uprising?*

"God damnit," Simone gritted her teeth. "This guy is persistent."

I now fight for freedom. I have been given abilities that allow me to censor those who hold power. I'm fighting the uprising in my own way.

This was all going downhill very quickly. Simone had to wrap it up before she gave too much away. She didn't wait for his reply before she started typing again.

Look, Anderson, I need your help, she typed as quickly as she could and punched enter. There was a brief pause – perhaps the internet died out – but then his response came through.

Go on, he said.

Hesslik is creating a giant electrical transmission device. Do you know anything about it? she typed, and leaned back in the chair, cracking her knuckles.

No, he responded, *I haven't heard of it. Interesting, though. What is he using it for?*

"Shit…" Simone cussed. She creaked back into position, scrunching herself over the keyboard.

He wants to make free electricity, but I think it's a load of shit and there's got to be a catch. Was hoping you knew where it was so I could look at it, but that's fine. I'll get another source.

Let me know when you do, he replied instantly, *that's got to be useful for the world. We can't let a Suneva invent it and claim it. It will only lift their image and further their agenda.*

"Right," Simone sighed, "he's full-on indoctrinated. What the hell kind of community did I create?" She could barely remember being that brainwashed, but then again, it was all archived – every turn of her opinion, saved in internet history. She closed the browser, resolving to never look back at that timeline as long as she lived.

That was one lead dead. What now?

Chapter 25
The Deserters

Celeste Leroux strutted her angry gait down a bustling peak-hour street in the city of Thessaloniki. Her ears were burning to the whispers thrown her way. Her face was known – Iva Argol. Her frown only deepened, her resolve growing to inflict justice on those who had abandoned their loyalty.

Chad was right, Celeste grumbled in her head. She massaged a small, pink flame between her finger and her thumb. *I can't rule a gang with cuddles and kisses. I need to prove my worth.*

Her steps were a storm, a hail-fire which caused crowds to scatter. She was physically hot, her Suneva ability to connect to heat boiling out of her control as she marched on.

Anastasiya walked in tow, posture slouched, hood over her face, hiding her identity and connection to the enraged French woman. She looked almost embarrassed, to Celeste, to be walking with her. This only added to Celeste's insecurity, further sparking her anger.

Celeste produced a key from her pocket. All Argol offices in each city had the same lock – except maybe that penthouse in New York, now that she thought about it. The office was in sight – a typical, five story building of white painted concrete and a flat roof. Grime streaked down it's balcony sides, dripping from overhead gutters.

Why couldn't Anastasiya get us closer to this place? Celeste grumbled as she closed in on the door. *The walk here was embarrassing. I didn't need to feel like this...*

She reached the door to the building. On its exterior, this appeared to be a regular apartment block with a singular entrance through a lobby – but the Argols of this city knew better. Inside was a corporate suite, and levels of offices which they rented out. Strangely, the books Yvon could find said that Celeste was still collecting rent from the tennants, so what had happened to the administration here? Were they paying the Argol treasury out so that their disloyalty wouldn't discovered? That was so *treasonous*, it made Celeste bend the key as she squashed it into the lock.

Celeste hadn't been this angry for weeks, even, and she hated getting mad, but these Suneva were idiots. Didn't they see that they needed a strong community for the Suneva to prosper? If they didn't follow her, then there would be no army to fight Hesslik, and there would be no new-age Suneva nation. She needed their loyalty now. This wasn't some selfish mission like saving Natalie and James was. This was serious, international business.

Celeste had spent over a week travelling Europe with Anastasiya, taking her to beautiful cities to check in on Argol hideouts and complexes, testing their allegiances to the grand Suneva cause.

The experience had mostly been great. The girls had been treated by willing hosts, feasting in mansions, penthouses, churches, and secret buildings all over the continent. They were met with smiles, open arms, and hospitality they'd never experienced before. Argol leaders worldwide were eager to prove their loyalty to the growing Suneva community, it seemed.

Except when they didn't. The Argols of some cities were beyond loyalty, seeing themselves as lone bastions for the Suneva cause in a vast sea of hatred, no help on the horizon. They sailed their ships further from the community wanting to help them, stubborn.

Celeste had found rather quickly that trying to wrangle together a Suneva community of this scale and nature was akin to scooping mud with a colander. No matter how hard you worked, you always lost some. You couldn't plug all of the holes either, and even if you tried, you ended up with *dirty* hands.

If she was ever to transfer the whole Argol community to side with Kuvalik, she would need unwavering loyalty to her decisions, and it seemed more impossible by the day. Would the plan to save the Suneva fail because of her?

A man lost his hand in Florence due to his stubbornness. His skin met her flesh-melting flames when he refused to cooperate. *How could it have happened in Florence?* she wondered after she'd done it. *Once the strongest Argol holdout in the world.*

She resolved to show her dominance. Only then could she ensure the fellowship she needed. How else could she have convinced the Florentines? They used to be a great Empire of the Kidin – an Empire built on lies and deceit. They couldn't trust a rat to eat their garbage, how could they trust her? They would have to, though, because they were *her* men.

Celeste had written letters to the command centre in Paris, to Michael Richard and other subordinates, outlying her intentions and asking them to rally the Suneva for it. Richard's replies were curt, but signed with his devotion to her plans. Other key leaders seemed to follow suit in their returned letters, and Celeste had confidence that at least the high ecelons of her regime would follow her orders.

The door of the Thessaloniki office flew open by Celeste's booted foot, crashing into the adjacent wall. The bang echoed as a shotgun, causing the inhabitants to jump and gasp. Frightened eyes fell on her.

Frightened looks. Celeste lingered on the feeling of power, letting it rise inside her, inflating her worth. She was the power these men feared. She was the one to guide them into the new world.

"Iva Argol?" one of the men gasped in his shock. He rose from behind a reception desk, slowly, with hands in the air.

The desk lay straight ahead of the door, laid out before a marble floor. To the left of the desk was an elevator and stair-set, and to the right was a den area with pool table, connected to an office space. A pool cue fell to the floor, releasing a crack which caused another jolt to shift through the room.

Celeste let the heat flow from her body, erupting in pointed, hot pink flames. Her eye twitched.

"Weren't expecting me, were you?" she asked, stepping her heavy combat boots into the lobby space. They boomed on the tiles, which came close to melting under the intense heat from her hands.

"We're still getting you the tenant rents, aren't we?" the man behind the desk stammered in Liktan. He was short, with darker skin and blonde hair.

"Rents? You could keep those if you really wanted. I don't care about money," Celeste said, stopping in the centre of the room. There were five people here – the man behind the desk, then two women and two men playing pool together. In the silence between her words, the television buzzed with the sounds of the Greek news.

"What's the issue then?" the man asked. "I mean…it's nice to see you…" He tried to save face, wincing.

"Save your shit for the toilet," Celeste scorned. "You changed your allegiances to Hesslik."

"We…" the man stumbled. He glanced sidelong to his counterparts in the den, whose faces dropped with realisation. He, however, wore his face with resilience, stepping around the bench. "That's right. We like his ethical approach to being a Suneva. We want to be a *part* of society."

Celeste growled, her brow furrowing so far it could have covered her whole nose. Flames licked from her mouth.

"How is everybody missing the message?" she asked with a deep growl. "Hesslik is going to shut off the threads. I don't know how much louder we have to yell it. Staying with me is the only way to ensure that there even *is* a Suneva community to be a part of. If you don't swear yourselves back to me, you're giving up everything."

She threw her hands down, the flame extinguishing. Celeste pleaded for the man's sense, but he would not give it to her.

"We don't believe that," he said, "it's nonsense. Hesslik has set up too much – put in too much of his own time – to destroy the whole community. It's garbage."

"It's not!" Celeste yelled, desperate. "I swear to Veritas, if you don't see the urgency in your allegiance to the Argols, then your thread is on the line. Actually…" She pointed a finger. "Not just *yours*, but *every* thread in the *world*."

"Sorry, Miss Argol, but we don't want to follow your regime."

"It's not a *regime*," Celeste sputtered, "and it doesn't *matter* what you want!" she roared, her finger pointing to each blank, dumb face in the room. "This is about the greater good of us as a race!"

The room was filled with the growl and ignition of her huffing breath. A pink flame formed at her exhalation, casting her expression in dramatic light.

"You burned a man's hand off, Tona Argol," the man said, his tone final. "We can't follow that."

Frustration beyond all else. Celeste's brain squirmed, unlinking, tangling itself in a tight knot behind her bulging eyes. Her muscles begged for release. Her throat wanted to scream. These people were ridiculous, *selfish* idiots. Her fingertips sparked with Suneva heat as they clawed into her own palms. Her lungs struggled to contain the hot breath which fanned the furnace of her deep anger. Her mouth twitched.

Release came.

She summoned her sword, and screamed. It wasn't a proud scream, or a defiant scream like that of a true leader. It was a shriek, the cry of a jealous child in defiance of their mother. Screaming, she rammed the pink-hot weapon straight into the marble reception desk – swinging it down from overhead.

It sliced straight through, turning the rock molten before it even touched the surface. She cut all the way down to her feet, where she had to stop lest she amputate herself. A tear of pure frustration and agitation burst from her eye, like a popped pimple. It oozed in a disgusting way, streaming thick on her cheek.

"You're *idiots!* You'll doom us all," she raged. "Hesslik is hosting his gathering here. It's the only reason he recruited you! You just handed him the key to this city, to do whatever he would like with it! This will be the end of Suneva."

She spun, manic, to those smug nutcases standing in the den, not even in fear of her. "How could you lose your faith in the organisation that made your livelihoods possible?" she barked. "Without my father and his father before him, you couldn't be standing out in that street using your powers. Your true identity would be hidden! You'd be run off into the fucking hills for your travesty to the Christian god. You lunatics! Get your heads out of your asses!"

Not a single response came to her onslaught. They refused to stand up for themselves – they had lost the fight – yet they did not accept their defeat. They stood tall, as if they didn't *have* to explain themselves to get out of this. Who did they think they were?

Celeste flung herself around to Anastasiya, searching for support in the girl's eyes. The Legendary shook their head, freeing it from their hood. They strode tall over to Celeste, determination and disapproval deeply intertwined in their suddenly stoic face. Celeste, manic and surprised, stumbled into the molten hot desk.

"I think you need to shut-up, Celeste," Anastasiya said.

"Wh...what?" Celeste stumbled, more frustrated tears betraying her.

"*Shut up*," Anastasiya repeated, "and listen to somebody else besides yourself for a minute."

"You don't even talk!" Celeste sputtered. "What have you got to..."

Anastasiya produced her *shath*, twin armoured claws, and lurched them to Celeste's neck. The French girl shut up.

"*Let* me talk, and I might," she scorned, and Celeste nodded. Her neck was released. "Now, I'm about to tell you things you'll hate to hear, but just be silent and take it," Anastasiya demanded, and without Celeste's approval, continued.

"There's a plainly obvious reason why you can't hold this community together, you know? It's because you're treating people like *objects* – like pawns in your grand schemes, being traded between you and Hesslik. You know what's really *dehumanising*? The sort of thing which leads people to resent you? Is not feeling like *you* matter to them." She stopped her rant to breathe, then blasted on.

"Do you know me?" Anastasiya asked, stepping up close to Celeste's confused face. "I'll tell you why I don't speak - because you never *fucking* ask me anything. You don't even think I'm a person, do you? To you, I'm just some tool. I'm just how you got around Europe in a week. I'm a tool which gives you an advantage."

"Do you even know *these* people?" she asked, throwing an arm towards the receptionist man. "Tell me his name, if you will, your *highness*. But I bet that you couldn't, because you never took the time to know who these people are, what their desires are, or what they want from a community. Instead, you just think of them as numbers, something you can and will *use*. It's sickening."

"I'm not scared of you, Iva Argol, and neither are these people. You don't have jurisdiction here. You can't just step into this city and pretend that you and the past kings of this phantom throne of yours are martyrs for the Suneva experience. That's a load of shit. Maybe in France, where the Catholics denounced the Suneva as human beings, you were revolutionary, but not here. You don't mean *dogshit* here. Greece is well enough integrated not to need the Argols, they just stay associated because it used to benefit them. Now it no longer benefits them, so they leave. Offer them something, Nerios-damnit! They won't stay because you're some queen and they're your subjects and you tell them to! They want ethics, so you're going to have to update your agenda, idiot!"

"So, you didn't liberate these people. They're Suneva with their own agency, with their own lives, who search for their own fulfillment. They owe you nothing. They're not your tools. They're their own people. Why would they follow you? You're being a total *bitch*."

Anastasiya gasped hard from the exertion of standing up for herself, but the satisfaction was deep within her eyes, bursting from her soul. Glory surrounded her, like the pink glow of her quatra. It overshadowed Celeste's flames, which had been extinguished for a while now. The Suneva in the room gravitated to Anastasiya's energy, inspired by her words and aura.

251

Celeste tipped over. There was no hope, there were only tears and pity. She slumped down the side of the bench, landing on the cracked marble floor. Her heart pumped just to keep her brain from turning to soup and leaking from her ears. Her entire sense of self-worth had just been destroyed. Was she really *this* unfit to rule? She understood how her father could kill a man when he took the job. She sympathised with him.

"Nothing to say?" Anastasiya asked. Celeste shook her head away from the desperate daydream. All spark was gone from her soul.

"I...I can't," she said, and started to cry heavily. The weight of disappointment in herself was too immense to hold in. How was she meant to feel worth *anything* if she couldn't do right the one thing she was trusted with? Maybe it was right of her to run away from this responsibility for all those years, calling herself Genive, hiding from her father. She would only ruin everything, anyway. She always wrecked things.

There was no sympathy from this crowd. Nobody appeared happy to see her like this, but nobody quite cared. Only Anastasiya was smug.

The man from behind the desk offered her a hand up, and she took it, if it meant getting her disgrace of a body out of his nice establishment.

"I'm sorry," she uttered between the sobs to herself. Crying didn't feel right, right now. It would never feel right when there was nobody who wanted to support you. It always felt like selfish, self-pity.

"Please...just...don't join Hesslik," she said to the man as she stood. He was much taller than her, and she didn't care to feel above him, anyway. "Kuvalik is creating a new nation. I...I was going to join it, and take everybody with me. He has the morals you want, but with the freedoms I have been offering..."

She turned to the other spectators, who had walked from their game of pool to come closer.

"Who are you all, anyway?" she asked past their eyes, staring into each soul. Their colours were pure – what little of auras Celeste could intrinsically read gave her that much to work with. "Why did you follow for these years? What are you looking for?"

There was no time for pity, only growing up. If she wanted these people, she would have to understand them.

252

Chapter 26
Systems Are Not 'Go'

I was so close.

I woke up in an unfamiliar bed in Paris. It was one of Celeste's hideouts, somewhere in the back alleys of the huge city, a bedroom high up in an apartment of a low-class neighbourhood. I hadn't found the secret to flying last night, but I was coming close. This wouldn't be one philosophy, but the amalgamation of a select few, and I was near to finding the right combination.

My search over the past weeks had strengthened my *Kiin* abilities, deepening my connection to the air. I had become efficient – able to leap twice as high off a single blast of air, and cushion myself from greater heights. I could pull up from a glide in half the time, with twice the intensity.

It came from a new understanding of what it meant to be connected to air. I wasn't *controlling* air anymore, yet I didn't believe I was quite a *part* of the system either. It was in between. There was still another level of complexity to be understood.

I opened the window to the Parisian apartment and admired the fresh, morning sun. Spring smells wafted in through the opening, filling my nose with delight. Crisp sun hit me, a warm breeze tickling my skin. I checked my pocket for the room's key, then stood out on the window's ledge, and leaped from it.

There was a gasp or two from below, but they needn't have feared. I streamlined myself, letting wind rush over my missile body. I plunged down, blasting off a tail jet, racing to the asphalt.

I rocked past a man's head, knocking his hat off, the asphalt now at eating distance. Then, a foot from the ground, changed the will of the air above me. I didn't *compress* it, I couldn't *command* it or *use* it, I had to *embody* it, and have it embody my will.

At whiplash speeds I pulled up, jolting my head and neck towards my arse. It was a rush, and incredible sensation. I pulled up so hard, with such ferocity, that I started to glide upwards, towards the peak of the next building.

I blasted down, letting the air embody my will, forcing me higher. I held my hands out, soaring to the adjacent apartment's stone gutter. At the pinnacle of my rise I met it with my hands, and grasped onto the stonework. I crouched onto the façade with my feet, then kicked up, summersaulting over the roof's ridge to land on its flat top.

I ran northbound, to meet everybody for breakfast.

I was met with a table full of steaming delights – coffee created by artists, scents wafting through the thin, morning air. Croissants, hot from the oven, a stick of bread with an assortment of cold meats and cheeses. The café was artisanal, with new-aged, metal stylings and jazz smoothly ringing from its speakers.

Everybody else was in a mood to eat – we had the full ensemble here, today, two weeks from Hesslik's Suneva gathering. Celeste had shown us this café, where she used to eat as a child. She sat opposite the window, letting us take in the view. Her trip to Thessanoliki had done something to her. She didn't mention what – and I assumed that Yvon, who sat by her side, bore the brunt of her emotional release – but whatever-it-was had forced her recent silence, revealing a reserved and sweeter young woman.

Chad slammed an abomination into his mouth – a ham and cheese croissant inside a baguette, whose insides were lathered in jam. An unorthodox combination for an orthodoxically hungry man, it seemed.

He and Simone would travel south tonight, to investigate one of Hesslik's server hubs in Lyon. Chad was confident that the computers held therein would reveal the location of Hesslik's free-energy device on the seventh of May, the Great Gathering.

In the day, however, they would join Natalie, Yvon, Boekidin and I, as we stayed in the city of Paris to intervene a festival and marketplace. Amalie Leroux had found her Sunevahood in such an event, where Eleni Floros, the great Suneva reader Surawelle, had detected her abilities. Eleni would be there today with her newest apprentice reader. She had given us the idea to speak here, telling us that there would be Suneva in abundance throughout the crowd.

Celeste would not join us there. She, instead, wanted to talk with her high-ranking men to gauge their responses to the Kuvalik plan, and to organise logistics about attacking the street festival in Thessaloniki. She was still adamant about changing her allegiance on the day of the gathering, in front of the great Suneva crowd, instead of beforehand.

Natalie lowered her hand from her utensils, and rested it limply over her chair's arm rest, palm in my direction. I took the moment to surprise her, resting my hand on her open palm. A smile worked its way across her whole expression. She had asked me to be her boyfriend, here in the Paris city streets just yesterday. I was surprised by the move, but of course accepted.

I stared, then, at the abundance of food stacked before me. Usually, there would be no time for staring, only time for swallowing, but recently I hadn't been all that hungry. I could only manage a single, plain croissant before my stomach gave up.

I was always one to lose appetite when nervous, and I had to put my lack of hunger down to the fact that I'd been on edge for weeks now whilst awake. Today was no better for my nerves, as I'd very soon be giving Kuvalik's speech in central Argol territory. This was something our plan hugely pivoted on the success of, and I was frazzled. My inability to scoff down the same amount as Chad made sense.

Still, Celeste seemed confident, given her rounds of Europe, that several Argol members would defect today to join Kuvalik. She would not only allow it, but encourage it, despite her refusal to publicly support Kuvalik yet. She had a plan up her sleeve, and I couldn't guess it.

We payed the bill, walked from the café, and split into our own parties. Natalie, Yvon, Simone, Chad, and I walked towards the marketplace by the river. I sucked in my nerves as we stepped the ancient streets – images from Olomb's mind bleeding into my vision. They contained scenes of boulevards from only a few years ago, when he came here to find Celeste, and of streets much older than that, of dirt roads, horses and carts, and men in old suits. Most disturbingly, Olomb gave me the sense that the girl I loved was evil, and that was the hardest hallucination to live with.

***

After helping at the markets, Simone and Chad had spent the afternoon travelling south, from Paris to Lyon. Simone had watched my speech, watched the way I transformed, became *somebody else* under the armour of Kuvalik. She wanted to deliver me to freedom, but knew that she was the one who encouraged this charade – she'd have to live with my discomfort till it was over. Her job in the crowd was to censor the naysayers, to alter the emotions rising from the speech. Silencing the enemy created a social feedback loop, whereby supporters felt more welcome to be vocal, eventually shutting down any attempts from audience members to be contrary.

By the time Simone and Chad arrived in Lyon, it had already hit dusk – the spring sun finding its place behind the buildings, letting the pink shine of sunset take the sky.

Hesslik's headquarters in this city, his main server room for his computer systems, was located riverside, in a lovely end of town. Chad and Simone found a local restaurant to eat at, with views over the slow, steady stream and passers-by.

In any other context, sitting at a table-for-two in a riverside, French restaurant would have been romantic, but Chad was as friendly and jovial as ever.

"*Master* will be waiting for us on the bridge before the building," he told Simone over a plate of lobster. Simone tied her long, blonde hair up behind her head, to stop it getting in her beef tartare.

"Who is this *Master* anyway?" Simone asked. "You don't seem to be the kind to keep secrets."

Chad smiled, and dug his hands further into the lobster's exoskeleton.

"Can't say." He winked past his mouthful. "That's the whole point."

"Why not?"

"There could be a *Kidin* anywhere." He eyed the room joke-suspiciously, pointing his fork at some of the other patrons. Simone tried hard to stifle her chuckle, but it squeezed out anyway. She willed him, through a strained mouth, to lower the implement.

"Is it the same deal with this mysterious girl of yours, too?" Simone asked. "We've only heard details about her. You're like the kid whose best friends all go to 'another school'."

"Oh, there's a different reason why I'm not revealing her identity," he said, stuffing what meat he could summon into his mouth. "You'll meet her soon enough, I reckon."

"I sure hope to," Simone said. "Whatever girl snagged your heart is worth meeting."

"Shucks." He used the word in jest, but his blush was real.

According to Chad, his *Master* hadn't yet disclosed the server room's address, but rather given him a meeting point to discuss it, as they feared interception by Hesslik. *Meeting in this city ought to have made the target obvious enough, right?* Simone thought as they traversed the riverside. Across the next road, just out of the streetlight on the bridge's corner, lingered a black figure on the footpath. A smirk grew on Chad's face at the sighting. This must have been the mysterious *Master.*

Simone and Chad crossed the bridge. For the occasion, Chad wore his biking leathers, with the distinctive helmet of *Lion's Foot* strapped onto his back, above the iron chain. Simone was instructed to wear her *stealth gear*, whatever that meant.

Zamelle had ultimately destroyed the Sunesca robe Simone had acquired in the Vochduh temple. Simone had worn the tattered garment for some time, but luckily the Salak handbook given to her by Salak Kallid outlined the design of a proper Sunesca robe, and Simone had chosen to make a new one. She used cloth of the traditional black – needed to capture light and heat for transformation, when she'd advanced that far – and crafted a gown with the traditional deep-section hood. She chose, however, to omit sleeves, stitching together a tie-up cape which draped over the shoulders and arms. She wore black clothing and sneakers underneath, absorbing all light incident upon her.

The shadowed figure strode into the light as Simone and Chad neared. They were tall – about as tall as Chad – and lean, in jeans and an oversized hooded jumper, hood pulled up to hide their face.

"*Master*," Chad greeted as he stepped towards them, into the pool of light on the street corner.

"You don't have to be *that* strict with yourself," they said. Their voice was deep, but clearly that of a woman. They carried a confused French accent, adapted to speaking frequent Liktan.

"Ah, but I do," Chad said, stepping up and putting a hand to her waist. Simone pursed her lips, unsure of what was happening. "Because you said I had to protect your name, so I do it with all of my heart."

The girl chuckled in French, and pulled down the hood of her jumper. Her face was striking – perfectly *imperfect*. It was slim, built with sharp, angular features, yet slightly *not* picturesque. The nose a little *too* pointed, the eyes *just* far enough apart to be off. It gave her all the more beauty. A familiar beauty, Simone thought, although she couldn't pinpoint it.

Even more striking, as the hood came down, was the scar of a horrible burn, streaking from the back of the woman's neck up to her ear and around to her collarbone.

Master's eyes met Chad's with intensity. Her arms swung up around his shoulders, hands resting on the helmet perched at his neck. They pulled each other in, eyes closing, and kissed deeply. A remarkably French kiss.

"Oh…" Simone recoiled, standing back. *There's got to be something kinky going on here, with the whole* Master *deal*, she noted, letting them kiss it all out.

They pulled away from each other finally, their faces giddy. Simone sighed. She hadn't experienced this kind of love yet, and that left her jaded towards it – especially since it had come to me recently, and I'd been lovey-dovey all over the house.

"So, *this* is your lady of the night," Simone remarked, stepping up to the two. "Salak Nera," she introduced herself, holding her hand out for the woman to shake. On closer inspection, this woman would have been Chad and Simone's age, even though Simone had pictured 'Master' to be someone much older. They shook the hand, but did not give a name in return.

"Lovely to meet you," they said. *Master* reached into her hoodie's front pocket, and produced a small slip of paper. She handed it to Simone.

"That's the address." *Master* said as Simone and Chad investigated the note.

Great, now I'll have to find a roadmap… Simone groaned internally.

"It's just there, across the road, five buildings down," *Master* pointed across the street. "See it there? The crème coloured face."

"You meeting us here wasn't about the directions, was it?" Simone asked, scrunching the useless instructions. Chad and the girl grinned. Simone rolled her eyes.

"I had to apologise in person for what happened with Natalie," they said. "I'm usually much more stringent with my sources, I can't believe I got you double crossed. The White Witch is clever."

"Amasos is cunning," Chad noted. "Not a whole lot you can do to combat destiny in action."

"Unless you're a Salak," Simone shrugged.

"Yes, well, we're lucky to have you around, Salak Nera," *Master* said.

"Are you coming on this mission too, then?" Simone asked them.

"If you need me, I'll know, but I shouldn't expose myself," she said. "My abilities are particularly recognisable."

Simone squinted, quizzing at Chad. He wouldn't budge on an answer, so Simone stuffed the directions into her jeans' pocket and pulled her coat closed. "Let's go then," she said to Chad, then turned to the girl. "Lovely meeting you."

"Lovely meeting you, Salak Nera."

Chad and Simone soon reached the door of the building, Chad now having donned his helmet. The building was a classic, period French piece of architecture, a structure in a row of identical buildings. Simone thought they must have been apartments, although, clearly Hesslik had converted this space.

Chad reached for the door's knocker, and Simone sharply inhaled, preparing to steal the sound. However, he stopped before banging it, and turned to Simone.

"I'm sorry if that was awkward," he rushed out, his voice modulated by the helmet. "I would tell you more, but her identity really *is* sensitive."

"Sure," Simone said. "Suneva politics, I get it." And she grabbed his arm, pulling it away from the door. "But what the hell are you doing knocking on the door?"

"I...uh..." Chad examined his hand with a quizzical stare, then chuckled nervously. "Love drunk...apparently. Although, I see no better ways in. This place shouldn't be too heavily guarded."

"Yeah, it's *only* his European server room," Simone choked. "At *least* try the window first."

"Busy street," he said, gesturing to the cars and people moving past. "Don't want the cops called. Door is probably the best option."

"And the guy who answers the door?"

Chad raised a finger, a smirk would have certainly been under his helmet, if his face was visible. He firmly planted his feet to the ground, and placed his hands onto the door. He waited, examining the vibrations he could inexplicably connect to.

"Nobody is behind the door," Chad concluded, and reached for the crack in the door by the knob. He gripped, then pulled away, telekinetically dragging metal from the lock structure. He held a finger to where his lips would be behind the helmet, and palmed open the door, gesturing Simone inside.

Simone held her hands before her as she entered, pulling the hood of her coat close over her face. Through her hands she could feel the energy in the building – ribbons of colour, dancing in her mind's eye.

Chad snuck behind, keeping his posture low, sensing for vibrations in the ground as they walked.

They were in a hall, which was only short, leading to a door directly ahead and a passage to the left, past a set of stairs which curled back towards the front door. Blue light bled in from the left-hand opening, dancing with different shades.

"Around the corner?" Chad whispered to Simone. On her fingers, in her minds eye, there was energy there; a red ribbon, the kinetic of somebody walking; a thin, silver string for the muted scuffle of their feet on the floor; and a white strip of light energy dancing around the source of the blue haze.

"Yep," Simone said, following the red ribbon, "coming this way." She ducked close to the staircase which lined the left wall, sneaking past the broom closet. Chad fell in behind, staying close.

"Cover me," he instructed, "it's about to get noisy."

"What?" Simone asked. "Why?"

"He's going to scream," Chad smirked, and stalked forward, pushing just ahead of Simone. He readied his right hand – in its peace sign pose – towards the open doorway through the cracks in the balustrade. He held his aim, waiting, tense.

Simone could see the kinetic ribbon waving towards the opening. She took her last breath, falling to silence, eyes wide.

The figure stepped out, a short man, oblivious to the fact he was being watched. He yawned widely, stretching his arms to the sky and smacking his chest. He rubbed his eyes wearily, and set a hand out for the rail of the stairs.

Chad tapped Simone's knee with his free hand, then fired his quatra.

A red bolt zipped between the columns of the balustrade, striking the tired man clean in the face. He swatted at his head by instinct, causing himself to lose his balance. His throat tensed, ready to scream.

Simone froze. What was more important? Stealing his scream, his fall, or the sound of him hitting the deck? She knew she could only choose one.

Yet she chose to try all three. The man exasperated, a grey ribbon dancing from his tongue. Simone latched into it, and ripped the energy from his mouth, causing the man's face to scrunch in greater surprise of his lost voice than his muted thread. He flailed with his hands, grabbing into the handrail with his left, and swinging backwards around it.

He fell into the face of the stairs, near the waiting Chad. Still holding the man's scream, Simone pounced to draw in the bang of his fall, exhausting it before it could echo into the room. The effort of converting multiple *sounds* was dizzying, involving far more concentration than multiple *kinetic* sources, even though the total energy sum was well below the maximum Simone could convert at once.

Chad wrangled the man, encompassing him in the tendrils of his chain. The man went to scream again, and Simone, having just caught her breath, grappled with the grey ribbon as it came, smothering the man's voice and sending a gust of air down the hall.

"Where's the computer?" Chad asked the hostage. Simone loosened her strangle hold on his voice.

"Why would I tell you that?" the man yelled with a hoarse whisper, straining to be heard.

"Because we're holding you against your will." Simone rolled her eyes. "Where's the computer room?"

The hostage chose silence, his hands squirming for his belt against the binds that locked them to his back. Simone's eyes followed the man's intentions, seeing that his writhing fingers were reaching for a weapon hooked to a holster. She threw her hand to the man's belt – a naturally uncomfortable gesture – and drew the weapon. Between herself and Chad, Simone held a thread-removal device.

"Wouldn't be much use against me," Simone quipped, and thrust the device to the man's neck. The hostage crushed himself up against the balustrades, eager to keep his distance from the dangerous prongs.

"Where is the computer room?" Chad asked again.

The man winced. "Follow me," he said, and rose with Simone's permission. Chad's hands keen at the binds, the hostage led his captors up the stair set. Simone tried her best to muffle their combined sound, but she found it difficult in such a quiet space. The Salak guide had taught Simone how to steal from multiple sources of the same energy type up to her personal limit, but it still required vast concentration. The effort of holding on to each footstep, the man's voice, and any creaky steps which groaned unexpectedly, was mind-boggling. Simone had gotten lucky when masking our footsteps in the Brooklyn factory, as she only had to make our ambush collectively quieter than the rain. Here she was fighting for total silence, and it was exhausting.

Through the haze, Simone could sense ribbons of energy camped above the floorboards, guarding the hallway past landing of the stairs. The streamers were dancing around the corner, from behind the wall which concealed their staircase. She paused, and cautioned Chad.

"Easy," he whispered. "Steal their movement, I'll take them out."

"You're assuming it's easy to hold down multiple Suneva," Simone grumbled.

"Isn't it?"

Simone had no reply, only the agonising strain of wrangling multiple tethers.

"I did jobs like this alone for years. Anything you do will only help," Chad smiled, and urged the party forwards to the landing step. The hostage was desperate now, rasping to yell at the top of their lungs. Simone grappled with his faint scream as best as she could, but with each step and creak she had to conceal, it was slipping.

"This floor?" Chad asked the hostage. Simone didn't allow the man to speak, lest his scream rang.

"He'll scream," she whispered. "There's guards around the wall. They're guarding something."

261

"Right…" Chad hummed, and eyed the man. "We'll still need somebody to get us into the computer, though. Do you know the password?"

The hostage squinted, and thought better than to try yelling again. Still, he gave no signal. Chad grumbled, and snatched the thread-remover from Simone, jamming the prongs deep against the man's flesh. Their eyes bulged, and they tried to whimper.

"Do you know the password?" Chad rasped. The hostage shook his head manically, which drew Chad's scowl.

"Good, he's lying," Chad nodded, then yanked the man to push him up to the closest balustrade. He yanked free a section of his long chain, and used it to meld the hostage's wrist to the wooden column. Chad then reclaimed his chain, and snuck to the corner of the wall which concealed the staircase from the rest of this new floor. Simone followed, still holding tight the hostage's scream.

"I'm counting three Suneva," Chad said, examining some field which he had access to. Simone didn't bother to count, choosing rather to concentrate on the yell which was slowly slipping from her grasp.

"Sure," she agreed.

"Let's do it."

"What?" Simone gasped, but Chad had already thrown himself around the wall, his chain extended long before him. Simone launched herself to catch up, using the hostage's scream to blast off the rear wall and draw herself to a halt in this new hallway. At the other end, away from the street, three Suneva now stood alert, weapons drawn.

Chad twirled, flinging his chain with one hand, and blasting a bolt of quatra with the other. The guards scattered – one leapt left, behind the balustrade to the upwards staircase, another grappled a bookcase on the right-hand side of the room and pulled himself behind it, and the last was left to skip over the metal linkages, determination striking his face.

Simone dropped the voice which she held, and the hostage's scream rattled aloud, shaking the floor. She focussed then on the scene before her, on the three men arrested in suspense.

"*Lion's Foot?*" the middle guard hummed.

"The very same," Chad nodded, and flung a bolt of quatra. The guard leaned away from the attack, hand racing to his back, from which he retrieved a weapon. A long snake of green-tinged metal unfurled in their hand and struck at the quatra bolt, capturing it for a flawless redirection into the wall. The wood splintered and shattered as the bolt's rings emanated throughout.

"*Cobra!*" Chad chuffed, and dropped his stance, his hands wandering to his hips. "You made it out of that terrorist stronghold?"

"It's a long story…"

"And now you're guarding a computer? Talk about a bear-market."

"This is no time for economics," Simone urged, and focussed on the energy in the room. The three assailants stood still in their equal analysis of the scene. If these people didn't actually move, there was no energy for Simone to harvest. She'd have to wait for them to will their limbs, and she could sense from their smirks that they knew of her powers, and therefore her intentions. The only movement was that of the copper whip, which oozed black ribbons and smoke to Simone's eye. She could not steal that energy from a quatra source.

"At least I don't need a Suneca to help me win a fight." *Cobra* smirked, eyes rolling to Simone. "Worried I'm too fast?"

"Two on three seems fair to me." Chad shrugged, then charged with his whip.

Energy exploded into the room.

Red ribbons danced from every limb, rising to the ceiling in a nauseating wall. Bolts of quatra flew from behind the mystifying curtains, aimed squarely at Simone. She shrieked, unable to grapple to the energy in her fright, and dropped to the floor. The bolts sailed overhead, colliding with the back wall and throwing the wood panelling to splinters and embers.

By Simone's head, metal crunched on metal as Chad's iron chain met *Cobra's* copper whip. The two knotted in each other, and *Cobra* heaved against the mess. Chad tried to maintain his footing, but couldn't against the smooth wood, and was thrown forwards.

Simone could see palms levelled at her again, and so she stole from the juicy, red streamer of the Chad's fall, converting it into a blast to throw herself against the leftmost wall.

Chad, given the extra time to fall, found his body again and leaned into his momentum. He rolled onto the ground, avoiding *Cobra's* quatra bolt which was aimed for his head, and abandoned his chain. His tumble finished at *Cobra's* feet, where Chad sprang up from his soles with palms outstretched. He caught the enemy in them, and threw him to the sky in a mighty shove.

Simone, who had stopped up against the wall to witness Chad's recovery, saw a blue bolt of black-hole energy racing towards her. Seeing her opportunity, she stuck a hand out to it, and channelled it through her body with her weight and step, sending it out her other arm and towards the flying *Cobra*. It caught the agent clear on his chin, and Simone was sure that his thread was disrupted as he crashed through the rear wall. Dust flew to fill the room, allowing Simone to jump up and land at Chad's side.

"Plan?" she asked.

"*Anything.*" Chad shrugged – and that was all he got to say before two quatra bolts sailed through the air. He ducked from their path, and threw a bolt of his own towards one of the sources. Simone could not sense nor see the sources through the dust, and dropped to the ground as the bolts roared overhead.

Then a red ribbon appeared, radiating through the settling cloud, a glowing betrayal to the hidden guard. Simone grinned, and yanked at the streamer to steal the man's motion.

"Left!" She yelled to Chad, hoping that he could sense the Suneva through the dust and fire on him.

"Right!" Chad said, either agreeing or totally misunderstanding the direction.

Unfortunately for Simone, the arrested guard had decided that he didn't *want* to move anymore, and the ribbon of energy between he and Simone sprang back into the dust. She could almost see his smirk radiating as she fumbled to release the streamer, but the guard had been too clever, and it disappeared as she held it. Simone yelped in pain as the force of her overdraft snapped back onto her soul. It panged in the depths of her heart, toppling her to splay across the floor.

She smacked at the floorboard with her palms, throwing herself up to her knees. She needed to stand quickly, to regain herself before danger struck, but her body ached, and she was wracked with a mighty sting from her muscles. She slumped, and just in time to narrowly avoid a quatra bolt, which slammed into the floor by her side, obliterating the boards.

This snapped her mind and body into focus, and Simone rolled away, landing upright on her arse against the left-hand wall. Before she could even comprehend so much, another bolt slammed into the wood an inch from her head, blowing the wall into splinters and shrapnel.

Simone screamed, and raced to her feet. The pain was gone now, but her heartrate was driving her dizzy. Chad had retreated to her level near the back wall, and redirected a bolt from the guard hiding behind the staircase on the left, to the one behind the bookcase on the right. Simone waited on the right guard to move his arm – to do anything to defend from the attack. She stepped towards him; hand ready for that ribbon…

Her foot fell through the hole in the floor.

She shrieked all the way down, watching in horror as two quatra bolts flew towards her helpless body. Chad tried to leap into their path, to cover for Simone, but he couldn't match their speed. The bolts zipped by him, straight for Simone's head. She stole some scrap of energy – some grey streamer of sound – and blasted air overhead to throw herself to the floor. She felt the heat of the quatra bolts as they just singed her cape. They collided with a window in the rear wall, shards exploding out and over the dark street.

Chad stared, shocked and deliberating what to do, before he caught himself. He turned to the guards, hand flicking to draw his massive axe.

"Well, if we're all comfortable destroying the place…" he said, and planted a foot to the centre of the room, squatting to grapple with his soul connections. He heaved, and the building groaned, then shook.

"Stop him!" the left-hand guard yelled to the other. They each blasted a bolt of quatra at his head.

"Catch!" Chad called to Simone. He swiped his axe to the blasts, managing to redirect one towards the trapped Simone. It was green, and she couldn't remember which of the guards had fired it, but she didn't have time to consider this. She took it through her right hand, and guided it through her vestigial quatra pathways, out of her left hand and towards the man behind the balustrade.

It might have been the guard's apprehension of Chad which had distracted him, but he hadn't noticed the quatra bolt flying towards him now. In fact, his avoidance of the energy seemed almost intentional, as if his senses – whichever he was using – understood exactly what was going on around him, but had failed to identify a threat. When he did notice the bolt, as it flew a foot before his eyes, he panicked. A fat sausage of red energy danced from his body, for which Simone had waited, and drew in hungrily. Caught by such surprise, the guard didn't think to abandon his desire to move, and sting Simone. He had no thoughts but self-preservation, which ultimately directed a bolt of foreign quatra square into his face. The boy's weapon smoked from his hand, and he stumbled to the floor.

He couldn't predict my redirection, Simone surmised, turning back to Chad. *I disrupted destiny…or something.*

From the dust and shadows of the far wall, a figure rose. Chad was busy redirecting a bolt when *Cobra* wretched himself up from his crater, whip twitching at his command.

"Watch out!" Simone yelled to Chad. By her side lay a chunk of wood from the window pane, and Simone's first thought was to piff it at the resurrecting man's skull. From her hand it flew true, striking *Cobra* square on the temple and forcing him off his feet. Simone latched onto the fat ribbon of his fall now – kinetic energy which the man could not rescind by his own will – and called to Chad once more.

"Juice me."

Chad nodded, and threw a bolt of his own towards her, before ducking away from an attack. Simone reached for the energy, eyes and aim locked to *Cobra*. It coursed through her body, redirected through her systems.

And before it made it out, she flicked her wrist.

The bolt zipped towards the right-hand guard. He hadn't been watching it, and just like his friend, he didn't even register its intent to obliterate his head. This time, Simone waited for a kinetic ribbon which didn't come – even releasing *Cobra* in anticipation. The bolt slammed into the right guard and knocked the soul out of him, setting him to his knees on the floor. *Cobra*, falling back into his crater, was met with a bolt of Chad's red quatra. His whip sublimated into black smoke his as his head lolled in defeat.

Chad laughed, roaring through his helmet and pumping his fist. He went to high-five Simone, then realised that she was still trapped with a leg through the floorboards, and jogged over to pull her out.

"Nice work," he laughed, yanking her up by the armpits. When Simone's feet finally found the solid floor, she skipped away from the hole, towards the three fallen Suneva.

"Yes, good work," Simone huffed. As she stood to catch her breath, Chad moved past her, sauntering over to the fallen *Cobra*.

"Where's the computer room?" Chad asked the man, holding him by the scruff against his crater in the wall. *Cobra* growled, his head rolling towards the left staircase.

"Why would I tell you that?" he wheezed.

"Well, depends how much you like your thread," Chad teased, and dangled the thread device from his pocket. *Cobra* scoffed, eying him.

"I know you. You wouldn't do that."

"Want to bet?"

Simone, having recovered, wandered towards upwards staircase. Now that the room's commotion had lulled, bar the squirming and writhing of the pitiful guards, she could sense and see energy emanating from here, the room's rear-left corner. A line of small, grey ribbons flapped to their sonic hum, writhing from under a door which neither she nor Chad had noticed before. The door's perimeter glowed in a blue haze, with white streamers dancing on the doorframe, complimenting the energy.

"There's something buzzing in there." Simone pointed to the door as she advanced. "It's either a TV or a computer."

As she approached, Simone sensed a third energy: a red ribbon flashed briefly from behind the door, its snake-tongue head glancing her mind's eye. It disappeared just as she noticed it, the owner shuffling to a stop.

She wound around to Chad. "There's a guard."

He nodded, and gently lay *Cobra* down, sleuthing over to Simone by the door. She reached for its handle.

"Be ready," she instructed, and Chad summoned his axe once more. "*Now.*"

Simone twisted the knob, threw the door open, and yanked at the ribbons of kinetic energy which formed in the room. Her grin grew as she tracked the streamers back to the Suneva in her grasp.

Only, at their end she found a black and white cat standing on a keyboard, eyes, ears, and fur alert. They bleated a confused meow as Simone released them, and leaped off the computer, trotting through Simone's legs into the battle-wrecked room beyond. Chad started to laugh, and Simone chuckled along.

"Okay, computer found," Simone hummed. "Could you restrain the guards? We might need their help with its operation."

"Sure thing," Chad nodded, and jogged back into the hallway. Simone sidled up to the machine, sneering at its strange composition. It was a huge beast, like an arcade game, with an inbuilt keyboard, joystick, rollerball, and cathode ray screen. Behind it, lining the walls, were metal cabinets buzzing excitedly with blue-green lights. Above those, hanging from the roof in a row, were five TV monitors. Three of them were off, the fourth showed static, and the fifth displayed camera surveillance of Hesslik's Caslte's front gate. The arcade-computer hummed loudly and happily, idle in the warm room.

Simone examined the screen. The system was logged in already, this was good.

It had physical controls, which, although not standard technology for home computers, meant the system *wasn't* Liktas controlled. This was even better.

The operating system was also not standard. This was some home-developed tech with an odd interface. Simone scratched her head.

"Maybe bring one of them in here…" Simone turned, calling to Chad over her shoulder.

"I might be able to work it out," he said, rearing his head up after chaining the last guard to the balustrade.

Simone shrugged, and stepped aside, gesturing to the alien controls in a grand wave of the arms.

"Be my guest, loverboy."

Chad stumbled over, squinting. He eyed the joystick, then the screen, the joystick again, and then turned his blank face to Simone. "I'll get the original guard," he nodded, and stalked out of the room.

There was a joystick on the machine, which Simone's hand worked its way towards. She toggled it, and found the monitor zipping up many levels of a menu. She quizzed, examining the new options.

Chad dragged in the original hostage, holding the thread-removal device to his collar. The man was shaking in nerves, eyes jittering, looking for an escape.

"There's surveillance footage up there." Simone pointed to the working television screen. "How do I control it?"

"The camera?" the man asked.

"No, the source," Simone clarified. "Surely there are cameras inside the castle. All I need to find – or not find – is the machine." She turned to Chad. "James described it to me, he even drew a picture." She reached into her pocket and pulled out an archaic scribble.

"I…I don't know…" The man squabbled.

"Who is the technician here?" Simone asked. The man pointed outside, to one of the men who lay in chains. Simone gestured to Chad, and he freed the current hostage, trudging outside after the pointed-to man.

Chad came into the darkness of the hallway. Annoyingly, his helmet had a tinted visor, although he'd become used to the darkness it provided. He spotted *Cobra* and one guard by the bookcase, but the guard tied to the balustrade had disappeared – perhaps they controlled an element stronger than iron, and already had their thread back.

"Which of you is the technician?" Chad asked.

"They ran off," *Cobra* grumbled, pointing to the descending staircase. "I don't know how to work this thing; I just protect it."

"No, you're smarter than that," Chad said. Through the floor, he could connect to the thrumming rumble of their hearts, and he knew that they were lying.

"It's you, isn't it?" He pointed to the right-hand man. Their eyes pried wide apart, and they shook their head unconvincingly. Chad reached for the thread-removal device and plunged it to the man's neck. They shrieked, then stiffened, cowering. *Cobra* went to kneel, to lunge at Chad, but the chain held him tightly down.

"It's your thread on the line," Chad said. "One of you can use this computer. Who is it?" Lips drew tight, expressions drawing grim. *Cobra* was clearly calling a bluff, but the right-hand guard didn't seem so sure. Still, he did not budge.

"Fine," Chad nodded, rolling his eyes. He grabbed the anxious guard by the neck, and turning the device's prongs away from the man's thread, he pulled the trigger. The device zapped at thin air – Chad couldn't bring himself to remove a second man's thread – but it appeared to produce the right effect. He became limp in Chad's grip, and slumped to the floor in his placebo shock. Any second now, the grief of thread loss would rock this man.

"Ready to cooperate?" Chad asked *Cobra*, whose eyes and mouth now hung wide.

"You've never had the guts…" *Cobra* coughed.

"You never tried me," Chad grunted. "Now why don't you help us out."

"Hey, I got to something!" Simone yelled from the computer. Chad stood, turning wordlessly from *Cobra*, and set off. Behind him, the downed guard started to moan in anguish.

"You just did that for nothing, you coward!" *Cobra* shrieked. "You can't just do that, you bastard."

"Did I?" Chad asked over his shoulder. "Check on him in a few minutes." And he walked through the door twirling the device around his finger. Simone had a new screen up, displaying some list of documents.

"I found lab reports," she said. "I couldn't get into the security. It was, obviously, very secure. Lab reports, however, are not. And look at this one…" She pointed to the first entry on the screen. This selected it.

"Touch screen?" Chad quizzed. "Futuristic, hey?"

"A bit of an expensive choice," Simone hummed, "but look at the top of the screen now." She pointed again, her finger now at a distance. "It was written today, by Vestas. And look at the topic. *Project Power, update one-hundred-and-twelve.*"

Simone scrolled using the joy stick, highlighting the text.

'*Entry 112*

Almost perfect working conditions for the energy transmitter. Electrical signals were transmitted successfully from this laboratory to the Melbourne Laboratory with a loss of 3W.

The machine, however, should be impossible to transport, which was one of the design requirements of its manufacture – and although I did not have a say in the system requirements, what purpose would one have with moving a global transmission device which works perfectly across almost any conceivable distance? Disassembly is required for transport, and the systems could fail if put back together as proper care was not taken to make joints separable.

This issue will be worked on, although with time being short, I'm not hopeful.

Vestas.'

"So...we still don't know whether the machine will be in the castle or in the parade?" Chad quizzed.

"Well, no," Simone said, "but we know that it's more *likely* to be in the Castle...probably."

"Probably," Chad smiled under the helmet. "That's good enough for me, let's get out of here."

"What do we do with all of these people?" Simone asked, turning from the computer, gesturing to the outside scene. *Cobra* and his accomplice still lay there, although both slouched dejectedly.

"I say we run before they get their threads back," Chad laughed nervously. "One guard already did, and ran off for help. Let's move."

"Agreed." Simone nodded solemnly.

They made their way down the stairs, footfalls silenced by Simone's energy stealing, then slipped out the door, sleuthing through the city's night-time shadow.

Chapter 27
What's My Name Again?

Natalie and I walked the Melbourne city streets, lights blaring down through the chilly night in late April, nine days from the Great Suneva Gathering. We were both rugged up against the bite of the coming winter, whose cold breath roared down the north-south corridor of the city. I held Natalie in one hand, and the wind in the other, splitting it around us to keep her warm.

She didn't usually ask for my help in crowds anymore, but she certainly never refused it. Especially not on a windy night, when the hydrogen – half of her remaining vision – blustered and swerved in patterns she couldn't follow.

Natalie's hand was warm. Our fingers fit together like they were made for the specific purpose. Holding her anywhere was always magical like that – two bodies made to be held by the other, two souls combined in the void-space between ourselves and the Gods. Every day that I spent with her I counted myself lucky to have so brilliantly stumbled into somebody so fulfilling – even if our meeting was the act of destiny, something I had so refuted.

Tonight, we were to meet Tom in a bar down a laneway by the state library. The description David was able to give me of the bar, in his exceedingly cool fashion and exhaustively selective taste for such establishments, sold it as drab, but *'well priced'*. He, for unknown reasons, could not make tonight.

No doubt, then, Tom's motivation was simple drinking. There was some event tied to the night too, some leg of a university pub crawl which Tom had been asked to come to by a girl he was seeing – and for whom tonight would serve our first introduction.

Tom, of course, knew that Natalie and I had been together for a few months now, and that our status was now official. He had cordially invited her along to the event, despite not having much to do with her recently. He seemed to harbor some miniscule animosity for her, and I couldn't figure it out. Natalie didn't have the opportunity to come forth to him about her Sunevahood the same way I had, and maybe hearing the information second-hand left him with a sour taste. Still, our friendship had continued strong past the ordeal of my own Suneva-outing, where I felt we might have slipped away.

We left the bustling crowd and raging headwind to turn right, off the main street, and into a small back alley, lined with cobbles. Puddles of chilled water lay in depressions, reflecting moonlight. Natalie reached for them with her dextrous fingers, holding to her connection, commanding the water to part from our path.

The bar was easy to spot in the dingy, stagnant way – music and lights poured from its door, the shadow of the bouncer extending into the street. He admitted Natalie and I, instructing us up the steps and to the right.

Happy hour was in full swing. Jugs of beer were filled to the brim by the barrelful, and held tight to chests like precious cargo as men struggled to their spots. They eyed each other like greedy birds, squawking through the crowd, sceptical of every limb and finger which moved in their way. The place was packed, with voices slurring and shouting above the music, drowning the ambience in joviality. A dim, red light cast the glow of fire over the patrons. Natalie tensed in my grip, overwhelmed by the ridiculous amount of activity. I held her close, parting the dense crowd through the thin, winding bar, looking for my red-headed friend.

I spotted his shaved, orange top in the most remote corner of the venue, his limbs spread liberally over the red leather couch of a booth. Next to him was a petite girl of east-Asian decent, her hair died from blonde through to pink at its ends. Her eyeliner, even from a distance, was offensive – great, huge wings which wrapped halfway around her head. This girl was striking, in every sense of the word. Luckily, Natalie couldn't develop any visual preconceptions of what she was being walked into. Tom waved as he saw me, and made room, letting us sit on the couch next to him.

Three finished jugs lined the table, although neither Tom, nor his date, appeared all that affected. He shook my hand with a smile and incredible vigour. He held his hand out to Natalie, although she didn't detect it, and his face flushed redder than his stubble. He wearily put the hand down.

"Welcome to the party, friends," he said. "James, Natalie, this is Rachael." He gestured his hands to the slim girl. She smiled and outstretched a very professional hand to us both. I took it, but Natalie waved and said "Hello, lovely to meet you." She'd missed many hands in the last two months, and waving saved face.

"Oh…I'm sorry, I didn't notice," Rachael apologised, giving Tom an immediately dirty look. The man sipped his beer, pretending not to notice.

"It's alright," Natalie smiled. "I'm just getting used to it myself."

"That's rough," Rachael sipped her cider. "What caused it – if it's not too sensitive to ask."

"I…uh…" Natalie stumbled, looking at me with her greyed eyes. Natalie had learned aura-reading from Surawelle during our time in Paris recently, and she used it now frequently to judge other's reactions without seeing their faces. She sensed my nervousness – it would have shown up as some colour to her fingers. "…got caught in Suneva crossfire." She completed her sentence. I tensed immediately, but it piqued Rachael's interest. She leaned across the booth, examining Natalie's eyes.

"You do know what Suneva are, right?" I asked. "I mean, it's very probable that you don't."

"I'm well read," Rachael said. I bit my lip.

That almost never means good things.

No, it often never does. Boekidin agreed. *Want me to go in?*

No! Geez, man. No invading Tom's love-interest's mind.

Boekidin hummed, sat back down quietly somewhere in the city of my mind. I secretly wished he would just jump over.

"So, how did you meet Tom?" I asked, diverting the potentially rocky course of the conversation. Both girls pulled from their trance and turned to me. Natalie squeezed my hand in a sign of relief. Tom, too, appeared to ease up.

"Tom and I both study computer science and electrical engineering," she said proudly and with a bold smile. "We have all of our units together. Nobody else talked to me except him, so I guess I just got stuck here." They shared a saucy look. Natalie smiled, clearly seeing something in their respective souls.

"There's a reason nobody else talked to you," Tom pouted, sitting back in the booth. "It's because she's so damn smart," he said to me. "There's always the one kid answering all the questions in the lectures, and its Rachael. Half of these engineering kids are too afraid to open their mouths except to eat. They can't handle the intelligence and the *boldness* of such an act. It blows their poor, mathematical minds."

"If Tom thinks you're smart, you must be *really* smart," I complimented her. "It takes a lot to make him feel inferior." I winked in Tom's direction, and he geared his return jab.

"But, James, I *am* perfect." He fed the joke. We laughed, the girls did not.

"How long have you been into computers?" Natalie asked.

"A while," Rachael said, sipping more cider. "I built my first one a few years ago. I've been designing applications for three years now, I think."

"Writing your own full applications?" Natalie asked.

"Yeah, it's super easy," she continued. "I just don't get why some of the people think it's hard. The lectures go so slow! It's like, how did anybody else even get into uni?"

A movement in the background caught the corner of my eye. A woman sleuthed through the crowd, with long, chestnut hair. The clothes looked wrong on her. Her face was from another time, an elegance I'd only seen in my childhood, from my village. It was her, wasn't it? It was my love.

She disappeared behind a portly patron, and didn't emerge on the other side. I rubbed my eyes, then my mind cleared. *Who did I think that was?*

Rachael was giving me an odd glance, although my strange change in attention didn't stop her mouth spewing forth fast paragraphs.

"That's absolutely remarkable," Natalie said. "Did you hear that, James? She's done work for the Australian Government's cyber security systems."

"Yes, remarkable," I droned, not having paid attention. "Anyway, I'm going to get some drinks. Who wants some?"

"I'll take one mate," Tom said. "We can share a jug."

"Probably not good for me to have one." Natalie gave me a pointed look. She had not had a drink since becoming blind. With such a dependence on her powers for sight, Natalie was concerned that she'd lose control of her soul or its actions if drunk. Either possibility was terrifying.

"I'm fine, I've got this whole glass." Rachael held hers up. I nodded, then slipped my way into the crowd.

The room was thick with people, bustling under the red lights. The music blared past the booth, disorientating, dizzying. I floated through the thick of it, brushing shoulders.

There she was again, to my left, in a group of friends. Her hair flicked, her eyes sultry, inviting me. I found myself lunging in her direction, I had to explain what had happened, I had to –

The face disappeared, becoming a tall, blonde girl. I stammered, bolt upright, and desperately looked for where my love had gone. *Why can't I remember her name?* My memories haven't been the same.

Their face appeared again, shifting through the thick of drunk university students by the booths. I pushed my way towards her, but she sunk down into the sea of people, and disappeared.

I found myself at the edge of the crowd, facing Tom, Natalie and Rachael in the booth. Rachael gave my repeated odd behaviour another interrogating stare, and my face flushed red.

I had to save the situation.

"Lager or ale, mate?" I asked Tom.

"Your choice, my main man," he said, waving a careless hand. I nodded, and made my way back towards the bar.

Who was this girl I was seeing? Why did I feel that I loved her? My mind was a haze, exacerbated by the dim lights, loud noises and slurred conversations spewing in a barrage upon the sea of people. I sailed my boat, half a man and half a dizzy mess, towards the bar, the lighthouse and beacon in the rough waters.

I slumped over the wood of the bar, hanging on for dear life, a log in a churning ocean. Beer would save me. The barwoman lifted her head from the tap, glorious chestnut hair flipped over her face as she looked to me. Sultry eyes, she winked. My heart was caught.

Then her face changed, and I found myself gripping hard into the bar for some sense of sanity.

James, you're getting anxious, but I can't see anything wrong, Boekidin said. *What are you seeing that I can't?*

You're not seeing the faces changing? I asked him.

What? No, I'm not. Not from in here…

The barwoman held her hand to her ear, an eloquent way to ask what I wanted.

"Jug of the house lager," I yelled to her over the noise. She seemed to get it, walking over to the taps with a new jug.

I just don't know who it is. I said to Boekidin. *I know her face...like she was my lover? I need to tell her something, but I don't even know her name...*

Your *lover?* Boekidin asked. *James, your lover, or Olomb's lover?*

I... my eye twitched.

You know your own life, mate.

It seems too personal, I argued. *I have to have known them.*

It's concerning that I'm being locked out of these delusions, Boekidin muttered.

The barwoman handed over my jug and a single glass – I felt it fitting, in my current state, that they'd assumed I was drinking the whole thing alone. I handed her the cash, then marched my way through the sea back to the booth.

I beached myself on its leathery seat, having spilled as little of the notorious cargo as possible on the way over. Tom eyed my single glass curiously, until I grabbed his old glass and filled it with beer from the jug.

"Thanks, man," he said half-heartedly.

"Barwoman was being all weird. Couldn't hear me properly," I laughed it off. He shrugged, taking his first sip.

The night stretched long, through all topics of conversation you could possibly imagine having with somebody you just met, right up to the point that it gets too personal, and you all decide it's time to head home. Rachael was lovely, past the odd looks she'd been giving me all night. She was, in essence, socially inept. She and Tom had a lot of interests in common, and she was cute, but she certainly didn't come across as outgoing or eccentric as Tom. It was nice to see him expand his horizons beyond the 'but she's hot' that was Penelope.

We exited the establishment just past midnight, not having had nearly as much beer in that time as I expected to. In fact, I stepped out the door relatively sober, at least compared to Tom and Rachael. The girl was very small, but amazingly held her drinks well.

I had to be in a good condition to walk, because Natalie depended on me. I couldn't let her down. I hadn't said it to her yet, because it was always too early, but I loved her. I knew it in the way that I could now look through her greyed-out eyes and see her looking back at me. I knew it in the feeling of holding her, in her caring for me. Being there for her excited me, and I was elated to lead her home.

275

The four of us walked uphill together, along the cobbled alley towards the main road and the library. A light drizzle came down now, flecks of water as cold as ice which covered the face like an unpleasant sheet. Rain filled the puddles on the roadway. Natalie became nervous. Usually water was good for her senses, but too much, with too much else to focus on, was never good.

We took shade under an awning on Swanson street, eyes set on Museum Station. Despite the late hour and low-levels of rain – to which most people had an extreme aversion – the street was still bustling with night owls. We waited for the pedestrian light to change, which sat a while away from our shade, but for which we were ready to pounce when the green man came.

I glared at the suckers out there on the other side of the road, waiting in the drizzle by the traffic light's pole, very slowly becoming wet. Some of them shivered. And amongst them was the familiar face again. Just as my gaze gleaned over her chestnut hair, she turned to look me straight in the eye. She did it with a smile so faint, it almost couldn't be seen, before pivoting back to the light.

It's not real, I told myself. *She'll just disappear.*

What's not real? Boekidin asked. *Who are you seeing?*

I glanced away, down the street, towards the river, and held my gaze there at the moving sea of lights. Momentarily hypnotised by the bright eyes of an oncoming tram, I almost forgot to look back, but when I did, the girl was the same.

Okay, don't freak out yet, I told myself, but I couldn't take my eyes away. Her form stood strong to defy the rain.

The light pole rang, the green man coming to its beat. The mystery woman took her first step onto the wet road towards us. Like opposing armies, the two sides of the street crashed towards each other. I took a cautious step out into the rain, away from the safety of the shop's awning. She bustled through the crowd, and I watched her, inching forward onto the wet road. I lost her once, then twice, as the tallest members of the opposing force drowned her in their height, but she returned on the other side of them. She was not an illusion, it really was her.

I froze, unsure of what I should do, but found my legs moving towards her.

I pushed through the front lines of the near sidewalk, storming past infantrymen. Like cowards they cleared, eyes scared. These were looks which frightened me dearly, although I had no time for self-pity. They feared me – the general who spent his years marching the rolling mountains of this land. The *Kiin* warriors who had fallen to my hand – they in all of their ruthless might held broken morals. Two societies now joined, with *Kiin* ethics and a *Liktan* egalitarian social structure. The end justified the often-horrifying means, but seeing the faces that I shoved aside, I had to resent my actions. I created aggregate peace, but at the cost of small social rifts. Rifts which I can foresee growing to my demise.

All of that time, and now, after the darkest hours of war, in the spring sun of this new Suneva community, I'd found my love. I could finally show her that it was all worth it.

She stepped off the gutter, onto the sidewalk on my side of the road. Nose held high, she pivoted so elegantly, turning north. I tailed after her.

"James!" I heard a voice yell from behind me. And then I heard it again, in my head. Repeatedly. Banging on the taught skin of my brain. Bouncing through my mind.

Odd. My insanity had called me by many names, when it flared, and James was never one of them.

"Tom, take my hand, run me to him!" a voice pierced my mind, cutting my skull. I could just about recognise this one, but no, it was lost on me.

My love walked calmly right before me, her hand hanging limp on a delicate arm as it swayed. I grabbed it with mine, pulling her back. She swung immediately, shocked. Her face was still her own, unchanged – it was her! Glee rocked my expression, streaming from my eyes as beams which lit her beautiful, framed face. She was stricken with shock – clearly the shock of seeing me. *It's me, Iris.*

Her hand tugged in mine, trying to pull away. She was overwhelmed. It had to have been close to one hundred years since she'd seen me. I only left her at the start of these wars, but who could have guessed she'd be ageless?

Then, I was ageless too. And now I was an ageless fool not talking.

"Iris! I know how I left you wasn't kind, I know…" Those damned voices were screaming at me. They called James in my head and out on the street. Would the Gods never leave me alone? The pushed at my gates with breaths of the insane. *I get it,* I growled to their cries. *James is important in some way, let me have my moment!* "…I know you felt that it was for nothing, and you gave me the ultimatum, but…"

"Get off me!" Iris demanded. She grabbed at my fingers, tearing them from her palm, ripping her hand free.

"Wait!" I cried. Arcs of lightning flew between the digits on my hand. I had to say persistent. I lunged again, grabbing her palm and falling to my knees at her feet. She yelped, tugging – I might have shocked her with a current from my nervous hand. Her eyes locked on mine and she did not lose my gaze. It was now her soul and mine drifting in and endless void. A sea of dull black guiding us. Crowd lost to the nether's end. Drowning in silence. A tumultuous ocean of peace.

"You said you'd never forgive me if I came back, and I never intended to do myself the heartbreak because I knew you'd hold true, but I stumbled on you here, and I have to ask for your hand again. We had *real* love."

"Screw this," a voice pierced the darkness. "Kuvalik…"

"Would you take me back?"

"*Olomb..*"

"I just can't see life having more meaning than this. I've seen all of destiny. I hold it in my hand, and…"

"*VASILLI.*"

The world bounced back – colours bleeding in reverse, sucked from the event horizon and zipping into place like mad, flying paints. I jerked bolt upright on my knee, holding the hand with a still Herculean grip. I turned to face the voice.

The Oracle Witch? It couldn't be…these were Kuvalik's memories invading mine again. Her tan skin, broad hips, face of such controlled prowess and rulership. Her greyed out eyes, shining symbols of her illness. A pawn to the Gods, rather than a listener. Possessed, and given power. Fallen to temptations too great. A cloud of imposition followed her every wake.

She shot a bolt of quatra from her slick palm. I caught it, an instinctive manoeuvre, but had nowhere to channel it. In my other palm, I held the hand of the woman I loved. A woman whom this quatra would kill.

The bolt was fast – too fast for my thinking. I tried to loop it through my body, around my chest and down into my legs, but its trajectory was too wide. It ran straight for my neck.

A breath was sucked from my lungs as Kuvalik's thread droned shut. But a second orange bolt came – one which I had no way of expecting or counteracting, and I had to take it to my own thread.

I went blind.

Then fire burned hot in my veins. It roared like a smeltery, turning my bones to liquid metal, forcing me into a puddle on the stone floor. I growled in extreme agony as Maiki was torn from me.

The sensation was not only of my thread snapping, but all of my ligaments tearing at once. Muscles weak, I was a bag of flesh in an oven. I seared, and seethed, groaning loudly.

Then, suddenly, it was all over, and I came to. Rain dusted my face. I was shockingly wet, lying in a puddle, right next to a tram stop in the Melbourne CBD.

Where had I just thought I was? Who did I just think I was? I was fully aware that whole time, wasn't I?

There was a girl sat on her ass by me, eyes aflush with fear. She backed herself away, dragging her skirt over the wet stones. Strangers grabbed at her arms, pulling her upright.

Strangers. There was a perimeter of them, like what would form for a busker or performer, only nobody was chanting or cheering. Everybody was stunned, and maybe they were yelling? I couldn't quite hear right. Shock gushed around in my head, cool like mint, blocking my senses. For each shocked face there was an equally angry one staring me down.

My god. I looked to the struggling girl. She was tall, with chestnut hair, but the face wasn't what I'd been seeing – and what I'd been seeing wasn't something *I* had seen before. No…it was what Kuvalik…or Olomb, or *Vasilli* had seen before. I'd just fallen hard.

So hard that I'd assaulted a girl whilst drunk on a busy night out, in front of a crowd. Someone had a mobile phone out. I didn't want to know which of the emergency services they were calling. None of them boded well for me.

"I'm so sorry," Natalie said, although it wasn't clear to whom, with the direction she was facing. "He must have taken the wrong meds. He just had an episode. Are you okay, you're not hurt, are you?"

Ouch. I peeled myself from the ground. *Throw a mental illness into it too?*

"Just get him *away!*" The girl demanded, although, she must have seen the change in my expression – whatever level of confusion my face was showing now – because she almost looked sorry for me.

Natalie grabbed my arm, and Tom grabbed her arm, and soon I was tugged off. My legs were wobbling, and my world was swimming. We breached the circle, and somebody shoved me hard on the way through, although I barely noticed almost falling over. My head rolled on my neck and my eyes snapped shut, but my legs kept strolling under me.

Already plastered in my memories were the faces of men and women gathered. Caricatures of hatred, judgement, and anger, rendered to the wall of my mind in a thick layer of shame and a smudge of confusion.

Yet, in this concrete memory, just now being formulated into the foundations of my city, was a growing, intense fear. Somebody had called the police, right? Everybody had seen my face. I'd be found, soon enough. I'd go to jail. There were severe consequences to the insanity that came with holding

Kuvalik's thread. Consequences much more severe and life-staining than simple mishaps of identity.

I couldn't go on like this. There were only nine days until Hesslik's gathering, but I couldn't exist between three distinct memory sets any longer. One incident was one too many.

I had to get rid of Kuvalik's thread.

Chapter 28
Haven't I Done Well

"Why did it hurt so much to get torn from my thread?" I asked Boekidin aloud, my eyes rolling, my head hazy as I lay in bed the next morning. The night was over, but anxiety hung over worse than alcohol. I was groggy with cringe, rubbing my eyes and nose. There's only one chance at a first impression, and Rachael must have believed that I was legitimately schizophrenic – no matter to Natalie's ramblings that I housed two souls. Two souls, three minds. Kuvalik, Olomb, and myself. It was madness.

Except now, it seemed, my memories were jumbled. I had the very distinct sense of being incredibly embarrassed, the face of the girl as she cowered and yelled at me, and the discerning stares of onlookers, but I could remember no more. In fact, most of the last two months had swept away from me. I had brief memories of snuggling with Natalie and feeling her embrace, specific moments of being in Paris, and of the Melbourne Ethnic festival. I could remember the Void and learning from the library, and fleeting moments of nerve and anxiety at having to deliver speeches as Kuvalik.

Almost all of my experiences past those, however, were lost. The most of what I could remember now was a vague emotional record of how I'd been feeling. I was left impressively confused, gathering details of my life from Simone and Boekidin just a few minutes ago.

I'll be honest James, I think you did that to yourself, Boekidin said. *Although, we couldn't have known it. My god, this place is a mess. Even Kuvalik's mind looks a shambles. There's so much rubble here.*

"What do you mean?" I moaned. "What did I do?"

Well, you bypassed sleep by going into the Void, he said. I could hear his feet shuffling through debris in my mind's space.

280

"And? What's the problem there? I've never felt better…well, except for now."

Except for now, he tutted. *Do you know what sleep does for the brain, James?*

"…consolidates memories…" I wearily admitted – my school psychology class had taught me that much.

Yes, exactly, Boekidin said. *James, you bypassed your memory consolidation and flooded your body with quatra to venture in the Void. Do you want to know how your memories have been consolidating themselves?*

"Not really…"

With quatra. I don't think you needed to draw quatra to exist in the Void, but you did, even after your arm was healed. All that energy had to do something, and it appaears that you used it to weave your memories into your soul, including those of Olomb's memories which came to you. Natalie obstructing your thread just cut you off from all of them, and now they've vanished from here. With some meditation, you might find them again in your soul, though, but I'm not sure where they'd be if they're not in your mind.

"You didn't notice this happening?" I coughed, desperate.

The mind and soul live in the same realm – the slip. The memories looked super-clear from in here – and they were coming here from what I could see. It was almost as if the Void was making them better. I'm sorry that I couldn't see it was the opposite.

"No, it's not your fault." I sat up on the bed. My head bobbled, desperate to just roll off my shoulders and smash across the floor. I managed to hold it in place. "Tess tried to warn me of the risks of quatra use. She said that I had to monitor it, because uncontrolled quatra use could lead to seriously bad consequences. I guess this is what she meant."

I don't think she meant this, buddy. I don't think anybody could have foreseen this at all, Boekidin hummed. *At least there's only eight days to hold onto Kuvalik's thread.*

Eight days, I hummed, my head throbbing at the thought of it. Only eight days until Hesslik's gathering, was I strong enough to deal with another of Kuvalik's episodes? Even though I couldn't recall the progression of the hallucinations – which in itself was frightening – it seemed that they now could strike at any time with incredible tenacity. How many more would I get over eight days? And how badly would I continue to embarrass myself and my friends? What if it happened on stage…?

James, don't have stupid thoughts, Boekidin advised unsympathetically, and it sparked a protest within me.

"They're not stupid thoughts," I grumbled. "I don't know that I can do this."

281

And what's the alternative? Boekidin hummed to me.

"I can rid myself of Kuvalik's thread."

You wouldn't.

"Yes, I absolutely would." I stood up from the bed, somehow set towards this objective.

James, that's stupid and brash. You can't do that.

"I can," I nodded to myself, rummaging through my closet. "The Void killed my memories, and it killed the likely many experiences I had as Kuvalik. Luckily I preserved something of myself, and I'm not going to lose myself to his memories again. I can't be falling into hallucinations. I can't deal with it."

Think for a minute, James. You're thinking too emotionally, Boekidin advised, and I could hear his claws scratching at his helmet. *The Void might have destroyed your recollection of our plans, and that's fine, I'll reeducate you: our entire plan hinges on the Suneva people gathering behind Kuvalik, their ancient leader. We need Kuvalik to be present at Hesslik's rally for that to happen. What happens if you remove his thread from your body? The dream will die.*

"It won't die," I rebutted. "The ideals are still there, Boekidin. We've made a society to match what we've heard that the people want, right? They'll follow."

I don't think you understand the importance of the icon, Boekidin cringed. *Kuvalik is a very powerful icon to draw people in. Hesslik is an icon, and Argol was an icon. We need a face.*

"And the *White Witch* and the *Shiverman* aren't good enough?" I protested. "We've even got a Legendary, and the Vochduhvlad. People have seen me transform into Kuvalik…"

And they'll want to see it on the stage.

"Then we tell them that one of Hesslik's agents took the thread from me. We play the victim."

You know that Hesslik will go to lengths to prove that's a lie. Boekidin shook his head.

"Then I'll make it the truth," I resolved. "One of his agents *will* remove the thread."

No, Boekidin snapped. *No, James, this isn't happening, and I won't play nice to your delusions. You're strong enough to hold on for eight more days! Just hold on!*

"You're not the one going through this Boekidin," I snapped back at him. "Tell me that I wasn't divulging badly into episodes as Olomb. Tell me that truthfully, and maybe I'll reconsider."

Boekidin fell silent, growling to himself. *James, this whole thing is bigger than yourself,* He said, his voice stern and considered. *The future of a united Suneva rests in your hands. This isn't just your dream, James Grey, a man who has been a Suneva for about a year. This is my life's dream, mate. The consequences of destroying Kuvalik's thread are bigger than yourself, they're bigger than any of us can imagine. I'm begging you, mate, don't destroy this chance we were given.*

What would it destroy? Kuvalik was a relic of the time of destiny and the Gods' control over us. He was an icon, but his disappearance would be just as iconic – or at least that's how I could justify it.

"I'm not destroying anything," I argued. "There's no place for destiny anymore, and don't underestimate Zamelle's ability to guide a crowd. She's just as iconic."

And his consciousness? Boekidin stabbed again, his voice roaring in my skull. *You'll destroy that for sure. It can't live without an active thread. That's five-hundred years of a plan gone.*

"What, and five-hundred years of life wasn't good enough for anybody?" I scoffed, throwing on clothes. I was determined to bustle myself out the door – if I wanted to blame Hesslik for this 'tragedy', I would have to go where his agents were stationed, to Vestas' lab. "This is *our* plan now. Destroying that rickety-old mind is exactly the point. I don't care about it."

This…this is unbelievable, Boekidin growled, then stormed off somewhere, bashing his feet within my mind. *Let's see just how much Natalie likes the movement being put on her shoulders, and how much she'll appreciate Kuvalik's death, hey James. I'm telling her right now. In fact, I'm telling all of your friends right now. You won't get a chance to go forward with this.*

"Fine, do it!" I yelled. "I'm giving myself some god-damned agency over my mind and body here. Tell them that, would you?" And I trudged for the door, throwing myself through it and out of the house.

I lept onto my bike, swinging it around the driveway, roaring the diamond beast of a thing up the street. At some point in the last two months, in some scene which had not been saved to my mind's memories, I'd built a bike out of diamonds. I wasn't inclined to question this, rather, I just put the fortune to good use and slammed at the pedals, burning the tyres hot on the cooling asphalt.

I crossed by Kuvalik's house, ditching down the hill and skidding through the back-street gravel tracks. The bike bounced over a gutter, and lept down into a cul-de-sac road, at the end of which stood the alley for Vestas' laboratory compound.

I abandoned my bike in the mouth of the alley, running on the front gate. I didn't check to see for a guard in the gate's security box – I'd have to be caught if I wanted a thread removed – rather, I connected to the air and thrust myself high off an impossible blast, somersaulting over the barbed fence.

I was amazed at my power, but the memories of recently training my connections were there for me to access, somehow. It seemed innate as I threw the blast behind me – I wasn't using the air, and I wasn't a part of its system, but I was somewhere in between the two, on a joint plane of cohabitation and control.

No shout came from the guard-post as I vaulted it, and I paused to scan for my entrance. The roller-door was closed all the way to the concrete, and the side entrance might have been viable, but I couldn't know if Chad's wall of rock still stood on its other side. My eyes naturally found the roof's maintenance entrance standing tall above me, and I knew that I had to take it.

I ran towards it, sizing up the building. There was a pipe halfway up the face of it, a refuge to bisect the leap. With my new connection to air – with whatever memory I had of it beyond a feeling – would I need the pipe?

Surely not.

I blasted down on the air, *with* the air, sending my un-armoured body into a frightening bound. Rising just past the pipe, and at the top of my arc, I blasted down to the concrete again, giving me a powerful second burst, but it wouldn't be enough to reach the roof.

Feeling the pressure, and seeing the drop, I summoned my staff in my left hand and sliced it into the building's corrugations. It gripped in nicely, and I used it as a springboard. I flipped over its pole, and using my momentum to rip it from the wall, spun it onto the roof with my body.

Landing on a roof on a cloud of dust and air, I realised my urgency still. Boekidin was going to tell everybody of my plan, and he knew where I was. I had to be quick.

I bolted for the door I could see. Taking no chances, I ripped at the carbon present in its hinges and blasted my staff straight into its wooden face. The whole door imploded inwards, snapped in half by the prongs of my staff and torn clean off its weakened hinges. I barreled down the staircase, sure to make a fuss, and ran into the television-and-lounge area.

Still, nobody sat here relaxing. In fact, as I skidded to a stop in the room's centre, I could hear no voices at all. None called from Vestas' office, none chirped from the other hallway. What gave? Extending my hands into the air and sensing for its presence, I couldn't determine any silhouttes either. It was like the whole office was on a holiday!

But I did sense one thing, and it not only gave me urgency, but gave me purpose.

The computers were here, just down the hall that I faced.

Simone and Chad were only able to obtain a washy conclusion of the electrical-transmitter's location in their mission. Now, eight days from the gathering, there would have to be solid answer as to its location, hidden somewhere in the updated lab files. I grew a grin of glee, I *could* get something useful to our mission out of this experience, and that could *surely* be a worthy justification for coming here. Sending air behind me, I blasted into a sprint, straight for the cubicals and computers.

I burst through the door to the offices, and with all of my afforded grace and none of my utility, vaulted off the floor with a strong blast to soar high over the first cubical wall and its fake, plastic plant. Spotting a vacant chair near a vacant computer in the totally vacant room, I spun a soft cloud to land on, and crashed my ass into it. Sitting now in front of the machine, I calmly reached for the on-button, then mashed at it.

The old box stirred into life, buzzing and whirring to fathom its own existence. The little green cursur flashed and summoned text to bumble across the screen. I sat with blood rushing, begging the thing to work faster. It gave a frighteningly feeble grumble in response, threatening to blow itself up from the effort of loading. I needed this thing to boot – I wanted to be found, but not before I had my answers. Not before…

"Who are you?" an unconfident voice stammered from before me. Slowly, I raised my eye line over the cubical wall and around the plant, to see a single visor on a Suneva helmet staring back at me. "Hands in the air," they demanded, pointing the barrel of some weapon towards me.

The computer finally loaded, flashing the log-in screen at me.

Time to improvise, I guess.

"I'm Operative…" I scanned my brain, raking for a fake name. Boekidin would have been able to give me a good fake name, if only he weren't trying to stop me. "Operative *Bear Paw*." I said, struggling to keep my face flat.

"*Bear Paw?*" the guard hummed. "Like *Lion's Foot?*"

"I'm the replacement," I smiled quickly. "Sent from Hesslik."

"To do what?" the guard remained skeptical, and they kept the barrell of their weapon pointed squarely at my face. Reaching out to my connections, I could feel a great mass of carbon in the device. It had prong ends, situated in wound springs, bursting to fire upon me at the pull of the trigger. I flinched at the sight of the thing.

"What is that?" I asked him, unable to hold composure. The guard eyed me with suspiscion.

"It's a thread remover," they quizzed. "New standard issue."

"Man, I've missed the newest upgrade, hey," I joked, trying to hold my character. This guard held a long-range, taser-like thread remover – this must have been what *Master* was trying to get Chad to intercept in New York. There was a factory somewhere making these things that we'd failed to find and disrupt. I steeled myself against the nerves – thread removal was what I wanted, after all.

"What's the mission, *Bear Paw*?" the guard repeated.

"I need to back up Vestas' lab reports on a hard-disc," I spewed out. "You know, after all of those leaks…"

"You couldn't do that from *anywhere* else in the world?" they quizzed. "Why come here?"

"Because I need some of the files *only* saved in this system," I said, hoping that this was true. I watched for a change in the guard's face, but they held it straight behind their visor. "You know that not everything is shared between the computers."

"Not a lot is shared," The guard narrowed their eyes. "Not after Anderson."

"Exactly." I pointed a finger, smiling along – although I was hoping that *this* particular thread of laboratory reports *was* shared across the system. Otherwise, I'd be doing all of this for nothing. "So, I need to access his files."

"Alright, go ahead then," the guard nodded, letting his weapon's barrell droop. They turned to leave.

"Wait!" I stammered, and they stopped dead, eying my strangely. "I don't know the password."

"You *don't* know the password?" They pivoted on a stamped foot, eyebrow raised.

"No…no…" I coughed, searching for a lie. "The password list got stolen off me. I got intercepted by…the White Witch…and her friends."

"Right," the guard hummed. They eyed me, bouncing between their feet, tossing up their next action. I waited in a sweat – further investigation would lead to thread removal, which was ultimately what I wanted, but seeing Vestas' lab report before that would help everybody out. It would also give me something positive to go home with, which was more than I could claim with the removal of Kuvalik's thread.

"Here," the guard said finally, and trudged over to the computer. They made sure to take a wide berth around my seated ass as they came to the keyboard.

"You're a life-saver," I smiled, sitting back. "This will go straight to Hesslik."

"Oh, I'm sure." They rolled their eyes, typing the password in secrecy. The guard themselves took control of the mouse too, setting it whirring to find the directory full of Vestas' posts. He pulled up a set of files assorted by date, which he left to my devices. "Here you go, *Bear Paw*," he hummed, stepping back.

"Ah, thank you," I nodded dumbly, scooting right up to the computer desk. I immediately scrolled through the directory, finding the most recent file saved by Vestas under 'Project Power'. I opened it.

Unfortunately, I was unable to safely take apart the machine. The time spent trying to make it transportable would have been better spent improving its efficiency. Hesslik will have the remote to activate it from the stage. Luckily, the same technology which makes the transmission possible also makes this level of wireless control possible.
Vestas.

My eyes lit up in relief, a smile building on my face. I'd found something useful! I sighed relief, sitting back into the chair.

Back into a set of prongs which crested my neck.

This was both perfect and horrifying.

"I know that you're Maiki," the guard said, and I stuck myself still.

"You did?"

"Yes." And they said no more, holding the prongs tight.

"Yet you let me view those files?"

"You won't get a chance to use them," the guard slicked, and I peered back to him, the prongs biting into my turning neck.

"Why's that?" I asked.

"Because I'm going to be the Suneva to take Maiki's thread…"

Hooray! I cheered. This was *exactly* what I wanted.

"…and then I'm going to lock you up until the celebration is over."

That was *not* exactly what I wanted.

"Not scared of the White Witch busting this place open to break me out?" I eeked. Sensing the buzz of the man's finger against the remover's trigger, I searched up the pipeline for that second eclipse of the moon. Deep in my mind's sky it lay, that second thread, and I drew on the power which it begged me to use. Kuvalik's soul replaced my own, and I summoned all of my conviction to keep my mind straight.

"No, I'm not scared," the boy answered after an uncertain pause. "Anything to keep you from the castle."

Just then, another Suneva appeared in the entranceway through which the guard had initially come. Their face fell to shock, and they spoke.

"James!" they said – although the voice didn't match the movement of the mouth, and I knew this voice as somebody elses.

Boekidin? I hummed in my head.

You don't have to get rid of Kuvalik's thread! he yelled, rushing his words. *His mind is already dead. It can't give you more memories!*

What? I stammered. The two Suneva before me were talking, but I couldn't focus enough to hear them. My head swam. *What do you mean his mind is dead?*

It was powered by his thread, which Natalie neutralised. Without any power, it died, and so did his memories. I mean, you still get to keep the ones he gave you, but your ordeal is already over! Natalie saved you.

Cheese! I cussed, feeling those prongs firmly planted in my neck. I sweated. *Can you help?*

I can try, let me...

Pain engulfed me. First electrical, then purely visceral. My spine was ripped from my body, bump by bump, pulled out of a hole at the base of my neck. I could feel the blood, hot, rotting, dripping, a river oozing down my back. Flesh torn thread by thread in an instant, passed over a grate of knives.

This was the pain of having a soul ripped from the body.

"*ARGH!*" I screamed, throwing each limb in every direction involuntarily. The thread of Maiki called at me through the thick haze of pain, and I connected to it immediately.

"Help me grab him," the guard said to his mate, and I had to act quickly. His arms grappled at my flaccid shoulders, and the other Suneva stepped across the dusty carpet.

I collected my swimming head, my sight coming back finally. I saw only one move right now, whilst gripped in hands, and went to execute it.

I threw my hand up to my captor's neck.

They weren't sure how to react, their claws tightening around me. I summoned a bolt of quatra, ready to slam it into their thread.

Only, I didn't summon quatra. None came to me. The sensation was empty.

"Oh no," I uttered aloud. I found a bolt of quatra flying at me from the back-up guard, and I thrust my free hand to it. It was redirected through my body, slamming into my captor's neck. Their armour shattered away, raining like glass, leaving me to leap to my feet.

The original guard stumbled away, crying his confusion as I stood. This new guard – a Suneva in dark grey armour – blasted two more quatra bolts straight at me. I threw my soul into the air around me, begging my thread for quatra to blast me away.

I connected – air rushing from my palms to push me out of the bolts' paths. Still, it was a terribly weak blast, and the connection was awful at best. In no condition to fight, I turned and ran.

"Hey, get back!" the grey Suneva yelled, but I was long on my way out. I threw air behind me in a pathetic gust, running out the door by the power of my feet, and slamming it closed behind me.

I zipped down the hallway, forcing my sprint as fast as my legs could carry me. Just as I raced into the TV room, the door behind me slammed open, the guard stumbling in my tail. I connected myself to the system of the air, willing it to throw my body towards the next doorway and around the corner, but I just didn't have enough power behind my swoop. Instead, I slammed face first into the far wall of the room.

Head spinning, my soul growling its rage through the panic, I flipped over and off the wall to have a quatra bolt slam into it just where my brain had been. I stared for a second at the scorch, then my attacker, and finally caught my senses and jetted off again.

I sprinted down the next hall, and clawed my way around following corner, flying up the staircase. Bolts of quatra careened in my tail, but were poorly aimed, scorching the walls by by side. I lept out the maintenance door, running across the roof for its aprupt end. Guard on my tail, my feet acting to my usual command, I vaulted myself from the gap.

The stupidity of that decision only came to me once airborne. With my connections weakened, my eyes bulged at the short fall, towards the *hard* asphalt ground which was coming faster.

I summoned all of my might, drawing every tether of connection afforded to me, and reached for every ounce of wisdom I could remember from that damned void library. I became a part of the system of air, both a controller and a member, and tore at the flow of air above my body.

I jerked, pulling into a long arc towards the sky. It was weak, just like everything else I'd tried just now, and the ground came fast. I could see my head smashing into it, my skull cracking, my brain painting the whole yard pink. I gritted in with all of my soul – it felt like I was sucking quatra out of a straw, when all of my life I'd been sculling the stuff from the bottle. My arc changed, I jerked again, and my nose just scraped the sandy asphalt as I pulled away from it.

I laughed my relief, holding tight to the stream of air as it pulled me over the barbed fence and past the guard's hut. I let myself fall from the pull, releasing the air and commanding a cloud apon which to land. It was a rougher touchdown than usual, and I landed painfully on two scraping shoes, but it was done. I straddled my bike and tore away, off around the corner and away to safety.

I had made a grave mistake today.

Chapter 29
Your Princess is in Another Castle

I slept restlessly that night, my second night of consistent regular-sleep since the months of void-dreaming. My dreams displayed a drugged-out version of my memories before me in slow, arduous detail. I saw my spine, long and juicy, being torn from my skeleton with a set of rusty pliers. Olomb slumped over a chair, unconscious, watching. His dream girl in the distance, crying. I tried to use my powers to escape the moment, but I was too weak. My air blasts were simple piddles, streams less powerful than a baby's breath – just like they'd been when I started. And in this dream, my friends stood watching on in the distance, their faces strewn with hatred, sporting large, comical frowns. They jeered through mouths which did not move.

The next day, in Kuvalik's old house, I would learn my friends' actual responses to my stupidity and brashness. Strangely, and against my expectations, I was met with compassion and understanding. There was a reverence for what I had to experience in carrying the thread of Kuvalik, and for how I suffered in doing so.

"I understand that it was difficult for you, James," Celeste said over her tea, "but Kuvalik's image and name *is* important, it's what we've been rallying people behind. It's what *I* have told some Argols to look out for already."

"We had the foresight to show that I was Kuvalik's vassal," I countered – although now it was hard to remember, did I show myself as Kuvalik to satisfy my ego, or because it was a good idea at the time? "I'm not sure that he needs to appear for the cause. Plus, getting rid of Kuvalik transitions us out of the reliability on destiny. It's all us, now. Us and the Suneva people." My speech was uplifting, but didn't turn Celeste's frown. She hummed her contemplation.

"I think it's better that Kuvalik was taken by one of Hesslik's Suneva," Chad pointed out, stretched across his bed of bean bags. "It's like Kuvalik fell as a martyr against Hesslik's regime. He always has, anyway – once cut down by plasma, then killed as a consciousness and a thread. That's the spin I'd take away – and *quickly*. We've only got a few days to circulate it."

"That's my job, then," Simone peeled herself from the couch. "Spreading white-lies on the internet, that's my specialty."

***

Dreams were terrifying – I'd forgotten that over the last two months. The Void was a lucid space, a place where the brain worked as expected, where reality shifted infrequently, but physics was always at least consistent. My dreams, however, created worlds of disturbing time distortions and failures in logic. Stuck on an Athenian street, lanes of the road devoid of movement, pocked by the blemishes of war and bloodshed, I saw Hesslik standing with a mean grin. I tried to run towards him, but my footfalls were weak, and I ran like I was being held by a demon. In his hands was a red buzzer, and he reached to press it.

I drew a breath, and all turned to blackness, *peaceful* blackness. I had reached the end, killed, with no air left to draw. I hung, no more than a floating consciousness in a field incomprehensively dark, not even the colours from behind your eyelids to light a path.

What now? I asked, but there was nothing. I did not breath, there was nothing to do. This was death.

Although a faint whisper whirred and rose to my ears – *James, James, James* – it cried, louder and louder. It forced me to fall into myself, crushing at my chest.

I woke in a sweat, drawing a sharp, huge breath of air. *Six days till the gathering*, my mind spewed at me. Nerves rocked my soul.

My name was called again, just as loud as in the dream. I gasped in fright, scrambling to pull the sheets close. Mum barged in the door, and called my name right at my face.

"Yes, yes, yes!" I stammered, weary and frightened. Her face drew guilty at the sight of me.

"I'm sorry, I didn't think you were sleeping," she apologised, then threw something at me. Before I knew what I was catching, it was in my hand – the new portable house phone. I stared at it dumbly.

"Nick Athanas wants you," Mum said, then shut the door. Darkness set again. I eyed the phone wearily, before putting it to my ear.

"Hello, Mister Athanas?" I said into the device.

"So, you're home, then," he said. His voice was flustered, breathy. I looked to my alarm clock. *Seven in the morning, on a Saturday? No wonder I'm so tired.*

"Where did you think I'd be at this time?" I asked.

"I thought you'd be with my daughter. I thought you'd be behind this latest adventure."

"Latest adventure?" I asked. "She didn't have any plans. I saw her yesterday."

"Well she's gone," he said. "Taken a suitcase and everything. Left in the middle of the night."

"What?" I stumbled alert in the bed, trying to gain my bearings. "Did she say where?"

"She left a note, but she wrote it in *Suneva.*"

"Tess hasn't read it?" I asked. I put the phone on loudspeaker as I lunged at my closet, searching for clothes.

"She's not up yet. I just woke up myself."

"I'll be right over," I said into the phone, and hung it up. I called Chad at Kuvalik's house to tell him to gather the forces to meet at Natalie's. I ran for the door.

"What did he want?" Mum asked as I soared by her face. I handed her the phone.

"Natalie's gone missing," I said as I sprung through the door and ran for the diamond bike.

"Gone missing?" Mum called down the hallway, but I was long gone.

She didn't tell me that anything was wrong, I stressed to myself on the short ride. *We were doing fine. Young people in love. Or…at least, I don't remember a lot of what actually happened. But the whole experience was very emotionally satisfying. Oh Omercronius, what have I missed?*

I wanted to be there for her, I truly did. My heart sank that I might have failed her on something, or that she didn't feel comfortable confiding in me. I wanted to provide her with that kind of comfort and trust. Why couldn't she dump her crap on me?

I parked the bike in the drive of her house and proceeded to fling myself through Nick Athanas' doorway. He bolted up in surprise as I showed myself in, with little more than a point to the letter on the kitchen bench. I gripped it between my sweaty fingers and read its ancient script.

You have cheated Gods, but even the strongest minds cannot win a war with the immortals.

I've talked to you once Maiki, where I told you that everything is not as it seems. You should be advised to hold those words dearly. Do not interfere in my work. Do not express your freedom in the realm of Gods.

The damage you are doing to yourself, and to everybody you could possibly care about, is larger than you could imagine with your short-sighted, ill conceived goals.

We are not benevolent lords in a game of chess, like I would have some of my Suneva believe. We are the great protectors of the Suneva, of humanity, and of the interests of life itself. We are Gods. We are the Universe.

You cannot play games against Gods and win.

"*Cheese bloody damnit!*" I seethed, and perhaps too loudly, for I forgot that Ms Floros was still asleep in the back room. Nick gave me a stern look before jogging over.

"What is it?" he whispered. "What does it say?"

In that moment, everybody else – Simone, Chad, Celeste, Yvon and Anastasiya – piled through the door, each with shocked expressions.

"Bloody hell, what is this, the *circus*?" Nick growled.

"Something's going on," I said to the group, ignoring his quip. "Let's take this to Kuvalik's house."

"What is it?" Chad and Nick asked in unison.

"Amasos left us a note, through Natalie. She's possessed again – and this letter tells me that it's much worse than before." I held the note and stormed towards the door.

293

"I'll get your daughter back, Nick." I turned to him, heart filling with determination. "I've done it before, I'll do it again."

"Wait!" He grabbed my arm as I neared the front of the house. I halted, turned by the force of his grapple. Everybody else seemed to pause halfway out of the house, intent on his word.

"Give us a moment," Nick commanded of the teenagers jammed into his door. They silently backed through the portal, flat faced, and Chad closed the door behind them. Nick turned me to him with urgency.

"James, listen here," he said. "In all of this shit, I'm powerless, okay?"

"Yes," I agreed. His look turned stern – as if he were the only person allowed to acknowledge his weaknesses.

"You are my power," he said. "I know that I told you to step down before, to leave this to authorities, but I'm not sure that was the right thing. You brought her back because you know how this magic shit works, right?"

"That I do," I nodded.

"And I've seen the way the Natalie looks at you. You love her, don't you?"

Of the memories that I'd been afforded, the admission of love for Natalie Athanas was one.

"Yes," I agreed. "I love your daughter." Nick nodded to the admission, more to hide his smile and his concurrent anxiety.

"Good. I'm glad," he said, "because this time I'm not just throwing you overboard to go and get her, I'm *trusting* you to bring her home safely."

"I take your trust very seriously, Mr Athanas." I nodded.

"Thank you." He patted my shoulder. I swung towards the door.

"Oh, and James," Nick called after me, and I paused, "stay safe, please. Do it for your Mum… I know how much she worries."

"Ha, Mister Athanas, if I died doing this Suneva shit, my Mum would *kill* me," I coughed. He chuckled lightly, although his heart was still set with panic. I opened the door, and stepped out to see my friends.

All turned to see my exit, except for Chad. His head rolled back as he fell over.

"Woah!" I shrieked, rushing to him. He toppled like a felled log, slowly towards oblivion. I blasted air at the ground, giving him a weak cushion to land on. Once again, I overestimated my new power – it was still difficult to draw from my thread.

Just think of how weak you'd be if you weren't *so close to flight*, Boekidin said. *Good thing you went into the Void so often…kind of.*

I'm only one book away from flying, I know it, I replied absently, kneeling to Chad's side.

His eyes darted open as he hit the mud. They were nervous, running in circles. His face was stiff, and he inhaled sharply to sit up in the dirt. A circle cleared around him, his manic movements repelling onlookers.

"Oh God," Chad gasped. "It's got me again, James." He grabbed my arms, shaking them. "The current is flowing over my head. Oh man, it's so *strong*." He stood suddenly, yanking me from my squat to my feet. His eyes darted for an exit, glaring at the front gate hungrily. "It wants me to stay with you guys."

"*Sweet Cheese*," I mumbled, grabbing his shoulders in return. "Pull yourself together, man. We'll sort this. Just do what you want to do for..."

"But I don't *know* what *I* want..." Chad stressed, throwing me off him. "How can I *know* what I want when I can't be sure if my ideas are mine?" he shifted away, towards the gate. I grabbed him with both hands, my weight barely able to hold him.

"Dude!" I shouted. "It's literally been two seconds. Have *confidence* in your brain. Have *confidence* in your own decisions."

"Why is this happening?" he asked me.

"I don't know," I said bluntly, turning to the group. "Let's get to Kuvalik's and we can sort this out."

"*It* wants me to go to Kuvalik's!" Chad freaked. "I can't do it..."

"*Sweet cheese*," I cussed, "trust me, I have free will. At the very least, trust Simone..." I pointed to her, standing at the back of the assembled group. She'd already pulled her home-made black robe on, ready for whatever was to come. "And get in her car."

I pulled Chad to the vehicle and threw him across the backseat. Simone drove him, Anastasiya, and I quickly back to Kuvalik's house. She parked the car in the garage, and I rushed Chad inside. We pushed our way through the dark and ominously empty house to the living room, where I threw Chad down onto the couch. He flopped onto it stiffer than concrete, like a steel plank with the face of a frightened deer welded on.

"If you can't trust yourself, trust my directions and nothing else," I said to him, and he nodded slowly. "Sit here until we figure this out. Ask me or Simone when you feel the urge to do something."

I stormed towards the door as Chad's own car arrived, piloted by Celeste and Yvon. I opened the door for them, letting them into the cool, dark space. I turned on the light and the heater as I made my way back to the couches.

"Good to see that they made it," Simone said, coming up to me. "What do you think is happening?"

"Clearly Chad's back under the black hole's control, I just don't know how it could have happened," I frowned. "I might need you to control us if things go south any faster."

"Control Chad?"

"Any of us," I clarified.

"You think you're *all* falling?"

"It's possible," I hummed, and stepped away to kneel by Chad.

Although I didn't get to exmine him – there was a thump in the hallway, a weight smashing against the floor. I threw my head around to see Celeste falling across the hardwood. Yvon dropped what he was holding to help her up, but Celeste was already shooting to her feet atop of groggy legs. Her eyes swam in her head.

"Not you too…" I grumbled. "What the hell is going on?"

"Veritas, what are we doing here?" Celeste said, her breath rushing. Her head glanced about, searching for an exit. That's when I felt Simone's exhaust air ride across my face. "I know what we have to do, James. I know how to solve this all!"

"Do you now?" Simone raised an eyebrow, then leaned over to me to whisper, "exact opposites, her and Chad, hey?"

I tried not to laugh, but my head turned to Chad's woeful display next to me, and I couldn't help but chuckle at the juxtaposition.

"Don't hold me back, Simone," Celeste growled. "We need to get to Paris. I've just remembered how much *work* there is to prepare for this gathering. I need to get to my throne, then we can chase down Natalie."

"Not happening, Celeste," I shook my head, standing. She fitgetted against her magical constraints, fire pouring from her eyes in her gaze towards Simone. "You've been ruling the Argols from here just fine, but I'm going to need you to take a seat so I can figure this out." In truth, I couldn't remember whether Celeste was controlling her throne from here, and I didn't quite care if it was a lie.

"Why should we listen to you, James?" Celeste spat.

"Because I have free will. I'm destinyless."

"And you think you know better than *Gods*?" she quizzed, struggling to break free. "Veritas must know something about what's happening up there. Why should I trust *you* over them?"

It was a valid point, but I had no patience for arguing. If Gods could do to anybody what Amasos did to Natalie, it was reason enough to distrust them with our lives and politics. The era of these Gods was over.

"Unless you want to turn into Natalie, I suggest you stop struggling, and sit down," I advised more firmly. This sparked her rage intensely – Veritas plucked her strings with precise, practiced fingers – and Simone struggled to hold the girl's insane energy from bursting.

Yvon then grunted from Celeste's side, falling to his knees next to her. He growled there, his pain roaring through the house, his hands gripping at his face. Now I was frustrated, blood roaring to my face.

"I said stop resisting, Celeste!" And I slammed my foot onto the ground. "We don't have time to fuck around with what the Gods want. We have a plan."

She refused, instead opening her mouth to spit a hot, pink flame. I flicked my staff into existence, and used the extra connection it afforded me to spin a dismal eddie and deflect the hot sparks.

"That's it, no connections for anybody!" I barked, and marched onto Celeste's position. She wrangled with her invisible restraints, growling at the gates like a tied dog in a muzzle. She didn't dare throw fire onto my bare skin. I stomped around her held body, thrust a hand to her thread, and fired a bolt of quatra. Celeste's eyes swam back in her head, then her whole body seemed to droop into a floppy mess as Simone's grasp fell away. Celeste crumbled into an unconscious pile upon the floor.

I turned to Chad, my staff pointed at his staring eyes, and blasted another bolt of quatra. It slammed straight into his face, sending his body into a stupor as it melted atop the bean bags.

"You!" I tugged Yvon to his feet by the shoulder. He yelped in pain, still grappling with his face. "Get inside my head, now."

"That would have been easier from the floor…" he whined.

"Fine, *whatever*, just get in there."

"Okay," he nodded, and scooted himself over to the closest wall, pitching his lazy body against it. I marched back to the couches, taking a stiff seat upon the nearest one and preparing myself for meditation.

Celeste awoke, gasping groggily. She peeled herself from the floor and stared up to me with lost eyes.

"What's going on?" she asked. "My head feels so heavy."

"You're all being manipulated," I growled. "Get on a bean bag, sit down, and shut up. I'm trying to…"

My ears were assaulted from all directions, hundreds of objects smashing, as if the entire kitchen had fallen on its side. One thousand plates of fine China dropped from a skyscraper all at once, pulverised to dust by my feet with a wicked screech.

The noise kicked me out of visual consciousness, blackness reigning as fragile items met their fates around me. A carcophony of destruction, it rang on, drawing my head into another reality with it.

The world swam around me, coming properly into place as stone dust flew into my face. I fell away from it, pulling myself out of the sediment cloud. The Void Guardian stood before me, tablet in hand, but then so did Simone. My sight crackled like a television, struggling to hold onto either reality as the truth. I was both in the *Vochduh* void library with the Void Guardian, and in Kuvalik's house at once, unable to tell which body I controlled.

"What's going on?" I asked to the Guardian, and through my shaking vision I could see Simone respond to the question. I smacked the side of my head – like you might do to a TV box when it plays up – and the static seemed to fade. I had to hold my concentration to *stay* in the Void.

The Guardian threw down the tablet which he held in his hand, causing it to rain as dust across the floor.

"What are you doing?!" I roared, shooting up and grabbing the next tablet from his hands. He let me have it, throwing the tablet with me attached into the ground, sending me spinning across the floor and rubble.

"You shouldn't be here. Neither should your friends, and neither should *this*," the Guardian harked.

"You're destroying history!" I stammered, and stood again. My frustration had built to rage, and beyond what had happened to my friends, I wasn't going to let this haughty imbecile destroy what stood here. I launched myself at him, straight for a tackle.

The Guardian evaded me easily, stepping aside and smashing the next stone over my head. I felt the whole impact, my skull screaming at my brain, my whole head spinning off my neck. I was ejected from the Void totally before I even hit the floor, the static of my vision buzzing me back into the real world. Everybody stared at me, now in a sweat across the floor.

"Omercronius *damn* it!" I yelled, grabbing my head. It no longer throbbed, which was nice, but I was still infuriated. I leapt back atop the couch, crossing my arms and trying to force myself into meditation. I had to get back into the Void before the Guardian decided what to do with my body.

"What happened?" Chad asked.

"I think the Guardian sabotaged us," I rumbled. "Now please, I need quiet, I need to get back in there." And I strained with balled fists, tight enough that I threatened to snap my own tendons. Entire lungfuls were being expelled and demanded in the effort to control my breath and doze off, but my furrowed brow kept me planted in reality.

James, calm down! Boekidin warned, sidling up to some bench in my mind-space. *Take it easy. Think about the first time that we travelled to the Void together. We climbed up the pipeline, remember? Let's try that again.*

Oh, I remember the pipeline, I nodded along, more aggressive methods of void-entry coming to mind. I stood quickly, my plan hatching.

What are you doing? Boekidin asked, but I ignored him.

"Chad, punch me in my left shoulder."

"What?" he and Boekidin stammered in unison.

"Punch me right where it hurts, as hard as you can." And I stood, baring my back towards the American boy. Chad cringed, sinking into the bean bag, unsure of what to do.

"Won't that hurt?" he mumbled.

"I can heal, I know that much," I assured him, "but right now I need to get into that *god-damned Void*, and the pain will throw me into it, I know it."

A bucket of water was thrown over my head, and I shivered to the sensation. *Bonjour,* Yvon greeted, getting himself comfortable. *What do I need to do?*

Are you sure about this, James? Boekidin asked.

"James, I don't want to punch you…" Chad bit his lip, slowly pulling himself up.

"*Everybody listen to me!*" I growled, and both my mind and the room fell silent. "I'm the one without destiny here. Listen to me for a few moments and I'll get this sorted. Just trust me! Chad, you need to punch me just next to my left shoulder blade. Boekidin and Yvon, when we get into the Void, Yvon goes for Celeste, Boekidin goes for Chad, and I go for Natalie. Got it?"

The room remained still, eyes shifting between Chad and I.

"Well…alright then…" Chad grimaced, and he wound his fist.

I was starstruck with pain instantly, the impact of Chad's fist ringing out over my whole body, my vision shining with white speckles as I struggled to stand, and instead fell. Impact again, the pain flared, buzzing over my body in flying annuli. White and red bands up a pipeline, surrounding my vision. I clutched onto them – those bands of my thread- dismissing my *urge* to scream, throwing my soul up my thread.

I came to, being dragged across the ground by my feet, the dull sky of the Void encompassing my static-buzzing vision. The Guardian had me by my ankles, towing me across the grey sands. I could smell the sea beyond our path, only one or two dunes removed.

"No you don't!" I growled, and tugged with my legs, gripping my palms to the loose earth. The Guardian stumbled for a moment, but I couldn't hold myself down, and he yanked at my ankles, forcing me along.

"There is no place for you here, on the land of the Void," the Guardian said. "You're going back where you belong."

I went to yell back at him, some scathing remark, but my head was relieved of a huge weight, as Yvon materialised standing next to me, his body wet and dripping. Quick to react, I lunged at his legs and hugged them tight. Suddenly we were both yanked towards the Omerconian sea, whipping around the Guardian as the body of water struggled to pull Yvon back.

I was held at the end of a tether, the Guardian grounding me by my ankles, and Omerconius pulling me towards the sea by Yvon's legs. Meanwhile, my vision buzzed between realities, the static of it just barely keeping me immersed in the Void. Water whipped off Yvon, but the force of its pull caused the Guardian to fumble, dragging him along.

Then the Guardian grew a wicked smile across his filty head.

He let go.

I was snapped from my anchor, flung towards the nearest dune by the pull of the sea. Yvon crashed into the sand first, then smashed my body into it behind him. We tumbled together across the crest as the tug of Omercronius dragged us forwards – faces and flesh ripped at by the plants on the sand.

We cleared the scrub, flying towards the crest of the next dune, the last one before the sea - before we and all Suneva met our fates. Through my tumbling, swimming vision, I locked onto the plants resting there. If I let go of Yvon to grab them, he would be flung out to sea, and losing sight of me, could not enter my mind to leave the Void.

There wasn't time to ponder it. Yvon slammed into the sand and shrubs, and my face met them just after him. I bounced off the dune, the tug of fate ripping me away from it. Desperate, with one last chance, I released my right hand from Yvon's leg and slammed it to the sands, then waited for the first contact with *anything*.

I felt something, and I clenched my fist around it.

My soul was tugged, my arms nearly ripping free of it, held between two extremes. Yvon had whipped himself around my hand, now grappling with both of his mits to my arm. I was stretched to my soul's limit as the water cascaded from Yvon's body in thick streams. I could feel the tendrils of my soul snap, their taught weave held between the vices of a torture device. Peering around, more just to focus away from the pain, I could see the Guardian running towards us. He sprinted through the sands.

The last drop flew, and Yvon and I crashed into the sandy ground.

"Run, man, *run!*" I coughed out a mouthful, spitting dust away. "Run, run to Celeste!" And I scuffled to my feet, tearing the Frenchman from the cold beach and to his own. "Quickly!" Despite his fright, he caught my messege, shooting a salute before running off around the beach temple.

As I turned, the Guardian reached the foot of the dune, and he marched himself up it with eyes glued to mine. I stumbled back, falling down the dune and onto the wet sands below. Rising the crest, his robes flapped in the dull wind, but he stood there still. Finally, I had the confidence to stand on my own feet before him.

"You should have left long ago, when I told you to," he barked from the sandy peak.

"Well…maybe I don't care what you think," I stammered, not sure of my next move. Behind me, the waters of Omercronius lapped and waned, their fates calling to me. I shouldn't have stood so close to their edge. "Who are you to decide what happens here?"

"I am the guardian of this realm," he repeated, but his meaningless explanation drew my annoyance.

"So?" I huffed. "Who gave you that role?"

"I have always had it."

"Show me *why* you have authority," I scoffed. "You threw the White Witch into the control of a God, you destroyed a library of ancient texts. I'm not sure you have anybody's best interests, or safety, in mind."

"I don't need to justify myself to you," the Guardian spat. "You've caused trouble by existing here. I have nothing to say to you." And he stepped down from the knoll. I wanted to back away from him, but with the ocean behind me, lapping towards my heels, I was forced to stand my ground.

"If you throw me into that ocean, the Suneva will be wiped out," I said, planting my feet to the sand.

301

"I will only protect this realm and its interests," the Guardian said with his stone face. "You're disrupting the way that things must be, here."

"What are the realm's interests, then?" I scoffed, the water slowly chewing its way up the sand behind me. "The death of its inhabitants?" But the man had no answer for me, he just advanced with his blank stare.

So I leapt on him.

It was a visceral intinct, to claw at his face, to bring him down. If he had no answers for me, then I had no time for his farting about between elitist silences. Although when I was upon him, my hands refused to meet his robes. Instead, my whole being phased through his, and I rolled across the sand behind his apparition.

"I think you're forgetting that this realm is merely a representation," the Guardian scolded, turning to face me. "What you do here has greater consequences than steps in the sand, but not everything here can be commanded by your touch." He reached an arm down to me, but I scuttled up the embankment, away from his grasp. "I am more than a man, I am a *mechanism*, that by which this realm and the Suneva will survive. You do not accept your fate, but you have no power to stop me from enacting it, and I will make you submit to it."

Around me the dull sky cracked with lightening, and the Guardian's eyes glowed to meet it. The entire atmosphere swirled amber and red, like the clouds were embers burning through space and time. My gaze was transfixed, totally unable to look away, as a scene unfolded across the painted red daylight.

It was my father's last breath – it seemed to take up the whole of the sky – playing before me, unavoidable, all encompassing. I felt it in my hands, that *connection* I'd had to his breath with no label to call it. I held desperately to the feeling of it, watching the rise and fall of his chest.

Only when the breathing stopped, it was clear why he had died – I'd held his breath too hard, and I had stifled it. With untrained hands, just over two years ago, I'd murdered my father through my soul connection. It must have been true – the memory fit.

And now, as if the reflex to such news, I was gagging on blood. Cold and purple, it spluttered from my mouth, raining from the orificies of my face. I was drowning in a spring of it, coursing from eyes, mouth and nose. I gagged, sitting up in the sand - pulled from the vision of my dying father to find my boddy being dragged across beach. My hands rose to clog the deluge, but by covering my nose, blood instead burst from my ears, staining the beach with a purple, thick line.

I went to yell instead, to protest, but all that left my mouth was a gurgle of deep indigo spew. The water drew closer and closer, its gentle reach climbing further up the sand with each outgoing wave. I had to do something.

Conviction, I reminded myself. *This place is abstract. Just have conviction – you have no destiny.*

There is no blood, I yelled to my head, although being certain of a falsehood didn't make it true. *My soul is strong. I control my soul. By my willpower, there is no blood.*

Blood poured still, past my hands working to clog it. I could feel the wet sand under my skin now. The Guardian dumped my feet on the water's edge. Nightmares played for me in the skies. I gurgled desperately, fighting blood for breath.

There is no blood! I screamed, and there was no blood. There was *never* any blood.

"I did not kill my father," I yelled, then. It might not have been true, but here, in a world without destiny, only convictions mattered.

The clouds seemed to close, returning to their dull grey. Images bled from the sky.

I shot to my feet, which the Guardian had, for some reason, abandoned in the lapping water.

"I can touch the Guardian," I hissed in a crazed smile. The Guardian, who stood facing the dunes, turned with fright, amazed to see me up.

I reached, grappling his arm in my palm and jostling it towards me. It came, and his body followed, stumbling into mine and spinning us around. I yelped with delight, and attempted to push him away into the ocean, but he grappled me in return. We were locked in a tight embrace, a wrestle on two feet.

"I knew this was a mistake." He tugged at my body. "I thought Omercronius was helping when he sent you, but Amasos was right all along."

"So, you *are* working for Amasos." I gritted against his grip, our chests crushed together in a tight stand-still.

"I'm working for the balance of this realm," he seethed. "There's something building in the Suneva. I can feel it. You know nothing of it. Amasos does, and the other Gods are too cowardly to face it."

"Amasos is evil," I rebutted.

"Amasos is *selfless,*" he insisted. "They're prepared to relinquish their control to save what we have."

"Give up their control over Suneva? Abandon destiny? Sounds familiar," I remarked.

303

"You don't understand the threats to this world."

"Then stop talking in cryptic messeges and *tell me*," I ordered, shoving the man back successfully, deeper into the shallow tide. His ankles wetted in the water, which swelled and lapped around him. Omercronius was thick to this man's presence.

The Guardian squinted, eyeing me, still. "You couldn't possibly understand…" he remarked.

"God, you're unreasonable!" I whined. "Think I'm that dumb?"

"This isn't your place!"

"You really think I'm that thick? That I can't understand something on the scale of this place?" And I advanced on him.

"It's not *your* place to understand it," he repeated, side stepping my advance to position me out to sea. I stepped sideways with him, keeping my back to the sandy dunes.

"That doesn't answer the question, *numbnuts*," I growled, face red, soul spiking with emotion and will. "*Answer me!*"

But the Guardian remained silent – his mouth dumb, drawn to a frown.

"That's it," I burst. "I've given you time to explain. You can't give me an answer, so you don't get to answer." I went to shove him, but he threw fists to my palms and shoved me back harder. I stumbled in the sinking sand.

"You cannot affect me. You don't know how this world works."

"You threw my girlfriend out to sea to be possessed by a God," I spat. "You stand in the way of a whole race of people who I, for whatever *damned* machinations of *this* body of water…" I pointed an accusatory finger to Omercronius. "…have come to be a saviour for. You think you can stand in my way forever…?"

"Yes."

"Fuck you," I seized. I grappled for his body. *He cannot touch me.* I set to convictions, making it so.

Unfortunately, it didn't work like that. His hand scratched into my arm, tearing at the fabrics of my soul. I roared, and he slashed again, ripping at the same spot. I focussed my will, forgetting the pain, and with one final effort, kicked off the dirt, forcing him with a mighty shove.

The Guardian lost his footing, and tried to grapple me down with him, but I ducked from his arms, rolling backwards up the beach. He lost his balance in the water, tipping backwards from my shove right off the edge of the shore-like bank of sand.

304

He fell back first into the sea. Like a bar of hot iron dropped in a vat, the water around his body bubbled aggressively. The swells rushed to it, storming the Guardian's being, grabbing it in a whirlpool. He flailed, mouth bobbing under the surface, brine choking his lungs.

The rip charged, raking him under the surface, crashing out to sea. The Guardian disappeared from sight.

I screamed, finally letting my soul relax. It fell onto the sands, desperate. I drew on quatra energy, which seemed to come from all around rather than my thread. The fabrics of my soul started to reknit, reforming strong with my convictions.

There would be time to mourn the loss of the library later. For now, I had to help rescue Natalie, Celeste and Chad.

***

I ran to the Amasosian sea. My connection to the Void was fading, my eyes struggling past the static which would plague me as a wicked tiredness took my body. I was fighting a deep sleep in every moment. Keeping my conviction defined and true was mentally taxing.

I crumpled at the edge of the black, basalt cliffs. I could spot Natalie immediately, a ghostly white radiating from between two of the three apostles in the bay.

I struggled to comprehend the magnitude of the water's ferocity. It boiled as if the sea floor was the core of the earth. Waves crashing into the cliffs sprayed well beyond their peaks, way over my head, raining down on the grasslands behind me. The swell was tremendous, so strong that with each rip of the current, the sea floor was sucked bone dry, before flooding upon release.

Bodies were flung helplessly in the soup of destruction and control – all except Natalie, who sat in its epicentre.

There was no way I could do anything about this now. Defeated, vision and hearing shifting between two worlds, I ran over to the Veritan sea to collect Yvon.

I saw Yvon flailing on a rowboat – an innovation of Boekidin's - out in the rough seas of Veritas. He had tied its bow to the shore by a rope, secured to a sharp rock, and paddled towards an anomaly in the waters – a whirlpool around a column of air. I'd seen these before, with Suneva centrally inside them. They represented something, but I didn't know what.

"What's in the whirlpool?" I shouted across the bay. The sound travelled far with my newfound conviction. Yvon talked back directly to my mind as he sifted closer to the anomaly's edge.

"Celeste is in it," he said. "Her thread is blocked. I think this is what happens."

"Huh," I smiled, "that gives me an idea."

***

I returned to the world with a gasp. My brain was too tired to stay awake, scrambled from the experience of keeping me in the Void. It was physically taxing, and where there was pain, quatra could rush. I couldn't risk building more of my body from the substance, after what it had done to my memory.

I flopped onto my stomach, clawing my way up the wall to stand, but I immediately fell. Chad slung my arm around his neck, and hoisted me to my feet. He slopped me onto the couch, where I lay in exhausted pity.

Celeste sat on a bean bag, contemplating something. In the house, faces were weary and exhausted. We had been tested, but we'd averted the disaster.

"Did you rescue Natalie?" Celeste asked me.

"No," I mumbled, barely able to speak. "The sea was too...*rough*. But rough doesn't do it justice. The rip emptied the whole bay and flooded it."

"How will we save her soul?" Chad asked. "Our plans are so dependent on her. I know we *could* do it without her, but I don't know how."

"We can't do it without her," Celeste sighed. "The movement was built on her – and Kuvalik, but we can't fall back on him now."

I gulped, but managed to interject.

"I can save her," I said, all went silent. Heads from other rooms turned, and gathered close.

"The seas in the Void can't touch a blocked thread's soul," I mumbled. "It happened to you and Chad in the Void just now. The seas moved around you – it wasn't even a struggle to pull you out."

"So, we have to block her thread?" Chad asked.

"Yes," I said, "one hit is all it will take. Boekidin, Yvon and I are going to have to combine our might to fight the sea, but we can get her out of it.

"You already had a plan for getting to Natalie in the castle, right, Celeste?" I asked. She quizzed momentarily, then lit up.

"Yes," she said, "it's why I wanted you to help me find Chad – I needed the perfect team to execute it."

"Of course," I agreed, scratching my head. I'd forgotten that we'd recovered Natalie by accident – that we'd originally planned to storm Hesslik's castle to extract her. "Have you still got the blueprints for the castle?"

"I've got good maps," Simone added. "I have the Anderson leaks saved."

"I had her location determined by scouts," Celeste said. "I mapped her activity in the castle. I know where she sleeps."

"I'm the scout who did it!" Yvon piped up, his chest puffed and confident. "I can tell you exactly where she was."

I'm probably more helpful, here. Boekidin said. *I did analyse her mind to find that Amasos had her under a spell. And I lived in the castle.*

"And Boekidin was tracking her too," I added to the group. "He probably knows the most, actually. But still, we should go to Paris to get all of your original plans, Celeste. We need all of the information we can get, and whichever Argols want to join us."

"Perfect," Celeste smiled, her fingers pent. "Let's get those blueprints."

"Anastasiya, can you get us to Paris?" I asked.

Episode 5

The End of an Era

Chapter 30
Mr Argol

Four days until the gathering.

There were four days.

My heart was pounding. I could feel the crush of existence weighing down on me, with just my convictions to drive it away. No destiny anymore, no chance, just our own choices.

And I was at the spearhead of the choices, the amalgamator of plans.

Pressure was building. Was this the reason Kuvalik had chosen me? Did he know that I would eventually lead the charge, with or without him?

There were only four days until the gathering, because it took Anastasiya two days to transport us to Paris. She had only just started creating power stones as we fell to the Void Guardian, and even then she barely had enough for a one-way journey.

I couldn't fault her though. We planned to be in Europe just now anyway – only, with Natalie on our side.

We made our way once more through the catacombs, guided by the new tunnels Celeste had cut through with Chad's help. During our recent stay in France, she had converted the pathway into a well-lit, spacious passage for what she hoped would be an inviting community centre.

Or, as inviting as a secret mob office deep under a mass grave could be.

As a posse in the tail of Iva Argol, we quickly brushed past the levels of security we met, although many faces appeared surprised to see us. The closer to the epicentre we came, the more frightened the guards appeared to be upon spotting us. Some guards looked to want to resist our passage, but were yanked aside by fellows and sternly whispered to. Something was wrong.

We came on the grand office, standing outside its great, mahogany door. "Ms Argol," the orange Suneva with the mace greeted us. I remembered having the distinct feeling that he would end my life, the first and only other time I'd ever seen him.

He gave us the same look this time. He did not let us pass.

"Step aside, Terogar," Celeste said, "I'm going into my office."

"I'm afraid you don't have an appointment with *Tano Canivaer*," The guard replied sternly.

"Well you can tell *Michael* to get his head out of his ass," she instructed bluntly, coming close to the guard's visor. "He's done well running things, but I'm back to lead this final charge."

"I'm afraid…"

"Oh, shut it," she hissed. "Simone, could you hold him, please?"

Simone, not one to be bossed around, liked Celeste's change in attitude. Before, it might have been "Simone, hold him," to which she would not have responded because she was essentially a God. A 'please', however, Simone was fine with, and complied enthusiastically.

The guard, stuck still, was helpless as we barged through into the flaming throne room. Thick, bright yellow flames, as tall as the ceiling, illuminated the glass behind the desk. Michael, a red-haired man with a burly figure, sat in the chair on the stage, talking on the phone. He looked to us pointedly as we entered.

"I'm sorry, give me one moment…" he trailed off in Liktan into the phone, covering the receiver with the palm of his hand. "Oui?" he asked, his nose up.

"Thank you for taking care of things here, Michael, but I've come to direct this final part of my plan upon my throne," Celeste said, hands upon her hips. Naturally, we all followed her pose. We were a beacon of power.

"Uh…" The man attempted to supress his snooty chuckle. "I'm afraid you can't do that," he told us, then raised the phone to his ear.

Celeste reached out, gripping into the oxygen within the phone and tearing it away. It crumpled to dust in Michael's hands, and he turned to eye her dangerously.

"Funny," Celeste said, sauntering up to the desk, "I gave you temporary powers to govern the community whilst I took care of important matters. You've done well, and I appreciate the work, but you have to step down."

This time Michael actually laughed. He stood over the desk, laying his palms flat on the table and adopting a smug grin.

"Honey," he started condescendingly, "you sat in this seat for three weeks at most, then you went running off, away from commitment to hang out with your friends."

"What?" she gaped.

"Three months I've been here. Three months I've been the leader. All you've done is galivant around Europe scaring communities into submission and ruining our name."

"I…they were slipping away," she defended.

"You expect to come back here, *four days* before the biggest day in our lives, and take control?" he coughed. "You want to implement a plan in four days? I've been working for *months* on an attack plan, you selfish idiot."

"I gave you our plan months ago!" Celeste rebutted. "You and my advisors were writing back with your support and commitment! You've had plenty of notice to enact my plans." She was trying to keep her anger down, and it was easier without Veritas chewing in her ear, but I could feel her blood brooding. "I came back here only a few weeks ago, even. I've been feeding you with continual updates and goals on what you should be achieving!"

"A plan to defeat the Argols and join under Kuvalik, the soul behind Olomb, the traitor to our people?" Michael scoffed, slapping the table. "I mean, I've heard of selling out, but that's pure treason."

"Then why play along with it for so long?" Celeste growled. "You have no right to deny my plan *now*! It's for the prosperity of the *Suneva people*. It goes beyond this organisation!"

"Beyond the Argols?" he tutted. "You have truly lost your way *and* your right to rule."

"I've been listening to the defectors," Celeste scowled. "I know why they're leaving. I know what the future of the Suneva *should* look like. Now, step down."

"You can't make me," he said, standing back and crossing his arms. His mouth adopted the pout appropriate for such a stance.

"Yes, I can," Celeste insisted.

"You're no longer the leader here. You've been voted out about, let's see…" He flipped casually through a calendar on his desk, landing his fat finger on a card. "…about a *few weeks* ago."

"…voted out…?" Celeste deflated.

"Being a *Monarchy* is really bad for image, you know," Michael said. He clawed his way around his desk, coming to sit on the front of it, overlooking us from his high perch. "What really killed our *legitimacy* as an organisation was when *daddy* lost his thread and his *seventeen-year-old daughter* took the throne, rather than an eligible leader.

"As a democracy, with the best picked leader, we stand a chance in this new world. You think you understand politics, little miss, but you don't know the half of how this world works."

Celeste's gut was a furnace - her defeat had quickly turned to pink flames in the stomach, which she fought to keep down. Composure would go far today, even if she could burn half this man's face off. *Don't make him a martyr*, she thought.

"My father wouldn't agree to this," she said. "Did you throw him out, too?"

"Actually, he voted for me," Michael smiled a devilish grin. Celeste's eye twitched, and her flame was released, a pink jet which careened off her finger. The floor started to scorch under it.

"How can you hold a vote without telling me?" Celeste spat. "How could you vote without me putting up my case."

"Oh, well that's easy," he smirked. "Because you gave me limitless power, and because you've been uncontactable for months, dear." His voice was at the pit of condescension, a whirlpool of arrogance. "Barely in one place, untraceable. Plus, you've been talking directly to me and my inner circle only. Do you really think we passed any messages on?"

"Holy *cheese*," I cussed. The whole room had grown unbelievably tense, quatra hanging thick in the air. It buzzed with the building emotions, responding to each soul's power, dancing down from the Void. Each spirit in this room was connected to an element, tethered to the physical.

"What's he saying?" Simone asked me in a whisper. She couldn't speak Liktan – it never came to her as easily as it did me and Natalie.

"He's saying '*no*' in a lot of creative and condescending ways," I whispered back, readying my hands to feel for the air around me.

"If you don't hand over power, you've just doomed the Suneva race. You know that, right?" Celeste reasoned.

"Oh no, on the contrary, I have a plan that will *work*," Michael hissed. "None of your bullshit. None of this 'mass thread removal' conspiracy. Just a simple, targeted attack on Hesslik, using the most current of information.

"You know, little miss," he continued demeaning her, "your desperation for leadership really is pathetic. It would lead some to believe that you're just power-hungry, rather than benevolent, wouldn't you agree?"

Celeste quelled herself, the flame on her finger extinguishing. Next to me, Simone pulled up the hood on her hand-made cloak, shielding her face from the light. She had told me that this helped her focus on energies, and I tensed for what might be coming.

"May your flame be strong, Michael," Celeste said formally, in French, turning her back to him, "I'm going to collect my plans and speak to my father."

"I'm afraid…" Michael went to say, but the rest of his sentence was squandered as it came. Simone stepped forward, her hand stretched towards his mouth.

"You've had your say," she told him in English. Finally, his façade cracked, red anger streaming into his face. Michael's mouth screamed, but no words came. "Aw, don't like having your power taken away?" Simone cooed, matching the man's arrogance.

"Go, get what you need and who you need. I've got this," Simone nodded to Celeste. She seemed hesitant to move, but finally nodded, wading towards the side door.

"Thank you, Simone," she said finally. "Yvon, come help me."

"Sure thing," he nodded, and skipped by her side. The two of them disappeared into the next room.

Michael furiously banged at the desk, but it was difficult to entertain a silent tantrum.

"You're Amasosian, aren't you?" Simone turned to ask him.

"*WHY DOES THAT MATTER?*" he barked with a voice rasping and cracking. His scream filled the room - a man working to be heard.

"Hah…" Simone chuckled.

"What's so funny?" he spat, now held in place rather than silenced. His body stilted in ratcheted movements, jerking awkwardly in its kinetic struggle.

"You think you're very smart, Monsieur Richard, but you're just a pawn. You're being used by a God to sabotage everything you hold dear."

"What are you on about?" he demanded. "I'm just trying to legitimise this community by kicking out a spoiled, arrogant, hot-headed brat. I.."

"The age of destiny is over." Simone ignored him. "This is the age of *justice* and *freedom*. What will you do when you gain your mind back?"

She tugged at his response, shafting it as Celeste and Yvon emerged from the side office. Michael climbed down from the stage, silenced and with his will to move restored. He barged towards Celeste, but Chad stepped into his path. Michael tried to yell at Chad to move aside, but he couldn't. Enraged, he materialised a heavy, yellow flame between his palms.

Simone switched to steal his movements again.

"You can't keep us from doing what we have to," she said to him. "You unfairly took the rights of others, so yours will be taken. This is *fairness*."

The flame still boiled in his palm, although now a spew of words screamed from his mouth to join it. His body twitched unnaturally, as threads of energy were

313

stolen just as they formed. Chad blasted a bolt of quatra straight into the man's neck, and Simone let him fall to the floor with a pitiful thud. He groaned.

"Let's go, I've got the plans," Celeste said.

"What about some support?" I asked. "I mean, he won't give us any troops…" I pointed to the red headed mess on the floor. "So, who will help us?"

"We've got plenty of power between us," Celeste gestured to the group, "but it's not *power* that we need if we're following this plan. In fact, it's the opposite."

***

"Why would I be useful?" Adam Leroux asked in Liktan. He sat in his office in Marsielle, on the dusk of the fourth day until Hesslik's great Suneva gathering. Somewhere near the roof his thread-end floated, teasing him. He was still a strong, capable man, but the spark of flames missing from his gaze fuelled his despondence.

"*Because* you don't have a thread," Celeste said. She moved her way around to her father's desk, as we all stood and sat awkwardly throughout the rest of the room. Adam Leroux was slouched in his chair, playing with its height adjustment lever.

"Think about it," Celeste perched herself next to the computer, "Natalie can detect threads and identify their Suneva from kilometres away. We need somebody who can't be detected no matter what."

"You've got the Sunesca." He pointed to Simone, who sat up quizzically, unsure as to why she'd been pointed to.

"But we don't have an experienced tactician with Suneva reflexes and combat skills - who successfully planned, executed and personally led heists like these for decades," Celeste emphasised. Adam's ego did well to be boosted, but he was still unconvinced. He sat further into the reclining office chair.

"We're all going in with blocked threads," she kept at it, "you'll be on par."

"But why do you need another?" he asked. "Aren't the…" he pointed to us each on turn. "…*six* of you enough for a sneak mission?"

"Hesslik and his men won't harm the defenceless," I added, and Argol turned to me. "I know it seems odd to put faith in their morals, but it's the only think they've got. You, however, can still redirect bolts, and your thread will never come back online to give us away…"

He grumbled to the mention of his perpetually inactive thread. I cringed, but continued.

"*If* our threads come back on too early into the rescue, you and Simone can run ahead and secure Natalie. Between the two of you, somebody should be able to attract and redirect a winning shot to diffuse Natalie's thread. Then it's up to Yvon, Boekidin and I to go into the Void and…"

"*Boekidin?*" Adam coughed. "I thought that bastard died."

No hard feelings – I did order his thread removed, Boekidin sighed.

"His body certainly did…" I petered out.

"How do you plan to go doing all of this *Void* stuff anyway if your thread is blocked?" Adam asked.

"Easy," I said. "I don't come into the castle. I can save Natalie from anywhere."

"Seems…cowardly…" Adam hummed.

"It's tactics, sir," I said, offended. "If the Green Dragon would like to show us how it's done…"

"Let's see those plans," he interrupted, turning to his daughter and holding his palm out for the folder she held. "I'm not going on any mission I didn't personally devise."

Chapter 31
The Castle of Silence

The Greek spring moon glowed bright and full in the midnight sky, casting the night-time shadow of Mount Olympus over the Electric Empire stronghold. A building which felt deeply familiar to me as I stared over it. A building that *I* had ruled from for a long while, before I had abandoned it to wait for the Suneva reprise.

I would never receive more of these memories, of Vasilli's life that I did not live. Oddly, knowing that made me reminisce them positively, and wished I hadn't thrown the opportunity away. The grass is always greener in your memory, before you burned it off.

Celeste had me examine the plans for the building. Memories which lived in my mind, which I had not actively seen, told me that the layout was correct. I could visualise the rooms printed on the card, I could see myself walking the halls.

She and her father reworked tonight's plan together. Celeste's grand opinion of her father was well founded, it seemed. Above all, he was a leader, and he understood the strengths of each members, and how to use them.

Adam scrapped the idea of a mass invasion with safety in numbers, instead preferring to strike with a compact group whose abilities would suit. Boekidin – as much as Adam hated to admit the usefulness of the Shiverman – was the most acquainted with the castle's layout, so he would have to guide the insurgence leader. Boekidin had to be within sight of me to enter the Void through my head, so that put me in the castle. This made sense also, as I might be carrying memories about the castle's history which could help us out of a sticky situation.

Adam saw the senselessness in trying to neutralise Natalie within the castle and having to transport her out after causing a commotion. Instead, and much to the protest of Anastasiya, he ordered that she join Boekidin and I, teleporting Natalie out to this hill where the rest of the party would wait in ambush. Anastasyia would then teleport back for the remaining insurgence members.

Simone was to be the last to venture with Anastasiya, Boekidin and I. She would perform her usual duties of concealment, however would also be useful in sensing for energies when the rest of us had our threads blocked. In the event that the plan went south, her Sunesca powers as a *Kiin* would put her on par with me to escape. Adam trusted that I had taught Simone well enough in the art of air.

We'd measured my and Anastasiya's thread-block-retention throughout the day, and found that at worst, we had five minutes and thirty-seven seconds to conduct the whole mission. At the castle base, we were to block each other's threads and start the stopwatch.

Celeste palmed the jade stone given to her by Anastasiya, which would guide the *Kida* back to the ambush, and watched Aastasyia, Simone, and I climb down the mountain. Together, we walked through the white night, down the forested hill, to the castle in the valley.

Boekidin had determined the best entrance for us to use, which combined the best cover with closest proximity to Natalie's quarters. There were closer entrances to the ambush point, but they were often more heavily guarded, according to Boekidin, or had open fields on either side.

The entrance we staggered down the mountain towards was the Chef's garbage area – which would clearly be out of commission at the stroke of midnight. As we walked, I sharpened a sword – one made of an atom-thick diamond blade, with an iron hilt crafted by Chad. This was the 'break through doors' sword – the replacement for my staff and my control of carbon.

Tall trees ran the entire slope of the hill, providing excellent cover from the moonlight. I stopped my sharpening, letting my thread – still weak – lie idle. Anastasiya did the same.

Unlike the rest of the castle's perimeter, the forest which clung to this hillside came all the way to meet the castle's wall in the valley. The trees hugged up against the tall, brick fortification, lining a covered pathway to approach by.

There was no actual breach in the wall here, and we would have to climb it. Simone led, stealing the wind's energy to create her own gust, then leaping high and grappling into the brick wall with sharpened silicon claws. She crawled into the top, then offered a hand down to help Anastasiya and I over.

"Start the stopwatch," I whispered to Anastasiya. "Three, two, one…"

We shot each other with a blast of quatra, voluntarily letting it slide through our pathways and into our necks. The sequence started, five minutes and thirty seconds on the clock.

"What if the White Witch felt that?" Anastasiya asked.

"Doesn't matter," I said. "She can't track us now. Come on, let's go…" I grabbed her by the waist and hoisted her up to Simone, who threw her over to the other side. I leaped up to meet my sister's hands, and she gave me the same rough treatment, stealing the great thud I made as I crashed into the muddy ground.

Simone used my sound energy to gently lower herself on a cloud of air. I picked myself up, handling the hilt of the sword.

We'd landed in a small courtyard set in darkness, protected from the moonlight by thick limbs of trees overhead. It was closed on three sides by the castle and its wall, with one side half-open through a hedge. Indigo shadows darted behind swaying trees, covering the scene in a dance of dark limbs. It made me instantly uneasy.

The entrance to the castle was a metal door atop a platform-like stage. Two dumpsters were parked to the left of the platform, and between them and us was a small vegetable patch with tomatoes coming into bloom. This would be the entrance to the kitchen.

I sleuthed towards the door, stepping carefully around the plants to throw myself onto the platform. I rolled to my feet, and helped Anastasiya up as Simone stole from some unknown source and propelled herself on a blanket of exhaust. She came to land next to me, and sensed for something.

"No kinetic, or sound, or big lights in there," she analysed, "but there is a large source of heat. Somebody might be cooking and standing very still."

317

"Probably just some overnight, slow-cooking," I joked, reaching for the handle. "Any people, Boekidin?"

I can't feel any minds, He said to me.

"We should be good," I said, and gripped the knob. Simone tensed in anticipation, ready to soften any sounds. I turned it.

To my surprise, there was no latch or lock. The door opened smoothly and quietly inwards. I slipped in, around it.

The kitchen was dark, bathed in blue and white moonlight which drifted down from a massive, modern sunroof. The same shadows of overhead trees had found their way in here, sprinting across the room as evil imposters. My peripheries fired, my instincts gripping themselves, but I managed to stay calm.

Nothing spooky here, keep calm, Boekidin said. *Now look right, you need that door over there.*

The kitchen was designed with a single, long island bench surrounded by appliances. Up the left wall ran a set of washers, driers, fridges, and sinks. On the right side sat a row of stoves and ovens – one of which appeared to be on, roasting away. Beyond these was another metal door. I held the sword near.

"The door," I whispered to the girls crouched behind me, pointing. I started to move.

"*James!*" Simone whispered urgently. I stopped, my face white. "Can I have Boekidin?" she asked.

I exhaled loudly, calming. "*Cheese*," I exclaimed, "I thought I'd just walked into something. Don't scare me like that."

"Sure," She said unapologetically, "I think it would be better if Boekidin rode in my head, if I'm the one sensing the dangers."

"Sure, sure, take him." I slouched to the ground. Boekidin passed from my mind, making my head fractionally lighter upon my shoulders. It was a difference that could only be felt if you knew what you were waiting for. With a lighter skull, I continued my sleuthing, sticking below bench height to reach the door. Simone and Anastasiya tailed me.

Simone forced her way to the front, predictably, and after a moment gave the hand gesture that the coast was clear. She opened the door.

Revealed was a dusty, dark hallway, only lit by the faint light at its end. The walls were made of unevenly cut stones, both old and worn.

"Hey, I know this place," I said, a memory of Kuvalik's forming. This wasn't an episodic memory, like the ones which controlled my personality, but rather a spatial memory. I tried to tap into it.

"This is the back hall from the kitchen…"

"Clearly," Simone interjected.

"I remember it being a main passage between the kitchen and the dining room, used by the cooks."

"What comes after the dining room?" Simone asked.

The map appeared in my head, places I'd been. Clearly, it wouldn't be up to date, but a sense of familiarity with the castle we were sneaking through was well appreciated in my mind.

I could imagine the dining hall in my head. Tall, stone walls, lots of arches. Cooks' entrance to the south, main entrance to the north, cloisters on the west side, which housed the dormitory.

"Left entrance," I said, "then there will be cloisters…"

"What's a *cloister*?" Simone asked.

"Uh…" I tried to access the memory, but realised that the memory didn't tell me this – it assumed that I knew what I was referring to. "No idea," I said. "Looks like a quadrangle…I think."

"Then?"

"Those are the dorms…I think."

Simone started to walk, and so Anastasiya and I followed. The door, now closed behind us, let no light through, shielding our silhouetted figures from onlookers in the dining area.

"Boekidin says you're right, although the dining room has more connections than you remember," Simone whispered. "He also says that a cloister is a Roman piece of architecture, and refers to a covered, square walkway around a central quadrangle space. From the Latin word for *enclosure*."

"Good on you, Boekidin," I hushed under my breath.

We came close to the end of the hall, where Simone stopped us again with a hand gesture. She closed her eyes, locking into her connections.

Then she urgently backed herself against the wall. Anastasiya and I followed.

Simone held a finger to her mouth, and peered back out to the dining room. She toed quietly towards it. In my nerve, I checked the timer. We had two minutes left.

Two minutes, I internally screamed. *This whole time took two and a half minutes? I glanced at Anastasiya. If she wasn't such a good witch, we'd have more time. Cheese.*

I snuck after Simone, and pulled Anastasiya along. The *Kida* wasn't prepared for the tug, and was surprised to see me move, so fell into a heavy footstep. Simone glared in fright to the sound, unable to do anything now that it had rung out. She squatted into the shadows, and I sidled up beside her doing the same.

"*Two minutes,*" I whispered urgently.

"*Shit,*" she whispered. "*There's movement to the left. We can't go in...*"

But we had to go in. I gripped at the hilt in my hand, my crude sword of diamond and iron. Dissolving my fear into adrenaline, I toed along the wall into the light, sticking up against the left corner of the hallway.

I pulled my head around the corner.

There was a cat. It meowed a greeting.

"What?" Simone coughed. "Again?" She seemed perplexed.

"It's just a cat," I said. "Come on, no time!"

We really didn't have time. I edged my way around the dining table – a massive slab of wood running the whole length of an equally impressive room. It was old, and to my memory, original. Massive stone walls ran from the ground, meeting in a series of arches, which formed a row of domes. Each dome had its own skylight. Four skylights, one for each God.

We worked our way between the wooden thrones and the arches, which dropped from the roof, to the left-side exit. Two large, wooden doors admitted access to the cloisters.

The bar to the door was set aside of the doorway. It appeared rotten from years of disuse.

"They don't ever lock it?" I asked, expecting Boekidin to be in my head.

"People *live* here, James," Simone replied. "How could they live in a place where all of the doors were locked? Clearly Hesslik doesn't expect break-ins in the living area."

"I'm glad he doesn't," I responded, "especially right now." And I stepped ahead of Simone to palm the latch. Her face furrowed with her mild annoyance, and I shrunk away.

"It's safe," she urged me on. "Open it."

I nodded, pushing the huge, wooden panel ajar and faxing myself through the gap.

Midnight light rained through the series of open archways around me. The world was painted in blue, indigo, grey and black. Trees which hung over the courtyard stood like stone sentries, but their shadows did not dance in the still sky. The light remained eerie, and was punctuated by soft voices, smothered by the stone walls.

"To the right," Simone instructed as she joined me. She and Anastasiya moved past.

"Can't you hear the voices?" I asked. "I think they're coming from that way."

"Just act natural," Simone instructed. "We're wearing regular clothes. We're guests."

"Why didn't we use this tactic before?" I sighed, jogging to catch up.

Embossed on the outside walls of the cloisters were new windows and doors, each with locks. At this hour, the many that we passed had blinds drawn, with lights out. However, one of the first rooms of the right-hand corridor had yellow lamplight etching the perimeter of their window. It was from this room that the voices came. I could hear them clearly now.

"Dude, you can't hate it," a nasally young man said in broken Liktan. "Acid jazz is the future of music in…"

"It's not even a genre," a female voice retaliated. "Half of it is regular jazz, just a bit different. The other half is full blown disco and funk. That's not a genre, it's a mess."

"But…"

I left the conversation behind, humored to hear the people here talking about regular life, rather than the soon end – or new beginning – of the Suneva world.

Simone led us past two more doors, then drew us to a halt with an outstretched arm. Nervous, I eyed my stopwatch. It read twenty seconds. I showed it to her.

"We wait," she whispered.

"For what?" I asked.

"Until the end," Simone said. "Then we know Anastasiya will come online in the seconds after. We can't risk waking Natalie before we're ready to take her away."

"Okay," I said, and tried to stand idly by, but with each second my body was rising with adrenaline. The stopwatch ticked its black hands over its white face, little by little. My nerves spiked.

What if Natalie blocked Anastasiya's thread before I got my own one back? Simone couldn't get all three of us out of here if it went wrong. Natalie could want to kill us in her state of possession, for all we knew.

The timer ticked. It came to five seconds.

321

Anastasiya stiffened, her eyes shooting wide. She grabbed her neck, and eyed me like a frightened deer.

"I'm back on," she whimpered.

"*Shit*," I and Simone uttered, and we both lunged for the door's handle. I grabbed it first, and tried to turn it, but it hit the locked latch, ringing a *clank* which was all too loud for the situation.

She already senses us, The thought thrummed into my head. I produced the long, diamond sword, and held it to the gap in the door. Sharing a glance with Simone, I raised the weapon, then slammed it through the door's deadbolt.

Air plummeted from Simone's palms, the sound of the crude cut coming as little more than a dropped tack. With unsteady hands, I pulled the door towards us.

The space behind the door exploded into blinding white light. I shrieked, yanking the door the rest of the way open and grappling everybody to the ground. A white bolt of quatra sailed from the room, overhead, and landed itself on the pole of an archway. The stone there cracked and burst into a dustcloud of masonry, obliterated and sublimated on impact. The crash and crumble reverberated throughout the chambers, and windows of rooms slowly started to flicker into illumination. My stomach sank.

We peeled ourselves from the ground, peeking into the room. A silhouetted figure stood disheveled by the back window, veins glowing white through the surface of their skin. Without hesitation, Natalie raised her palm again to fire.

Simone, Anastasyia, and I slipped into cover around the side of the doorway, sitting our asses to the dust. A moment later, the bricks above our head flew out of the wall, sent flying into the cloisters to turn into dust and magma. Hot specks of stone rained over us.

"Get in there!" Simone ordered to Anastasiya. "Save the day!"

"I can't..." the girl whined in her soft voice. "It's too dangerous, it's..."

Simone growled, "if you don't..." another explosion rocked the wall, shattering the glass into deadly hail. Simone stole the sound, using it to blast a jet of air into the debris. Glass fell away from us, and dust kicked up into a cloud, concealing us just as other Suneva emerged from their rooms.

"If you don't," Simone stated again, "then all of these kind people will capture us, and we'll be in for *much worse*." She grabbed the Legendary by the shoulders. "Bloody *believe in yourself*." She shook her.

322

Anastasiya was almost at tears, but she did as Simone instructed. Anastasiya stood to peek into the room, over the destroyed wall, and reached with her extended arm into the dusty abyss. Her body disappeared, pulled into a sphincter in spacetime.

Simone and I twisted onto our knees, peeking our eyes over the rubble. Natalie appeared confused, as the prime beacon of Suneva energy disappeared. Anastasiya fell out of space on the bed behind the White Witch, and sprang onto Natalie's back. She drove Natalie into the ground, all while she reached out with an unsteady hand.

They both disappeared in an anomaly – light and sound stretching around them, growing bulbous to fit their bodies through the backstage of the universe. As soon as it appeared, they were gone, and Anastasiya's fingers finally fell off the edge of the bubble and into the destination.

Simone and I slumped on the dusty ground, the cloud cover still strong. We could see lights flickering into existence all around us.

"Now what?" I asked.

"She comes back for us," Simone said.

***

Celeste checked her stopwatch. It ticked over to five minutes and thirty seconds.

She raised her binoculars, peeking through the blind darkness of the forest onto the now-moonlit stage of the castle. She caught the quadrangle with her eye.

"Come on," she muttered.

There was an explosion of white light, illuminating a cloud of dust. The sound of the explosion followed, bellowing, ringing around the valley.

"No!" she exclaimed, throwing the binoculars down.

There was another blinding flash, she saw as she turned to the rest of the group. Their shadows were sprayed across the trees, their faces radiated with a thin strip of divine white.

Celeste palmed the luck-stone Anastasiya had given her. Glimmering with pink quatra, it called to her. It gave her a feeling of intense, suffocating dread. The image of a bolt of quatra ramming through Simone's chest. Her blood sprayed, painting walls red.

Celeste couldn't look away from the action after a vision like that. She raised the binoculars and spun on the loose, needly soil. Her binoculars weren't pointed in the right place, and she had to wave them about to find the scene of the action.

Celeste's gaze landed upon the main gate, with its concert stage. She turned her head left, stupidly, away from the castle, and towards the forested hills.

On an outcropping, where she'd stationed her men the last time she attempted this plan, she saw an anomaly buzz into life. Light distorted, like wavering air off a hot road. The sphere bulged, fingers wrapping around it from an invisible source. Fingers were followed by a hand, and then by two bodies all at once. The Legendary *Kida* and the White Witch fell across the field.

Natalie was practically glowing white. With no hesitation, without even supporting herself off the ground, she aimed her peace-posed hand and blasted Anastasiya with a perfectly true bolt of orange quatra.

The legendary slumped into the mud, defeated. Natalie sauntered over to the body.

"Veritas damn it!" Celeste screamed, throwing the binoculars. "Follow me. *Run.*"

***

Footsteps advanced from all directions, all drawn to the destruction. Voice chatter carried through the crisp air. I held the sword for dear life.

"What if she doesn't come back?" I asked, head spinning with fright. I crawled past Simone, finding refuge behind the destroyed wall of Natalie's quarters. Simone joined me, crouching out of the passageway's sight.

"She will," Simone assured.

"She doesn't seem reliable."

"I never thought you'd mention it," Simone grumbled.

The door next to Natalie's opened. Steps landed on the doormat. A sigh huffed loudly, a light held in their hand.

"Can you steal light?" I whimpered. "You know; make us invisible?"

"I can just steal heat, now. Light is next," Simone said.

"How come you've never used that?" I asked.

"It's not been useful yet."

The inquisitive person stepped into the dust cloud, yawning.

"Zamelle?" they called into the room, then the sight hit them. "Amasos! Zamelle, what's happened?" they cried.

My arsehole clenched.

324

With bounding steps, they ran into the room, over the rubble, past the burning and melted stone.

They leaped straight past Simone and I, not even acknowledging our presence. My eyes were wide, filling with airborne dust. The need to cough and splutter and cry and run was palpable, a solid chunk swimming in my brain, screaming for release.

The Suneva, a tall, young man, examined the bed and the back window. He held is light to them.

Then he turned.

We locked eyes.

"*What the...*" he yelled, before Simone stole his last word. The man's hands immediately went for a peace-sign pose. He fired a bolt of quatra.

I lunged to catch it, redirecting it back towards him. Instictively, he dodged the bolt – although one's own quatra did not pose a threat – and it careened into the back window.

The rings emanated through the glass, which proved too much. It shattered outwards in a rain of commotion. The man dropped to the deck, covering his head from shards.

"That way!" I yelled to Simone, leaping to my feet.

"Where does that go?" she asked me.

"Somewhere better," I said, connecting to the air, willing it below me to blast through the window.

Except, I couldn't connect to the air, because my thread was still blocked.

Instead, I ran towards the ledge, shoving my hands down like an idiot as I jumped forward. Clearing no air, and having put all my weight in front of my feet, I flailed my hands ahead to catch onto *anything* before I planted into the floor. There were three things ahead of me – the man, the bed, and the window pane.

I tripped over the man as I accidentally kicked him in the head, I crashed my knees into the bedframe, and with my body swinging forward from the impacts, the window pane was what I caught.

Glass shards pierced straight into my right hand – the left still wielding the sword.

I screamed louder than I thought possible, alerting everybody in earshot.

Simone grabbed me by the shirt, tugging me off the window. My palm was red, gushing with blood. Her face was stern. The man shifted, so she kicked him in the head again.

"Hold still, keep screaming," Simone ordered, and I could only oblige. She stole the force of my scream, using it to connect to the silicon in glass. Used her connections to tear the debris from my hand.

The resulting residual oxygen left in my skin burst into deadly licks of flame – whose heat she stole as she swatted them away with a gust. "Don't use your hand," Simone instructed, throwing herself through the window.

I followed suit, fist tucked into a tight grip, stepping up and through the pane.

The fall was longer than I expected before I jumped. I looked in dread as the ground approached and I had no realistic way of *not* breaking my legs. Pain was coming, more than I was in now.

Then I slowed, Simone stealing my motion to soften my landing. I landed fine on two feet.

"Thanks," I said with a wobbly smile.

"Now where?" she asked.

"I don't know, you have Boekidin," I said.

We were walled in, standing on the edge of a massive floral garden, bordered by the stone walls of castle buildings. No gate, fortification, or forest in sight above the tall rooves.

"Ach!" I gasped as my thread pounded into existence, spurring my body with heat and life, and most importantly, sparking my connections. I was no longer dumb, running about with no sensation of where I was, with no ability to affect my path. At my fingertips – half of which now lay splayed and bloody, distracting me from a lot of their sensory output – was a spatial representation of the world through air. I smiled, then immediately frowned and whimpered because of my pain.

"I'm online," I croaked to my sister, who had already started running ahead. Her black cloak flapped in the night. She was almost invisible.

"Hurry up!" she ordered, and I ran along, sprinting to catch her.

I glanced behind us, to the broken window, to see a dozen people shifting in the room, a few looking through the pane. I eeked.

"Where?" I puffed.

"Over," Simone huffed, pointing to the roof we were running towards. I realised that I couldn't figure out which way was north. We'd entered through an eastern entrance, right? Which way was east?

"You can make it?" I asked. The roof was tall.

"You taught me how to," she said.

Behind us, yelling. A door banged by the entrance to the cloisters. People rushed out of it, into the gardens.

"Can *you* make it?" she asked me. As I peered up to the high, terracotta peak, coming fast, I wasn't certain that I could.

***

Iva Argol rushed the field, armor on, sword drawn, all of her connections available and at full force.

The now armoured Zamelle Menas had the blonde, Russian *Kida* draped over her shoulders, carrying her away down the grassy, muddy knoll.

Iva fired her bolt, hot on the tail, footsteps of literal fire. It flew true, right on target.

Zamelle flung herself around, shoulder-mounted girl and all, limbs flying, and caught the bolt with a free hand. She redirected it through her leg, ending her pivot with a face-high kick which sent a white-blue toxicated bolt back at Iva.

Iva rolled from its path, and fired again. Zamelle's bolt tore through a nearby tree, turning the bark to magma and flames. There was a mighty crack as its trunk crashed into the earth, then it started to fall.

Zamelle caught this next bolt, too, but there was a barrage on its way. Three more bolts, two red and one purple, barreled through the trees. Yvon as *Riskidin*, and Chad as Ferrad, stormed through the forest, firing wildly with abandon.

Zamelle was forced to drop the body of Anastasyia to counter the heavy assault. Three Suneva firing on her, three bolts at a time. She danced gracefully, a flow of kicks and grabs, spinning like a whirlpool. Her movements were fluid, calculated, informed by sight more powerful than light. She fired on some, but caught and toxicated others, sending them back to the attackers with fierce accuracy.

Ferrad grappled with the earth underfoot, flipping it, throwing it, giving it motion. The ground shook and flew in large chunks towards Zamelle. She dodged, rolling, amassing water from the soil. She created a whip of liquid, using it to slice through boulders of dirt.

Iva growled a Suneva shriek, letting a pink flame billow by her side. Zamelle could not get away.

***

327

I coated my injured palm in carbon I stole from a hedge, simultaneously setting the plant alight. I eyed the jump, still sprinting.

Simone concentrated, and suddenly the noise of the crowd faded to naught. She blasted down at the ground, leaping with extreme grace. Pushing off once more mid-air, she propelled herself onto the roof, landing softly. Simone had been practicing.

I followed suit, letting my will mix with that of the wind. I became a part of its desires, altering them to align with mine. The wind rocked past my palms and soles – certainly not as fast as it once did – and launched me high. I bounded again at the top of my arc, soaring, desperate.

I wouldn't make it; I'd not gotten high enough. Heart pounding, I prepared to grab onto something – any protrusion in the wall, but had my hand scream at me in pain.

My body dropped past the roof edge. I summoned my staff – more on a whim than by any thought process – and swung the blunt end down into the gutter. The base of the prong caught, and I swung towards the stone wall.

My motion was halted, exhaust fanning through my hair as Simone took my speed before I could slam into the castle. I climbed the staff, ignoring the intense pain, and flipped myself onto the roof.

It was a long, peaked roof. From here we could see the castle wall – just beyond this building's end and across an opening. We sprinted for it, legs slamming the terracotta tiles. The noise was insane, boots smacking on loose, old clay. It drowned out the commotion of the crowd, who may have been running beside us. I didn't dare look to find out.

***

Zamelle appeared strong, but was succumbing to the commotion. Her extreme connection to destiny had allowed her remarkable feats of luck and agility in battle, but luck was wearing thin.

Without destiny, Iva noted, battles like this were more difficult. It was all up to you – no helping hands to guide your impulses, no genius tactics executed with half a mind. You could only rely on your own skill.

And with skill they were winning.

Zamelle dodged an intense flame, whipped water at a rock, and fired a bolt of quatra. Another one came, and she redirected that, then another, then fired on Ferrad.

Finally Riskidin was able to slip around to her backside, enclosing Zamelle on all angles. She cried a departed howl in her frustration, which echoed its ghostly claim over the whole valley.

Spines shook in the might of the scream. A call so inhuman, so inorganic, so innately unnatural that each surrounding heart skipped a beat as their brains processed it. The sound caused only one natural instinct to arise with furious intensity – *run*.

It pounded Iva's brain, making her falter. *Run. Run. RUN.* It beat at her skull. Her flames died.

All action ceased. All stood still in the aftermath.

Except Amasos. They smiled through Zamelle's teeth, forcing their White Witch's arm to fire orange energy upon a shocked Iva Argol.

Iva's lungs hadn't caught up to her. Her heart hadn't kicked in. She wanted to raise an arm to the bolt, but couldn't fathom how to. The scream had knocked her out, ceased all of her functions. An action of destiny spread sonically, Amasos had tied her down.

Iva's father leaped in front of her.

Adam took the bolt through his right arm, flying through the air, and ejected it from his left.

The aim was off – it missed Zamelle by a long shot, and she howled laughter in her demonic, two-toned cry. She shot again, this time at Yvon.

But Adam Leroux wasn't a man with bad aim - the Green Dragon had a perfect aim. He was renowned for it.

Adam's redirected bolt flew towards its target – Ferrad. He absorbed it through his axe, leaning into the new trajectory, and ejecting a toxicated orange-red bolt from his left arm.

Zamelle spotted it, firing another of her own bolts at its path.

But like-bolts didn't destructively interfere, she found out, they *accumulated*.

Her bolt was absorbed into, and increased the power, of the toxicated bolt with which it collided. The double-size bolt of orange-red quatra hit Zamelle square in the chest, bowling her backwards across the muddy, needly forest floor. Her armor shattered off her body, spreading like broken glass.

An unconscious Natalie lay in a crater of her own making.

The opening at the end of the castle's run revealed itself to us – a corrugated metal roof coming into view, jutting below the castle, just before a large field of mud. *The concert ground.*

As I ran, a sonic wave enveloped me, crushing my soul. A deafening, harrowing Suneva cry. I hit it head on, and my legs fell from under me. I blasted air at the roof, softening my land into a roll. Simone screeched to a stop, grabbing me under the arms to haul me up.

"What was that?" she yelled.

"Natalie – but not good," I whined.

"No, I mean you falling over."

"Oh…" I blushed. "I don't know, that's never happened before. There was something different about that scream."

"Fine. Come on," Simone ran off again, leaving me on my feet. Huffing, I kicked back into a sprint behind her. My legs hurt from the fall, my palms hurt from the glass. I was running on pure adrenaline, fueled by fright.

We reached the end of the building, and I leapt off the terracotta with Simone, blasting onto the iron roof with a thud. I eyed up the next drop, and without hesitation, vaulted for my freedom.

I dove, air rushing over and under my body. I prepared for the pull up, gripping into the air flowing over my head, ready to clamp down on its will, to be yanked upwards.

Simone followed, diving by my side, her black cape billowing behind her. We both prepared to swoop.

But we ground almost to a halt instead, hanging midair.

We dangled peculiarly, drifting slower than falling dust, all parts of the body stopped equally. Not pulled by a rope, nor yanked by our feet. It was as if somebody had simply stopped our *ability* to fall.

And as I craned my head, I realised this was *exactly* what had happened. The taller of the two Sunesca twins stood on the concert stage, smug grin riddling his lean face.

"I'm afraid I…" he said in his greasy, two-toned voice, but his words were cut off.

"*I'm afraid* you need to shut up," Simone yelled at him.

"What's the secret to beating a Sunesca?" I asked Simone. "Surely you know it by now."

"There isn't…" she went to reply, but her voice faded to nothing and we fell out of the sky. I put my hands out to protect my head, and immediately screamed as my cut palm pressed into the mud. I tumbled upright, but was halted again.

"Freedom is not so far away," the Sunesca said, "but your actions prohibit it."

Simone growled, attempting to shift her limbs. They responded only in spasmodic jitters, which my body didn't seem to recreate. "You're a fucking *idiot*," she slammed him. "Do you ever listen to the stupid shit you say?"

"Have you considered my ultimatum?" he asked. "You seem conflicted about your purpose still."

"I know my bloody purpose, you selfish prick," she spat. "I'm here fighting for *justice*. You're just some edgy, black-wearing, self-hating, egotistical, dimwitted, narcissist who wants to drain the world for self-gain."

The Salak smirked at Simone's outrage, shaking his head and stepping forward – only, Simone stole his movement after the second step, her exhaust whipping right across my face. The man's booted foot hung in the air, his body forward of his rear foot.

"You clearly don't understand my…"

"James, there's one way to distract him," Simone said to me, completely ignoring the Sunesca. "You shoot him with bolts until we're out of his range."

"But I can't move my arms," I argued.

"*A little rude to interrupt me when I'm speaking,*" the Sunesca said.

"Oh, shut up, we don't care!" Simone yelled. "James, I'm going to do something that might hurt."

"*What?*" I stammered.

"I'm going to steal *all* of your motion," she said. "Your body's energy system will kick up, I'll hurt both myself and this idiot, but you'll get *one* moment to hit him. Use it."

"Okay…" I agreed.

Then my insides snapped, burning alight. With all the pain I was in, I did not need this.

But I could *move*.

In the moment I had, I swung my arm to face the Sunesca, who was groaning, cringing in his own pain. I blasted as many bolts of quatra as I could fit in, sending a smattering barrage in his direction.

Then I kicked off the ground and ran.

The Sunesca dodged the bolts, redirecting the ones that came to his body. I drew my staff, aiming it backwards, firing upon him with blind aim and fury. Simone and I charged towards the gates with our freedom.

I stopped my blasting to ready my connections. My will connected to that of the air, and I blasted it down, launching myself clear over the gate. Simone followed, landing cleanly.

"Where to?" Simone puffed. I had to trust by now that Natalie had been taken down, even if the haunting, limb-stopping scream would have pointed to the alternative.

"A close, secluded spot," I said. "I know a place."

Chapter 32
"Oh, That's the Title of the Book!"

The great sea shattered rocks
Who on her waters sat.
Black, tall, they crumbled to her might
Like sand on a dune to the desert wind,
Swept.

A blinding light extinguished out at sea
The beacon replaced with a clearing,
A whirlpool, twisting, down to the bedrock. Thirsty.
A girl trapped inside.

Between the shadows of three idle witches:
Rockfaces, tall, held by sickly bottlenecks
Fighting the waters which made them.
One fell.

Bodies lay on the surface
Buoyant as the dead
Churning under crashing, cavernous waves.
Obstacles to be avoided, but lives to be saved.

I rowed my boat, hands gripping oars raw.
Boekidin had built it
Ever the engineer;
For months with me
He wasted his talents here
Meticulously working machines
Mending that which made destiny obsolete
The driving cog in a genius plan
To save the Suneva from dire hands.

Rope secured me to the cliff face
Which threatened to melt under the heat of a God.
I rowed through fluid violence.
Letting the current take my course.

My boat tipped and rocked.
My head cocked.
Fright.
I held the oars for life
One slip, and that would be it
The water would eat me alive.
Current catching me
A bath of acid no soul could survive
Not even those who rode the waves,
The vibrant dead.
Particles in the ocean;
Products of reactions, not sentient thoughts
Citing destiny for their fortune.
Forced to do against their root delights,
Held in perilous plight,
At the end of their tunnel, a false light
Dark White.

I came to the whirlpool
A spinning torrent of blood, it painted the ocean pink
Red with rage, a wound for an almighty
Whose tantrum crashed and roared.

Their power greater than they could fathom
Their cries crushed two worlds
This and the real.
A child given supreme power,
Justice dead for their will to rule.

My vision seized
Buzzing, rapping
Static zapping
Pulled between worlds
I retched my mind
Pushing dizziness aside
Resolve, I harked
Conviction, in my soul.
And two worlds phased to one.
The Void.
But my mind was worn.
This would take its toll.

My love lay face first on the sea's rocks
Her soul battered
Her spirit knocked
I rode the boat toward the ground
Through the current, round and round
Dizzying, my head spun
My eyes swum
I crashed.

The hull was fine. It would be *fine*
How else was I meant to take that line?
To descend a boat into a column of air
Who would dare?
A boat could be rowed with a *little* water inside.
Of course it could
To a faring seaman this was but bricks and mortar.

I loaded her in. Her body supple, shaking.

Her skin was brilliant to hold
My fingers came alive.
The world snapping from this dull grey lie
When I held her soul to mine.

Another trick of the master sailor
Was to ride one's boat into a wall of water.
Not a wave, but a literal wall.
At ninety degrees to the rock.
Built by celestial carpenters.
Magic whirlpools.
Everybody threw their boat-bound girlfriends into them.
Especially with a broken bow.
There was no question. I had to act now.

Ass to the seat, hands to handles, hull to the sand
I gave the boat more torque than it could stand.
Press with the legs, like I'd done so many times before.
Often in a regatta day's core
With feet in the stretchers
My mind wandering. Pain to come.
A day of fun.

The bow, forced to the water, was caught
The current pulling it away
And thankfully, the rest of the boat came too.
We whipped up the funnel. Steam from a stack, pushed to the top.
No looking back
Currents to face.
To the cliff, a race
For at any time, her thread could come back online.

Like the starting blocks all that time ago.
Heart thumping, I pressed to the legs.
Go.

Waves battered the vessel

Spray flying high
A God attempting to claw
Me from my perch.
But I resisted,
Like I had so often now.
My strength could hold me here,
It could change worlds.
I would not succumb to this God's white curse.

At the face of the cliff
Ropes dropped from above
All I had to do was keep the boat still
Natalie, sleeping in the prow
Could not know of our peril
Her soul silent

I hooked the ropes to the boat's mounts
Their clips, made of soul energy, rusted
They cried under stress
Rope burning in its own twine

White
The cliffs thrown in light
Did my vision flicker again?
To cast me into the seas
When my body failed me
As it fell from my command?

Conviction.

No, there *was* light
And the sea came to meet it.
Striking the white cliffs
The waves wrapped about the vessel.
Tentacles with snide grip
To seek their vassal
Whose eyes glowed.

"Harder Boekidin!" I yelled
And to the deck fell
As the boat jerked in the air
My heart crashing to despair

I held tightly to the wood
Securing my lover.
But I was no match for arms of the divine
Who seeped their way between the cracks of my grip
Wrestling me to slip.

The reigns of the ship tugged.
Boards of the hull shrieking in pain
Their agony mine
I could not lose this girl again
Not for a third *fucking* time.

"To hell, Amasos," I called
My yell piercing the depths of the bay.
The sea roared, rearing its head
Strangling my frame with its fluid legs.
Prying my limbs with its own
Tearing me from saving a soul.

Boekidin hauled, crank whirring
The ropes called, tears stirring
I hunkered down, courage failing
The sea rumbled, grip gaining

Then the tentacles snapped.
The light went out,
Cliffs returned to black.
The boat shot up with a mighty shout
As spinning returned to the cranks.
The sea would not have her on this mighty day
Nor me.

My friends on the ground had lined the way
To pull us from the wretched sea.

Hull to the clifftops, I threw Natalie from the boat.
And I dragged her across the grass.
Through the forest.
Past the mountains.
Into the library, I lay her down fast.
And there,
Without even a stolen kiss
I fell onto my ass.

Chapter 33
Day of the Black Suns: Part I

The day of the Black Suns had arrived.
I stirred awake, my heart racing. My blood had turned to an emulsion of dread and
adrenaline shooting through my veins.

I was in a sweat.

Natalie shifted in the bed next to me. She let out a soft, tired groan, and
patted her hand across the sheets before finding mine. She held onto it, squeezing
as tightly as her tired body could manage.

"It's a big day," she said.

"Yeah..." I hummed, my voice sewn with anticipation.

"Be calm," she said, "and sleep, we have an alarm."

"How can I sleep?" I asked. "I keep dreaming of falling out of the sky. My
whole life has been about the Suneva recently. I can't think of anything else – and
it all could end!" I looked to her, but her eyes were closed, her hair frizzed over
her face. "I mean, what are we doing sleeping? It's already..." I looked from the
light coming through the blinds to the alarm clock by Natalie's bedside table. "Five
thirty in the morning..."

Natalie hummed, turning fully over to face me. I expected to see her deep
blue eyes when she opened them, but I was greeted by her grey, unfocussed
blindness. It was particularly jarring when I needed comfort. Amasos could talk
through those eyes.

"Stop worrying and come here," she instructed, arms wrapping around me, pulling me into the sheets.

We kissed.

***

The city of Thessaloniki buzzed. Natalie, Celeste, Anastasiya and I sat around a small table at a café, seated under the hot, spring sun, watching the people bristle past.

Anastasiya thumbed green, infused stones. Her nerves looked beyond mine, which seemed almost impossible. Celeste was weary too, her eyes sleepless. Only Natalie seemed to be calm. *Probably because she can't see any of it*, I surmised, trying to pick at my plate of mushrooms, eggs, and toast.

That said, the mood in the street was abundantly cheery. Happy faces sifted between obstacles along the closed street. Food trucks and vendors were driving in, engines buzzing between event organisers in high-visibility gear. Members of a band walked past, instruments slung over shoulders. The whole thing was surreal – none of these people *knew* that their threads ended today.

"You all need to calm down," Natalie said. "We won't fail this."

"What makes you so sure?" Celeste asked, her stare dirty.

"This event isn't what we thought it was." Natalie said. "It's really fun. There's rides, and traditional food, song, and dance. There are Suneva using their abilities in the streets like nobody cares. Hesslik has put together a great day."

"Is that Amasos still talking?" Celeste squinted. Natalie sighed.

"After coming back from being totally possessed, this is cheery," Natalie said. "We don't have to break in like we thought we did, either. We can just enjoy the show and steal the stage when we need it."

"We'll still need my men," Celeste grunted. "I've got the Thessalonian Argol branch on my side – after taking the time to learn their worries – but they're not enough to help us storm the stage. I think you're underestimating the security here."

"I am the White Witch. Next to me sits a Legendary of Teleportation." Natalie sat tall, smugly. "James can jump over buildings. You can control the hottest Suneva flame ever produced through heat control. I think we'll be fine to take the stage."

"That's the plan, anyway, right?" I asked. "Make our way to the stage then teleport up?"

339

Anastasiya nodded meekly, and blushed away from the attention.

"We'll still need a force to keep us safe in the crowd." Celeste said, breaking up her waffle with her hands. "Once people see our faces, we'll be in for trouble. Especially if Hesslik has his Sunesca here. He's bound to have taken at least one of those odd twins."

"We're in more danger from our threads being recognised than our faces," Natalie reasoned. "I don't think it's unreasonable that Iva Argol shows up to the largest Suneva gathering in history. As for myself and James, well, we hopefully have more supporters in this crowd than we know. Things have changed over the last few months. Hesslik will have a hard sell palming us off as terrorists to be extinguished."

Celeste grumbled, biting down on her sweet breakfast. She scanned the crowd skeptically.

"I'm finding my men before I go anywhere else. I'm worried about what Michael is doing to the rest of them. Amasos controls *both* sides. This could be a mess."

Natalie nodded.

"It's concerning," I agreed. "I can't imagine what they'll plan to do past creating chaos."

"That's probably just it," Celeste grunted, "and *if* we get caught by any of them before Hesslik's speech at one-thirty, you better hope we can get away and back in time. We still have to take that remote control off Hesslik before he uses it." The remote, outlined in Vestas' lab reports, would help Hesslik activate the free-energy device from the stage.

"Legendary of Teleportation," Natalie said bluntly, pointing in the roundabout direction of Anastasiya. "We can get to the stage from anywhere in sight of it."

"Fine," Celeste grumbled, finishing her plate, "let's go get my Argols. Then we can enjoy the festival like you want to."

***

Simone, Chad, and Yvon camped in the hills surrounding Hesslik's castle, playing cards in their tent.

Chad's got a flush. Boekidin warned as Simone went to put all of her money in. *He's not bluffing.*

"God damnit Boekidin," Simone cussed aloud, throwing her chips to the centre. She had a better hand, but could control her face.

Yvon had thrown his cards down some raises ago. He now played with the tent's zipper, poking his head in and out, taking in the view of the castle.

Chad, smugly grinning, lay his hand upon the table. A *straight* flush. Simone huffed, setting down her full house.

Told you, Boekidin cooed.

"That's a straight flush, bird-brain!" Simone growled as Chad raked in the chips. He threw them above his head, dancing in the shower of gold.

"Don't you guys think we should be doing something?" Yvon twitched. "Anything?"

"We've got a few hours till we have to strike," Chad smiled, patting Yvon's back. "Sit down and relax."

"But why don't we act now?" he asked. "It seems stupid to sit here and wait."

"We give Hesslik too much time to react if we strike now," Chad said, picking up the deck to shuffle it.

"And we risk getting caught," Simone added. "We can't do anything if we get locked up. This attack has to be precise." She turned her wrist to eye her watch. It was ten in the morning, and Hesslik's speech would be at one-thirty. They planned to enter the castle at one. Her heart spiked just thinking about it.

"Surely we can run in and permanently damage the device?" Yvon asked. "Just go in there and start ripping out parts. Burn them."

"Vestas has all of the parts to build a second one," Simone said. "I had Anderson get me the full lab reports. I've been reading them."

"So why hasn't he built a second one?" Yvon whirred. "Wouldn't it be a stupid idea *not* to have a backup."

"He's afraid it wouldn't work properly," Simone said, taking cards from Chad. "Vestas has had trouble getting the single device to work at all, let alone a second. Replacing parts causes it to break down – but it's broken down range still gets from here across to all of Europe, the Middle East, and North Africa."

"Fine," Yvon huffed, sealing the tent back up, "but why are we here then, when Hesslik has the remote?"

"Because we *are* going to destroy the machine," Simone said, "*and* it has its own switch, too… so two locations can turn it on. We still don't know *who* will activate it."

"Okay, okay. Fine." Yvon slumped down, gesturing Chad to deal him cards. Chad smiled. "Still seems *wrong* to sit here not doing anything."

"All good plans are about timing," Chad said. "You can always do the right thing, but if you do it at the wrong time, it can be like it never mattered at all. Patience in the face of adversity – waiting for the correct opportunity - is what makes success."

"Huh…" Yvon quizzed, and palmed his cards. "That's pretty wise for the guy who usually has the silliest ideas."

"Thank you." Chad nodded to the backhanded compliment. "I try."

Yvon eyed his hand, expression beaming. Yvon had a terrible poker face.

***

We danced.

The festival was joyous, an explosion of excitement and Suneva energies. Live music wafted through the street, hijacking the streams of scents from every cuisine around the world. Traditional *Liktan* goat stewed in a pot somewhere, served in chunks with rice and cabbage. Faces glowed in all directions, smiles and happiness creating a canopy of rainbows which shrouded the whole affair.

The Suneva community was ecstatic on this day, and Hesslik had made it the perfect gathering. That in itself made me anxious. How could we upstage this display with a *speech*?

Celeste's Thessalonian bodyguards hung nearby. They were enjoying the festival, and she was enjoying her time with them. Adam Leroux had joined us now, too, and he chatted with the previously Argol men and women of this town. He had a way of talking which was utterly captivating, hanging the small crowd helplessly to his words. Along with him, Adam bought his wife, Juliette Leroux, and his close associate and friend, Alexis LeGrand, who had defected from Michael's Argolian vision as soon as Celeste was voted out.

Natalie and I were nearby dancing. There was a small music group performing a traditional Suneva dance that we hadn't tried before, and a middle-aged woman had detached from the group to teach us the moves, then roped us in.

Natalie, even using quatra-sight, was a magical dancer. Her limbs were fluid, perfectly controlled. She understood her body. She knew how it moved and where its parts were. Her smile was radiant, her step full of bounce.

"Iva Argol? Et Naxaer?" I heard in my peripheries. I turned to the voice, to see a frantic man and his friends approach Celeste. They had their *shath* weapons drawn.

"Just Adam, now," Mister Leroux said in Liktan, shaking the man's hand.

"This seems important," I said to Natalie, splitting off from the dance. She stayed on, legs swinging as the snake of dancers slithered on.

"We don't know what to do," the frazzled man said. He addressed the question to Celeste, rather than her father

"Michael's plan is crazy! And he's got thread removal devices to neutralise anybody who won't go through with it."

"What *is* his plan?" I interjected, making my way to the circle. A reverence passed through the newcomers.

"First is to remove your and Celeste's threads…" he said. Celeste and I immediately drew our weapons, her long sword exploding into pink flames. The man's hands flew to the air to protect his face.

"Woah!" he shrieked. "*We* don't want to do it."

"Fine," I said, keeping my weapon held. "Why, and what else?"

"He thinks that your plans are compromising the future of Suneva, and getting in his way," The man answered honestly. "He wants to set apon ruining the festival. He wants to break in with large numbers, force our way to the stage, block the threads of anybody who gets in our way, and take down Hesslik before he can pull the trigger."

"That's his idea that he kicked me out over?" Celeste grumbled. "Make a mess and remove threads? Who does he think he's going to convince doing that?"

"He says that if you don't want to fight for the full rights of Suneva, you don't deserve to be a Suneva."

"This could be messy," I said to Celeste, and she hummed along, nodding.

"What's your name?" she asked the man.

"Karilik, Tona Argol," he said formally.

"Which branch are you from?"

"Barcelona, miss."

"And these are our Barcelonan Argols?"

"Yes," he said.

"Do you know what I plan to do?" Celeste asked Karilik, and he shook his head. "I'm going to help Kuvalik and the White Witch take the stage and stop Hesslik," she said. "No intimidation. No thread removals. We just need protection. Will you and your Suneva help?"

"Yes, absolutely," he nodded.

"Then take this…" she said, handing him a strip of paper. It had an address on it. "This is the Thessalonian clubhouse. I have the city's Capo in there assessing the situation as it develops. He'll want to know that you're offering your help."

Karilik nodded, and went to gather his Argol force, but turned on his boot. "What are you going to do after this, Iva?" Karilik asked.

"I'm going to join Kuvalik," she said. "All over Europe I've seen that Suneva want peace and ethical conduct, but they also want their rights. I will take what I've learned and fight for our rights in this new coalition.

"But," she continued, touching his shoulder, "follow who you want into the new world. You have a choice now."

"What do you think, Naxaer?" he asked her father, who smiled to the conference.

"Olomb continued to tell me that the Argols were a temporary fix to the Suneva community, and that one day, when the time was right, he'd spearhead the community the Suneva world needed.

"I think in light of recent changes, the Argols are becoming obsolete. As much as it pains me to desert a community which generations of my family have built, I think it's time to move on. We are about community, and a better one is coming."

Karilik nodded. "Thank you, Naxaer, and Iva," he said.

"Tell any other possible defectors to find me or the Thessalonian Capo," Celeste said. "We could use any of the help we can get."

"For the Suneva people," Karilik nodded. He walked his crowd away.

Celeste squinted, watching them leave. She rubbed her chin.

"Interesting," I noted.

"Great," she corrected. "It might get easier to gain support from old Argols than I thought."

"Wouldn't have predicted that after your trail across Europe."

"Not exactly…" she blushed, "but this is good…very good."

***

Simone checked her watch again. *Quarter to twelve,* she read from its face.

"We're got forty minutes till we move," she said to the group.

"That's like, forty more games of big-two," Chad grinned, "at the rate that I'm beating you losers."

Only Chad could be so jovial. Simone lowered her hand, rustling towards the edge of the tent, where she joined in Yvon's habit of opening the zipper and peering to the castle in apprehension.

"We'll be fine," Chad said, "just relax. We've got this."

"I know," Simone sighed, slumping back into the tent, "it's just so weird, how everything led to this, you know?" She picked her hand back up, lazily analysing her terrible set of cards. "I'm not even a part of destiny, but somehow, in a year, I went from Suneva enemy number one to fighting for their survival. What kind of a weird story is that? How did I end up so nervous on *this* day?"

"It's the kind of story we're all grateful for," Chad said. "You grew up and found your purpose. Even then, what you think your purpose is will always change." He placed his card down first, the three of diamonds. "The world is dynamic. Things you care about one day will vanish, or fade away, and you'll go down another direction. I suppose the important thing to realise is that there are plenty more directions to go, even if you feel it's too late.

"So, I don't know. Today is big right now, but if we fail, you'll always have something else to look forward to. That's the way it goes."

"Damn," Yvon commented, putting down the two of spades – possibly the stupidest play at this point in the game. "Which old man gave his mind to you for all of this advice."

"I have a feeling there will be plenty more of it today, my French friend," Chad smiled. Simone passed her turn, and Yvon placed his hand, smiling broadly with his double-threes.

Simone checked her watch again. *Eleven forty-six,* it read.

"Time is moving so slow," she noted aloud.

***

The morning moved quickly, danced away down the lively street. The crowd thickened, filled with all of the world's accents speaking broken Liktan. Natalie was approached by many Suneva – some who knew of her title, and asked for blessings, and others who had no idea who she was, and commented with surprise at the strength of her thread.

Celeste's Thessalonian men, joined now by legions of other Argol gangsters, sifted through the crowd inconspicuously, watching for our safety. The festival was lively, but I couldn't help but feel the tension in the quatra field. Nobody had ever amassed this many Suneva in one place. The possibilities were explosive, and the energy reflected that.

Adam Leroux had disappeared an hour ago to talk to the Thessalonian Capo, Tano Kessivaer, about the tactics in facing the Argol threat to the festival. They were using the information given by the newcomers to decipher the plan, and counter it.

Then I heard his voice again, yelling from behind me. Natalie and I turned from the food vendor we were talking to – an old *Vastas* man from Adelaide who had us rapt in his story – to face the commotion.

"They're striking now," Adam cried to Celeste, Anastasiya, and the gathered Thessalonian personnel. A brigade of men and women marched alongside him, behind the Capo Kessivaer. Adam left them, jogging over to Natalie and I. We excused ourselves from our enthralling conversation and met Argol in the street's centre.

"They're about to strike," Adam said to us. "Coming from all entrances."

"How can we help?" I asked.

"You don't," Adam instructed. "Get yourselves, Celeste, and Anastasiya through to the centre of the crowd with the Thessalonian guards. Take the stage only when Hesslik starts speaking. Any sooner and you're in hot water."

"Are you kidding?" Natalie asked. "I'm not going to run away from danger and risk the entire crowd's safety. I'm the *White Witch* – I'm an aspirational spiritual figure to the people I've talked to today. Do you know how bad it would look if I ran from the danger?"

Adam went to speak, but Natalie continued on, unable to see his lips move in protest. "And, I don't mean to be arrogant, but I'm particularly good at deflecting attacks…even when I'm not possessed."

There was a pause, as Adam waited for her to be finished. He finally raised a finger. "I appreciate that, Natalie, but we have plenty of force. We warned Hesslik's guard captain and let him in on the plan. He was particularly sceptical, but has reinforced the barriers."

"Won't that leave the middle of the festival relatively unguarded?" I asked, and Argol winked.

"He must know that you're going to try something, but he's evaluated his threats. I've given you an opening, so use it!"

Behind him, Argolian men and women thrashed into a chaos, running off to allocated sections of the street. Crowds moved aside for them like water in a boat's wake. A shroud of deadly anticipation rocked through the masses as footings were lost and gained.

All around, the music died, leaving room for the thousand voices of the crowd to ring out and be squashed in the sky. A hush descended in the newfound quiet, rippling its way from the silent performance stages throughout the street.

In a clear, blue sky, on a hot day with the sun shining down, an arc of lighting cracked. It roared its way from the heavens – seemingly from the sun itself – and ripped the ground behind the main stage into a cloud of dusty debris.

The shadow of a figure bobbed through the mist. Tall, slender, with little lightning-bolt horns adorning their helmet.

Hesslik was taking the stage.

"*Cheese*, he's starting!" I cried, and looked to my watch. *Quarter past one*, it read. "He's early. Come on!" I grabbed Natalie's hand, with Celeste and Anastasiya in tow, and rode the wake of the passing guards towards the street's centre.

"He must have heard about the Argol attacks and moved it all forward," Celeste puffed, running behind me. "That's…actually a great contingency move."

"It's a great move on all fronts," I agreed. "Come on."

We forced our way through the crowd, Celeste's guards struggling to keep up. They straggled as people bunched in behind us, eager to get closer to the stage. The audience became denser as we travelled through them - everybody was keen to hear what the *Fara Hesslik* had to say today. I roughed my way through the audience, shoving people aside with a hand and shoulder. I was greeted by understandably annoyed grunts and gasps, and a few choice comments.

"Blind girl coming through, move it!" I yelled as a saving grace, before bowling through Suneva tall and small. Hesslik stood firmly now on the stage. He stepped up to the microphone, to a raging applause. Clapping elbows caught me across the ribs.

"Welcome, Tona and Tano, Ladies and Gentlemen," He greeted, a sly smile behind his yellow helmet and distinctive, cyan eyes. "Welcome to the last day of the Suneva world as you've known it. This afternoon, we step into a new era of our people."

***

At least five games had passed, all of which had been lost by Yvon, and won by either Chad or Simone. At one point, Boekidin had asked to play, using

347

Chad's right hand to hold his cards. Of course, with such a strategy, he could never win, but he enjoyed being a part of the game.

Simone glanced at her watch again. *Quarter past twelve*, it read. But it had been ten past twelve at least two games ago, and games just *didn't* take two and a half minutes – not with the amount of time it took Yvon to choose his terrible hands.

And he's a bloody Kidin, too, Simone grumbled in her head. *How can he be this bad at a card game? He can see all of our hands through our eyes.* Maybe he hadn't even thought to cheat like that. Such a possibility was even more perplexing.

Still, annoyed at the slowness of time, Simone furrowed her brow and tapped her watch face.

The second hand jumped.

Simone jumped.

The second hand did not continue to move.

Simone tapped it again, and the hand shifted, ticking, but ran quickly to an exhausted stop.

"Oh *my* GOD," she cracked. Her eyes, ears and face became hot, pounded with boiling, iron blood. Her stomach fell through to the centre of the earth, taking her legs with it, which turned to tense, limp noodles. Her hair stood on end. Pure fright.

"Hey, don't reveal a good hand!" Chad playfully scorned. "Now we know you'll win this round…"

"Jesus, this isn't about poker!" she snapped. "My watch is broken! Oh *fuck* us, my watch is broken!" She leaped for the tent's zipper, shoving her fingers around it and yanking. The zipper was stuck. She tugged, roaring with frustration and anxiety.

Chad calmly wrapped a hand around her waist, pulling her from the exit. With a controlled grip, he delicately pinched the zipper, and gently pulled it open. He raised his eyebrows to Simone, but she'd already halfway bounded out of the opening, her brain in a mania.

There were massive, silver energy ribbons spewing from the castle. Silver-grey for sound – something was playing over the speakers. She caught a single word of it. *Welcome.*

"He's started!" she cried. "God almighty…"

"That's you, Ms Sunesca," Chad teased. Simone lunged for his ear, pinching it.

"No god-damned joviality!" she roared in her adrenaline induced fit. "We have to run!"

Chad nodded, letting the armour of Ferrad take control of his body. Yvon emerged from the tent, already as Riskidin. His metal replacement arm to match Ferrad's bronze replacement shin.

Simone pulled her black Salak robe over her head, and launched herself up the nearest tree. Gathering sound from the speakers, she kicked off into a nosedive, down the hill, towards Hesslik's concert ground gates. Chad and Yvon sprinted underfoot.

***

We shifted through the masses, slow going. The Thessalonian Argols had managed to find their way back to us through the sludge of the crowd, and were parting them with greater efficiency than we could manage on our own.

It was an oversight to stick to the back of the street, away from the stage, for so long. I was kicking myself as we muscled through. Nobody had fired on us yet, but *somebody* wouldn't take kindly to being roughed around. I knew it. I could sense it, through my own convictions.

On the stage, I could see Hesslik's guards grow tense. Sly fingers were pointed in our direction – to our massive, fluid movement through the crowd towards the stage. Weapons were summoned.

Hesslik's initial speech was short and sweet. A welcome of sorts, with introductions to the six Suneva who lined the stage. Simone, through all of her time as fairysmog, might have known these figures, but I only ever knew Vestas and Boekidin to be the other high-ranking officials – and neither were here. Hesslik stepped aside as one of his cronies, a Suneva of bright orange armour, by the name of Tona Vasteric, took the podium. She spoke, and through my passive ears, it seemed like she was talking about money, or economics.

"What is this, a presentation?" I rambled to Natalie. She shrugged, getting knocked by some stranger she couldn't see. Crowds were her nightmare in her blindness. This would have been terrifying.

"There's a number of speeches…I think," Celeste said, then pointed off stage, "and look, a band too. We've got more time than we think."

I fell into a man who formed a solid wall, coming to an impasse. We were so close to the stage – definitely close enough for Anastasiya to get us there easily, now.

"Teleport from here?" I asked her.

"Maybe a bit closer," she said. "I can't see the ground. It's hard to tell where I have to land us."

"You're too short to see the stage, anyway," I grumbled. "I'll lift you up."

The man in front of me, tired of being pushed into, turned with mean-set eyes. "Are you alright, there?" he asked. "I'm trying to listen to..."

"How many things are going to be said, here?" I interrupted. He was taken aback.

"I'm sorry?"

"How many speeches, and music, and whatever else, before the end?" I asked again.

"Every committee member is making a speech," He said, "then there's the band, *Na Quatra Taevo*, and special guests, and..."

"*Great*," I said, and shoved him aside when he wasn't expecting it. I marched through. "Lots of time," I said to the group, "let's get closer."

***

Simone blasted past the concert stage, into the first great hall of the castle. Riskidin and Ferrad were hot on her tail, their combined footsteps ringing like a stampede. Simone took some of the sound energy, but couldn't find a way to use it. Instead, she just focussed on running as fast as her legs could move.

The hall ended in the great theatre room, where Hesslik has hosted his New-year's dinner. The entrance was at the second level, but Simone didn't care. She vaulted the balcony, leaping off and finally finding a use for those noisy footsteps. She glided to her fall, coming to a halt at the room's centre.

Left, through that entrance, then follow it to the back of the stage, Boekidin said. Simone nodded, and waited for Ferrad's massive crash onto the wooden floor, and Riskidin's to follow. She slammed down a flurry of air, snapping away off a cloud of dust into the hall, leading the group around.

This castle was disastrously unguarded – and even if there were guards, Simone didn't care right now. She'd steal their motion, somebody would blast them with quatra, that would be it. Even if they couldn't neutralise them, it didn't matter. You didn't need to be a Suneva to smash apart a big machine. That's all they needed to do.

Around the back of the stage, Boekidin instructed her left, up the stairs, and into a grand, marble lobby. At its centre stood a massive, black marble statue of the Mark of the Black Suns.

On the right, Boekidin called, and Simone followed, swinging around a large marble column into what could only be described as a hospital hallway. Sanitised white walls and linoleum floors ending in two large, swinging double doors.

Simone threw a torrent of air towards them, casting them open, crashing them into the plaster of the walls behind.

Ferrad and Riskidin followed through the doorway, but were ground to a halt. At the end of this hallway, beyond the doors, was a wide open room containing a device like a massive, black, electric donut. But standing centrally before it were two repulsive brothers, whose hands arced with electricity and flames.

In their hands they held Simone, Ferrad, and Riskidin's motion. They smiled slyly.

***

Celeste, Natalie, Anastasiya and I adopted our armour, causing a gasp from the surrounding people, whose faces fell between excited and terrified. Mothers huddled their children away, others, with starry eyes, held them to the White Witch, their spiritual idol.

I grabbed Annikida by the waist, and threw her over my shoulders, giving her a perfect view of the stage. Zamelle and Iva huddled in, holding me closely by the Legendary's instructions.

"Do it!" I yelled. "Quick!"

Annikida held her giant, spiked hand out to Hesslik on the stage. She clenched the fist, hanging onto the fabric of time and space.

In a moment, I could see their eyes lock. Hesslik gave her an approving nod, with a helmet-hidden smile.

"*Mina athios Fara,*" she muttered – *My true Fara.*

Oh no…

Chapter 34
Day of the Black Suns: Part II

Annikida tugged on the fabric of space, expanding it over us before I had time to let go. The crowd on our outskirts slimmed to mere lines, which flopped like noodles in a vast ocean of perception. The world around us both opened into cross sections of itself, and closed over around us, forming a snake through which we flew.

Her enormous hand clenched my wrist tightly. I tried to struggle free, but couldn't escape before we were spewed out the exit of the wormhole.

Annikida landed on her feet, skidding to a halt. I fell to the ground beside her, with Iva and Zamelle grappling onto my trunk. We slid across a great, stone floor, before grinding to a stop.

"No! Why?!" I yelled to her, flinging myself to my feet. We were in the lobby of the ancient Vochduh temple, high in the mountaintops of Macedonia. I could feel the energy of the coalescing demons behind me, near the king's quarters. Wind buffeted through the opening.

I fired a bolt of quatra, but Annikida disappeared, re-emerging from space-time about a foot to the right.

"You can't cheat Gods," she said, in a two-toned voice that was half hers, and half of the voice I'd heard in Christina's head – the voice of the God Amasos.

I roared, firing again. Zamelle raised her hand to join in, but Annikida had already formed her handhold in the universe, and sucked herself into it before the bolts could reach her body. She had truly vanished, not reappearing.

My backside burned hot, the temple erupting into a dazzling pink light. Iva roared a Suneva shriek, flames bursting from her palms, sword, and mouth. Her rage was incomprehensible. She swung the hot sword into the stones, melting through them like butter.

"Hey!" I called. "Watch it! That's history!"

"*We* are fucking *history*," she spat. "Good lord Veritas, I *never* trusted that halfwitted *idiot* of a Legendary." Iva ran the sword again through the stones, and a pack of demons descended towards her.

"I can't believe I didn't sense it," Zamelle growled. "How could Amasos hide that from me? They made me powerful enough to sense almost *anything*."

Another rip in spacetime appeared, right between Zamelle, Iva and I, and the fright of it appearing threw us to our arses. Annikida stepped out of it, flinging Simone, Riskidin and Ferrad across the stone.

Simone clawed at the ground, her face red, her eyes bulging. She pushed off the body of Ferrad – who had stuck himself into the stone – screaming. Her cry filled the temple, demonic enough to curse souls, piercing enough to vaporise eardrums. Her hands gripped for their connections, violently thrashing.

My whole world suddenly plunged into darkness. Not midnight darkness, where your eyes would eventually adjust to the soft indigo, but *real* darkness. The total absence of light.

There was a shot of quatra, and the fizzle of smoke burning.

Then the blackness cleared.

Annikida was gone. Replaced by Anastasiya, who lay unconscious across the floor, black smoke rising from her body. Simone slumped to the stone, her eyes red, her yelling transpired. Dust rained around, settling in its final resting place. Everybody sat up, armour peeling off bodies, curious eyes taking head counts.

Then the room erupted into screams.

More frustration and rage than any one confined space had ever seen. The result of a dozen shaken bottles of hot anticipation erupting into an emotional shitstorm. Fire streamed across the ceiling. Bolts of quatra flew into oblivion. The place became nightmarishly cold, despite the immense flame. I crawled towards the cliff, peering out to the abyss. So peaceful.

"Everybody stop it!" Chad roared. He stomped to the centre of the chaos, and planted his boot to the stone. The sound cracked throughout the lobby. The demons rolled in, ribbons of charcoal dust and smoke, stealing the activity. He stepped over to Anastasiya's body, and ripped her side bag off her. Chad then sauntered over to the open ledge and threw the bag over the cliff, flinging enchanted stones across the valley.

"Far out," he continued, "who shot her?"

"I did," Natalie said.

"Toxicated bolt?" he asked. "You know…the unconsciousness."

"White," she answered.

"Jesus," he coughed, and knelt down, feeling at her neck. "She's alive. You're lucky - but her thread is destroyed."

"I know," Natalie admitted.

"*She's* lucky." Celeste pointed to the body. She stormed towards Chad and Anastasiya, swinging her sword.

353

"We'll get nowhere by killing her, or throwing shit around," Chad urged.

"We'll get nowhere *anyway*," Simone shrieked. "She fucking sabotaged us! That useless idiot. She was *way* too stupid for the power she held. I *knew* she couldn't be that dumb."

"Yes, fine, we all figured it out now," Chad agreed. "She played us, and nobody picked it up. Now we have to find a way back."

"We can't! It's over, Chad." Celeste slumped, having exhausted herself. "All of my life spent fighting for these rights, and they're *fucking* over!" Her rage – the façade she wore so often – faded fast. She started to bawl. Her fists clenched at the stone. Yvon rushed to her side, and was not thrown away.

"I thought it was over when we lost Natalie for the first time, but it's not," Chad said. I turned from the cliff, walking to join him. As I stepped past Simone, she shot up and grabbed me by the shoulders.

"Any ideas, James?" Chad asked, but I was truly focussed on Simone, who now had me held in place.

"What the hell is *this*?" Simone asked, spinning me around a pointing to my thread's mouth.

"What, my spine?" I asked.

"No, you've got two little prongs in your neck."

"I do?" I asked, craning my head to see them. Simone grabbed my neck and straightened it.

"Yes," she stated, "how did you not feel this?"

"I don't know," I shrugged.

"How didn't *you* feel this?" she asked Natalie, although without being able to see, Natalie had no idea she was being addressed.

"Natalie," Simone called, and it piqued the White Witch's interest, "James has tiny little prongs in his neck. You didn't feel these?"

Natalie blushed instantly. "How handsy are you assuming I get?" she shyly protested.

"You're blind – pretty handsy," Simone said matter of factly. "Now, if I'm right about what these are..." She grabbed onto them and yanked them from my spine.

Breath. My eyes shot from my skull as my mind and body expanded with air. Pain, whose void was immediately filled with the greatest relief. My spine was reamed back into my body, making my meat-bag self fuller, taller.

A second thread at the base of my neck reappeared in my mind's eye. A lunar eclipse uncovered again, setting my vision to the mark of the black sun. *Kuvalik.*

"You got shot by a gun to remove the thread, didn't you?"

"Yes," I stammered as energy rushed into my body. My connections soared, the full power of air returned to me. The scars on my hand, below the bandages, were drawing energy, healing completely. I could feel it.

"Vestas developed thread tasers – designed to block a thread, not remove it," Simone said, walking away. "I saw it in the reports Anderson gave me."

"You didn't feel like mentioning that?" I spun.

"I hadn't seen any. I didn't think he'd produced them yet."

"Oh…oh man." My head became woozy with the full stream of energy my threads were affording me. I stumbled, falling over a rock. A demon glowed, stealing my fall, but as soon as I hit the ground, I was thrown into visions.

Not visions – I hadn't had visions since walking the Void. These were *memories.*

Memories I had seen before – Olomb falling out of portals. I'd always been shown his memories after teleporting with Anastasiya. I now saw myself fall onto my arse from six separate instances at once. Six memories overlapping.

"A fourth spatial dimension?" I heard myself ask to him – one of my own memories, of the first time he trained me. He taught me the peace-sign pose. One finger direction for each spatial dimension, and a palm for the fourth.

"I'm a living consciousness kept alive by black hole energy," Olomb said to my memory, although I experienced the words from both perspectives at once. "I opened my mind long before this stage. You would do well to open yourself to new possibilities, Maiki."

My mind zipped to the scene of depression-era New York, standing with Tanivaer Argol and his son, Seros.

"I need a man of your talents," Argol's voice rang, before the scene meshed with itself, strangely dreaming to its end, where I extended my hand towards the tree.

And where my hand gripped, space time bent around it, and I pulled myself through the anomaly. My mind zoomed out, back to the six overlayed memories.

The sensation of the world at my fingertips when I used his thread; the feeling of everything being so connected, so much closer, all of the threads *right there*, and the field being so small yet so expansive.

These weren't feats of Kuvalik's prowess as a witch. They were symptoms of a soul that sensed in four dimensions.

Kuvalik was the Legendary of Teleportation.

I awoke from the strange thread-backlash with a startling gasp. I lay on the floor of the temple, head directly under one of the massive, bored skylights, staring at the last sector of the sun overhead. My face bathed in light, the silhouettes of all of my friends surrounding me, and the demons lurking on the roof.

"Kuvalik was the Legendary of Teleportation!" I yelled, and shot up to sit on my arse. The air was responsive to my hands, as powerful as it had been before. I felt a deep sense of elation that rushed my body, because, above all, this was *hope*.

"What?" everybody seemed to utter at once.

"That's how he kept buying tea as a ghost, and how he found me in Hesslik's lab, and how he travelled back to Melbourne faster than your flight, Celeste, and how he travelled around the world as an old, decrepit bastard with no god-damned issues. It's how the whole thing makes sense! He is connected to all destinies and senses the quatra field in four dimensions – that's how he knows *everything!*"

I panted, catching my breath from the arduous rant. There was stunned silence from my audience.

"He didn't want to just *tell* us that?" Celeste asked.

"No," I said, "just like every Legendary, really."

"Can you get us back?" Chad asked, his face shining like a thousand stars.

"I…I certainly bloody hope so," I said, standing. All rose around me.

"Will this help?" asked one of the demonic voices in the room. A flying book broke through the air, flung towards me. I jumped, high off a burst, and caught it before it went overhead and slid off the cliff.

It was the book I had set down on the podium in the Void before they all got destroyed. The one I believed – as much as all of the other books I set upon that podium – would contain the secrets to flight.

"Oh my goodness!" I shrieked. "I mean, no, it won't help – but I can't believe you have it. Didn't they all get destroyed."

"Not this one," the Salak – whose voice I recognised as *Kallid*, replied. "This one was kept under the throne of the king himself. A past king must have placed it there."

"O…okay," I said, my vocal chords failing in my excitement. "I'll have to read this…later."

"Yes, *later*," Celeste said, "you've got to learn how to teleport – and you've only got a few minutes."

"Well, maybe the *first* page," I said, my excited fingers dancing for the cover.

"*James?*" Celeste scorned, slapping my hand. I resolved to open the book, anyway. "What will you *really* learn from the first page?"

"These monks were concise," I said. "The most important line of each book is always the key finding – that way, you know if the text will interest you…"

"Why *now?*" she complained.

"This…" I flipped the book open, looking at the first line. It wasn't written in a language I could read. "This is a last act of destiny. The fact that I get handed this book right now, to me, seems a long time premeditated. It *may* be important to us *right now*."

I held the book the way that I'd handled the tomes in the Void. I had an ability to connect to it, like I had done in that realm. Drawing quatra, I powered this connection between myself and the author. The text, unexpectedly, came to me.

I have discovered that control of air is not solely about the forceful, or peaceful, combination of wills, nor about control over the element, nor about being the air, and having a fluid soul and spiritual state. Perfection of the Vochduh arts lies somewhere on the plane between these three points. The only word I can use to describe it, is existence.

"Amazing…" I uttered.

"What is it?" Natalie asked.

"The one book I needed to read," I smiled.

"Okay, great." Celeste snatched the tome off me, handing it to the demons. "If you don't figure out how to teleport us, there won't be a point in having read it."

"Okay…yes, I'll do that," I stammered. I had barely learned to use air in the half a year that I studied under Kuvalik - how would I learn to *teleport?*

Faces looked on, surrounding me in a circle, each full of hope. Rage had been funnelled into acceptance, then crammed into a tiny box of possibility. They were desperate for me to succeed.

Gulping, I stashed away the thread of Maiki, and drew instead on that of Kuvalik.

357

The world expanded. A familiar feeling, now that I'd drawn on his thread so many times to give so many speeches. A breathless oasis of the quatra field, larger than the eye could perceive, lay at my fingertips, like the edges of a web to a spider's feet. Distance compressed, wrapping around itself like folded paper. Thinking about it, I could perceive far-off places, see far-off, familiar threads.

I wouldn't know how to do this by myself, but knowing that I *could* do it unlocked a familiarity – procedural memories that the old man's soul had stashed in my mind without me knowing. The less obvious way he'd melded his experiences to mine.

A great thrill of cognizance panged as I danced through the wide, far off quatra-scape. I found one thread I knew intimately well – that of my student. *Hesslik.*

"I can see Hesslik," I said. "I can get us to Hesslik, if I can figure out how to…you know…compress space."

"Yes, yes!" Chad whooped. "What about the castle? We need the castle, too."

"Are there any threads that Kuvalik would know by the castle?" I asked. James and Maiki might have known castle-dwelling Suneva, but Kuvalik was the only one of us who had the capacity to sense and smell threads. He was all I had right now.

"Annikida might have left something," Yvon suggested. "When she went to the wrong hill with Natalie, it was out of her sight. There had to be a marker."

I was ripped from my sensation by his stroke of genius. All turned to Yvon, equally surprised.

"Yes," Celeste agreed. "She gave me a quatra-infused stone…" And she turned to eye the body of Anastasiya, searching for a magical rock to show me, but the bag was gone. "Although Chad threw them all away…"

"Sorry!" he gulped.

"We don't need the stones," Natalie said. "Her teleportation leaves a big enough smear in the quatra field to be sensed for miles."

"That's right!" Simone agreed. "She was too afraid to teleport anywhere near possessed-Natalie. That's how we got found here in the first place."

"Maybe you can sense her trail?" Natalie suggested.

I shifted back into the quatra field, letting the vast pastures of its being roll under my fingers, interconnected in the strange web of the fourth dimension.

Yes. There was a large smear of pink near Hesslik. I latched onto the smell, scrolling further, taking bridges between the field's spaces through the fourth direction of travel.

Then I saw another, much less powerful, wrapped around a large mass. Maybe the castle, maybe the surrounding mountains. I couldn't know – I didn't know how to read the depressions and expansions of the field.

"Got it," I said, keeping the vision solidly in my mind's eye, "everybody grab onto me now."

"Are you sure you want to try it for the first time with everybody?" Yvon asked. "You don't want to test-run this before zipping us all through space?"

"No," I interjected. Although my confidence was far from high, something told me that I'd either get this right the first time, or I wouldn't get it at all before it was too late. Like learning some difficult, physical trick, it always worked the first five times, then never again. "Grab ahold everybody."

My head became heavy, and hands squeezed to my body.

I believe in you, James, Boekidin said, entering my mind, *you've got this.*

"Thanks, Boe." I nodded. I gripped onto the largest pile of hands on my body that I could find, then extended my left hand out into space. I could touch the field there, at the smear. I could feel the earth where it was. I could see myself being there. Hand outstretched, I grappled onto the feeling, and I tugged on the destination.

As I pulled, I became astutely aware that I was not pulling myself towards the point – rather, I was bending space itself, pulling the ground at the castle towards the ground at the Vochduh temple. Like folding a piece of paper to touch the other side, instead of propelling myself to the destination.

The world crashed and spun around me, the whole plane of existence twisting over itself above my head, folding into its own gaps like hyperdimensional origami. The castle's ground careened towards me, and I could see it now, coloured around the tips of my fingers. I was no longer looking through the field, I was staring at a grassy floor. The hole expanded.

I crashed into the earth as I fell out of it. *I never did have smooth landings,* I reminisced.

On top of my body landed all of my passengers. I coughed and crawled from the crush as people made their way to their feet. I had landed us in the forest, by the hillcrest where Anastasiya had brought Natalie. And, probably by choice, where Simone had apparently set up her tent.

"Holy shit, it worked!" Chad yelled, ecstatic. He yanked Yvon to his feet, but Simone was already halfway running down the hill, zipping away without them. Yvon saluted me, mouth agape, before they both took off after her.

Hands grabbed my face. Natalie turned my head to hers and kissed me full on the mouth. I blushed.

"Handsome and smart. What a catch – even if I only get to enjoy one of those," She joked, "Now get us to Hesslik, please."

"Done," I said, standing off the mud.

Celeste let the armour of Iva take her once more. "Armor on, guys," she instructed. "We need the spectacular entrance."

"Yes, of course," I agreed, summoning my armour, getting a shock of surprise as gold, silver and black gleaming plate took my body under it. It locked into place, and I waved my hands about, sensing the field.

I found Hesslik immediately – reality was still folded over from the last time Anastasiya hand jumped from here to Thessaloniki – the remnants of his cyan smear on the field were right above me, the way that the three-dimensional world had orientated itself. I reached towards it, gripping in.

"Hold on tight," I said, and I felt four sharp hands cling to my body. "Here we go."

I pulled the two planes together. It happened in almost an instant, the distance was so narrow. The cross section of reality flopped onto my head, coming down like a crushing meteorite. I winced as it fell towards me, irrationally fearing my fate.

Then we were ejected from the space sphincter, crashing onto the hard tarmac ground – myself first, then Zamelle and Iva atop of me. We were in an empty section of the parade, amidst a row of closed vendors. I stood, to see that we were once more at the back of the crowd. We wouldn't be able to push through in time.

"Oh no," Iva noted as she stood. "Can you get us to the stage?"

"I don't know that I trust my skills," I said. "That's where I thought we were landing...oh dear."

Zamelle stood, her eye slit shining an intense, divine white. I recalled, through what memory I had of the past three months, Zamelle strapping herself to my back, and me leaping us up the Grand Exhibition building for our first speech. It gave me an idea.

"*Not forcing of wills, not control, not being the air, but something greater,*" I whispered to myself. "*A point between the three. Existence.*"

"What was that?" Iva asked.

"We're flying to the stage," I said.

"What?" she coughed.

"Flying," I asserted. "I…" I considered the weight of the two girls. Perhaps I was being too ambitious. "I'm not sure if this will work, but…"

I switched between the thread of Kuvalik and that of Maiki. My senses of the quatra world faded, replaced by the atmosphere at my palms.

I extended my grip, hands out, feeling my connection. It was strong, now. The air danced around my fingertips. It had its own will, like millions of individual energies all connected to a great hivemind. Beyond its will, there was my control of it. I could be the central brain, I could give each node energy to move in certain ways. I could *change* their will.

If I could change their will, then I *was* a part of their system. I could *be* the air, and move as it did. I could feel myself as a particle in the random struggle of molecules, perfectly elastic.

Then there was the point between the three, and I could just sense it. The point between control, combination of the hivemind's will, submission, dominance, *being*, asserting. There was a point in there where I wasn't simply the air, and the air wasn't just an extension of me. We both simply *were*.

We both existed, and shared energy.

I opened my eyes, and my feet were no longer on the ground.

"*Veritas*," Iva gaped. It was hard to see what Zamelle thought through the blinding white of her face, but she did step closer.

I hung precariously, not even believing the feat myself. The air and I shared an existence – I'd reasoned that – I just didn't understand how that allowed me to control my position. Was that part of the deal?

Somehow, by only believing it, I was able to lower myself – to change my relative existence with the air. This was a strange way of thinking. It wracked my brain.

"Okay…hold on," I wearily instructed. "We're flying to the stage."

Without hesitation, the girls wrapped themselves around the bulky, metal frame of Maiki. I closed my eyes, preparing the mindset again, and changed my state of existence and energy within the air.

We rose, the girls' long, Suneva claws digging into my armour. I winced, and the lack of concentration almost caused me to falter and fall, but I maintained myself.

I stared at the stage, where Hesslik and I locked gazes. He continued to talk, but I could see the awe writhing its way across his face. I smirked smugly, rising higher.

Then I really flew.

I kicked forward, not blasting the air, not by any force or wind, but simply by existing elsewhere, creating the supports under me, by changing the energy of the system to allow me to occupy it at this elevation and speed.

Naturally, wind thrust behind me, surging me forward. It was exhilarating, totally mind blowing. I swooped close to the crowd, blowing through hats and hair. I pulled up, soaring towards the sky. I had captured the attention of the public. Heads turned, craned towards the clouds, fingers pointing. I had won their admiration.

Then I dove straight towards the stage. It was almost a *lack* of existence in the air which allowed me to fall at speed. Zamelle and Iva screamed as their stomachs dropped through their armour. My grin, however, was unstoppable.

Hesslik's guard raised their weapons. *Oh...I forgot about that,* I gulped. Suddenly, we were falling into a sea of bolts. I barrel rolled, and shifted pressures, bouncing myself between lines of travel. Zamelle freed a hand — her other one gripping in for dear life — and countered what she could. Her orange bolts flew true, destructively interfering with attacking hits, destroying them mid-air. The crowd marvelled at her skill.

I swooped under the gantry which held the lights and speakers, allowing Iva and Zamelle to blast bolts downwards. I passed the stage, pulling up vertically behind it and letting us drop the distance to the ground. I threw down a cushion of air to catch our fall, and Iva and Zamelle let go.

I dropped the thread and armour of Maiki, letting Kuvalik take his hold of my soul.

***

Simone, Ferrad, and Riskidin ran onto the castle grounds. Their feet were flying furiously. Even more so than being late, they had little time, and a formidable opponent waiting for them.

Simone ran for the concert stage — hoping to take the door — but Ferrad pulled her by the shoulder.

"No doors," he instructed through his panting. He sprinted to the left of the great hallway, up a section of gardens before the next building. Simone slowed, suddenly overcome by frustration. There was no entrance there – what the *hell* was Ferrad panning on doing?

She ground herself to a halt, almost intent to sprint back to the stage, when she saw Ferrad's plan unfold. Grappling into his connections, and blasting his hands forward, half of the building's wall caved in.

And he did it again to the next wall.

"Great plan!" Simone yelled, sprinting to catch the group. They piled their way through a wake of rubble, rocks thrown aside haphazardly by Ferrad's control over earth and stone. They ran on, through a short garden to the next building. Walls burst, crumpling in before Ferrad as he launched himself through them, explosions of dust clogging halls. Simone stole the sounds of collapsing stone to clear the air, allowing them to see their path.

The fifth wall they crashed through was the last, as the group landed in the lobby – much faster via the direct route.

"Prepare to blast the Salaks," Simone yelled as they charged across the marble floor, towards the hospital-like hallway. Their steps rang, thunderous as an apocalypse, a pack of bulls charging. Simone stole the energy, launching herself feet-first through the doors and into a running land.

There was nobody in sight – only the hallway and the machine in the end room took up her vision. She truly expected at any moment to feel her energy drained – to slow mid-stride, pushing and gasping for movement, but she continued to charge. This was- of course – a trap. She knew it, but had no other option but to run into it. Everything about this situation would *have* to be a trap, because Hesslik and his people weren't idiots.

The three of them burst through the open door to the machine's lab – Ferrad choosing to take the whole plaster wall with him as he shouldered his way through it, casting the room in a spray of dust.

It was in this moment, staring at the glowing, electronic donut, just metres from grasping it, that their energy was robbed of them. Simone, now halted past the doorway with her friends, relinquished her *will* to move. These brothers would get nothing out of her, and she would wait for the perfect moment to surprise them.

"*Don't move…*" She went to advise her friends, but her words were stolen before they rang.

"Welcome back," a familiar voice said – words crawling like crude oil across sea-water. Garbed in black Salak robe, the speaking Salak – the slightly taller of the brothers – peeled himself from the darkest corner of the room. He was joined by an almost identical figure, who appeared from the opposite dark corner, face illuminated by the light of the giant, buzzing donut.

"Yes, hello," Ferrad greeted jovially. "I'm Ferrad, this is Riskidin and Salak Nera."

The brothers gave Ferrad an identical, confused squint.

"Well, it would be *rude* not to introduce yourselves to your guests, no?" Ferrad suggested, an eyebrow raised beneath his helmet.

"I…" the Salak on the right hummed, "you are an odd one."

"I'm not the guy dressed in a black robe squishing myself into dark corners," Ferrad replied simply.

This quip cracked a condescending laugh from the Salak on the left, who's fingers buzzed with electricity. "Fine," he hummed. "I am Salak Festro, this is my brother, Salak Terrak."

"Oh?" Simone sang. "Because in my head, I've been calling you Salak *Dickhead.*"

"Funny," Festro harked with his greasy tongue. "You really are eloquent, aren't you, Nera?"

"Go sit in a dark corner and impress some kids," she spat back. "You're getting in the way of progress for your own, selfish bullshit. You just want to be king in a world of slaves. What happened? Didn't your Mum love you enough?"

Festro chuckled to the accusation, stepping forward with a leisurely, calculated gait. He reached his palm out to caress Simone's chin, and it sparked with liquid electricity. Simone stole his motion, forbidding the contact, and jerked back.

Festro furrowed a mean frown, and ripped an electrical arc from of Simone's kinetic movement, and launched it straight into her neck, his eyes glowing with scornful intent. Simone screamed, but her cry was stolen by the brother, Salak Terrak, whose hands flamed.

"You and me, we're not so dissimilar, Nera," he said, his words slow and enunciated, his voice splitting into its two tones. The flow of charge stopped, and Simone could finally breathe. No longer satisfied with sitting still, she went to move – to lunch for his neck – but her motion was halted. She silenced her will, then moved again, locking her and Festro into a jittering dance.

"Yes, we are," she tried to force out, but only a whisper of her yell could be heard.

"No, you're *just* like me," Festro teased with his demon voice. "We both want something, and we have no qualms about stealing the freedoms of others to get it. What gives you the right, over my brother and I, to steal free will for your own gain?"

"I'm creating fairness and justice," Terrak allowed her to speak. "You're fighting for domination. It's fundamentally different."

"Ah!" Festro raised a finger near her head. She, once again, stopped his hand, and he let an arc of liquid electricity rip across her face. Terrak allowed Simone's scream to ring out this time. It shrieked through the hallways, human, of bloody murder. Simone wanted to slump into the ground, but Festro wouldn't allow her that dignity.

"You hinder me, *Nera*, you will face pain," he sneered. "Now, you see Nera, if your ideology was *so* just, and *so* righteous as you claim, you wouldn't need to steal the free will of others to implement it, would you?" he slicked. "No, if your path was, *truly*, the utilitarian good for society, then nobody would stop you from implementing it." He stepped back, away from her face – although she could no longer bring herself to look at him. "But it's *not* the great path you think it is. It is simply you imposing your own views on everybody else. You're not righteous. You're an idiot."

Simone sniffled, still fighting the pain of the shock. Her body had spasmed, and she was sure she'd been scarred. Her neck and face were hot, burning. The brothers didn't even afford her the dignity of crying – her weak sobs of agony stolen, powering a yellow palm-flame. She tried hard to think of a next movement, but found standing still to be the only action she could imagine.

"Actually, you're wrong," Ferrad spoke. Festro eyed his brother scornfully. "You see, change isn't ubiquitous, because society isn't uniform, and individuals don't always care about the utilitarian good if that good doesn't help them, or if it disproportionately helps others."

"Shut him up!" Festro ordered to his brother in his slimy voice.

"Most people are passive participants in whichever paradigm happens to rule society. They don't quite care to make change. They are doing okay. Other people – leaders, visionaries, and small groups - see brighter futures. The problem is, they're seeing their own bright future, and they don't all agree with each other."

"I'm trying!" Terrak protested.

"So, any shift in paradigm will never satisfy everybody. A lot of people won't care one way or the other, and a minority will be incredibly resentful towards the change, but it will never be a ubiquitously *willed* change. The fact that Simone has a vision which is contested is simply a fact of society. But the change she offers will provide a shift in power, allowing the weak to have stronger voices. It's an inherently equalising paradigm. Making it – on the whole – more ethical."

Festro discharged an arc of electricity straight at Ferrad's helmet. Ferrad did not flinch, he did not yell, he did not react in any way, except to wear the same smile under his helmet. The arcs grounded themselves through his metal leg in a show of sparks and fury.

"Would you *shut up*?" Festro growled.

"Not until you admit that your argument is flawed," Ferrad offered.

"Jesus…" Festro cracked. "Steal his god-damned voice, Terrak!"

"I can't!" Terrak pleaded. "The ribbon is black!"

"*Black?*" Festro quizzed, spinning on his booted heel to face Ferrad. "Quatra powered?"

"Yes!"

"Quatra powered voice…" Festro stepped up to the frozen Suneva of earth. "A Suneva of Sonics. How interesting."

"Thank you," Ferrad smiled.

"It's just a shame that we'll never get to learn about such abilties. Any moment now, Hesslik will push the button on his remote. And, if that fails, we'll just pull the lever," He pointed to a lever on the top left side of the donut. It was long and black, with a great red ball on the end. It looked like it would be a lot of fun to pull.

"Now we wait," Festro smirked, leaning over the machine. "Are we having fun?"

***

Zamelle, Iva and I marched onto the stage from its rear. Hesslik's associates scrambled to the sides, leaping from the platform. Hesslik ordered his guards to lower their weapons, although they remained on edge, ready to fire. Hesslik wore a smug, knowing grin as we approached. He stepped stage left, out of our way and towards his microphone.

Walking onto the stage felt something of a theatre performance. The crowd were enthralled. The golden armour of Kuvalik, which covered my body, glimmered intensely in the sunlight, throwing gleams of golden glow across the audience. There were several cheers from the crowd, but many more stunned faces. Rumbles of "Kuvalik" and "Olomb" were whispered in hushed voices.

I had finally returned to liberate my people; the time was right.

"Ah, Maiki dressed as Kuvalik, thank you for inviting yourself onto the stage," Hesslik greeted sarcastically into a standing microphone. "If you'd like to hand back the White Witch, and get Tona Argol off my stage, I'd kindly appreciate it."

"Your event is impressive, my student," I congratulated him. I stepped up to the main podium, taking charge of the other microphone there. Hesslik gestured a slice of the neck to on off stage technician, hoping to cut my mic.

"I am Kuvalik – Legendary of Teleportation, and once great *Fara* of the electric nation. It is a great day to see the Suneva of the world gathered," I said, and my sound projected down the whole street. Apparently the microphone wasn't cut – at least, not yet.

"Yes, the gathering *I* organised," Hesslik asserted. "The people *I* amassed through massive worldwide reworking of Suneva communities."

"I always believed that the time would come for the Suneva communities to reform," I said. "The Argols did their job to combine people in the time of requirement…"

"A requirement left by your abandonment of the people…" Hesslik interjected.

"So, you do believe that you're talking to Kuvalik now? How interesting," I quipped. I was without the old man's mind, yet I was surprisingly competent in my impersonation of him. Wearing the armour of Kuvalik, with its golden gleam, gave its wearer an innate authority. There was a sense of leadership, determination, and chivalry in its glow.

Hesslik frowned at my quip.

"It is time to create the community that I knew was coming. Hesslik has done a fantastic job gathering the Suneva, but the ideology he presents is at the exclusion of an entire legion of Suneva who he failed to accept or encourage to integrate. What we need is a combination of the Vochduh morals the Empire is built upon, with the rights that the Argols hold dear."

"*They* would have us compromise our ability to fit into society by being stubborn, un-integrating, and needlessly dangerous to life," Hesslik argued into his microphone.

"Excluding them as outsiders has created a rift in the Suneva. We seek to unify, not to divide. We are, however, *all* Suneva. If we are to form a strong community, to create strong guidelines of action, morality, and to generate a cohesive culture and family, we must act cohesively. We must be one family."

"He's deluded," Hesslik stormed his microphone. "We are the future of Suneva right here. There are Argols at the gates *right now* trying to upturn this festival."

"And there are Argols defending it," I added, "working together with Hesslik's guards to hold back a crazed, indoctrinated, and most importantly, *manipulated* individual leader. With one cohesive community, these extremist indoctrinations don't occur. When we welcome all, there is never a reason for somebody to turn away and seek other, nefarious open arms."

"That's it," Hesslik grumbled. He drew his weapon - a long snake of red plasma coalescing from the immediate sparks on the jagged sword. It quivered and cracked with extreme energy. "I've had enough of this. I did not invite a possessed terrorist up to the stage to talk through a dead man's mouth about extremist ideologies. Get off my podium."

Hesslik advanced on me with a whip of hot plasma. The red energy cracked once into the stage – a warning – which cut a clean, glowing line through the metal.

"Hesslik killed Olomb in his impatience, and plans to destroy all of the threads *today*, any minute now," I rushed. "He rewired Vestas' brain for discovering the plot, and murdered Boekidin when he found out. This is not the future you think it is. It's a very short one."

"Lies," Hesslik declared, marching on. "Boekidin died, he was not murdered. Olomb was, like, five-hundred years old. I have done *everything* in good faith, including build a world-wide *free-power* transmitter. This is the gift from Suneva to humanity which will secure us a place in society."

"Don't believe him," Zamelle yelled, rushing forward. "Join us. Fight *now*, or you lose your threads."

Then Iva ran to join her at my podium. Hesslik halted, and gave a hand signal to men on the stage's sides. A hail of quatra bolts were fired, flying our way.

I ducked.

Zamelle spun into action. Her white eye basked the audience in its intense divinity, and she repelled the shots of the ten-or-so shooters, meeting each on-target bolt with one of her own.

"I, Iva Argol, pledge myself to the new coalition," Iva fumbled with her words, and fired a defensive bolt on a guard. I joined in, blasting Kuvalik's purple bolts to the attackers. "I will fight for our rights as a people in the new world."

She was torn from the microphone by the immediate action surrounding us. We were hopelessly cornered, firing bolts at an enemy which seemed to grow. The heil of fire was strategic, forcing us to the back of the stage.

"It's time for the moment, my fellow Suneva, that we give our gift to the world," Hesslik continued, as if his stage wasn't a ludicrous mess.

"*No! Fight!*" Zamelle ordered.

Hesslik produced the fateful remote, holding it and its large, blue button up for all to see. "This is the moment of power. The moment we gain our acceptance. We *will* be ourselves in this new world…"

The firing stopped, suddenly. The guards, who bordered the stage, appeared to slow dramatically. Their faces were determined, but paused.

"Demons?" I yelled.

Then the stage's roof caught alight in dazzling blue fire. A fire so hot, that its core burned invisible.

"*Zirrus?*" Zamelle coughed.

Hesslik had paused, to observe a tall, black and purple Suneva clamber onto his stage, fighting his way out of the audience.

"The Legendary of Time!" I yelled to the crowd.

"Legendary of Time?" Hesslik scoffed. "What is this, a fairytale? You think gathering the White Witch, the Legendaries, and the Shiverman will make these people change sides? You're deluded."

His hand raced for the button.

And then it stopped.

Zirrus growled, holding a field of men and the *Fara Hesslik* near a standstill. His grip on this many people was strained, and he groaned to maintain it.

"Get the device off him!" Zirrus ordered.

"You came to help us?" I asked. "You seemed so…"

"I had to own up," he croaked. "Now get that thing off his hands!"

"How?" I plundered. I swapped out Kuvalik's thread for my own, immediately more comfortable as my usual senses came flooding back to me. This elicited a gasp from the crowd.

"We have taken the basis of Hesslik's ethics system to design our own code of ethics and conduct," Zamelle said, taking the stand as I nervously approached a time bubble. "Maiki, the *Kiin King*, has personally been involved in preserving the system that Olomb tried to implement so long ago – the dream

369

culture, as it were – before social revolutions diluted the Suneva and our awareness."

Zirrus had once told us never to stick any part of one's body into time bubble, lest you wanted your limb ripped off. Heeding his guidance, I formed a long, diamond rod in my hand, and prodded it gently towards Hesslik's frozen grip.

"Iva Argol will help us further to preserve our rights in a world that might not accept us for who we are. It is important not to give up what makes us Suneva in the fight to integrate."

I met resistance as the diamond crossed the threshold. I powered my connection to its atoms, holding their conections and form across the entropy barrier.

"Iva!" I called. "Help me heat up this rod!" She had successfully sped herself up through a time-bubble before, and my mind raced to the conclusion that she could help with it now. Iva sprinted over.

"Unfortunately," Zamelle said, "it might be too late for our vision."

***

"There's trouble," Vestas said, entering the room from the darkened, back entrance. He paused in surprise at the sight of hostages. "Oh…" he huffed, "hello Lion's Foot."

"Hi boss," Ferrad cheerfully replied.

"There's trouble, boys," Vestas continued. "Maiki and friends assaulted the stage. Then the *Legendary of Time* showed up. Apparently Kuvalik might also be the Legendary of Teleportation. Many witnesses say they saw him coalesce from nothing with the White Witch and Iva Argol."

"What's the trouble?" Salak Terrak asked. "Why doesn't Hesslik just push the button?"

"He's caught in a time bubble," Vestas said.

"Of course," Festro nodded, and jogged over to the lever.

"*No!*" Simone, Ferrad, Riskidin *and* Vestas cried.

Everybody stared pointedly at Vestas.

"That's not the only trouble," he said. "Somebody has tampered with the code. It's going to send the thread-destruction signal global! It will be a disaster. And, for once, I think the lot of you…" he pointed to my friends, "aren't behind it."

"Oh no, they're innocent," Festro waved a wrist, flinging his hand for the lever casually.

But his grip didn't make it.

There was a loud crash of metal on stone, as he, Terrak, and Vestas found themselves flung sideways, falling towards the left wall of the room. Salak Terrak clawed for the lever as he passed, but missed it as Simone finally found her senses, and stole the reach of his arm. Vestas tumbled along the floor, before landing in a pile atop of the two Salak on the left wall. Somehow, Festro kept his grip on his energy ribbons firm, holding the supressed wills of Ferrad and Riskidin tight.

A new figure walked into the room, dragging their hand along the floor, gripping hard at their element. Tall, attractive in the most unique of ways, and with a scarred burn down her neck. In her hand she held a great, bronze hammer of a *shath*. Ferrad's eyes glistened.

"*Master!*" he yelled. "I mean...babe!"

"*Amalie?*" Yvon cocked his head. "*You're* Vectra?"

"Vectra?" Simone yelped. "You're going out with the Suneva of Gravity?" And she eyed Ferrad sharply. He managed a shrug, despite the pull on his movements.

"Big, important secret to keep," he said.

Amalie let her armour flow over her body, becoming Vectra. The form was similar to Iva's, but with bronze and white plating covered in zebra striping. She intensified her hold on the Salaks and Vestas, who groaned and writhed under her grip.

"How did you find us?" Simone asked.

"I gave my man an infused stone a long time ago. It's how I always find him," she said, then turned her attention to the enemy. "You crossed the wrong group. That lever is *not* getting pulled."

***

Iva heated the rod, and I held its structure. The atoms were begging to become plasma, trying to break free, to do *anything* but stay in a lattice. I used quatra to deliver them order.

Slowly, I pushed the rod further into the bubble, towards the device. Zirrus strained under the effort. Tops of buildings had set alight in an incredible display of the transfer of entropy. The air around us was heating, bubbling dangerously. I was afraid that the time-bubbles themselves might heat beyond their usefullness, allowing Hesslik to act.

Even still, Hesslik's finger was moving now, slowly but surely.

Finally the rod touched. It transferred heat immediately to the plastic casing, melting the device and throwing it into semi-real time. The remote jumped away from the hot rod, across Hesslik's fingers.

And it settled, teetering on the edge of Hesslik's hand. I panicked.

"You!" I yelled to an audience member, looking him directly in the eyes. He glanced about himself, stunned that I'd summoned him. "What's your name?"

"Stephen," he answered.

"Stephen, can you catch the device? It's going to fall."

"I..." Stephen stammered. He found himself being thrown over the barrier by his friends, and he scrambled up onto the stage, squatting below Hesslik's hands.

"Whatever you do, *don't* push the button," I warned.

The device made its last nudge. It fell over the edge.

It spun towards Stephen's nervous hands, tumbling over itself in song, a dangerous dancer.

Stephen caught it, fumbling momentarily, fingers churning about the button. They grazed its surface, threatening to push. I gasped.

Then the man found his grip firmly on the sides. He whooped, raising it to the air in a cheer. The crowd roared.

***

Salak Festro clawed his hand from the ground, which rippled with electrical arcs, sparks flying off like water from a fountain.

Then the arcs ceased, and he gripped at a new element, one that neither Simone, nor my friends, could have guessed that he controlled. He let his hand slump, driven into to the ground.

With it, telekinetically controlled, the lever clunked down.

Chapter 35
Day of the Black Suns: Part III

A scream tore through the crowd like a wave, crashing into all the amassed Suneva at once. Thread death, on a global scale. Those more connected in the audience wailed, stabbed through the hearts and hands.

My spine was yanked from my body, twice. Two whole sets of bones ripped out of a tiny tear in the skin. A whole network of senses hacked from my fingertips, inverting my hands, degloving them, and towing the skin out through my neck.

I, along with everybody else in the street, slumped to the floor, groaning. Voices started moaning, then crying, and shouting, as realisation hit.

Hey...I'm alive, A voice stammered in my head. It was the voice of Boekidin.

What? How? I asked groggily, still perplexed in a sensory daze.

My thread wasn't connected to anything, was it? he asked smugly. I would have replied, but a scream broke my concentration.

"I...ah!" Stephen shouted, dropping the device. "What have I done? Oh god, you said not to..."

"Calm," I grabbed his shoulders, standing. His frightened, scarred eyes met mine. "That wasn't you. There was an external switch."

"How do you know?" he whimpered.

"Nobody pressed the button," I said to him. "You didn't press it."

I jumped up, running to the microphone.

"For what it's worth," I said to the crowd. "Stephen didn't push the button. There was a switch on the device in Hesslik's castle. It was a failsafe."

My next thought was to Natalie, my blind girlfriend. I whirred my head around the stage. It was littered with bodies – those of guards and friends, sprawled on the ground, moaning.

Amongst them I found Natalie. Unlike the deposed and devastated who composed the floor around us, she was standing and silent. Her greyed eyes were wide with awe, pointed towards the sky.

"Natalie!" I ran up to her. "Natalie, are you okay? Aren't you hurt?"

She was wordless.

"Oh my...oh my," a voice whined. I twisted to the source, to see a young woman wrestle the device from Stephen's hands. Pretty face falling to disgust – an enraged regret – she took the remote and threw it to the floor, then smashed it with a booted foot. The woman turned to me, their chestnut hair twisted about their face.

"James Grey, what the hell did I do?"

"Who the hell are you?" I quizzed, spinning to the rest of the stage. Nobody else seemed to find this woman's existence, nor aknowledgement of my name, surprising.

"Hesslik?" They waved their hand over their face, giving me a dumb look.

"Hold up…you're Hesslik?" I coughed. "A young woman."

How the hell didn't I see that? Boekidin quizzed. *I was in their head for well over a week.*

"Why does that surprise you?" she asked.

"Because…I don't know." I crumpled my brow. "Everybody called Hesslik *him*, and *he*. Even Boekidin's confused. I just didn't think…"

Her face went red. "Hesslik *is* a man, but I'm not. That makes sense, right?"

"Sure," I shrugged. "I can deal with that – not that it matters anymore."

"You still…why did I do this?" she asked, her face red, distressed again.

"You were possessed," Celeste cut in, her voice groaning. She peeled herself from the stage. "Your mind had been conquered."

"But, I mean, I wanted this, right?" Hesslik asked, desperate, clawing at herself. She huddled close to Celeste and I. "The ethics should have worked…but they didn't, right? What else were we supposed to do?"

"Stuck it through," I said, squirming away from the crazed woman. "You should have built your Empire on your laurels, and dealt with problems as they arose."

"It's too late now, though," Celeste grumbled.

"I can't believe it," the girl said, panting, realisation crashing into her. "I can't believe I actually did it. Now it's over…"

"It's not over," Natalie spoke. We snapped around, turning to the blind girl who was about to walk off the stage.

"Ah!" I gasped and sprinted to her side, holding her back as she stretched towards the edge. Natalie resisted my touch, reaching beyond the stage with a long, extended arm, grasping for something I couldn't see.

Her fingers twiddled in the air, gaining for extra length. I gave in, lifting her forward, over the stage's lip. Her hand grasped at nothing, but in her grip appeared a glowing, holy light.

"Woah…" I gaped, stepping back, setting her down on the stage. Natalie's hand was hot with light, which she held to the sky, white brilliance creeping from between her fingers. "What is it?"

A silence rapt the audience, who had also turned to marvel at the the White Witch. In her hand, she appeared to hold some undead aspect of divinity.

"Hesslik…" Natalie called, not turning her head, unable to see.

"It's *Helena*," she said, gulping. "My name is Helena."

"You're a girl?" Natalie quizzed. "Well, anyway, *Helena*, pass me a thread removal device."

"What are you holding?" Helena asked.

"My thread," Natalie said. "I'm holding my thread. You can't see *all* of this?" And she threw her free hand before her, into the atmosphere of disappointment, awe, and loss which hung above the audience.

"See all of what?" I asked.

"The sea of souls," Natalie said, her skin flushing with goosebumps. "All of the threads in the world, just hanging here. Thousands of lights in a black sea. More vibrant than a night sky. A milky way of threads just *here*, and you can touch them. You guys can't see this?"

"No…" I said, staring out to the sky.

"Aren't you blind?" Helena asked.

"What will a thread-remover do?" Celeste quizzed.

"Run it backwards," Natalie instructed. "I can feel what's missing in my thread. It's missing its *buzz*. It's missing the part that makes it a connected thread."

"Clearly…" somebody squirming on the floor noted. We didn't pay them attention.

"I…I'll have to get Vestas out here to run it backwards," Helena said. "Only he can reprogram with his hands like that. We didn't make them re…" her face dropped to a frown. "He can't control electricity anymore," she pondered, chin deep in her han. Then an idea sparked. Helena jogged to the podium, tapping the microphone. Its awkward screech echoed through the street. She winced, then leaned into it.

"Hello," she greeted the crowd. "Just me, *Fara Hesslik*. It appears that our friends here, whose efforts I have spent vast resources combatting, were right about one thing: my plans for today's festival had been compromised, and likely were for a long while. I will launch a full investigation into the matter." She paused, nodding back to us. "Now, will anybody be the day's saviour and help the White Witch? Has anybody got one of the *really old* issue thread removers?" she asked to

375

the crowd. Those in the street who weren't wailing in grief and pain were surprisingly silent. "You know, the *super* old ones, the first ones I produced? The ones where you have to enter the formula? Nobody can help the White Witch?"

People rustled in the audience, but no civilians would realistically have that device. Helena scratched her chin again, turning to the guards about the stage. She stepped over to a man who lay stage right of the podium, and fell to her knees at his side. Helena shoved her hand inside the holster which hung from the man's jeans. From it she produced a large, clunky device with two prongs.

"Old issue holster," she explained, before we could ask. "Made for bigger devices." And she jogged it over to Natalie, who stood mystically, glowing orb in palm. Helena fiddled with the device.

"What you're asking for is the *opposite* of this equation, right?" Helena asked.

"I think so," Natalie said.

"You don't want it backwards? You want it flipped, right?"

"I guess," Natalie agreed. "Give me the *opposite* in magnitude, not time."

"Good," Helena smiled, "that's easy."

She fiddled with the screen, then pressed a hidden button on the device's underside which caused a miniature keyboard to flip out on a lid.

"Woah, look at that!" I uttered to Celeste. I'd never seen anything like it.

Helena played with the keyboard, then closed the device, handing it to Natalie.

"Reversed the signs," she said, and placed the black brick in Natalie's free palm. Helena, however, refused to let go, her grip lingering as she turned to Celeste and I.

"If this works," she said, "then I sign myself over to your coalition."

"What?" the three of us asked in unison.

"You need me for this to work," Helena said. "You might have a big chunk of the Argols and my supporters who would follow you, but you don't have everybody. You want unity of the Suneva? Have me as a founding member. You'll have your unity in my loyal followers, trust me."

Celeste and I stared at each other for a moment, not sure what to say. If Natalie had eyes that could see, I was sure she'd be sharing the same glances.

"We'll talk about this later," I said, "I'm sure you've just lost a *lot* of public support for *this*." I gestured to the crowd of disheartened, soul-dead ex-Suneva. Helena grinned, releasing the device.

"You leave the explaining to me," she said. "I'm going to need everything you and your friends know about today, but I will conduct a thorough investigation as to what has transpired here, for the people." She winked, and stepped aside of Natalie. I shuddered.

"You *are* right, though," I agreed. "This *will* work better with your support."

Celeste nodded, although I could tell it pained her to agree with anything the former Hesslik had to say.

"We can't deny that you've got a way for bending truths, Helena," Natalie agreed. "Now to see if this works. Wish me luck."

In her left hand, she held her thread, the magical light of its orb squeezing through her fingers, radiating its divinity. Slowly, she reached around her head, and held it to the most pointed bone at her neck's base. Fumbling blindly for the button on the thread-device, she raised it to the same place, holding both tight to her spine.

Natalie pushed the trigger.

***

The room was silent, bar the screaming. Suneva had fallen to the floor, but Simone remained standing, unaffected, teeth gritted. In the commotion, Salak Festro had lapsed his concentration, and she lunged at him.

Vestas, a middle aged-man, clawed his way out of the pile of Sunesca. His face a mess of tears, he fell onto his machine, flinging the lever back to *off*, switching it to-and-fro in desperation. Finally, he switched it into full-off, and broke the lever from its hinge, lobbing it across the laboratory.

Simone lunged on the Salak brothers, and she kicked Festro straight in the face. Overcome with rage, her eyes glowed a serious red. Hot like magma.

His nose bled, and he coughed loudly, flailing. His arms reached, retching. Finally, on the next blind kick, he got purchase on Simone's foot, and he leveraged all of his weight to throw her to the floor.

Simone's head smacked against the stones, and her brain swam in the echo of her collision, her vision running. The world seemed to grow distant, falling away from her through a tunnel. The whole thing was fading to black, clinging onto a comfortable, soft breath.

Festro stumbled to his feet, his bloody head swaying against the castle wall. His frown turned to a sick grin as he lunged forward with his fist, straight towards Simone.

Adrenaline kicked into her system, grinding her woozy vision into grainy clarity. Simone was sure she was dying, falling through the tunnel, but suddenly it didn't seem so likely. Foremost in her vision were ribbons of red kinetic energy, streaming from the attacking Salak.

She channelled them through her palms, converting them in her soul to align her will with the will of the air around her. This was a technique I'd tried to teach her, which had only connected to her mind in this moment of conscious crisis.

The resulting blast was so intensely powerful, that Festro was instantly blown backwards through the sky, crashing into the roof before dropping to the floor with a sickening thud. His brother rushed to his aid.

"Come on, you," Chad said to Simone, jostling his arms between her armpits and lifting her slowly from the ground. "Before they stop us."

"Huh?" Simone groaned. She could hardly comprehend what was happening through the spinning haze of her mind.

Chad slung Simone's left half around Amalie's shoulder, and took her right side on his. With Yvon jogging up the rear, they fast-walked themselves down the corridors of Hesslik's castle.

"Where…where are we going?" Simone moaned.

"Into the new world," Chad said.

"No…really," Simone implored. She passed under the black marble statue in Hesslik's lobby. Her frazzled brain marvelled at its size.

"I'll call Argol, see if he can tell us the plan," Chad said. "We'll go into town, get you to a doctor – do something responsible."

Simone's boggled head had to agree with Chad. That would be a good idea.

***

The crowd was hushed, even those groaning had stopped to watch the White Witch, as she held divinity and destruction in her opposing palms, pressed tightly to her neck. She pulled the trigger.

The device buzzed, a shock running across her spine. She yelped, fumbling forward, her eyes closed. The light extinguished from her hand. In a blink, I swore that I saw it shatter to dust, rising in the wind. I ran to grab her as she stumbled to catch herself from falling.

I grasped Natalie's arm in mine, but she found her footing in the same moment. I let go, and she stood tall, her spine straight and stiff. She pointed her head to the sky, and opened her eyes.

They burned with white light.

It cast wide onto the street, pure white, depriving the darkest corners of the city's shadows. Men and women shielded their faces, peeking from beneath raised arms at the beams of salvation which poured from her soul. One man at the back started to cheer, and then another joined, whooping. The joy spread, rippling through the street festival. A thunderous applause rose, drowning the dread, lifting the shadows from the dank corners. It echoed through the city, bathing Thessaloniki in a roaring stormwall of sound.

Natalie closed her eyes, breathing deeply. She let her heartrate settle, before stepping up to the podium.

"If you can see the sea of souls above your head, you can grab your thread and those of your friends," she advised. "We can take back our souls, but I'll need all the witches who can see and grab the souls, and all thread-devices we can find. Hesslik has agreed to join our coalition. Let us welcome ourselves to the new Suneva era."

Episode 6

In the Face of Victory

"Hesslik has joined your coalition?" a voice raged in the near crowd. From the stage we could see a distressed man with fire-red hair barging his way through the mess, creating a wake of bodies. Riding behind it was Adam Leroux, running to catch him.

Michael Richard pounced onto the stage, storming straight for *me*. Confused, I tried to leap from his path, but he lunged, grappling my waist and throwing me to the floor. I hit on my shoulder with a hard thud, feeling a pang of pain as the healed muscle groaned.

Natalie held an open palm to his torso. Michael stiffened to a halt, hands in the air, before reasoning that she clearly wasn't a Suneva – despite the white-light spectacle – and didn't pose a threat. He scoffed, and yanked a pistol from his trench jacket.

"Woah!" I yelled. "*Cheese*, no need for that!"

Micahel swung the weapon's end towards my face. Instinctively I cowered, and he grinned, letting the barrel rest there, before shifting to aim it at Helena and Natalie, then finally Celeste.

"How *fucking* dare you," Michael scorned. "You just ran the Suneva into the ground, you stupid, selfish *bitch*." He stormed towards Celeste Leroux. Natalie blasted a bolt of white quatra towards his advance, and it tore through the weapon he held, obliterating its contents down to the handle. Celeste screamed, throwing herself to the floor. The bullet did not fire.

Michael growled, and turned to Natalie. "It was *you* wasn't it?" he raged. "This was meant to be *my* day! I was destined to lead the Suneva into this new world. Amasos told me! They pushed me to head the Argols. The plan was right."

"You made a deal with the God who set this all up," Natalie said plainly. "Be thankful that you weren't possessed. Many were."

"Give me back my thread, you stupid girl!" he ordered. The stage ground silent, uneasy glances falling between each set of eyes.

"You guys don't *possibly* think he deserves his thread, right?" Helena asked.

"Do you deserve yours?" Celeste asked, shooting a seriously scornful look. Helena appeared confused, more than anything.

"We don't have a framework to say *which* actions deserve a loss of a thread," I added. "I don't think we can afford to discriminate. It would be unfair. Not until we define this coalition's rules."

Celeste and Helena grunted, but Natalie smiled.

"If you can find a witch who can see the sea of souls, and find a reprogrammable device, you're more than welcome to your thread, Mr Richard," Natalie said. "I've got a lot to re-attach here before I move anywhere."

Michael grunted. His eyes, although missing Suneva flame, still carried a regular dirty scornfulness. He trudged off the stage, brushing past Adam Leroux, who came to join us. Adam handed me his mobile phone.

"Chad called for you," he said, "and he wants to know what the plan is now."

"Thank you," I nodded. I took the device.

***

We walked through the castle halls at the set of night, all exhausted from a day of returning threads to citizens. There would, of course, be more tomorrow, and likely for a long while to come.

I had teleported us here – although it was harder to do than I had experienced the first time. Kuvalik's thread seemed to resist me, where it hadn't before. I had taken the burden of carrying it again, as I couldn't have just left it in the Thessalonian streets.

I also didn't mind the concept of teleportation, nor learning how to use it properly.

"I'll put thread-attachers into production," Helena said as we scaled the main hall. She had already pushed out the alert on her channels for Suneva to mark the point where they had lost their thread, and to find an accomplished witch to help reattach it.

Natalie had to be dragged from the stage and be forced towards the castle. She had spent her entire afternoon sifting through the masses with witches and reprogrammed devices, reattaching the threads of the fortunate. Of course, all the Suneva of the whole world were perhaps too many threads to reconnect as a single witch. This was where Helena's expertise for global operations was useful. It became quickly apparent, even just from the way that she held herself and commanded respect, that she would be important for the success of the coalition.

Simone, Yvon, Chad, and Amalie had joined us, and told their story.

"I can't believe that *Amalie* was the mysterious *Master*," I commented. "I thought we'd lost the Legendaries, really."

"You never convinced Nick, but you had me," Amalie said. "I just didn't want to be directly involved, not after Hesslik captured me." She turned a greasy glance towards Helena, who either didn't see it or chose not to acknowledge it.

"I thought I was doing the right thing for what I saw as the utilitarian good for Suneva," Helena said, formally. "I'm sorry you got caught up in my plan."

Amalie didn't take this to be much on an apology. She grumbled, stepping back to her sister.

We soon reached the lobby, where Boekidin had chased me during my first heist here. Then, from there, Helena walked us towards the laboratory, through the double door and hospital-hallway.

At the end of the hall, in a room whose walls had been blown open, a slim man with a balding head worked on a device. He jumped at the sight of us, using his body to shield the machine.

"Who are you?" he demanded as we approached. Helena let herself slip into the armour of Hesslik. The transformation didn't appear as strange as I thought it would. She was a tall woman already, and her long, chestnut hair streamed into the helmet as it formed over her head. Still, I couldn't help but feel in danger.

"It's just me, Vestas."

"You're a woman?" he asked. Hesslik sighed.

"Why is *that* the biggest question of today?" Hesslik huffed. "I should be glad that the attention is diverted to *that* of all things, anyway."

"What's happening here?" Vestas asked. "Why are they all walking *with* you."

"We're forming a coalition, under Kuvalik and the White Witch," Hesslik told him, before letting his armour slip back off, becoming Helena once more. Their voice shifted in pitch during the transformation – although Helena seemed to talk in a deeper register than most women anyway. "I'm here to investigate what happened. Simone, Chad, Yvon and...the Legendary of Gravity, here, are witnesses. What can *you* tell me that happened?"

Natalie hummed before Vestas could speak. She walked up to him, in his position guarding the machine, and touched a hand to the back of his neck. She nodded to herself, before prancing gracefully into the room. Vestas regarded her with confusion and suspicion, his body stiff.

"Salak Festro did it, I think," Vestas said. "I trusted him with the machine, and when I came back, it had the code for thread removal in it.

"When I came out here to tell him so, he didn't deny knowing about it, so I found myself siding with these four…" he pointed to those of my friends who had been in the castle.

"Ah," Helena said, and turned to us, sharing a sly look, "so, you're saying that Festro was the one to input the code into the machine." She turned to us, grinning. I wasn't sure how to respond to the connotation. "When did you first notice the code?"

"I checked the machine two hours before firing," Vestas said. The lab was suddenly thrown into a teal, glowing light. Natalie held the orb of Vestas' thread in her palm. She walked over to the scientist. "It didn't have any code in it then, and myself and the Sunesca were the only people in the castle for those hours. I don't believe it was this group here who did it, either. I think they actually had good intentions."

"And it wouldn't have been his brother, Salak Terrak?"

"Excuse me for suggesting it," Vestas prefaced his next claim, hand to his heart. "But Terrak was fine in the head. Festro was demonstrably sociopathic."

"I see," Helena smiled.

Natalie sidled up behind Vestas, and without so much as a warning, stuffed both the held thread and the reattachment device to his neck. She pulled the trigger.

Armour immediately flung itself around his body, and he gasped in shock, stumbling from his machine. Vestas was quick to regain himself, comfortable in his armoured body.

"Thank you, Tona Menas," he said to Natalie. "What…what equation was that?"

"The regular one, just inverted," Helena answered.

"About which axis?" he asked.

"Amplitude," Helena said. "I just made the signs negative."

"Oh…" Vestas' face turned to a sudden shock, "but some of those terms…" he worried, "some of those terms weren't for the thread removal. They were stabilisers. And the shifting constants would have done best left as positive, because…"

"It worked, didn't it?" Helena said.

"Yes," he admitted, "but I'll need to fix it before you start doing it en masse. You can't just zap any old signal across a thread. You don't know what it'll do."

"Where did Festro go?" Simone asked Vestas, shifting the focus. His face fell to concern as he eyed her, trying not to focus on the electric scar which hugged her face and neck.

"His brother scooped him up and took him away. After how you left his face, I could only assume he took him to a hospital," Vestas put out a casual shoulder, leaning on the device. "Now, I'm no medical expert – although I am a doctor in thermophysics, an electrical engineer, and a quatra scientist – but hospital is probably your next destination. You took a very serious hit to the head."

"We took her just before," Chad said. "They admitted us, she's alright."

"I gave her a healing stone, too," Amalie said, producing a veiny, white rock from her backpack. It glowed with pinkish quatra. Simone and Vestas shared a cynical sneer.

"Oh well, not a day to be refuting witchcraft, I'd say," Vestas shrugged off his attitude, thumb pointed to Natalie. Simone nodded her own shrug, and palmed her stone tightly, which lived now in the pocket of her black jeans.

Natalie then grabbed my hand and pulled me away from the group. Nobody seemed to care as we snuck out – even though Natalie was yet to reconnect the threads here – as Helena opened another line of investigation to the witnesses of Festro's actions.

"I want to show you something," she said, and led me through the lobby, down one of the entrances I'd not ventured. After a small, glass hallway through the gardens, we arrived in the church-like dining room. From there, she led me through the cloisters, and into what was left of her dormitory.

My blood still lined the windowsill. I coughed at the sight of it, peering to my hand, which had recovered remarkably well through my singular trip to the Void. So well, in fact, that I hadn't felt it hurt at all today. I had scars across my palm now, though.

Natalie released my hand, skipping over the debris towards her nightstand. I wearily followed, carefully lifting my feet past broken bricks, glass, and chunks of sharp wood.

She picked up the pot plant that rested atop her bedside table, and I was surprised not to have noticed it until now. The plant in the small, clay pitcher was mesmerising. An enchanted tulip, of purple-pink colouration. It glistened, even without light. I'd once drank its tea.

"Omercronius!" I gawked, and she handed me the pot with a smile. "How did you get this?"

"I pushed past the compulsions," she said. "It was the first time I was lucid to the fact I was being controlled. I saw this plant atop the spire, and it seemed to connect me to you, and then I knew I had to save part of it."

"I can't believe it. Thank you," I said, putting the plant aside to hug her.

"You kept me going through the possessions," Natalie admitted. Her palms found my face, and they caressed it. "I'm sorry that I destroyed the Vochduh texts."

"I'm sorry that you had to fall into possession three times," I said, "but it all worked out. I'm glad it came together like this."

She smiled deeply, her cheeks becoming rosy. That always warmed me.

Chapter 37
The Return of the First Lost

Adam Leroux welcomed us to his house in Marseille. It had been a long week spent in Thessaloniki and Athens, helping Suneva find, and be connected to, their threads.

During that week, Simone and I stopped by the Vochduh temple to check on Anastasiya – who we came to the realisation that we'd stranded on the stone ledge of the city for a couple of days. When we arrived, however, she was gone. Salak Kallid explained how, once the demons realised we weren't returning, they'd thrown her off the edge of the cliff and gorged on the energy of her fall. According to them, she landed safely and ran off, and that was all we needed to know.

Through Hesslik's empire website, and whichever Argol communication channels that Celeste could command, the story of Festro's betrayal was spread. The official story, typed up by Simone, stated that Salak Festro was recruited by Amasos – with whom he communicated through possessed Amasosian Suneva – to destroy the Suneva and frame Hesslik for the atrocity. The report warned of the dangers of destiny through reconnection, and outlined the coalition's policies towards freedom of will, and how all Suneva should expect to have their free will restored soon. Designing a system to save all of the souls from their respective void-seas was *not* something I was looking forward to.

Adam invited the whole group of us to his house – Helena, Natalie, Celeste, Chad, Amalie, Simone, Yvon, Boekidin, and myself. We climbed the stairs to the top floor of the three-story, terraced home, at the head of which rested Argol's study, and behind that, his bedroom. Natalie peered around the space with her quatra sight, and eventually settled on Naxaer Argol's thread with a glowing grin.

"Here it is, found it again," she said, reaching up to the corner above Adam's computer. Seeing her struggle, Chad made his way over, and lifted her up and onto his shoulders. From the new height, Natalie stretched easily the corner of the room. She plucked the thread, and its greenish glow seeped from the cracks in her fingers.

"I said I'd get this back for you eventually, didn't I, Mr Leroux?" Natalie asked, and he nodded, his face a painting of elation. Adam's eyes followed the faintly glowing orb with ecstasy, and he picked the reattachment device from Helena's hands himself, putting it to his neck.

"I hope we don't have too many hard feelings, Naxaer," Helena said, to which Argol had no response but to roll his eyes over her. He pulled the trigger as soon as Natalie had the thread to his neck, and his soul was immediately ignited. Green flames spittled from his fingers' tips.

"We have hard feelings," he said to Helena, and sighed from his nose. "But a lot of people have hard feelings with me, too. When your decisions affect people's lives, you get used to not being liked. You've got to live with that." And Adam patted her on the shoulder, as if soothing a confused child. Turning from her, he reached for Natalie and drew her into a hard embrace.

"I know none of you like the idea of destiny," he said, releasing the blind girl and gesturing to us all, "but I'm glad that it introduced me to a group of such determined, exceptional young Suneva. I was beginning to doubt the strength of the community, but you bought me back my daughters and reminded me what was important. Thank you."

***

Adam and Juliette took Chad and Amalie out for lunch at their favourite spot in the city. Chad was acutely aware of the luncheon's purpose: the famous *'what is your purpose with my daughter'* talk. I could only imagine that Yvon had gone through similar, although I didn't want to ask - such a line of questioning could bring on anxiety in any young man.

Celeste, Natalie, Helena and I were gathered around Adam's study desk, where Yvon hunched over a large piece of butcher's paper. He had in his hands a collection of coloured pencils and markers to jot down our ideas – we were prepared to design the name and logo of our new coalition. Simone sat nearby on Adam's personal computer, updating Hesslik's site, converting it into the coalition's broadcast and information destination.

"Okay," Celeste started, "clearly, we're not calling it *The Empire of the Black Suns.*" This was met with universal nodding, apart from Helena, whose discontent shone in her near offence. She spoke up.

"It's a reputable name," she argued.

"Yes, the society in which everybody had their thread removed."

"In an *explained* attempt of espionage," Helena rebutted, but nobody responded to her plea.

"We're not exactly about *the Black Suns* anymore though, are we?" I questioned. "I mean, we are refuting destiny, and all. Maybe it should be more about the people?"

"The Empire of the Black Sun *People?*" Helena suggested, but we all shook our heads. Yvon tapped his pencil and stroked his chin-shadow.

"Forget the *Empire* part," Yvon said, "that's like, the bad guys in a fantasy story." We all nodded, Helena reluctantly. "And forget the *of* part. We're not an Empire *of* people, we're a Coalition *for* them. That's much more inviting."

"Yes, that's really good," I said, patting his shoulder. "You're good at this."

"Thanks," he said, blushing. "I try."

Why not 'The Coalition for Suneva? Boekidin suggested to me. *That's nice and simple.*

"Oh," I smiled, "*I* just had a great idea…"

Hey… Boekidin whined.

"Why not…" I set my hands before me, creating tension. "The Coalition for Suneva?" I waited with a large smile and wide eyes, wiggling my eyebrows up and down. It didn't quite catch on.

You deserved that reaction, Boekidin grumbled.

"I'll do you better," Yvon said, and started to sketch. He outlined the mark of the black sun – a perfect replica only from his memory. "Make it simpler, nobody likes a long name." Yvon then outlined four circles surrounding the mark, just off the corner of each quadrant, then a larger circle around the whole drawing. His arm then raced back and forth across the picture, filling the space inside the large circle between the shapes with black marker. When he was done, he held it up for all to see.

"Why not, *The Suneva Coalition*," he said, admiring his work.

"That's a good name," Natalie agreed. "The drawing, though, I'd have no idea."

"Why the four circles?" Celeste asked, pointing to the white dots about the mark. "I thought we just agreed that the black holes were out."

"They're not black holes," Yvon clarified. "They're the four ideologies of the Coalition. Maiki's Vochduh ethics, Kuvalik's Liktan culture, Iva's Argolian rights, and the White Witch's spirituality."

"Ah," We all exhaled in resounding admiration, except for Helena, of course.

I can already see Hesslik having a problem with... Boekidin started, but was cut off by Helena.

"I'm not sure I like that bottom bit." She pointed to the tail of the black sun mark, which was excluded from the circle and coloured black. This started a heated debate, on whether the stylistic choice to colour part of the Mark black was more importat than the superstition regarding the shading of spiritual symbols.

Simone didn't have an ear for it. She sat on the computer, reworking the face of Hesslik's website. Helena had expected that Simone could re-write the damn servers, but she was no *Tom*. Simone knew HTML code, and that was it. That's how she got Fairysmog's blog up and running.

With half an ear, she heard the new name being decided upon, and typed it into a line of code for the webpage title. *The Suneva Coalition*, the title read, in a futuristic, italic font. She smiled, opening another piece of code. Soon they'd have to draw the logo digitally and upload it.

Simone watched the number of readers fluctuate. The current front screen article – that of Hesslik's investigation and of the Coalition's base promises, was gaining a staggering number of views. The popularity could only be explained by a high human viewership, not just visiting Suneva.

Sceptical, she opened a new tab, and loaded the infamous paranormal investigation site that she had built and moderated for many years. Simone logged on as Fairsmog.

She had promised Celeste, quite a while ago now, to use her leverage to sway the opinions here towards the Suneva. She'd forgotten to do it, having focussed on her journey into a Salak, and wished now that she'd given it time.

Hesslik's article was linked as the header to every thread, with hundreds of heated discussions being bumped onto the front page.

Simone opened one, but reading the responses of these close minded, fear-driven idiots made her blood boil. The range of responses was surprisingly diverse, but overwhelmingly unsympathetic. She grew frustrated at her own complacency in abandoning this community to its own ends. That had been a massive oversight – one which Anastasiya had also called her out on. Simone gritted her teeth to it - worst of all, she had created this place.

Simone could just shut it down, the thought came to her, but it was immediately dismissed. Destroying this place would only force the bubble of hatred operate elsewhere – somewhere where she couldn't monitor or control it. This was the problem with the internet, she realised. In the real word, a Salak could censor people's movements, their voices, and their image. On the internet, Simone had no power to make things her way. This was deeply ironic, she laughed to herself, attracting attention from the room, as this site *was* her expression of power and freedom for so long.

"I'm laughing at a memory," Simone had to awkwardly explain to me and the group. We then diverted our attention, to continue our argument with Helena about the specifics of blasphemous Suneva symbols, and why they didn't matter in the new world.

Then something caught Simone's attention, a pop-up window came to her screen – a message from an instant chat, the kind she didn't remember programming into the site the last time it happened. The message was, again, from Anderson.

I trust you've seen the news of the Coalition, and the survival of the Suneva, Anderson's message began. *I suppose we should be glad that the Festro guy didn't succeed, he seems more dangerous than the Suneva.* Simone grumbled, realising that this community's opinion of Sunesca must be even lower than that of Suneva, now.

I would like to formally offer you a place in what's to come. The Suneva have defeated destiny, and are adamant to be a part of the world, this means that they can and will run wild. If they want to live with us, it's time that we developed the technology to make the world an even playing field. The data I stole on New Years have helped me to design a few pieces of equipment you might find interesting. They're only ideas now, but with your help, could become reality.

Will you help me usher the start of the New World?

Simone closed the tab immediately without logging out. She finished her changes on the newly christened Coalition website, and shut down the computer. Her eyes were drawn wide.

She turned to us, to warn us of something ominous to come, but saw our faces. We were joyful, yet argumentative, gathered around the flag and logo of our making. The new Coalition was exciting. We had hope for it, strewn into our passion, visible on our faces.

Simone decided not to tell us – not to ruin our mood. She shuffled across the room, towards the stairs.

"Where are you off to, Simone?" I asked.

"The website's done, for now," she said, her voice gravelly. "You just need to upload your logo into a small enough file. I'm going for a walk."

"Thank you," Helena smiled.

"Stay safe," Celeste said, waving with a smile.

"I will," Simone agreed, and trudged her way down the stairs, feeling the darkness of guilt surround her. Would these crazy zealots have existed if she hadn't created a platform for them to congregate? Had she caused the demise of our Coalition before it even began?

Simone stepped out the front door of the Argol household, into the shining midday sun of late spring. She felt the light on her skin, and around her body. It bounced between the molecules of air she could sense. It warmed her. It was hopeful, inspiring.

So she stole its energy, absorbing it into her exhaust. Her skin turned to midnight, the surrounding air cooling to black smoke - dancing as spiralling, radial tentacles to her body. She pulled the hood of her Salak robe over her head.

And Simone bounded into the city.

Chapter 38
The Return to Home

I put on my finest shirt. It was crisp, floral, mainly pink, and fit too tightly to be the shirt of any self-respecting young man. I pulled off a shark-tooth necklace under the collar – a token I'd picked up from Natalie's Mum in the few times I'd seen her.

Natalie liked this shirt, anyway. She could feel my body under it, and according to her – she once told me whilst biting her lip, that was the most important measure of its utility. I'd wear it every day just to hear her say *that* again.

"James, I…" Mum barged into my room. I pivoted to face her. "*Jesus*, don't you use your legs anymore?" she whined. I peered to my feet to see that I was levitating – something that I no longer thought to be strange. I grumbled, altering my existence within the air to step back onto the ground, and slouched there.

"Legs don't seem as useful when you can fly." I shrugged.

"Well, in my house, there's at least *some* rules left after you spent a year dismantling them, and I want feet on the ground. I'm not having you teach Simone how to fly, and then having the two of you track muddy feet across the ceiling."

Of course, the notion of learning to fly only to walk on the roof didn't make sense, but I smiled and nodded. "Sure, sure, feet on the ground, mud in the carpets. Understood."

"Good." Mum nodded, then handed me an envelope. It was the kind with the little plastic window to denote the address, the kind which held a letter so official that there was no person paid to bother with writing your name and details on the outside of it. I gulped, unsure of what to expect, but took it from my mother.

"Are you ready for tonight?" I asked her, waddling about to my desk for a letter knife.

"Well, I'm dressed for it," Mum hummed, gesturing to herself, "but the way that Nick Athanas talks about you – I'm not sure I'm ready to squeeze your inflated head out the front door once the night's done."

I smiled, my cheeks growing red. The compliment was almost enough to diffuse the anxiety induced by holding the envelope in my hands. With a steady knife, I peeled it open.

"Don't worry," I laughed to disguise my nerves, "you both hate the Suneva-magic-nonsense."

"He seems to like it."

"He likes that I brought his daughter home," I corrected. "Nick hates the rest of it, believe me."

"Good," Mum huffed, "the man is sane. I wonder what he thinks of this ridiculous year of adventures from the two of you?"

"You can ask him yourself," I suggested, and with steady hands, pulled the crisp paper from its casing. My address and name appeared first, printed in the most beaurocratic of serif fonts.

"Oh, I'll make sure to ask." Mum tapped her foot. "I'm glad none of you died. Simone told me that she went to hospital, and look at that scar on her face. Will that heal?"

Probably not. I thought, but didn't say. The letter which unfolded before me was from a university, the same which Tom now attended. My eyes buzzed, my skin sweated, and I scanned for the important words.

We're delighted to tell you that you've been accepted…

"I got into Law!" I yelled, throwing up the letter for Mum to see. I leapt from the ground, air sweeping up my body to levitate it towards her. She grumbled at my egregious and just-banned use of powers, but swiped the letter from my outstretched hand anyway to read it. Mum snorted with a great, face-wide smile, throwing the thing down with stars in her eyes.

"James, congratulations!" She threw herself around me, squeezing the air from my lungs and forcing me back down onto the ground. Even on release, she held me there to the floor. "You didn't tell me you'd applied."

"I know, I just didn't think I'd get in." I smiled broadly, not even believing it myself. I snapped the letter from the bench where it landed, and read it again just to make sure. "It must have been the Suneva connections. The Vice-Chancellor was at Hesslik's rally, you know."

"The…of course." Mum's eyes rolled, although the admission wouldn't diminish her smile. "So, all of this Suneva business is over now, right? You went and *saved-the-day* – and yes, I'm proud and all of that, I'd be lying to say that I wasn't – but I was worried for a second there that you were going to throw away the chance at a normal life. Normal life begins now, right? …"

I laughed nervously, shrugging away from the woman. "Ha, no, actually…" I said. "I'm leading the next Suneva movement, a Suneva Coalition. I need this law degree to write laws surrounding the ethics codes I helped create. It's all serious business."

Mum frowned, sighing. Her pensive fingers naturally found their way to her brow. "Serious business? Will you get *paid* for this serious business, James?" And I went to answer, to raise my objections, but Mum steamrolled through on her tangent. "It's time to start looking at the bigger picture – you're not living here forever! And don't tell me you dragged your sister into this, too."

"I might get paid, sure," I said, but Mum's furrowed brow reeked of her scepticism, "but taking responsibility of the movement I helped to create, it'll look great on a resume." I jiggled my eyebrows, and Mum seemed to accept this answer, relaxing herself against the doorframe. "Imagine reading that on a resume – ethical leader of the world's Suneva Coalition. Mum, the law firms will be snapping me up. I just need four-or-five more years under this roof, and four-or-five more years of Suneva politics to pull it off."

Mum hummed, nodding. "That's a reasonable plan," she admitted. "I don't trust that you'll give up your Suneva-business when it's done, but it's a good plan." And she went to walk out the door, but turned all the way back around, hands grabbing at my shoulders. I stood pin-straight in her grasp, not sure where this would go. "And just so you know, James, I *am* proud of you. I know I've never said it, and I never was interested in the stakes of what you've achieved when compared to the risks, but you've achieved a *lot* just now. I just don't want you to be caught up and lose sight of building your life, you know?"

"I know, I know." I nodded, and grabbed my Mum's hand, squeezing it. "And thanks for that. I needed to hear that."

"Do you know what Simone's plans are?" she asked me.

"Simone's going to finish her sociology degree. I think she's on the way to getting into honours, or something." I scratched my head – I think she got accepted into that course when my memories weren't saving. Either way, I wasn't a reliable source on it. "She'll do *just fine* in sociology though. Trust me, it truly is her calling."

"Good." Mum nodded, then left for good this time, striding her way out into the hallway. "Meet me outside," she called as she left, "I'll start the car."

"Will do," I called after her. It was nice, finally, to give my mother hope in me and my direction after it had been so frayed and tested this past year. I prepared the rest of my oufit with a bold smile, knowing that I'd finally made her satisfied, if not happy. Shoes secured to my feet, I connected my will, convictions, and identity with the air about me, changing my existence within it, and levitating off the floor. I thrust myself out the door, swooping through the hall and flying out the front of the house. Zipping between the trees of the yard, I pulled up by Mum's passanger door, and she yelped in fright.

"Feet were touching the floor in the house," I said, my smile cheeky. "They did it *at least* once."

***

Nick Athanas welcomed me into his home with open arms, embracing me with them as I attempted to enter his door. He kissed my cheek even, before setting me inside the house to cordially greet my mother. Nick had invited my family over for dinner – although Simone was out tonight, working on some group assignment for her course.

"Maria, lovely to see you," Nick greeted my mother. "Thanks for making it."

"Thanks for having us," she smiled. "I hope it's nothing too fancy. I don't think I could cook well enough to return the favour."

"Don't be silly," Nick said. "The way James talks about you, you'd be making much better food than the *crap* I'm about to serve you." Mum chuckled, but turned to give me a stern eye.

"I sure hope that James didn't say that in some sort of comparison of your cooking…" she accused, and I winced away.

"James is better than that," Nick chuckled, "give him credit. Now, come and have a seat around the coffee table."

Natalie entered from the hall past the kitchen, her posed hands sensing me in the field. Behind her came Tess Floros, who balanced herself against a sturdy walking stick. Having refused to be reuinited with her thread, Tess now bore the full extent of her age, but she smiled with it, finally free.

Instead of taking my seat as instructed by Nick, I jogged over to Natalie, and gave her a great kiss and hug, snuggling close. She smiled deeply in my arms, her grey eyes resting upon mine, peeking from behind ill-tamed, thick hair. She wore clothes of comfortable materials and mismatched colours, as appearances didn't really matter to her anymore.

"Hi Maria," she called over my shoulder. She moved aside of me to say hello to my mother, her posed hands guiding her through the field. Nick came up to me now, patting my shoulder and pulling me aside to the kitchen's island bench. He reached down into a drawer of the island's cabinet, pulling out a crepe-paper wraped package. He handed it to me.

"What's this?" I asked, aweing the package. Being an experienced guesser of presents, and a frequent feeler of that left under the Christmas tree, it was clearly some item of clothing inside the paper in my hands.

"Open it," Nick said, and I obligued. What emerged was a shirt louder and more vibrant than one I had ever owned. It was perfect.

"Why?" I asked. "But, thank you! You know my tastes so well."

"You brought Natalie home, mate," he said, patting the shirt in my hand. "You're a good kid, and I appreciate you putting yourself on the line."

"Thank you, Mr Athanas," I said, unsure of how else to express my gratitude. "You didn't have to get me anything."

"I picked the shirt!" Natalie shouted from her place with my Mum. "I mean…Dad helped, but he can't take the credit." And she left her conversation with Mum, swaying on over towards me. Mum followed, just to see what the commotion was about.

"I described the shirts." Nick shrugged.

"Oh, that's nice." Mum pointed to the gift. "Did you say thanks?"

"Of course." I rolled my eyes. Natalie's hand met mine, and it crawled its way up my sleeve.

"It should be the same fit as this shirt," she said, and smiled, her blind eyes finding mine like they always could. "How did I know that you'd wear this shirt tonight?"

"Eh, you're magical," I teased. "That must be it."

To this Natalie kissed my cheek. When she pulled back, she stayed lingering on my arm, holding it dearly.

"Well, we could probably all sit now to eat. The food's good." Nick scratched his neck, trying to move the night along. "And you know, Maria, I heard you've got good alcoholic taste. Come have a look at *Cellar Athanas* and tell me what you'd like," He said, and walzed from the kitchen to the left of the house. Mum followed, and together they ventured off into the next room. Natalie and I took our seats at the table, waiting for the feast.

***

Dinner wound long, with the lamb, salad, and baked deserts of the table joined by coffees and cigarettes as the night lingered, on into its darkness. Mum was relaxed here, melted to her seat under the guise of Nick's enthralling stories about nothing. He had praise for me to my mother, things she'd heard before, but which still brought a smile to her recovering attitude. Tess was sure to chime in herself, as an ultimate Suneva authority, to praise Natalie and my work over the last year. A lot of it was lost on Mum, but she appreciated it none-the-less. I was her darling boy tonight, and I made sure to squeeze her arm and whisper that I loved her. And she responded, surely, by saying that she knew, and that she loved me too.

Nearing midnight, Mum decided that she'd best be off, and went to tow me along as she bid her hosts thanks. Mr Athanas, to my surprise, offered that I didn't have to go – I could stay over tonight. My eyes and Natalie's beamed with delight, before toning our faces to immediate, yet appreciative, disinterest. Two young lovers could never be too careful showing enthusiasm for such deals around adults. With that sorted, Mum departed, leaving me with a kiss and her love. I gave her the same, after which both Nick and Tess retired themselves to bed. Natalie and I found ourselves alone in the kitchen – alone with a set of unclean dishes, which Natalie insisted that we spritz up and pack away.

Then naturally, with heartbeats and hormones high, alone in a sleepy house at the dead of night, we migrated to Natalie's room. We giggled as our socks shuffled on the carpet, any attempt at sneaking thrown to vein. Natalie threw herself onto her creaky bed, and I lay myself on top of her, letting my body sink into her curves, my elbows to the side of her arms, my hands in her hair.

She cupped my face with her palms, feeling the ridge of my jawline. Then she went to take off her jumper.

"Wait," I instructed, holding her hands down.

"Why?" she asked, her voice breathy.

"There's something I want to show you first."

I tumbled off her, onto the bed beside her. Natalie flopped her arm around my stomach, moving her chin up to my chest.

"What is it?" she asked.

"Just close your eyes and relax," I said, forcing myself immediately into deep meditation, and waking my soul in the Void.

We rested under a dull grey canopy, lying on a rocky outcrop within a thick forest of the Void. A sea sloshed in the distance, a God who could no longer trap us. I pulled myself up, then leaned down to Natalie's sleeping soul. I touched it, connecting to her. Natalie twitched, then gasped, her bright blue eyes coming awake as she sat up startled.

"James, you know I shouldn't be in here long," she said, looking about before resting her gaze on my face, "and we were just getting comfy." She tugged at my void shirt, beconing me to the ground. I kissed her forehead, then stood and pulled her up.

"I know," I said, "but you don't get to see much these days, and I found something that you *have* to see. In fact, you'll be the first Suneva to ever see it."

"I…" She smiled, then caught onto a flaw in my logic. "How can I be the first?" she asked. "Haven't you seen what you're taking me to?"

"Fine, first *other* Suneva," I grumbled. "You would have woken up to the sight, too, but I couldn't drag your soul all the way up this mountain." I gestured to the landscape around us. We stood halfway up a rocky, forested mountain – one of the rocks at the centre of the Void continent.

"Believe me, with the amount of bodies Boekidin and his teams are going to drag out of the seas, this will become prime *Void-tourism*. You'll want to see it before it becomes just another destination."

"I...okay," Natalie agreed, with slight hesitation.

We embarked up the steep slope, thick and rugged with meaty plants. Her eyes lit to stars, as she bent to see and smell the flowers and leaves, all vibrant colours which I couldn't know. It was a forest of remarkably beautiful shapes, and scents, and feelings. A mountain which represented the pure emotion of ecstasy, fully in bloom.

I dragged her up the rocky, fertile face, all the way to it's top, where the forest turned to a jagged, grassy meadow, nestled on the piles of void-stone.

It was here that a great tree grew. It's trunk thicker than a human was tall. Its branches spread in patterns that shifted as you turned from them – a labyrinth of connections twisting continuously past the sky itself, breaking the surface into the Void beyond this. Crashing through the planes of reality.

"Wow," Natalie gasped. "It's...creepy." She frowned. "It's not actually that high, so why does it look to be going on forever."

"I don't know," I said, "but that's not the point. Look that way..." I grabbed her shoulders and turned her around, towards Omercronius.

There, in the desert beyond the next mountains, lay a temple – one of the many temples that my dad had alluded to with his map. In its entrance courtyard, drawn as a mosaic on the tiled floor, lay an image of the White Witch, cast into this realm for eternity. I smiled broadly, admiring my work.

"Is that me?" Natalie asked, gripping at my arm.

"Pretty impressive, hey?" I chuffed. "I drew it with perspective and everything. You know the way how they have to draw arrows on the road really long?"

She shook her head, her smile radiant, chuckling through her nose.

"James Grey, you are peculiar, but I love you for it. Thank..." she said, before her soul collapsed on the mountain top.

"N...Natalie?" I gasped, reaching down to her body, shaking it back and forth. Her soul was limp in my arms – I couldn't sense its energy.

"Oh *cheese*..." I worried, mind skipping over her anxieties at spending long periods in the Void. My heartrate spiked, and I grabbed her hand.

"Natalie?" I called again, and I felt the connection to her soul rise – that one so familiar to me, which had connected us over a year ago. But this time, *she* tugged on the thread between us.

And she pulled me from the Void with a passionate kiss.

Epilogue

Hesslik, Zamelle, Iva, Ferrad, and myself mounted the stage of the street festival in Melbourne, basking in the late spring sun. The Legendaries Zirrus and Vectra stood at the rear of the platform, gazing stoically over the audience in their gleaming armour. Riskidin squirmed in the front row of the crowd, giving us an enthusiastic thumbs up.

The banner he had designed flew behind our heads, hung from the stage gantries. It flapped in the low breeze, demanding presence.

Simone was out there somewhere, amongst the people. I tried to find her, but she'd become adept at stealing light since continuing her training with *Salak Kuul*. Now, if Simone didn't want to be seen, it was likely that you'd never spot her.

Months had passed which we'd spent establishing the rules and agenda of the Coalition. It had taken hours of argument between us each day, clutching to find the point of compromise we were all happy with. Boekidin was the great intermediary who drew all of our minds together. He was familiar with all Suneva ideologies, and passionate about them equally – he even helped Helena and Celeste see eye-to-eye.

Then it took a team of lawyers for us to understand how these laws and ethical rules could be enforced, and how they would fit into existing legal frameworks and societies.

Antithesis to my mother's concerns for my income, the government of Australia had taken interest in our cause. With the promise of a Coalition and a new world, Suneva became daring, and ordinary people had started to discover their own connections which had so far lain idle. Suddenly, cities of the world were finding themselves inundated with vocal and novice Suneva, often resulting violence and outcry from both Suneva and their protestors. Governments needed experts to help them deal with, and legislate, these newcomers. Miraculously – although, as Helena would argue, naturally – they came to us.

The Australian government, the most overrun by the new influx of Suneva from their ethnic population, gave us a central office in Melbourne, and a small portion of taxpayer money to fund ourselves. Soon after, we had an offer from Greece, then Italy, and France, and Malta, and then every other country bordering the Mediterranian – the traditional Suneva homelands.

Suddenly, this venture of leading the people I cared about *could* be profitable, and it *could* be my life. Mum was less than ecstatic that things turned out as they did – that I never would be turned away from this magic nonsense – but she certainly made an effort to be supportive.

The new laws we'd created, which Simone released on our website today, were a carefully constructed amalgamation of Vochduh ethics – both my own and Hesslik's interpretations; of the rights that Iva and the Argols believed the Suneva should preserve; and of the spiritual rules that Natalie deemed to be followed for the safe use of quatra. They were soon to become law in this country, with many others to follow the same framework. This was an important and exciting time, and we were its drivers.

I approached the microphone on the stage. We had organised this festival to be our official opening – the Coalition's official welcome of Suneva into the *New World*. It all started today.

"Suneva of Melbourne, and of the world," I began. "It's been a long road to our re-emergence in society, starting hundreds of years ago with Olomb, and his soul, Kuvalik. It was the final act of destiny that this time, our re-emergence coincided with the wake of the White Witch, the Shiverman, and the three Legendaries – and, unfortunately, the tragedy of the great thread stripping.

"The New World cannot be built without sacrifice. By the nature of Suneva, of what we represent to most people, this shift will be difficult for the world. It is, however, *necessary*, so that you have the *freedom* to be who you want to be, wherever that may be. Sacrifices are required to protect others from us, to protect Suneva from their own abilities, and to protect ourselves from discrimination and hate.

"We fought diligently for your rights, so that we could preserve the Suneva way of life. This shift may be difficult for some of us, as we become accountable where we might have otherwise held greater freedoms, but nobody said that gaining acceptance was easy.

"Remember that you will be rewarded for bringing your best self into this world, and that you will benefit the whole community by doing so. Be brave in the face of danger, be calm in the face of anger, be kind in the face of hate, and enact fairness in the face of injustice."

I paused, and the audience broke into applause. News cameras squared on my image, with reporters talking into lapels, earpieces, and great, fuzzy microphones. I skimmed the audience, seeing the range of emotions on the faces of the amassed. Most were joyous on this day, but many others were reserved, or critical, with arms crossed.

Then I spotted Simone, her hood pulled over her head. Our eyes locked in a brief, silent moment, and she nodded to me. Her body then vanished, becoming totally transparent in a glimour of light, like air rising off hot tarmac. I nodded back to where she had been standing, swallowing my apprehension.

"It's with great pleasure, that I welcome you all to the New World."

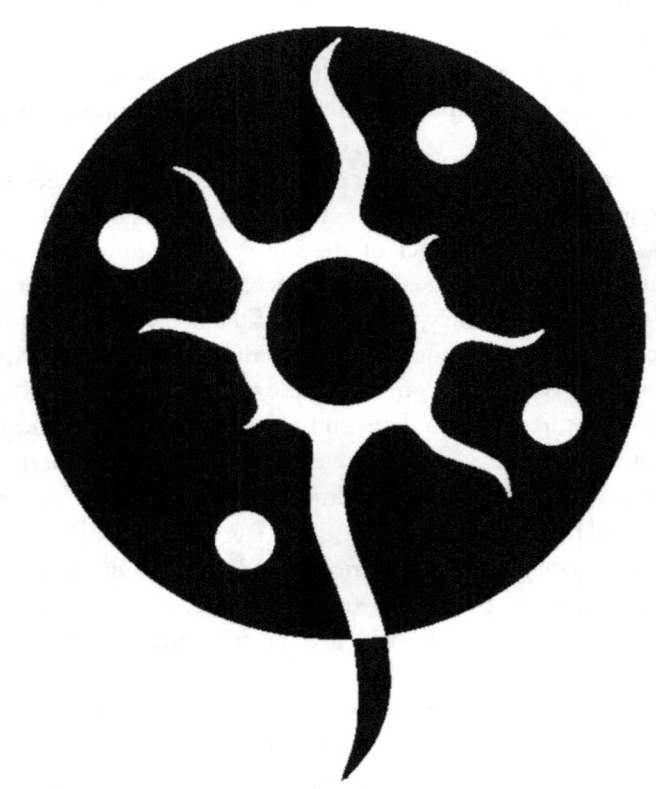

The Empire of the Black Suns Series:

I hope you've enjoyed The Empire of the Black Suns series. Stay tuned for *Volume VI: Dawn of the Red Sun*, and future unrelated works by Alexander Mackie.

About the Author:

Alexander Lewis Mackie is a young and aspiring author emerging from Melbourne, Australia, whose stories aim to address identity, rights, and justice. He penned his first draft novel at the age of eighteen, and wrote through his university degree in the hopes of having his works published.

Now working as a Railway Systems Engineer in his home city, Alexander is continuing to write in the genre of fantasy, and hopes that his stories and characters find interest with passionate readers.